We hope you enjoy this book. Please renew it by the due date

You can renew it at w\
by using our free librar

Otherwise you can pho\
please have your library

You can sign up for email reminders too.

NORFOLK COUNTY LIBRARY
WITHDRAWN FOR SALE

NORFOLK ITEM
30129 091 040 601

NORFOLK COUNTY COUNCIL
LIBRARY AND INFORMATION SERVICE

JOFFE BOOKS

Joffe Books, London
www.joffebooks.com

First published in Great Britain in 2024

© Joy Ellis 2024

This book is a work of fiction. Names, characters, businesses, organizations, places and events are either the product of the author's imagination or are used fictitiously. Any resemblance to actual persons, living or dead, events or locales is entirely coincidental. The spelling used is British English except where fidelity to the author's rendering of accent or dialect supersedes this. The right of Joy Ellis to be identified as author of this work has been asserted in accordance with the Copyright, Designs and Patents Act 1988.

Cover art by Nick Castle

ISBN: 978-1-83526-363-1

AUTHOR'S NOTE

An Aura of Mystery is my very first novel. It has sat in a dusty box file, and on an old floppy disc for over twenty years. I was very much a novice writer, but since childhood I'd had a fascination with mysteries, especially those with a supernatural element. So, I wrote one of my own! It's very different to my current work although, as there is a strong police procedural theme right through it, I think you can see the direction in which I was heading.

I wanted to keep the supernatural side of the book believable, so I did a lot of research into the subject of colour therapy and auric sight; seeing auras, the coloured life forces that surround all living things. I also looked into medical conditions caused by chemicals released into the brain during head traumas, and invented one of my own, the Azimah Syndrome. I found it all incredibly interesting and wove it into a murder mystery that became *An Aura of Mystery*.

There was publisher interest in it, even way back then, but cross-genre was not popular at the time, and it never went any further. Even so, I wrote a sequel, *The Colour of Mystery*, and then committed them both to the attic! Over the years, they have haunted me, and a few months ago when I was not feeling well and could not concentrate on new work,

I resurrected them. My assistant Luke managed to convert them into a workable manuscript, and I read them again, for the first time in two decades.

I was absolutely over the moon when Joffe Books offered to publish them as vintage work from my archive! Or maybe that should read, attic! They are exactly as they were, with no changes or attempts to bring them up to date, so they do reflect the age when they were written.

They will always be very special to me as my first step to becoming a writer, and I do hope that you enjoy them.

Joy Ellis

CHAPTER ONE

She was in a place that she did not recognise. Somewhere dark and threatening, and she was not alone. Someone was with her in the stinking room, and a feeling of dread twisted her gut into knots. Then there was a scream: a sound that seemed to come from far away. It began softly, as a ghastly keening, and then it intensified into a terrified shriek.

Fighting fear and bedcovers, Ellie McEwan struggled to find the switch to her bedside lamp. She prayed to God for blessed electric light, and sat up, shaking uncontrollably, and pulling the duvet tightly around her.

Glaring pictures in red and black flashed like strobe lighting behind her eyelids each time she blinked. The images were so strong that she did not trust herself to stand. She desperately wanted to get out of the bedroom and escape the memory of those horrible visions.

Still shaking, Ellie pulled on her dressing gown and stumbled towards the kitchen. A warm drink and some comforting music from a late-night DJ should help. She managed to drop the tea bags, and splash water everywhere.

'It's okay, it's okay!' she told herself. 'I'm safe, I'm safe in my own home; it was just a horrible dream.'

As she plugged in the kettle, the back of her hand brushed the wall tiles and a sickening bolt of memory flared up. Her back to a tiled wall, freezing cold, and that awful something, just out of sight, but giving off those dreadful emanations.

Ellie's hand jerked away from the wall and her elbow caught a pottery mug, sending it crashing to the floor and dispelling her demons across the quarry tiles.

Sweeping up shattered Denby, she felt normality creeping back, along with a host of other emotions, and she started to cry.

She roughly brushed the tears away. She'd done enough damned crying recently and didn't need bloody nightmares to set her off again.

It took her a few minutes to successfully make a cup of tea. The shaking was subsiding, but it was not easy to do anything with a snotty nose and tear-blurred vision, especially things that involved the use of boiling water.

Clutching the drink, she tentatively went back into the bedroom.

Huddled in the duvet, she felt shaken and frightened. The telephone beckoned to her, but who could she call at two in the morning? She had lots of friends, but they nearly all worked, and she could not bring herself to worry them at this unearthly hour.

She wanted a hot water bottle and a teddy bear. She wanted her mother back, to hug her and reassure her, and tell her that everything would all be all right in the morning. For a moment she felt a hand gently stroking her hair. Yes, Ellie wanted her mother back, but Florence McEwan had passed away only six months ago, six weeks before Ellie's live-in partner, Stephanie, had left her. Her reason had been to 'find herself', but the grapevine at Oneidas Packaging, where Steph had been an inspection line manager, had taken some delight in informing her that Steph had taken Michelle from quality control to help her in her quest. As Stephanie had never been the kind to search her soul for anything, yet alone hug a tree, Ellie had hoped that after a three-year relationship, she might have warranted a little more in the honesty department.

Memories and remembered conversations started up a familiar internal dialogue in Ellie's head, and found her once again agonising over Steph's departure, and the void she had left behind. That led to thoughts of her mother's long illness, her departure, and the more permanent void that she had caused in Ellie's life.

'Hell! It's no wonder I'm having nightmares,' she sighed. 'It's got to come out somewhere, so why not in bad dreams?'

The next day found her feeling vulnerable and easily upset. She was uncharacteristically snappy with her staff and distant with the customers. She even considered bunking off early. It was her own flower shop, so there was no reason on this earth why she shouldn't, except she couldn't face going home.

After the staff had gone, she arranged the next day's orders and endeavoured to start some accounts. The figures swam around the page and refused to add up, so she closed the ledger and stared at the clock. It was only 6.45 p.m. She knew she couldn't stay at the shop all night, and there was precious little left to do, so she gathered up her coat and bag, and reluctantly locked up.

Her car was parked a few roads away, and as Ellie slowly paced the paving stones towards it, she realised that she badly needed someone to talk to. The way she felt right now, going home to an empty house was no longer an option.

She opened the car door and threw her things onto the passenger seat. Climbing in, she slipped her mobile from her pocket and rang Gill. Her closest friend's crackly car-boot ansafone declared her unable to come to the phone right now, as did Ellie's brother's state-of-the-art version.

'Sodding machines! Why is there never a bloody human being around when you need one!'

Her frustration was bringing her closer and closer to the ever-present tears.

Throwing the phone down in her lap, she thumped the steering wheel with both fists, and cursed Steph. If she'd still been around, at least Ellie would have had someone to talk to, somewhere to go . . . and she couldn't face another night of awful dreams.

Dreams! With the word came the answer. Thinking of Steph had brought a fleeting thought of her nemesis, Carole Cavendish-Meyer.

Carole's dislike of Ellie's ex was legendary, but more than that, she was the one person Ellie could turn to without feeling foolish. Dreams, tarot, runes, dowsing, in fact anything esoteric or other-worldly, and Carole had some knowledge of it.

The older woman picked the phone up on the second ring, and after Ellie had given her the briefest of explanations, simply said, 'Get yourself down here, right now!' and hung up.

It was a good forty-five-minute drive from Weybridge to Compton at that time of the evening, but she set off with more enthusiasm than she had been able to muster all day. The traffic on the A3 towards Guildford was heavy but moving, and she could cope with that.

Ellie thought about Carole and smiled. They saw each other perhaps once a month, and had a comfortable friendship that thrived without living in each other's pockets. In her early seventies, Carole was an unusual mix of Lady of the Manor, and the woman who sold jellied eels on Southend seafront. She was honest to the point of rudeness, and had probably earned the title of 'Bloody old cow!' from more shop assistants than anyone Ellie had ever met. Few people liked her, but then few people knew her.

She had met Carole through the flower shop. None of the staff wanted to serve the 'bad-tempered old bat', so it was frequently down to her to attend to Carole. One day, the delivery driver, who was inundated with timed orders, asked for help with some long-distance deliveries. Ellie, who often stepped in on occasions like that, found herself carrying a huge bouquet of flowers up the garden path, between a profusion of pansies and polyanthus, to the door of Snug Cottage. She was confronted by a grim and suspicious looking Mrs C-M saying, 'Well, I hope they are going to last better than the last lot did. Come on, girl, bring them to the kitchen.'

Ellie had duly followed her through the hall and into the kitchen, where she placed the flowers on a huge scrubbed pine table. Turning to leave, she gasped with unconcealed delight at seeing a tangle of spaniels, curled up in a furry heap, in a huge dog bed next to the Aga.

And that was the start of a beautiful friendship.

Blue lights up ahead explained why her speed had just dropped to under 20 mph, and her mind wandered back to Carole.

She had invited Ellie to her home for a meal one Saturday evening, and it was then she had met Vera: Carole's partner of twenty-five years. It was with some trepidation that she had arrived, with a pretty hostess bouquet of double tulips and Dutch freesias in one hand, and a bottle of Merlot in the other. She should not have worried; the evening had been far better than she had ever dreamed. The food was delicious, and both conversation and copious quantities of excellent wine flowed freely. Gentle, witty Vera counterbalanced the abrasive, acid-tongued Carole, and their deep friendship shone through their apparently argumentative banter. More dinner parties and lunches had followed, then occasional theatre trips and shopping expeditions.

During this time Ellie had become very fond of the two capricious women. She soon saw beyond their eccentricities, and discovered that they possessed great intuitive powers, not to mention some rather mysterious skills that fascinated Ellie, but they were things she did not pretend to understand. The talent that amazed Ellie most had been Carole's natural aptitude for clairvoyance. She was completely blasé about it and passed it off as being a 'family thing' from her mother's side. She had declared that if Grandmother Hobbs had been born a century earlier, she would have been burned at the stake. Her mother had also enjoyed witch-like tendencies, although Carole, who refused to speak of her family any more than that, had emphasised that bitch was more appropriate than witch.

Carole constantly amazed her young friend with matter-of-fact statements about areas of her life that Ellie had never shared with either of the two companions. Both women had travelled extensively, often to wild and dangerous places. In Carole's case, an early and disastrous marriage had found her trekking the world, living with the most primitive of people, while her young husband endeavoured to teach them modern methods of irrigation. Some of her beliefs had certainly stemmed from these indigenous people who still possessed more natural wisdom. Vera had been born, and lived, until the age of nineteen, in India, and embraced many of the ideas and principles of their culture. Together, there was little in the way of the esoteric that they had not explored.

Initially enthralled, Ellie had soon come to accept the quirky pair and their strange beliefs, and often consulted them when she had a problem of some kind. They were easy to talk to, their advice was always sound, and she knew she could trust them totally. Once, Vera had been showing her some little wonder that was dear to her heart — she didn't remember exactly what, maybe a blackbird's nest, or some freshly discovered wild flower in the orchard — when she gently took Ellie's hand and said, 'You also have a gift, my dear. A very special one. It's just not the right time yet. Don't be frightened by it when it shows itself, and use it wisely; it is very precious.' She had said no more, and it had left the younger woman wondering. She was sensitive to atmosphere and situations, but no more than most artistic people.

She had never understood, and as she sat with dozens of other motorists waiting for the traffic to flow again, Ellie felt sad that she had left it too late to ask.

Her thoughts went back to the previous year. She had been driving back from London, having just done a quote for a society wedding. Approaching the slip road at Cobham, she had the distinct feeling she should stay on the A3 and get to Compton as quickly as possible. She comforted herself with the knowledge that it was Carole who always said, 'Trust in your gut feelings and go with it, even if you don't know why.' She certainly would not laugh at her if she had got it wrong.

But she hadn't got it wrong. Ellie had arrived in time to see the tail lights of the ambulance, taking Vera on her last country drive through the leafy lanes of Surrey that she loved so much.

Carole had stayed behind to gather up their five spaniels from the orchard and was preparing, somewhat unenthusiastically, to make her way to the Royal Surrey County Hospital.

Vera had had a heart attack, not totally unexpected as her health had always been poor after some neglected childhood illness. Ellie had helped Carole with the dogs and then driven her to the hospital. She remembered babbling on about cardiac massage, and how the paramedics might be able to save her, but Carole had sat ramrod straight next to her, and said she knew Vera had passed over, and she didn't really know why they were racing to the A&E anyway. She was perfectly aware of what they would find when they got there.

Of course, she had been right. Vera was dead. Carole had said, 'I told you so,' put some money in the Scanner Appeal collecting box and demanded to be taken home.

If she hadn't known Carole so well, Ellie would have been aghast at her apparent lack of emotion at the loss of her dearest friend. But she did know her, and realised that Carole's grieving would not be done in public.

The traffic hold-up miraculously disappeared, and in a very short time, her VW Passat estate car was bumping down the unmade-up lane to Snug Cottage.

Half an hour later Ellie was curled up on a soft, cushiony sofa with a muddle of spaniels, and a large gin and tonic. She tried her best to describe the nightmare as clinically as possible, but she couldn't conceal the fact that she had been badly disturbed by it.

Carole tilted back the sparkly Waterford glass, reached for a top-up and stared hard at Ellie. 'Did I ever tell you that I've always considered you very sensitive?'

'I don't understand that statement. I never, well, I don't see things, or hear voices.'

'It's not always like that.'

'So, what do you mean?' Ellie asked.

'With you, Ellie, I honestly don't know. I've always had very strong feelings that you are incredibly gifted in some way, but it just hasn't presented itself yet.'

Ellie drew in a surprised breath. 'That's exactly what Vera said! I never understood, and then . . . well, it was too late to ask.'

Carole sipped her drink. 'We talked about it a lot, but she knew no more than I do, my dear, but I feel this awful dream has something to do with it. I just can't make the connection. Let me think about that for a while. I need a little time to consider.'

A wicked grin swept over her face. 'Let's call up Vera and see what she thinks, shall we?'

'Carole! That's awful!'

'My dear Ellie.' She indicated towards the sleeping spaniels. 'The boys and I do nothing of importance without consulting Vera first.'

Ellie gazed into her glass, noting the tiny air bubbles clinging to the lemon slice. 'I'm sorry, Carole, I guess séance, and things like that, kind of frighten me a bit.'

'A séance! We don't need one of those to talk to Vera. I can simply ask her if she would like to join us, that's all, and I cannot think of one aspect of my dear Vera that would frighten anyone. She is the gentlest of souls.'

'It's just that she's dead!' exclaimed Ellie.

'Oh, that . . . well, yes, but only in a way. She's around as she always was, just on a slightly different plane now. At least I can communicate with her easily. You really mustn't worry — even the boys love to feel her around them, and if animals are comfortable with her, then you certainly have nothing to fear.' She paused for a moment, and then in a soft voice, more reminiscent of Vera's than of her own, said, 'It's the living you have to worry about, Ellie. Not the dead.'

The last sentence hung in the air.

A puzzled frown passed over Carole's face and she got abruptly to her feet. 'Another gin and tonic, dear? Perhaps we'll stick with this kind of spirit tonight, and you must stay over . . . no driving tonight for you, young lady. Now, tell me, how is that awful brother of yours? And have you had any more thoughts about extending your floristry empire? The last time we met you were bursting with ideas!'

Carole handed Ellie the refilled glass. The slight tremor in her hand and her abrupt change of tack had not gone unnoticed by Ellie, but she welcomed it, and soon launched into the new plans for her business.

The slightly uncomfortable moment was apparently forgotten, and the evening passed, a delightful mixture of easy conversation, Gordon's gin, and soporific canine snoring.

When Carole proclaimed it was time to climb the wooden hill, Ellie realised she had slumped down in the cushions and was half dozing with her glass resting on her chest. 'I'm so sorry! How rude of me.'

Her friend laughed, one hand trying unsuccessfully to brush dog hairs from her crinkled cords. 'I'm glad to see that the peaceful atmosphere seems to be having the desired effect on you. Let's adjourn, shall we?'

Her guest bedroom was a welcoming hotch-potch of florals and chintz, velvets and fringes.

'I'm afraid Digger comes with the bed.' Carole indicated to the little blue roan cocker, already nestling happily in the duvet. 'Now, as all this is a bit impromptu, I've left one of my nightshirts on the radiator in your bathroom, and there's plenty of towels and new toothbrushes, just help yourself. Sleep well, dear, I'm sure you will tonight.' There was a pause. 'Thinking about it, as tomorrow is Saturday, why not stay on for the day? We could potter around the antique shops, and you could help me take the dogs for a good run over the Downs. In fact, stay for supper, then push off home if you need to.'

The two friends hugged companionably.

'Tomorrow sounds absolutely great, just what I could do with. Peter and the girls can manage the shop. There are no big weddings, or anything complicated this weekend, and if I go mid-evening, there will be plenty of time to get my Dutch flower order together and faxed over before their deadline. Thank you, Carole. I'd love to stay, and I really appreciate this.'

'Nonsense, you're always welcome, you know that.'

The older woman strode off down the hall with an entourage of furry bodies at her heels. 'Come on, boys, out into the garden and be quick about your business, it's damn cold tonight!'

Digger stayed put. He was the only one small enough to use the now defunct cat flap, which gave him the rare privilege of doing his business when he chose. Besides, it really was a damn cold night.

Ellie washed perfunctorily and pulled on the baggy nightshirt. It smelled of flowers and felt warm and comforting. She snuggled down under the duvet, and with Digger's body providing a gentle and reassuring pressure against her legs, slipped into a deep and dreamless sleep.

* * *

Outside in the orchard, Carole stared into the frosty night sky and pulled her old Barbour closer. Her shivers were not entirely because of the November chills. She had not liked the sound of Ellie McEwan's dream. Graphic and concise, Carole knew that, whatever the young woman may have decided, it was nothing to do with her broken relationship or the loss of her mother. There was no deep Freudian message there. It was simply a glimpse of something. Whether it was someone else's past horror, or something yet to come, she was not sure. Her gut feeling said the future, but for once she did not want to go with it; it was too horrible to contemplate, as it meant that Ellie could be in grave danger.

She shook herself, bustled the dogs together, and made for the welcoming light of the kitchen door.

As she strode back, she gave one last glance up into the night. 'Vera, I think our young friend is in trouble.' Her voice caught in her throat. 'I miss you, Vera.'

A light breeze whispered through the last few stubborn leaves in the orchard, and under one of the apple trees, Carole glimpsed the shadowy figure of a tall, slim woman with a dog at her side.

CHAPTER TWO

Saturday was crisp and bright, allowing the two women to do all the things Carole had suggested. Ellie felt refreshed and insisted on finishing off a lovely day by taking her friend to supper at the Poacher's Inn, before she headed back to Weybridge.

Ensconced in a cosy corner, they chatted amicably. 'It's a shame you can't have a little wine, dear,' said Carole, pouring herself a second glass. 'This really is a most excellent claret, they have a very good cellar here. Vera loved this place, you know.'

'Yes, I came here with you both one evening. It was the day after Monty, your oldest Springer died. You said we needed cheering up, and we'd have a little party to celebrate his life.'

'Ah, yes, dear Monty. He's with Vera now. He rarely left her side while he was on earth, and I know he'll not leave her now.'

Carole drifted into her own thoughts, and Ellie silently fought a battle with temptation over the red wine. 'God! I could murder a glass of that, but it's not worth the risk, not with all the driving I have to do, and frankly, I sank enough gin last night to last me for a month!'

'Well, at least you slept.' Carole smiled.

'And how! If Digger hadn't decided to push a cold nose in my face, I think I'd still be there now.' She paused for a moment, trying to formulate her words. 'You've been so kind, Carole, I hope you know just how much I appreciate all your help. The last six months have been bloody awful, and . . .'

Carole raised a hand. 'Now stop all this nonsense. I'm here when you need me, and that's all there is to it. Actually I think I should be thanking you, knowing what these rogues charge here!' She gave a sly wink to Paul, their waiter, who was one of the very few people that the irascible Carole seemed to like.

Paul smiled at Ellie and muttered something about old trout.

Ellie grinned and finished her last mouthful of salmon en croute. 'Worth every penny. How about dessert? I saw your eyes light up as the sweet trolley went past.'

They made all the usual comments about tight waistbands and faulty scales, then settled for a 'Death by Chocolate' with two spoons.

'I am replete,' sighed Carole, leaning back and sipping her coffee. 'Do you really have to go back tonight? Digger wouldn't mind sharing his bed for another night.'

'Hmm, 'fraid so. If I don't get back to the shop to collate my order, I'll miss getting it through to Kees the Dutchman on time. It's tough at the top!'

'Surely things are easier for you now you've put that manager in? Couldn't he do it?'

'Oh, it's certainly easier. I mean, have you ever known me to take a Saturday off before? It's a florist's busiest day, what with weddings and parties, and so on. No, the shop is doing fine, and I'm ready to step back a bit and concentrate on the plans I told you about, and Peter the manager is great, but he is not quite ready for the ordering and the buying. I juggle the orders between early-morning trips to the flower market at Nine Elms in London, and three suppliers, each having different connections to specialist growers, and I don't want to frighten him off just yet! Besides, it's taken the best part of a year to build a really good working relationship with my main Dutch wholesaler. Now, I'm getting good quality and fair prices, so I prefer to deal with him direct for a little while longer.'

'That sounds reasonable. You've worked hard on that shop since your parents died. It's not easy carrying on a family business, especially when one member of the family backs out and leaves you holding the baby.'

Ellie's brother, Phil, had apparently realised very early in his working life that floristry meant hard work, long hours, and very little financial reward for your labours, so he threw it all at his sister, and bought an estate agency.

She laughed and folded her napkin. 'I don't really blame him. He's not a bit like Dad, no love for the flowers, and he couldn't bear to be seen driving a van . . . not his image at all.'

'Bone bloody idle, more like!'

'Well, I can't really criticise. He's built up his own agency now, and owns a new Saab, not a five-year-old VW estate.'

'Probably got it all swindling and double-dealing. At least you can hold your head up; what you've got has been honestly earned. Anyway, I'm glad to see you letting go of the reins a little. Perhaps you'll ease up a bit too. I know you have a new business plan in mind, but leave a little room for yourself as well. The old adage about all work and no play is absolutely correct.'

Even the career woman in Ellie was forced to agree. Work was one of the main reasons that Steph left her. Ellie's social life came second to the business every time. 'You are quite right, Carole, and I'm going to try and balance my life a little better from now on. Do you know? I have a feeling I won't be at the shop much at all soon.'

She smiled at her friend, but the grin abruptly disappeared when she saw the ghastly expression on Carole's face. She seemed to be having trouble breathing and her usual ruddy complexion had drained to a putty colour.

'Could you get me a glass of water?' Carole whispered.

Ellie pushed back her chair and ran to the bar. Paul appeared from the back and swiftly poured some cold water into a tumbler. She hurried back to the table and found Carole still looking ashen. She drank deeply. After a few minutes her breathing eased and she seemed to relax.

'Whatever is wrong?' Ellie asked gently, giving her a little while to compose herself.

'Oh dear, I'm so sorry. Red wine and a peptic ulcer don't seem to get on.'

'Peptic ulcer! Why on earth didn't you tell me you weren't well?' Ellie was surprised, but not a little relieved at her explanation. For a moment she had thought her friend was having a stroke. Under those circumstances, an ulcer didn't seem quite so bad.

'Oh, it's very recent. In fact, Dr Littlewood hasn't even had the test results back yet, but he's pretty sure that's what it is. He's a bit of an old fart, but a good doctor nevertheless. He'll have it under control in no time. God, but I'm a silly old fool, now I don't have Vera to keep an eye on me.'

'Let's get you home.' She waved across to Paul, who was regarding them quietly from the bar, and he brought the bill to the table.

'Are you okay now, Mrs Meyer?'

'Fine, thank you, young man. Don't worry, I won't tell anyone it was your food!' Carole smiled at him ruefully, then added. 'It's all right, Paul, nothing to worry about.'

As Paul helped Carole into her coat, Ellie noticed the other woman staring at her with an unfathomable expression on her face.

'Are you sure you're up to the walk home?' Ellie asked.

'Yes, yes, the air will do me good. I'm just very embarrassed at spoiling a perfect day with my stupidity.'

'Don't be so silly. I'm only worried about leaving you now because of faxing over the damned shop order.'

In a very short time, they were back at the cottage, and Carole seemed to be her old, caustic self again. Ellie stayed for another hour, and when she felt confident the episode was over, said her goodbyes, and drove slowly between the potholes of the lane and out to the main road.

It was nearly eleven o'clock by the time her headlights spotted the sign for the A3. She was going to have to put her foot down if she wanted to get her order completed and sent off before the allotted cut-off time. She eased the VW into the outside lane and drove at a steady seventy. She couldn't risk getting stopped, but she didn't have too much time to spare either. As she searched for a music station on the radio, she vaguely wondered why Carole's ulcer had not been upset by the enormous quantity of gin that she had consumed the night before.

* * *

Carole had watched the tail lights of the VW until they turned out of the lane, then slowly made her way to the kitchen, and the warmth and company of the Aga and her beloved dogs. She felt sick and cold inside.

She hoped she had fooled Ellie McEwan with the ulcer story, although she doubted it. When Ellie had mentioned not being at the shop so much in the future, she had had a dreadful flash of foreboding. She knew that Ellie would not be at the shop at all. The thought had left her throat dry and her chest thudding. When Ellie went to get her a drink, she had closed her eyes and experienced the strangest feeling.

All was silent, and behind her eyelids she could see bursts of coloured lights, flaring and fading like mute fireworks. Hazy figures moved in and out of the lights, appearing and disappearing. Ellie had come back with the water, and the icy coldness had melted the wraith-like spectres into a mist, which spiralled around and vanished.

Huddled in front of the big cooker and hugging little Digger tight to her, Carole felt completely desolate. Her clairvoyance seemed to have deserted her. She had no idea what was happening or going to happen — she just knew that it concerned Ellie.

She couldn't have told the girl. What could she have said without frightening the life out of her? All she knew was that her friend was in danger, but from what or when she could not say. And so, she sat and waited.

* * *

At seventeen, Joseph Edward Saville had three major beliefs. About two of them he was correct, albeit somewhat indirectly. About the last, well . . .

First, Joe believed that there would never be another night like this. Despite the cold, he walked barefoot, toes tingling against wet, diamond-sharp blades of grass, his trainers hung by the laces round his neck. He was at one with the earth beneath his feet, and an intimate part of the vast black, crystal-studded heaven above him. He knew the intensity of his feelings was a direct result of the E's, but how he came by the incredible sensation was irrelevant. He had never felt so good. Too good to pile into the overcrowded Fiesta with the rest of his mates. Too good to try and share this emotion with anyone. Too good to explain.

He strolled across the old airfield, away from the deserted hangar that had been the venue for the party, his chest expanding with a previously unthought-of love.

He felt whole, complete and all-knowing.

Which brought him to his second belief. That he was destined for something special, something great. He did not know exactly what it was, but he felt sure that his very being had a reason of earth-shattering importance.

He walked in a trance, heart thundering with the significance of what he knew to be true. Reaching the end of the field, he climbed a steep slope topped by a sturdy wooden fence. Swinging himself up onto the rough palings, he sat and observed the late-night traffic hurtling along the dual carriageway to God knows where. He was apart from all this. He of the stone-washed Levis, and faded Mega-death T-shirt, was apart from the pointless rat race. The boy felt a stab of pity for the drivers.

'Lemmings,' he thought. 'All rushing onward to the same fate. Poor lemmings.'

With the certainty of his destiny before him, he jumped down from the fence and crossed three lanes of the northbound section of the A3.

Oblivious to the glaring lights and screaming tyres, he vaulted the crash barrier.

Joseph Edward Saville's third belief burst from his lips in a triumphant cry. 'I am invincible!'

On that score, however, the front bumper of Ellie McEwan's gold VW, travelling northbound at 70 mph, abruptly proved him wrong.

CHAPTER THREE

It was Justin's second day on the Rapid Response Vehicle. For the last two weeks he had been floating, doing holiday and sickness cover until John, his crew mate, returned from leave after injuring his back. He then received the news that his partner's condition was worse than the doctors had first thought, and he would be off work for quite some time. The powers that be had offered him Rapid Response, and he had jumped at the chance. He desperately wanted the motorcycle, but the ambulance service had not been overimpressed with his expertise, and gave him an Espace. Justin had never really taken too much notice of that kind of vehicle, considering it the kind of thing that rich mothers did the school run in. Hence, he had no idea of their capabilities until yesterday, his first day out in the new car, and he was impressed. It had been unnaturally quiet for a Friday, and his paramedic skills were not exactly stretched, but tonight he had a feeling that things would be a little hotter.

Cruising back to base from his last call, the M25 looked almost surreal. It was after midnight, steady, fast, purposeful, sometimes heavy traffic, then nothing for a moment or two. Bright lights, then darkness. He had a sense of virtual reality. His call sign and a burst of static dispelled the illusion.

'Bravo Two Zero. One vehicle RTA. Not known if there are any injuries. A3 Northbound, Wisley in the region of Elm Corner.'

'Bravo Two Zero, control. All received. Towards from M25 clockwise between junctions 9 and 10. ETA three minutes.'

The exit ramp was in sight and in less time than he had estimated he was braking at the accident scene. Someone had put a warning triangle up some way back from the VW estate, and although there were several cars on the hard shoulder, none seemed to be involved in the crash. A man and a woman had stationed themselves in the road, frantically waving torches to direct any traffic around the wrecked vehicle.

He felt a twinge of apprehension. It was a bit scary being alone on duty, no mate to bond with, no one to share the responsibility. He ran his fingers through his short fair hair, took a deep breath and allowed professionalism to take over. He grabbed his Ambu-bag and raced to do what he could.

There seemed to be only the driver in the wrecked VW Passat. A woman in her thirties, he guessed. Through the window he could see that she was unconscious, and from the amount of blood, apparently badly injured. The driver's door was jammed fast and he had to get the passenger side open to crawl in beside her.

He turned off the ignition, then checked her breathing and pulse. She was alive but he wasn't sure how long she would stay that way. There was a gaping cut on her forehead, her right leg was trapped, and there were possible chest injuries. It was hard to tell due to the state of the interior of the car. A piece of the crash barrier seemed to be lodged in with the debris from the car itself, and Justin could not see clearly enough to know exactly what damage it had done.

In a very short time, he had set up a line, applied a dressing to her head wound, and administered what first aid he could in the appalling conditions. Talking gently to her all the time, even though she seemed deeply unconscious, Justin reassured her that the ambulance was on its way, and to hang in there.

He extricated himself from the car, ran back to the Espace, and radioed in her condition. He was assured that a paramedic unit was close at hand. He was about to crawl back into the wreck when he heard a frightened voice call out, 'What about the boy?'

Jesus, he thought, and called back, 'What boy?'

'Over here, for God's sake!' A man, some fifty yards behind him, was standing, staring into the space between the crash barriers.

The boy lay, face up, tangled in iron sheets of twisted metal.

Justin recognised the peculiar emptiness that accompanied death. Even so, he scrambled over the wreckage and checked the vital signs. The lad was young, handsome, and very dead.

'Where are his shoes?' he muttered, half to himself.

The man with him was shaking.

'What?'

'He has no shoes on. Look, bare feet. I'm sorry, but I can't do anything here. I have to get back to the driver; she still has a chance. Listen, are you up to staying with him, just until the ambulance arrives?'

The man nodded mutely, then climbed in with the boy and gently took a lifeless hand in his. Justin wondered if the fellow had a son of his own.

Back at the VW, he checked the woman again and noticed a thread of consciousness returning. 'That's my girl, you're doing fine. You'll soon be safe, just stay out of it for a bit longer, until they get you out of here.'

Sirens screamed up beside him and blue lights flashed from every angle.

Thank God! The Cavalry.

* * *

A&E was calming down after the usual Saturday night riot of assorted wounds from the bottle over the head, the glass in the face and the boot in the ear. Vomit and blood had been washed away, and Staff Nurse Alex Cotton was heading for the rest room and a well-earned cup of coffee. As she approached reception the red telephone rang. The receptionist was nowhere to be seen, so with a sigh she picked up the receiver and watched her vision of a steaming hot drink fade into oblivion.

'RTA, four minutes away, two casualties, one female, head injury, trauma to chest and fractured right tib and fib, and a young male, suspected fatality.'

Alex gathered up the team. 'Is resus ready?' she called out.

'Yeah, it's free now. The ruptured spleen is just off to theatre.'

'Where's Jack?'

'Right here!'

Jack Barker, the casualty consultant, shambled out of Sister's office. At any given time of the day or night he managed to look as if he had just been washed up somewhere after a bad storm. Anyone who had ever worked with him, however, knew that his inability to do up his buttons correctly did not affect his reputation of being one of the sharpest and most astute Accident and Emergency consultants in the country.

'What have we got?'

As Alex filled him in, the porter called from the door that the paramedics were arriving.

The team, led by their crumpled maestro, proceeded to do what they did best. Skilled hands lifted, held, massaged, manipulated. Deft fingers inserted tubes and needles. Voices rang out. Feet scurried this way and that. Orders given. Orders accomplished. To the outsider it would have looked like Bedlam, but after nearly an hour, two consultants, two doctors, an anaesthetist, a radiographer, a sister, a staff nurse, three SRNs, and one nurse practitioner, gave Ellie McEwan her life back.

Not that any of them were sure what form that life would take; the only certainty was that it would be very different to the one she had woken up with that morning. They had stabilised her and ensured that her body was strong enough to endure the coming operations. A neurosurgeon would excise a piece of bone that was pressing on her brain, and an orthopaedic surgeon, with rods, pins and screws, would sort out the Chinese puzzle that was her right leg.

The chest trauma, at least, had been less serious than it appeared. It had proved to be a cracked sternum, one cleanly fractured rib, and heavy bruising.

As the trolley took Ellie to theatre, another took Joseph Edward Saville, to a more private place, to await the arrival of his parents.

Alex was exhausted. While you were busy, working on the adrenalin rush, it was fine but, when you stopped, the limp-rag syndrome took over. She had felt like shit even before the shift had started, and she cursed the fact that she had fallen in with the others and gone out clubbing till God knows what hour the night before. Her break was long overdue and she went to the locker room to get some change for the machine. Hurrying down the corridor, head lowered, hunting through her purse for the right money, she cannoned straight into a green paramedic uniform.

Justin helped her pick up silver and bronze that was rolling under discarded wheelchairs and oxygen stands. 'Looks like we are heading in the same direction. I've just been stood down for a while, I could kill a coffee. What a night!' The RR driver grinned at Alex. 'You look awful!'

'Thanks a bunch, J. I need you like a hole in the head. Speaking of which, your mates, Mal and Ian, said you went to that woman in the RTA tonight?'

'Yeah, you know what is really bothering me, the dead kid involved, he didn't have any shoes on. It was really weird.'

'Seems he was higher than Big Ben, perhaps that had something to do with it?'

Justin ignored the large 'Out of Order' notice on the drinks machine, fed some money in and thumped it strategically. Hot coffee poured into a polystyrene beaker. He repeated the performance and handed a cup to Alex. They both flopped down onto uncomfortable plastic chairs in the tiny waiting area that served the now closed plaster room. 'How's the woman?'

'She arrested once, but Jack brought her back. She's in theatre now, there is a depressed piece of bone sticking into her brain, but neurology seem pretty hopeful that when they get it away there should be no permanent damage.' Her voice softened. 'But you know, as well as I, what that could mean. Her leg's a mess, she's lucky that Royston is the orthopod on duty, if anyone can make a good job of it, he will.' The nurse pushed her dark fringe back, rubbed her eyes and stared at the dog-eared posters offering advice for a multitude of illnesses. 'God, I am so tired!'

'Too many late nights,' said Justin smugly.

'Oh yes, and of course, you stay in, drink cocoa and knit blankets for Oxfam, I suppose?'

'Not exactly, my sister's borrowed my knitting needles, but I do like a nice mug of cocoa now and then.'

'Sad man.' Alex drained her cup and got up to put it in the bin. 'Seriously, Justin, I think I've really overdone it this time. You said that accident you went to was weird, well, I had a few bizarre moments in resus tonight.' She sat back down and looked at her colleague, wondering if she should tell him. Well, she had gone this far, so why not? 'We were all working like crazy to get the McEwan woman stable, someone was calling for Hartmann's solution and Jack was demanding that we get a portable chest X-ray. I turned to call the radiographer, and I nearly fell over this old woman. She was standing up against the wall, just watching us.'

'Perhaps she was a relative, or a drunk wandered in by mistake,' ventured Justin.

'Oh, no, it gets worse! For all the world, I thought I saw a dog with her! A brown-and-white dog! Then Jack called out to me, I turned back, and she'd gone! Honestly, J, I had to have imagined it, surely?'

The man's face was serious. 'I suggest you slow down a bit, Alex, catch up on some sleep and give the late nights a miss for a while. You can't afford to be ill or have hallucinations.'

Her eyes were suddenly misty, and she was worried that Justin might think she was going to cry. 'It was so real, I honestly thought . . .'

'Don't beat yourself up, kid, you're just overtired. Get some proper sleep, okay?' He tossed his cup towards the bin, missed, and went to pick it up. 'Gotta go. Control will be sending out a search party. You look after yourself. See you.'

* * *

Justin sat heavily back in the driver's seat of the Renault. He stared out of the windscreen, not really focusing on anything. As the nurse had told her tale, he was remembering the moment when he had first looked into that car on the A3. There was just the driver. Then, as a vehicle had passed on the other carriageway, throwing light and shadow through the crashed car, he thought he had seen another figure in the back . . . it had looked like a woman, and something else. It had appeared to be a dog. Then nothing, so it'd just been a trick of the light, but after what Alex had said . . . He took in a deep breath. Surely he . . .?

'Bravo Two Zero. Collapse. Sixty-year-old male. Talbot Hotel. Ripley.'

Justin turned to the radio and put his brain back on duty. 'Show me attending.'

CHAPTER FOUR

Carole strode up the flinty, tree-lined path, and hoped the wind would blow the stink of the hospital from her. Phil McEwan, Ellie's brother, had telephoned her that morning and informed her of the accident. She had felt sick at the news, but at least the waiting was over. Her premonition had come to pass.

Carole suspected that he had rung several of Ellie's close friends, not out of loving concern, but to cut down on his own hospital visits. She kicked a dead branch out of her way and decided that she disliked him almost as much as she had Stephanie.

She had immediately called the hospital and had been put through to Intensive Care. After confirming who she was, she was passed on to the unit's sister in charge. It seemed that Philip McEwan had left specific instructions regarding Mrs Cavendish-Meyer. In the absence of any other relatives, he insisted she be made aware of all aspects of his sister's condition. Carole had silently fumed at this buck-passing, but asked if she could visit her friend. The sister said this would be welcomed, although her stays should be of a short duration to begin with. Ellie, she explained, was not yet conscious after the long operation of the night before. They could not tell how long she would remain that way, but a familiar voice was considered helpful. The senior nurse's tone had been compassionate when she told Carole that her friend had been very badly injured and, although she was stable, did not have a particularly good prognosis. She had gently advised Carole to prepare herself for a shock when she first saw Ellie.

Carole had driven straight to the Royal Surrey Hospital, noted that Phil was not there, and while waiting to be taken in to see Ellie, seethed at his shifting of responsibilities on to others. It was not that she would have done any different; she would have been there for her friend no matter what. She simply felt desperately sorry for Ellie, who frequently defended her no-good brother, and asked very little of him anyway. She deserved better from her only kin.

She had sat with Ellie until she was politely shepherded out when the neurological consultant arrived to check on her progress.

Looking out over the Surrey hills, through leafless branches and dark pines and ivies, she thought of the awful sight that had met her when she had taken her seat beside Ellie. She had never been in an ITU before and was shocked by the girl's appearance. Drips, drains and noisy machinery had surrounded her. Ellie herself, lay like a marble figure in some hi-tec sepulchre. Carole could still feel the distress that had swept over her, seeing her friend in such a helpless condition. She could have wept, but covered her sensitivities in her usual manner, with brusqueness and acidity.

She had gone back in for another half an hour, then left, at the nursing staff's request, to allow them to attend to their unconscious patient. They thanked her for visiting, and asked if she may be able to return the next day, as it was always found to be advantageous for someone in that state to have friends or loved ones around them. She had promised she would and left her telephone number in case of an emergency. Day or night, she had added.

She called to her spaniels, who were dashing this way and that in the busy and industrious fashion of gun dogs.

They had walked further than she'd intended and the wind was biting. Her old thorn-proof jacket felt about as thick as a net curtain, and she could hardly wait to get back to Snug Cottage and a roaring fire.

As the five animals and their mistress made their way back down the track, she thought how very different life had become since Vera died. She loved the dogs, and she was at her happiest when out walking in the countryside. But the life had gone out of all the things that pleased her. She was sure the sunsets were still as beautiful, and when summer came, the branches of the lilac trees, adorned with fragrant flowers, the ones Vera had loved best, would still captivate her with their heady perfume, but . . . something was always missing. The love that made the simplest things special had gone, and for all her offhand chat about being able to contact Vera, the woman herself, the flesh and blood had gone, and she was lonely in a way she would not have believed possible. In the eyes of the world, nothing had changed, but without her friend to share its wonders, the world now seemed a rather sad place.

Until Ellie McEwan had arrived on her doorstep, laden with concern over her troubling nightmare, Carole had been burdened with an uncharacteristic apathy. Small tasks were taking on the magnitude of mammoth undertakings. It was an effort to get up in the mornings, and some days, she barely had the energy to play with her dogs in the orchard, let alone take them on their daily constitutional. Dr Littlewood had pronounced her fit as a fiddle medically, and he was certain that her malady was caused by grief. Grief, he had explained, did not always hit at the moment of passing, or at the funeral as the coffin disappears from view. To share twenty-five years, then lose your soulmate, was like the amputation of half of your very existence. Give it time, he had said. Well, she had plenty of that. She had decided she needed a mission, a campaign to get her back on track. Working two days a week in the local charity shop did not seem quite her thing, and she was beginning to think that for someone who had crossed deserts in an old army land rover, and canoed her way up swampy equatorial forest rivers, finding something stimulating in her sleepy village could prove to be a challenge in itself!

Then Ellie had rung her doorbell, and although it would not have been the crusade she would have chosen, she felt her blood rising again. The girl had no family other than her useless brother, and she would need practical help. If she survived, she would need a whole lot of that! Carole had time and money, and she was happy to give both in abundance to get her friend back on her feet again. They would help each other.

As she towelled down her damp and dishevelled dogs, she felt the stirring of the old peppery Carole Cavendish-Meyer returning, and she welcomed her with open arms.

* * *

'Why don't you have a break? You've been sitting there for hours.' A nurse stared down at her.

'I'll have a break when I want one, young lady.'

'Perhaps I could get you a coffee?'

'Horrible stuff! Tea with milk and no sugar, please.'

Carole had been in a sort of reverie. Talking incessantly to the heavily bandaged Ellie, she had almost sent herself to sleep. At first, speaking to someone and receiving no reply had been difficult but, after a while, she fell into a dialogue pattern that needed no answers. She told Ellie about the premonition at the Poacher's Inn. How she couldn't explain it to her without frightening her. Said that the ulcer was all made up on the spur of the moment. She recalled how she had sat up all night in the kitchen, sipping tea and berating herself for ever letting Ellie leave Snug Cottage. She described how she had sat there with the dogs, desperately trying to make some sense of that strange, misty picture with the figures and the lights. It had been familiar, but just beyond her recognition. She recounted how, as the telephone had rung on the Sunday morning, she had known, even before she picked up the receiver, that it had been the accident scene she had witnessed.

She railed against Phil and his shoddy treatment of his sister.

She crowed with unconcealed delight that Stephanie had gone from Ellie's life, and assured her that someone far more suitable would come along; of that she could be certain.

She told tales of her travels. Stories of strange people and places. She spoke of Vera and her childhood in India. The trips that she and Vera had taken together, and the adventures they had shared.

Repeatedly, she told her silent listener that she would get better. The emphasis was on the 'would' and it was not a request.

'Mrs Cavendish-Meyer?' The voice was deep with an authoritative resonance.

Carole turned. 'Mrs Meyer will do.'

'Good afternoon to you, I am Mr Carl Thomas. Consultant in charge of Ellie McEwan. May I speak with you for a moment?'

'How long is this poor girl going to be in this state?'

'Why don't you come into my office?' He left without waiting to see whether Carole was following him.

Being careful not to touch the drip, she gently stroked the unconscious woman's hand. 'I'll be back before you know it.'

* * *

Mr Thomas offered her a seat and said, 'After a telephone call with Mr Philip McEwan, I am given to understand that you are probably closer to my patient than anyone else. Would that be correct?'

Carole looked fierce. 'Possibly, although I would like to know how he came to that conclusion. He never spends any time with his sister.'

'It appears he is a very busy man at present. Too busy to get here. There are a lot of reasons, Mrs Meyer, why people don't like coming into hospitals, I am not here to judge him. My concern is for Ellie. She needs friends around her and lots of support. Can you offer that?'

'Of course I can,' she snapped. 'I'm here, aren't I?'

Thomas kept his voice even. 'What I am trying to say is that I do not wish to put any onus upon you, if I have been misinformed by Mr McEwan, that is all.'

He watched and saw the granite-faced woman visibly soften. 'I am sorry, and I appreciate what you're asking. It's just that I do not like Philip, or the casual way he is dealing with his only sister's life. Ellie is a lovely woman; he has a responsibility to her and should be taken to task over it!'

Carl Thomas had the feeling that Mrs Carole Meyer would be just the woman for the job, but said, 'That is as maybe, but let's talk about Ellie.'

'I will help you all I can,' she said simply. 'Ellie has other friends as well, but I know that they have families and work commitments. I am sure they will do everything possible, as and when they can. I, however, have no ties except my dogs. Now, please tell me what you want of me, and exactly how Ellie is. I need to know the extent of her injuries and your expectations of her recovery.'

Thomas smiled at the frosty woman in front of him. He would definitely want to have her playing on his side, rather than as an antagonist. He quietly prayed she would not bump into Mr McEwan while on his ward. God help him! 'Ellie is very poorly. The neurological procedure was more difficult than was first thought. The piece of bone that was pressing on the brain was removed safely, but there was some "shrapnel" underneath, and there had been considerable bleeding. The fact that she has not yet regained consciousness is some cause for concern, but I have known this state to last for much longer than this, and the patient still make a good recovery. I do not want to raise your hopes too much, we will not know the full extent of the damage until she is back with us. She will heal physically; of that I am certain. Her hair will grow again, and a fringe will cover the scar on her forehead.

She might need plastic surgery, but that is something for later. The orthopaedic surgeon has done a remarkable job on her leg. The right tibia and fibula were badly broken. I can show you the X-rays if you like?'

Carole nodded.

Carl Thomas got up, went over to the light box, switched it on and beckoned her over.

'These are the first films. They do not need explanation, do they?'

He saw Carole Meyer heave in a shaky breath as she examined the plates.

'And these' — he changed the pictures over — 'show the work of a great surgeon! See, here, how he has pinned this, and with these supports alongside the bone, look, a brilliant job, brilliant!'

He noted that Carole still looked shaky, but remarked that the second set of pictures looked more like a leg than the first.

Sitting again, Carl Thomas continued.

'The chest trauma, the sternum, and the rib will heal themselves, she will be very sore, but fortunately nothing punctured the lungs. We do have a decision to make.' He paused. 'Whether or not to transfer her to Atkinson Morley, where they specialise in head injuries. Neurology are happy to wait for a while, and I agree at this time. If I am concerned at any point though, I will have her moved immediately. Are you happy with that?'

'I want whatever is best for Ellie, and I will leave it to your expertise to decide what that is.'

'I will monitor her very carefully, be assured of that, Mrs Meyer.'

'I appreciate that. Now what can I do to help her?'

'Keep talking to her. Get her other friends in for short visits. Play her some of her favourite music. We have a CD player, so if she has any CDs at home, they would be perfect. Most of all, always assume she can hear and understand you. It's all we can do right now.'

'You forgot about praying.'
'Oh, yes, and that as well.'

* * *

Back with Ellie, Carole decided she needed a master plan. There was much to be done, and it was obvious that Phil wasn't going to feature heavily in the doing of it. Although she would have loved to 'vent her spleen' in his direction, she decided that could wait until Ellie was better.

In her handbag she found an old shopping list and used the back of it to make some notes.

She needed to telephone Ellie's friend Gill and organise a visiting rota.

She must telephone the flower shop and check that Phil had informed them of the situation. She should also organise some flowers for Ellie, perfumed ones might help.

With a grunt she wrote down, *Telephone Phil McE. Keep temper in check. Ascertain what part, if any, he will play in E's recovery. Ask for key to E's house, she will need toiletries, the CDs, and hopefully clothes, etc.*

She frowned, because on the home front, she needed to contact her friend Marie Littlewood and see if she could assist with dog sitting and exercise. Oh, and petrol! That was urgent, and meals too. She hated ready meals but they would have to do for now. Finally, she scribbled, *Telephone G.K. to get temporary* . . . She crossed that out and wrote, *permanent cover for my Meals on Wheels run.*

Carole read it through. 'Okay, my girl, I'll soon get this organised. I have to go now, feed my boys, and make some telephone calls. You sleep until I'm back, and by the way, don't worry about that brother of yours. I won't make mincemeat of him just yet, even though I'd dearly love to!' The next words were very difficult but she said them anyway. 'I know he is not my favourite person right now, but I'm sure there is a good reason he hasn't managed to get here yet. I'm sure he loves you, and he'll be here soon.' *Bastard!* she added silently.

At home, she made short work of the list. Gill would call as many of Ellie's friends as possible, and sort out visits at varying times, starting with herself that night.

Ellie's staff at her florist's shop were stunned by the accident. Peter, the manager, no matter what Ellie might have thought, was up for a challenge and was going to do his best with the buying. They wanted to send the flowers that Carole had requested, but Peter pointed out they would have to wait until she was out of ITU. They did not allow flowers with all that expensive equipment. He made Carole promise she would assure their boss that they would look after her shop and not let her down.

Carole believed them.

Dogs, Meals on Wheels, and Sainsburys were dealt with, that left Phil.

Carole took a deep breath and picked up the telephone.

'I am sorry, but Mr McEwan is with a client. Can I take a message?'

Carole swallowed back the phrase that came to mind. 'My name is Meyer. I need to speak with him regarding his sister. I want a return call and no excuses. The number is—' She was cut off mid-sentence by another voice on the connecting line. 'This is Philip, Mrs Meyer. Is there a problem with Ellie?'

'Not specifically. Other than the fact that she is in a coma! Now, listen to me, young man. I don't know why you have not been to the hospital, but there are things to be attended to and I want to know just how much you are prepared to deal with and how much you want to foist off on to others!'

Philip was slow to reply. 'Look, I know I owe you an explanation, but I can't go into it here on the telephone. Suffice it to say that I cannot go to see Ellie right now.'

Enraged, Carole was about to burst in at that comment, but he stopped her. 'I said I will explain! Leave it at that will you!' His tone changed, anger subsiding. 'I will take over anything I can do from here. I can raise cheques for the shop, get her car insurance sorted out, deal with any legal stuff that might occur, in fact, whatever you need Mrs Meyer, the money is here for you, if you will be there for Ellie . . . please?'

As there were obviously more agendas here than she knew about, Carole simply said, 'Your sister needs you. I don't know what your problem is, but I suggest you address it! And yes, I will be there for her, but you can stuff your money.' For all her tatty corduroys and old banger of a car, Carole could have bought and sold Philip fifty times over. 'I need a key to Sefton Place. Ellie will need some of her things.'

'I have a set here. I'll send one of my staff straight over with them. Are you at home now? Oh, and thank you, Mrs Meyer, I—'

Carole made an exasperated huffing noise and hung up.

Philip's business was based in Guildford, and in less than thirty minutes, a smart young man was handing her an envelope containing Ellie's keys. Oh well, he'd been as good as his word for getting those to her. Now Carole hoped he would honour all the other things he promised, including explaining his reticence to visit his sister!

* * *

At the back of Snug Cottage was a flagstone courtyard. The walls on either side were red brick, and in the summer were festooned with swathes of old roses and clematis. They grew in such profusion that it was sometimes hard to see through the archway to the orchard. At the far end of the courtyard was a high ironwork gate that led through to a large lawn area, edged with trees and wide herbaceous borders. Nestling in the corner nearest the courtyard, where in good weather it attracted long hours of sunshine, was a summer house.

It was to that place Carole went before returning to the hospital. It was no ordinary summer house. It had been Vera's brainchild, and she had spent weeks planning its location and designing the layout. Hexagonal in shape, it was built of cedar, with big French windows to the front, and long narrow alcove windows in the sides.

It was their quiet room, a retreat where they could go to be away from the telephone, the TV, and the twentieth century. They had furnished it with a cane settee that had the biggest puffiest cushions Vera could find, a rattan chair with a brightly coloured blanket throw, and a table with upright chairs, where Vera could do her watercolour painting and Carole could read or study her tarot cards. Bookshelves nestled under the window alcoves and a long low coffee table sat in front of the settee. It had been their sanctuary, a peaceful place, and hardly a day had passed without them spending some time there.

Carole still went there every day and sat quietly with her memories, or sometimes she meditated in the glorious garden.

She opened the door and was greeted by a gentle perfumed warmth. She kept it heated right through until late spring, and frequently burned incense sticks to aid with her meditations. Switching on the old CD player, she waited until soft, tranquil music drifted around the room, then settled herself in the comfortable chair and took some deep breaths. She pushed away unwanted thoughts and lowered herself into a deeply relaxed state. She offered a prayer for her protection, asked for a ring of white light around the summer house and herself, then sank into a deep meditative state.

A strong smell of lilacs overpowered the incense, and Carole knew Vera was with her. The feeling of relief and happiness that spread through her body, warmed her soul. All too soon the calm was replaced by a sense of agitation and urgency. Behind her closed eyes, she saw she was being handed the purple satin bag that held her tarot cards. Tarot to her was a Universal Oracle, the best way she knew to focus and to understand situations. She had been taught to use the tarot as a small child by Grandmother Hobbs. The old lady had been a follower of the Craft, believing that no self-respecting witch was worth her salt unless she had a good working knowledge of the cards. Knowing that her only granddaughter had inherited her gift, she made sure she would learn properly and show due respect for the ancient symbols. Young Carole had taken to them with a natural aptitude and reverence that had pleased her grandmother, who encouraged her to use her talent wisely and for the right reasons.

Slowly she got out of the chair and walked across to the table in the corner. It was spread with a dark velvet cloth and in the centre was the bag containing her cards. She sat on an upright chair and began to shuffle her precious cards. She cut them three times, then began to lay them out, face down, in the pattern that was so familiar to her.

After a while, she turned them over one by one. She gazed at them individually, then as a whole. A story unfolded and she spoke softly to herself, of that which she perceived. Whispers around her encouraged her, and explained when she was at a loss to understand. Running her fingers over one card at a time, she named them and their significance, until she was satisfied that there was no more to draw from them. Words and feelings had flooded through her, and after blessing her cards and carefully putting them away, she felt drained.

She felt again the intake of breath when her fingers had touched the Tower. Its divinatory meaning was a traumatic change that will lead to a new awareness. Freedom gained only at some cost. Words spun through her thoughts. Danger, confusion, courage, confrontation. She had seen the High Priestess and the Hermit. Major Arcana, powerful cards. The most encouraging thing to come out of the reading had been the last card. She could not have wished for anything better for her friend. Strength. A beautiful card.

She thought of it now as she sat and stared at the empty table in front of her. A woman rides on the back of a lion; one hand grasps the animal firmly by the tail. She carries the caduceus, a staff of serpents, and at the top of this is a sphere of pure white light. In the background is a mountain over which the sun shines from a blue sky. Beneath the lion's feet is green fertile grass.

Yes, a beautiful card, offering Ellie spiritual and mental strength, great courage, the ability to develop latent power, mastery, defeat of negativity, and the ability to succeed and overcome all obstacles. *If* she could make it that far, and only if it was what she wanted.

Carole prayed, thanked her angels, sent love to Vera, then quietly closed herself down. She locked the summer house and went back indoors for a long drink of water.

It had been a revelation to realise that Ellie's fight would not finish with her battle to recover from the accident. At least Carole had no doubts that she would recover. This was just the beginning, the start of something else altogether. Something Carole did not fully understand and it made her feel very uneasy.

CHAPTER FIVE

True to her word, Gill Edwards was sitting with Ellie when Carole got back to the hospital. They had only met once before, at an anniversary party at Fleurie: Ellie's shop. Every year on the third of February, from when Phil and Ellie were tiny, the family had celebrated the shop's beginning with an open evening for their friends and customers.

The two women, united in grief at Ellie's misfortune, hugged as if they were old friends.

'I've spoken to everyone I can think of and left messages galore. With you filling in all the gaps and allowing for Ellie having some rest, I think I've got it covered.'

Gill looked tired and Carole remembered being told that she had some insidious form of arthritis, even though she was only in her thirties. 'I still can't believe it! Ellie is such a careful driver. God, we've driven miles together. It doesn't seem fair. Do you know what really happened? Phil was rather vague, and I didn't have chance to ask you earlier.'

Carole shrugged. 'I'll tell you all I know when we pop out for a tea later. I don't want to say too much in front of Ellie, we have to believe that she is aware we are here and knows what we are saying.'

'Fine by me.'

Gill and Carole sat either side of the bed. They chatted together and continually included the silent third member of the group in their conversation. They spoke of the time they had met at the shop and Gill asked why the florist shop had been named Fleurie.

'Oh, Ellie will tell you.' Carole addressed the rest of the conversation directly at their unconscious friend. 'Apart from being French for flower, your father named it after your mother, Florence, or Florrie, as she was known, didn't he, Ellie?'

'Ah, yes, I remember you saying,' added Gill. 'I really liked your mother.' Gill held Ellie's hand. 'You are a lot like her, you know.'

'Sorry, ladies. Ellie here needs some attention, don't you, my love?' The male nurse asked if they could give him ten minutes to check his patient.

They walked to the drinks machine in the corridor outside. Away from their friend, they were subdued and found themselves talking in hushed whispers.

'What are her chances, really?' asked Gill. 'I know you've spoken to the doctors.'

'They are cautiously optimistic, I would say.'

'What of, her regaining a proper life or just pulling through with heaven knows what disability?'

'I don't know, and neither, I think, do they until she wakes up. All her physical injuries should heal, even the shattered leg. It's the brain damage they are in the dark over. It is my gut feeling that she will recover, completely. I can't substantiate that statement, but I believe it.'

'Let's both believe that,' said Gill emphatically, 'and perhaps Ellie will hear us and believe it too.'

They took their drinks back to the relative's room and sat down.

'You asked how the accident happened, Gill . . .' Carole told her all she knew, and finished by saying, 'Apparently, several motorists missed him by inches. Ellie was the unlucky one who didn't.'

'Poor Ellie. The boy died?'
'Instantly.'
'Oh.'

A silence drifted over them. There seemed little left to say.

* * *

Anxious to organise some music for Ellie, Carole left the hospital in the knowledge that she was in good company and made for Weybridge. Sefton Place was a new development on the Brooklands Estate. Number 31 was a two-bed, Victorian-design house. Carole preferred old properties but was nevertheless impressed with the attention to detail that had been lavished on a comparatively small, modern home.

She picked up the mail and the local free paper, placing them on the hall table. Perhaps she should bin the paper. Ellie would not be around to read it. Taking it to the kitchen, she briefly scanned the front page. There was a piece about the newly proposed recycling plant that was causing uproar locally, but it was mainly taken up with the murder that occurred last month in Oatlands. Poor woman, thought Carole, you just cannot believe what some so-called human beings are capable of.

She shuddered, threw the paper in the rubbish, and went to look for some CDs.

Most of the artists were completely unknown to Carole, but she picked up some unfiled ones that lay on the top of the sideboard beside the hi-fi. If Ellie had been playing them, then it stood to reason, she must enjoy them. She released the one that had been left in the player and returned it to its case. Eric Clapton. At least that name was familiar. She thought he might be a local hero, although his music meant nothing to her.

She busied around checking the sink, the dishwasher, anything that should not be left for a long period. She threw the perishable contents of the fridge into the bin, then took out the black bag, tied it up and took it to the dustbin in the garden. It was obvious, even with her great love of flowers, Ellie didn't get much time for gardening. Carole made a mental note to get Scrubbs to pop over next week, cut the grass, tidy the flowerbeds, and wash down the patio area. Before she left, Carole walked briskly through the whole house making sure nothing had been forgotten. She could not help noticing that all the photos of Stephanie had gone. Not one remained. 'That's my girl,' she whispered. 'I hope they are in the bin with the other rubbish!'

* * *

At ten o'clock that night, Carole felt a gentle hand on her shoulder. She was used to the continual coming and going of the nursing team and had learned to almost shut them out of her communion with Ellie.

'She also serves, who only sits and waits.'

She looked up and gave a weary smile to Carl Thomas.

'I think maybe you should get home, don't you? You can't help her if you are exhausted yourself.'

'You're right.' Carole slowly rose both hands in a gesture of surrender. 'I hate to admit it, but you are right.'

* * *

Much later that night, in a comfortable, safe world of soft lights and shadows, a world protected from pain by a cocktail of chemicals, Ellie wondered why the angels were playing 'Tears in Heaven'.

* * *

As a little thank you for her loyalty, Carole was alone with Ellie when she woke up.

It was an unremarkable awakening, a return to consciousness for a moment or two before she closed her eyes again and uttered a small sound; something between a sigh and a groan.

But it was a start. The staff were delighted. There was much back slapping and when someone, rather courageously, hugged Carole, she decided it was time to go to the cafeteria for a cup of tea.

CHAPTER SIX

A week later, and Ellie was moved to a room off a main ward. Physically she was healing, but her state of mind was about as low as it could get.

Every professional available had talked to her, but Ellie was obsessed with the boy who had fallen from the heavens in front of her car. The boy she had killed.

No one had expected her to remember anything about the accident and, for the most part, she didn't. She had no recognition of Justin, none of being cut out of the car, and no memories of being brought to the hospital. But she did remember the angel-faced boy whose countenance had filled her windscreen for one brief second before he died.

That was bad enough, but there was another very disturbing after-effect of the accident, or maybe from her life-saving operation — she didn't know which had caused it.

It had been there from her first recollections of coming round. Bright lights surrounded everyone she encountered. Her whole world was a kaleidoscope of vivid multicolours. Focusing on inanimate objects was difficult enough, but if what she was looking at had any kind of life force, it was almost impossible. Initially, she had believed that things would improve and hopefully return to normal, but after days with no change, her hopes of ever seeing properly again were fading fast. Dark glasses helped, and most of the time she had the blinds down, but the lights were still there, although somewhat muted. Even her dreams were interspersed with explosions of light and darkness.

Ellie was profoundly unhappy.

She would have believed, if presented with the idea she would narrowly escape death, that she would be positively elated to be alive. She had been assured that, with hard work, she would walk normally again. Even though her head injury had been bad, and she sported a crescent moon of a scar that went from her scalp, then scooped across the top of her left eye, it was already apparent that in time it would heal and could easily be covered by her hair.

The bruises on her chest were now a dull yellow with a slight mauvy discolouration — another week and they would be gone. It still hurt to breathe deeply, but the pain was less every day. Even the ocular disturbance would surely settle in time?

So why did she feel that every part of her was depressed? Enough time had passed for sensibility to dictate that, yes, a boy had died in the accident with her car. But it was not her fault. No more was it Carole's fault for not making her stay over that night. It was not even the boy's fault. Without the drugs, he could have been the perfect son, but Ellie did not know. She did know, however, that she saw his face every time she shut her eyes, and that was the root of the trouble.

Her preoccupied state was interrupted by the dramatic entrance of Carole.

She laid an enormous bunch of flowers on the bed and declared, 'I've brought your florist's scissors. Let's see what the expert can do with hospital vases! Hah! That should tax the old skills somewhat!'

The colours that billowed out from the bouquet made Ellie wince with pain. She covered her eyes and began to sob. Even the things she loved most were hurting her.

* * *

Carole took the offending flowers away and asked a nurse to give them to someone else. Slowly, she went back to her tearstained friend, searching in her mind for the right words of comfort. She plumped up the younger woman's pillows, helped her lean back into them, and suddenly heard herself say, 'It's time for a talk, my dear, and I will tell you what I believe is happening. I will let you consider what I say, then, when you are ready, we will talk again. Do you remember what Vera once said to you about a precious gift? Well, let me explain . . .'

Carole spoke gently for nearly half an hour. Finally, she could see Ellie's eyes were heavy, and sleep was not far away. Silently, she left the ward, and asked the sister if Mr Carl Thomas was around, and if so, could she arrange for her to have a quick word with him.

Ten minutes later, she was back in the surgeon's office, but when asked if he could offer a medical explanation for Ellie's condition, Thomas shook his head. 'I'm sorry, Mrs Meyer, but I can't. Ophthalmology have assured me that her sight is not impaired. Be assured they have done every test imaginable, but it is nothing to do with her eyes; so it must be neurological. However, the brain scans have come back negative — there are no signs of haemorrhaging or any previously undetected damage. We are arranging for her to see a doctor from University College Hospital next week. She has been doing work on brain chemicals. She believes she might have some other documented cases of a similar nature. She's quite excited about meeting Ellie, and I think Ellie will be strong enough to see her by then. Her physical progress is nothing short of a miracle, you know.'

'Yes, I do know. But regarding her mental state, I have to say that I think you should leave her alone for a while. I believe this phenomenon, for want of a better word, is something that she will have to come to terms with in her own time.'

Carl Thomas thumbed through Ellie's notes. 'You could be right, but I'll let her see the brain chemicals specialist, and if I'm not happy with what she comes up with, well, we'll just monitor her and see how it goes. I won't admit defeat, but I have to say that this is something I have never seen before.' He paused for a moment. 'Mrs Meyer, I know you have offered to look after Ellie in your own home when she is ready for discharge, something that we are now considering. Do you feel you are up to that responsibility?'

Carole gave him a look that could have felled an ox at thirty yards, and he decided not to pursue that avenue further.

'We can offer a lot of support. Don't be afraid to ask. I will certainly sanction anything you may need.'

'Thank you, but my home is well suited for Ellie. I had a lot of work done for my partner. She had trouble with stairs, so I put in a ground-floor wet room, and the library would make an excellent bedroom cum study for her. I think she will be comfortable and safe with me, Mr Thomas.'

'I'm sure there is no one I would rather entrust her to.' He paused, staring at his desk and pushing a pen around. 'I get the feeling you have a theory on Ellie's sight problem . . . ?'

'I don't think it is a problem, well, not a medical one, but yes . . .' She took a slow, deep breath. 'I believe that Ellie had a near death experience. A doorway has been opened, and her life will never be the same again. She now has a gift, and she will have to learn how to live with it and use it. Right or wrong, I have said all this to Ellie, and left her to decide what she feels in her heart about it.'

'I have been a doctor too long to ignore NDEs. I have heard of them from the most varied cross-section of people. From frail old ladies to construction site workers. I would be a fool to disregard them, but I cannot begin to offer an explanation or a reason for whatever occurs.'

Carole smiled and said it was enough that he'd even acknowledged it and did not laugh at her.

'I wouldn't do that. After all, "there are more things in heaven and earth . . ." are there not?'

'Oh yes, Mr Thomas,' said Carole assuredly. 'There certainly are!'

* * *

Ellie had been moved to a different ward. It was warm and restful, with subdued lighting. She shared it with three other long-term trauma patients, all with eye problems. Carl Thomas felt that the side room she had been in was not helping, and that she would benefit from having others around her.

Sadly, there had been little change in Ellie's state of mind, but as Carole drove back to the hospital, for what seemed like the thousandth time, she decided it was the right moment to bring up their conversation of a few days ago.

When she arrived on the ward Ellie was alone, sitting in a wheelchair, her injured leg stuck out before her on a plaster board. She had her dark glasses on, and was listening to her CDs through headphones that Gill and her family had bought for her.

Carole felt a tide of compassion wash over her. For a while she stood in the doorway and surveyed her friend. She looked vulnerable and sad. Once so vibrant and full of life, now her head hung down, her once shoulder-length fair hair had been cut to a boyish crop, and the huge scar still looked livid and tender.

Noticing Carole, Ellie smiled weakly at her visitor and patted the bed next to her chair. She switched off the music and took Carole's hand in hers. She looked as if she was close to tears.

'I've been thinking about what you said.' Her voice broke, and she sobbed. 'Carole, I don't understand! How can this awful affliction be a gift? I can't see properly! It's horrible!'

Carole put her arms around Ellie and held her closely for a while, without speaking. She was grateful that the girl had taken the initiative and brought up the subject herself.

When she did speak, the cadence was soft and gentle, no hint of the irascible Cavendish-Meyer, and she caught the slightest hint of the perfume of lilacs drifting around them. She knew immediately that Vera was with them and guiding her words. 'Ellie, dear, it is a gift, make no mistake about that. It is simply in its raw state now. You have no idea how to control it, and it's frightening. Believe me, I can help you. Imagine something immensely powerful, like an airliner or a jet fighter. If you were put in the cockpit with no training, it would be terrifying. Now, imagine being taught how to fly properly, and the magnificent craft is yours to control, safely, enjoyably, and for the benefit of others. That is what will happen, I promise you. We can start whenever you are ready, and we will continue in the peace and quiet of Snug Cottage, as soon as you come home.' Carole squeezed Ellie's hand. 'You are going to be fine, just fine.'

Ellie wiped away the tears, squinted at her friend, trying to make out the familiar features through the pulsating colours. 'All right, if you can help me, let's start now.'

For an hour, until her roommates returned from their session in the hydrotherapy pool, Carole and Ellie worked together.

As the others hobbled and limped back in, light was dawning on Ellie in a very different way to what she was used to.

* * *

Carole left early that day, assuring Ellie that Gill's roster was operating successfully, and that she would have plenty of company. Carole told her that she had a long list of things to do, and an appointment to keep.

Ellie, having been put on her bed for an afternoon rest, had twenty minutes before her next visitors arrived. She closed her eyes and her mind raced through some of the things that Vera, no, not Vera, *Carole*, had explained. She had started doing some breathing exercises and direct concentration into some of the colour and light sources while Carole was with her. Lying quietly, she tried to continue defining and separating the colourful bursts. Almost immediately she noticed subtle changes and, for the first time, understood some of what her friend had told her. Perhaps she could find a way to control this?

She stared at Pauline in the opposite bed. At first, the teenager was inseparable from the glowing halo of coloured lights that surrounded her, but after a while Ellie managed to dampen down the flaring brightness until she could define the outline, and even some of the girl's features. Greatly heartened by this, she turned her attention to the ward aide who had just come in. But that proved too much for her. The woman was ablaze with a frenzy of colours that dazzled and glared at the sensitive Ellie. She closed her eyes and forced herself to take deep breaths. Relax! She continued taking deep breaths and recalled the conversation of earlier.

'Ellie, do you know how to meditate? It's very important that you calm yourself, lower your blood pressure, take charge of your body. It will help you understand what you are seeing.'

A few deep breaths later, she tentatively opened her eyes. The ward aide was still on fire, but there was a slight decrease in the intensity. Ellie felt her spirits lift, and experienced a surge of hope, the first positive emotion since the crash.

Carole had declared that she had been given the gift of auric sight, as a direct result of the accident. She had explained that everyone had the ability to see auras, but as we use so little of our brains or our senses, few people encouraged these skills. Ellie's ability had hit her like a hurricane, but with help she would be able to turn it off and on at will. The time would come when she would accept it as a natural part of her life, and she would use it like any other talent.

Carole had explained that what she was seeing were energy fields. Multicoloured images with layers, shapes and intensities. These emanated from anything with a life force, and that meant human beings, animals, plants, trees, stones and minerals. They were always there, like hidden halos, but it took either special cameras or a trained eye to see them.

That made sense. On the occasions when Ellie had been alone in a room, the strongest light sources surrounded the trees that she could see from the window. A bird flying past had appeared like a bolt of coloured lightning. There were even hazy lights around the box of grapes that Carole had brought her. She had no concept of what she was supposed to do with this new talent — that would come later. Right now, her main job was to tame the beast. When it was harnessed and safe, she knew she would discover how to put it to use.

Her thoughts were brought to an abrupt halt by the entrance of two small rainbow-hued bundles of light, followed by a taller figure, surrounded by a duller, less brilliant glow. Gill and the twins had arrived. Ellie held out her arms to the children and hugged them to her.

She smiled up at an amazed Gill, and said, 'I've got some really exciting news!'

CHAPTER SEVEN

Carole was ushered into a cosy room filled with books and crystals. The tightly packed bookshelves went right up to the ceiling. There was not an inch of space left anywhere — even the back of the door had a meridian and chakra chart on it. She sat in one of the two old leather armchairs and waited for her dear friend and guru to appear.

A bearded barrel of a man bustled into the room. He had a full head of white-grey hair, and peered over half glasses at her, before grasping her outstretched hand with both of his.

'Carole! What a lovely surprise. How are you?'

Pleasantries over, Professor Michael Seale stuck his head back round the door, asked Janet, his assistant, for two cups of tea, then settled down in the other armchair, facing Carole. 'I'd love to think you are here to invite me to the party of the year, but I've got the feeling it's business, am I right?'

'If anyone was going to throw the party of the year, it wouldn't be me, you old fool! And yes, I need information. A lot of it.' Carole looked him straight in the eyes. 'Michael, my friend, how long have you got?'

'All evening, if necessary. My last client has just left, and there's no one to go home to. I'm all yours!'

Tea arrived, and Michael told Janet to get away early. 'Now, we've got two choices, old girl. We can stay here, or talk in Chez Simone, two hundred yards down the road. Great moules, my treat.'

'No contest there, my friend, but we go Dutch. First, let's not waste the tea, and I'll tell you the bare bones of the story.'

* * *

Michael ordered a bottle of Sancerre to be brought immediately, while they surveyed the menu. Carole sipped the crisp white wine. 'Can't overdo the vino, Michael. I have to drive back to Surrey tonight and, guess what, I keep having nasty thoughts about car crashes.'

'Understandable after what you've just told me, but don't worry about this.' He pointed to the bottle. 'It won't get wasted. I'm on foot now. I moved last month to be nearer the consulting rooms. Home is just round the corner. Didn't you get my change of address card.'

'Yes, I just didn't know it was so close to here.'

They both chose the moules, followed by a salmon and pasta dish that Michael recommended.

'I'm amazed at what you've told me,' Michael said, gently tilting his glass and swirling the glistening liquid this way and that. 'I've only ever seen one similar case. A lad who had a potholing accident. He had all the right gear on but took a nasty fall. His brain got shaken up in his cranium, like whole peaches in a can knocked off a supermarket shelf. He was unconscious when they brought him up, and he stayed that way for two weeks. When he came round, he showed the same presentations as your girl.' His expression darkened. 'Let's hope she deals with it better than that young fellow did.'

'What happened?' asked Carole, unsure of whether she wanted to know the answer.

'Couldn't hack it. Thought I was a crank. I even got James Tasaki to talk to him, and James is the world's leading expert in auric sight, but the lad told him it was all bollocks, and hit the drugs. Died within a year of his accident. But then Jason didn't have you, did he?'

'Umm,' said Carole, pushing a mussel around in the delicate garlic sauce. 'I just hope it's enough.'

'Well, I'll tell you all I can about auric sight. As you already know, I was blessed from birth and I use it for healing. But there are other uses, and you'll need to see what your girl is drawn to. Would you like me to come down and see her?'

'I was going to let you have another glass before I threw that into the conversation! You've saved me the bother! Yes please, Michael, if you've got the time. I think it would help Ellie enormously to know that she is not alone with this ability. At present we are just helping her to get this under control, but I know that talking to you would be a massive step forward for her.'

'Who is "we"?'

'Vera is helping me.'

'Ah, good.'

Michael spoke at length, and finally they parted, having made a date for the healer to visit Ellie as soon as she was out of hospital.

Michael walked Carole to her car. 'Good Lord! This old bird is still running!' He patted the old Morris Minor estate. 'Give me a ring next week, and let me know how Ellie is doing. Don't mind me saying this, old girl, but get some rest yourself and keep yourself protected. You can't afford to be physically or psychically drained.'

'You aren't the first person to say that, Michael. But don't worry, I've got the constitution of an elephant!'

'Even elephants need sleep.'

'Yes, yes, don't fuss! I'll ring you soon with a progress report.'

* * *

Carole did not visit the hospital the next day. Gill had rung and said that she had arranged for some friends of Ellie to come up from the New Forest for a visit. As there were several of them, and Gill herself, Carole heeded Michael's advice and had a quiet day. She needed some space to evaluate what Michael had said, and to rethink some of the things that had happened since Ellie's visit after the nightmare. After lunch she took the dogs to St Martha's Hill and walked to the little church perched up on the high ridge. The wind blew her iron-grey hair, and she drew her scarf tighter under her chin.

Finding an old tree that had been blown down in the last storm, she sat on its horizontal trunk, while her spaniels busied themselves rooting through lime green moss and crinkly dead leaves. She missed her twice daily expeditions with her boys, although she knew that they were being well looked after by her friend Marie Littlewood. The view was wonderful, and she shared it only with the lord of the universe and five muddy spaniels.

She thought about Ellie. She did little else these days. Running a finger along the rough bark of the fallen tree, she wondered why she was constantly haunted by the feeling that Ellie was in terrible danger, but what sort of danger, she had no idea.

The girl was making such good progress, and Carole felt that she would very quickly come to terms with the auric sight. Ellie was strong and determined, and Carole guessed that, when she started to control it, she would take up the gauntlet and use it to the full. So where was the problem?

A powerful gust of wind ripped through the clearing, and Carole jumped up with its intensity. The bright day seemed to be blanketed over with dark menacing shadows, and the howling gale blew dead sticks around and hurled eddies of leaves in her face.

In seconds, the dogs were at her feet, cowered and frightened. Benjamin, the biggest Springer, scared of nothing, whimpered and shook at her side. On the other side of the great tree on which she had sat so comfortably, a strange figure was materialising. A whirling shadow of sticks and stones and every form of woodland debris shaped itself into what appeared to be human form.

Carole was frozen to the spot, as lights began to erupt from the apparition. Dark red, sludgy brown and grey — then scarlet and orange, and back to the sickening brown again. The form moved forward and bent over a dark shape on the ground. There was a sudden movement, and a bolt of silver grounded itself in the huddled shape on the grassy floor.

Carole prayed out loud. Shouted from her heart to whatever god was listening. Her hair was blown again, but this time with a warm breeze, and accompanied by the scent of flowers: the familiar smell of lilacs. A bright light entered the clearing, and the darkness swirled and faded. Leaves settled and the trees ceased their devil dance. There was a loud bark from the bushes, and a brown-and-white dog leaped towards the spot where the hideous blackness had been.

A howl of delight went up from her feet and then, fear overcome, the five canines rushed to the other animal, their tails wagging furiously. They met in a joyous melee, jumping and dancing, tussling and turning. Then suddenly, the dog had gone, and in the quiet, the other spaniels sniffed around in puzzlement. They ran quickly back when their mistress called them.

Carole sank back onto the tree. Her heart thundered as she looked up at the weak winter sun in an unusually bright sky.

'Dear Lord, Great Spirit. Give us your protection.' Her prayer continued all the way back to the car and on to Snug Cottage.

Still praying, she lit a fire in the study, poured a stiff scotch and phoned Gill. Her husband, Clive, said that his wife was not back from the hospital, but she had rung him some thirty minutes previously to say Ellie seemed in high spirits. She thanked him and hung up.

At that moment she missed Vera more than she ever had before. A physical pain in her chest reflected the emptiness she felt without her friend and confidante.

In the hearth, the flames crackled and leaped from the dry kindling to the jet-black coal. She stared at the bright sparks and remembered the ghastly lights that the man-thing had given off. No glistening life in it, just a sort of unwholesome luminescence. Colours that made her feel nauseous. The similarity to Ellie's nightmare was obvious, but what it meant was unclear and deeply disturbing.

The telephone shrilled out and Carole jumped. She was still very edgy from her earlier experience. Gill's voice flooded the line, delighted with the dramatic change in Ellie. She was thoroughly enjoying her friends' company, and two of them were staying on until visiting time finished. 'I can't believe the difference in her, Carole. She was almost the old Ellie, and she only mentioned the dead boy once all afternoon. It's really promising, isn't it?'

'Yes, I think we should expect a few backward steps — it's early days yet, but, yes, it's very heartening indeed.'

Gill hadn't managed to get anyone to go the next day, but Carole said she wanted some time with Ellie anyway, and it was no hardship for her to be there for most of the day. After hanging up, Carole took her drink with her to the kitchen, and prepared some supper. She was far from hungry, but decided she would need all the energy she could get, the way things were going.

* * *

To Carole's surprise Ellie's bed was empty. Being Sunday, she would not be having physio, and for a minute, a shock of fear pulsed through her.

'Is that Mrs Meyer?' called a young voice from the other side of the ward.

'Yes, who wants to know?' Carole turned, and saw a teenage girl wearing a skimpy nightie, and sporting a tattoo of a butterfly on her shoulder.

'Coo, touchy, aren't we? I'm Pauline. Ellie's gone off with some tasty geezer. He took her in the wheelchair. She said she had to meet someone outside in the grounds but wouldn't be long. So, you can wait, can't you?'

'But it's freezing outside! Whatever was she thinking of, and what's a "tasty geezer", for heaven's sake?' demanded Carole.

'Young bloke, sharp suit, or so Nurse Julie says.' Pauline pushed her dark glasses further back on her nose. 'Couldn't see him too clear meself, but he smelled good.' She laughed as Carole marched out of the ward.

After ten minutes of searching the grounds, Carole was shocked to see Ellie, huddled in blankets, and deep in conversation with her brother, Phil McEwan. A little way away, hands deep in the pockets of his sharp suit, stood the young man who had delivered Ellie's house keys to Snug Cottage.

Carole drew herself up to her full height, and like a battleship on a steady course, set her prow directly at Philip. The iciness of her demeanour must have forewarned him of her coming, because he jumped up and turned before she was anywhere near him.

'Mrs Meyer, excellent! We were just talking about you, and I have something to tell you. Please sit down. Ellie, you should go in now, it's very cold out here. Andrew will take you. Mrs Meyer will join you when we've finished.'

Words flooded from him in a constant stream, not allowing Carole to butt in on the one-sided conversation. Then he hugged his sister in a tight embrace and called Andrew to take her back into the warmth of the hospital ward.

'For heaven's sake man! Let's talk inside the building. This is no weather to be sitting in the bloody garden. It is December, in case you hadn't noticed.'

'I can't.'

'What?'

'I can't. I'm polyphobic, and I cannot go into a hospital.'

'Polyphobic?' Carole frowned. 'A fear of' — she paused — 'what exactly?'

'Lots of things. It means fear of many things, and this is one of them. Mrs Meyer, believe me, I tried on the night Ellie was injured. I was here for two hours, trying to go inside, but . . . I freaked, couldn't handle it. I'm sorry.' He shook his head. 'I find it very hard to tell people. I'm a businessman. I'd rather be thought of as a hard-arsed bastard than root-toot!'

'And Ellie, how much does she know?'

'I've had difficulties since I was a kid, constantly being dragged along to shrink after shrink. She knew some of it, but a long while ago I decided not to burden her with all my problems. I decided to put up a front. It worked quite well.' He shrugged. 'Until the crash.'

'What on earth would happen if you were ill or injured yourself?'

'God knows! I'm pretty much a recluse. I live over the main branch; it has a huge flat above it. So far, if I've been ill, the doctor has visited, and that's that. The staff run errands for me, and Andrew is my right hand, so to speak. He thinks I'm agoraphobic, and to a point, I suppose I am. I pay him to shop for me, drive and run errands, as well as work as an estate agent. He's very good and very loyal. I don't know what I'd do without him.'

'Hmm, well, I'd make contingency plans if I were you. I have it on good authority that he is a tasty geezer, so he may get swept off his feet by some little madam.'

For the first time, Phil laughed. 'Probably will one day, but I pay him enough to make him consider very carefully before he rides off into the sunset with a girl on his arm!' The smile disappeared. 'I apologise for my behaviour, and I appreciate your care, and all this help you've given my sister. Please understand, she could come home with me when she's discharged, but apart from the practicalities of the long flight of stairs to my flat, there are my disabilities to consider, and that is what they are. I would not be easy to live with. I wouldn't wish for anyone to share my world, especially my beloved little sister.'

'I wish you could have made the effort to tell me all this a little earlier. I could've saved a lot of the energy I spent on actively despising you! So, now perhaps we can discuss Ellie's future on a slightly more amicable level.'

'Certainly. I'll ring you next week. I'm afraid I have to go home now. I took rather a heavy dose of sedative to even get into the grounds here, and it's wearing off.' He fumbled in his pocket for a card. His hand shook as he passed it to her. 'My private number, whatever you want, just ask. You know my limitations, but there is not much that I cannot organise or achieve with a telephone, a huge database of contacts, and quite a lot of money. And Mrs Meyer, can I rely on you to keep this to yourself? About my difficulties?'

'Do I look like a gossip?'

'No, you certainly don't.'

Carole Cavendish-Meyer knew that she looked a lot of things, but an over-the-garden-wall chatterbox was not one of them, and from the look on his face, Philip McEwan knew it too.

Andrew appeared, produced the keys to the car, and prepared to drive his employer back to his hermitage.

As the silver Saab pulled out of the car park, Carole privately thought that it would certainly take a very special young lady to part Andrew from a Saab and his designer suits.

Back on the ward, Ellie was on her bed with her leg elevated. The nurse was just giving her some painkillers and a dressing-down for spending too long outside in a wheelchair. Carole thought the nurse was doing a pretty good job, so she didn't need to pitch in and help.

As soon as she had gone, Carole flopped into the armchair beside the bed. 'I suppose you are now going to tell me that I'm wrong about Stephanie, as well?'

'No, I think you're dead right about Steph.' Ellie smiled. 'And your opinion of Phil was perfectly understandable, given what he showed to the world. Even I never knew the whole truth. I thought he had got over most of his phobias, and had just grown into being self-centred — become a "Jack the lad" type. He has put on a very good act over the years, except that on a different level, I still loved him, and always knew he loved me.'

'What else is he frightened of, apart from hospitals?'

'I didn't know about the hospital thing. He was always frightened if he got too far from home, didn't really like going out much at all. He used to have a fear of birds, too. He would have an attack, a bit like asthma, if one came too close to him. Oh yes, clocks, and what was it? Ah, blood. I remember sharpening a pencil with a Stanley blade once, and I cut my finger. Phil went into shock. He was really ill and shut himself away in his room for the rest of the day. It was awful, poor kid, and because of it, he had a dreadful school life.'

'Clocks?' Carole looked puzzled.

'He couldn't cope with a ticking clock in the room. He'd stop them and put the hands to midnight. Don't ask why.'

'How very strange. Well, at least he's got in touch with you.'

'And he's liaising with Peter at Fleurie, doing all the admin and the books, and so on. The driver takes all the accounts over to him. That is a great weight off my mind.'

'Good. Anything to help keep you calm. Have you started meditating yet?'

'I've tried, but it was a bit hectic here yesterday. I used to go to yoga, so it shouldn't take long to get back into the habit. It was lovely to be with my friends yesterday, but I think I got a bit overtired. Staff nurse asked them to give me a snooze break mid-afternoon, just for half an hour or so, but I had a weird dream, so I didn't really get much rest.'

Carole felt a slight shiver lift the hairs on her arms. Casually she remarked, 'I'm sorry about that, did it upset you?'

'Not really, although it has stayed with me. I can remember it clearly. It was rather like watching a film. There was a wood, very pretty, and I seemed to recognise it. I was seeing it with my new sight, so everything was shimmering with green and gold light. Then this really strong wind got up . . .'

Carole dug her fingernails into the palms of her hands and forced a neutral expression to stay on her face.

Ellie continued, 'It got dark and stormy, and I remember feeling a bit frightened. There was something or someone lying on the path, and just as I, or the camera, was moving towards it, the whole wood was filled with this brilliant light. It was mauve, the colour of amethyst, and it engulfed all the darkness. Then you and Vera were there, throwing sticks for the dogs — all six of them. Benji, Orlando, Tug, Digger, Badger . . . and Monty! I woke up with the sound of barking echoing in my ears. It wasn't a "bad" dream, but at one point it seemed as if it was going to be.'

Carole realised the girl had not seen nearly as much as she had, and silently thanked God. 'So that was yesterday afternoon, and you slept okay last night?'

'Yes, my nap was at about three, I suppose, but I slept fine later, except the plaster on my leg bothers me at night, and who really sleeps well in hospital?'

Carole had been sitting on the fallen tree at three o'clock. What on earth was going on?

'Did you have a good day yesterday, Carole?'

'Oh yes. Got a few things done at the cottage and had some time with the boys.' Carole tried hard to push away all thoughts of what really happened yesterday at St Martha's, and Ellie's startling announcement about the dream. 'I saw an old friend of mine on Friday, his name is Professor Michael Seale, and he'd like to meet you. He has the same gift as you, Ellie.'

Ellie didn't answer straight away, then said quietly, 'Will he help me?'

'Yes, I'm sure he will. Let's get you a bit stronger, and then he will come down from London and spend some time with you. Do you feel up to doing some work now?'

'Of course, where do we start?'

The next hour was spent with teacher and pupil deep in concentration.

At the end, Ellie lay back, her eyes covered with a pair of shades that Carole had kept after a long-haul flight from the Far East. Carole then went to get them both some tea. She was surprised how quickly Ellie was gaining some control over the blinding lights and colours that flooded her vision. In the last hour, Carole had made her study and describe exactly what she saw around Carole herself. She then made Ellie mentally push the auras back, colour by colour, to form a gentle glow around her. In just sixty minutes, Ellie could make the flaring coronas recede to an acceptable level and hold them there for several seconds.

Carole took two polystyrene cups back to the ward and sat quietly talking to her friend. 'How do you feel?'

'My head aches terribly.'

Carole patted her hand. 'Then we won't do any more for a while. If you're up to it, we'll continue this evening, just for half an hour. You are progressing remarkably. Far quicker than I expected.'

'I don't feel as if I'm doing very well at all.'

'Believe me, you are. Now rest. Just lie with your eyes closed, and I'll tell you a bit about what the individual colours mean.' Carole spoke softly, and once again, caught the heady floral perfume drifting around them. She sighed and allowed Vera to guide her words. The soporific voice, different to her own, continued explaining what kinds of colours surrounded healthy people, angry people, spiritual people, calm, sick, injured, and so on. She also talked about the effects that colour can have, both physically and mentally. How looking at pink could weaken the muscles. About colour in merchandising, how deep green packaging made a product look classy, and orange made it look cheap.

She talked on, then saw that her apt pupil was drifting off to sleep. Carole smiled, silently thanked Vera for her help, and whispered, 'She's getting there, isn't she?' The smell of lilacs intensified, and Carole felt a warmth surrounding her. Yes, Ellie was moving forward into accepting her gift.

* * *

Ellie had been fascinated by what she had just heard, but her head was throbbing, and she felt herself drifting into sleep. Her arm fell over the side of the bed, her hand dangling towards the floor. Her fingers touched soft, warm fur. Instead of pulling away, she gently stroked the familiar back.

How ever had Carole managed to convince the nurses to let her bring one of the dogs in with her? She knew about Pets as Therapy dogs, but they were specially trained, and she couldn't imagine Sister Trenchard allowing a playful Springer on her pristine ward. A second later there was a slight draught on her skin, and then nothing but empty space under her hand. 'Oh, I'm only dreaming,' she thought, as she slipped into sleep.

* * *

Carole left Ellie sleeping and went back to her car to eat a sandwich that she had brought with her. Switching on the radio, she looked for a classical music station. She moved the ancient radio's dial backwards and forwards, never sure where to find anything and, not liking the cacophony of sounds she was picking up, left it on the County Sounds news bulletin.

Half listening, half drifting back to Ellie's odd dream, she heard there had been another death in Surrey. The newsflash said there were few details yet, but a woman's body had been found in the woodland that edged the Freeman's Golf Course at Woodham. The police were treating it as murder. The solemn voice was replaced with some giggly girl group, squawking about making love on a beach and Carole hurriedly switched off. She hoped the police would catch the bastard soon. It was not pleasant having this sort of thing happening on your doorstep. Placing screwed up foil and a sandwich crust in an old plastic bag, she locked up the car and returned to her friend.

That evening Carole coerced Pauline, who had no visitors, into joining in with a little experiment.

'Now, Ellie. I want you to stare at Pauline's aura. Work around her outline and describe what you see.'

Pauline, delighted to know that she even owned an aura, glowed like a yellow beacon.

'Gosh, she's very bright!' exclaimed Ellie.

'Right, look slightly to one side of her,' encouraged Carole. 'Now, push the brilliance back in towards the body, got it?'

'Yes, yes, that's fading a little.'

'How far out was her aura to begin with?'

Ellie concentrated. 'About three feet from her body.'

'And now?' asked Carole.

'About a foot.'

'Wonderful, hold that there. Is the aura completely surrounding her?'

'No. There are gaps in it.'

'Tell me where they are.'

'Her lower arms, wrists, hands, and her head, around the temples. It's very dull there.'

'Perfect!' exclaimed Carole in delight. 'All the injury sites! Pauline had sustained a blow to the head, resulting in temporarily damaged eyesight. Now watch.' Carole got up and walked over to Pauline. 'Tell me any changes that you notice.'

Carole whispered to Pauline for a few moments. Ellie saw red flashes spear through the yellow, then calm down, and a lovely orangey, pinkish blush spread around her.

Ellie described what she had seen, and asked Carole what had happened.

Carole smiled and told her that she had been very scathing about women with tattoos, which had made Pauline angry, hence the red sparks. She had then apologised, told her she had not meant it, that it was all part of the experiment and gone on to mention that Andrew had thought her very attractive. That had resulted in the tangerine and pink colours.

'Tell me one last thing,' asked Carole. 'Is it one solid colour band that you see around a person?'

'No, there seem to be layers. It's almost white against the body, then another colour, then a glow of another out from that. One colour always seems predominant though.'

'So, you can perceive three separate layers?' exclaimed Carole in surprise.

Ellie said that she could.

'Brilliant! Ellie, this is wonderful!' Carole was elated. 'It can take people years to come this far.'

'Great, but how do I turn the blessed thing off?' grumbled Ellie.

'Ah! Yes, well that's not quite so easy, but you are getting there, honestly. Now, rest those precious eyes!'

She handed Ellie the eye shades and gathered up her coat and bag. 'Time to relax. Is it tomorrow that you see this lady doctor from UCH?'

'Yes, crack of dawn apparently, she wants to do her tests at different times right through the day and into the night. Sounds like a barrel of fun, I don't think!'

'She could be tall, dark and gorgeous!'

'And she could be short, over eighty, and have halitosis!'

'I'll be interested to hear which, but I won't come in until Tuesday as you'll be exhausted after those tests. Now, is there anything you want from home. I can easily pop over tomorrow for you.'

Ellie couldn't think of anything, and Carole was given another day off. She sincerely hoped that it would be less eventful than the last one.

CHAPTER EIGHT

Alice Cross was not tall, dark, or gorgeous. Luckily for Ellie, neither was she short, elderly, or had bad breath.

In her late thirties, Alice was medium height, had straight fair hair that fell into a curtain over her left eyebrow, and piercing blue eyes. A cleft chin and dimples completed the portrait.

She strolled into Ellie's ward at seven on Monday morning, sporting a bright red-and-blue check shirt and navy chinos. 'Sorry to have to start so early,' she said after their introductions. 'I need a lot of graphs of your brain frequencies and an early morning one is vital.'

She produced a laptop, which she proceeded to plug into a socket behind Ellie's bed, and immediately began punching in information about her. 'I have taken a lot of info from your medical notes to save some time, past medical history and suchlike, but I do need to ask you a lot of questions. Are you okay about that? Do you think you're up to it?'

Her enthusiasm was so intense that, even without the barrage of excited lights beaming from her, Ellie would not have had the heart to say no.

'Then let's get the first graph out of the way.' She gently placed a headset on Ellie's crown and was very careful not to touch her wound. 'You won't feel anything, it's totally safe, non-invasive, and only takes about two minutes to do ten passes over the brain. I'll be doing these off and on throughout the day, and into the evening. I need to build up a picture from the readings.'

'What should I think about?' asked Ellie.

'Anything you like. The computer is delving a bit deeper into your brain waves than just your thoughts. It brings up activity through Alpha, Beta, Delta and Theta.'

'Is it similar to an ECG machine? I seem to remember those terms being used before.'

Alice pulled a face. 'Not exactly, although you are correct in a way. An ECG does multiple tracings of the electrical activity in the brain. My little baby here' — she patted the laptop with affection — 'doesn't need electrical connectors, it works with crystals and lasers. The information that it feeds back is very different.'

The morning passed swiftly, and Alice left her at lunchtime, saying she should endeavour to get some rest until she returned later to start the next session.

Ellie ate a light lunch, then dozed for what seemed only minutes before she saw Alice's glowing face above her.

'Sorry, Ellie, but we need to start again.'

The headset was back on before she had even fully woken, and Alice was sitting beside her typing fast on the keyboard.

A nurse appeared at her bedside, offering her the familiar little plastic cup full of pills. 'Time for your painkillers, Ellie.'

'Don't I know it,' she replied, wincing as she tried to ease her leg into a more comfortable position.

'Oh, hang on!' interrupted Alice. 'I need a graph every ten minutes after you have taken those, for about an hour and a half, I'm afraid.'

The next ninety minutes were taken up with graph readings and questions about her vision and her general well-being.

Alice was friendly; informative and humorous, doing her best to keep her patient cheerful through the long day.

As evening approached, she closed the lid of her laptop and sat back in the armchair. 'Interrogation finished, Ellie. Just a couple more scans later into the night, and we've completed all the tests. Tell me, have you ever heard of Azimah Siddiq Syndrome?'

Ellie shook her head. 'Not that I can recall.'

'It is very rare. I am doing a paper on it. So far, what I see here leads me to believe that you may have either the syndrome or something very like it. I'll try and explain.' Alice sat back. 'Head injuries and damaged brain cells, as you well know, can have terrible consequences, can rob you of your senses or your faculties, but sometimes they actually give you something extra, something that you never had before. Azimah Siddiq was an eminent scientist and surgeon, working in India in the 1980s. She discovered a link between certain damaged tissue and a chemical that is sometimes released at the moment of trauma. On the very rare occasions that this synchronicity occurred, it left the patient with some dramatic visual disturbances that proved to be visible images of magnetic fields surrounding all forms of life.'

'Auras,' whispered Ellie.

'Exactly! The chemical, simply known as Azimah, when reaching the damaged area, kickstarted this amazing ability. Well, I say "amazing" but I am told by the few surviving sufferers I have met that it is more of a curse. The good news is that, before she died last year, Azimah Siddiq managed to produce a drug regime that can suppress the disturbances to a manageable level.'

Ellie interrupted, saying. 'I am learning how to do that anyway, Alice. I don't want any drugs.'

'But, Ellie, that's impossible!' Alice looked amazed. 'You cannot control this on your own!'

'I can and I will. I've started in a small way, and I will get on top of this . . . without drugs. Alice, how many recorded cases of this are there?'

'Maybe thirty, worldwide. I've met eight sufferers, not including yourself, if this proves to be what has happened here.

I have been privileged to read Azimah's notes. Her documentation is most impressive. I met her once before she died, she was an amazing woman; it's a terrible loss to science and to humanity.' Alice was genuinely upset and her voice had a wistful quality as she said, 'I want to continue her work, if only I can get the funding.'

'I hope you do. Have any other sufferers beaten it without drugs?'

'No, not so far. Then there is the problem that the full syndrome has other presentations. The olfactory system is disturbed in some patients; they experience odd smells that aren't there. Some have other sight disturbances; they seem to witness things that others can't. Because of all the bright lights that they see anyway, it is very difficult to describe, but they do "see" things that others present don't. There are other more complex medical issues as well.' She considered what she had said, then continued. 'Do you have any other similar symptoms, Ellie?'

Ellie decided not to mention the smell of lilacs, and shook her head. 'No, no other symptoms.' She looked at Alice, carefully reducing the flaming halo around her face. 'And I'm going to be fine, without Azimah's drugs.'

Alice left that night with reams of graph paper in her briefcase, and promised to visit Ellie again, when her findings were confirmed.

Ellie liked her and sincerely hoped she would get her funding; then as Carole had predicted, she was exhausted, and fell into a dreamless sleep.

* * *

Breakfast was barely over when Ellie had a visit from her consultant, Mr Thomas. He had just come from a morning meeting with her orthopaedic surgeon and the neurological team. It had been decided that Ellie could go home. It would take a day or two for her discharge to be arranged, and for him to be certain that she had everything in place to assist her recovery.

'I shall be committing you into the very capable hands of Mrs Meyer, and frankly, my dear, she appears to be streets ahead of me with her preparations for the next stage in you getting your life back. She really is an extraordinary woman!'

'You won't find me disagreeing with that, Mr Thomas!' said Ellie vehemently. 'She has been my rock, ever since the accident.'

'And will be in the days to come, unless I'm very much mistaken,' replied the doctor. 'Now, I suggest you work with the physio, and get yourself geared up to leave us. Use the wheelchair and venture out of the ward for a while. You'll be feeling a tad institutionalised, I'm sure, so spread your wings a bit, and do a few tours of the hospital.'

After he left, Ellie decided to take his advice, eased herself into the wheelchair, and made her way to the nurses' station. Having told them of her intentions, she embarked on her first solo voyage of discovery along the hospital corridors.

It felt strange to begin with, but she made her first port of call the little chapel, and sat for a while enjoying the quiet, away from the hubbub of the main hospital. She then continued her trip, surprised at how many people she knew after her lengthy stay there.

'Hey, Ellie! How are you doing?'

Ellie looked up to see one of the nurses who had cared for her soon after she regained consciousness. Jean Brady was an older woman, with a beaming, kindly face and short curly grey hair.

Before Ellie could answer, Jean said, 'Go sit in the waiting area, just down there.' She pointed further along the corridor towards the Maternity Department. 'I'm on a break in five minutes. I'll buy you a coffee, and we can catch up.'

Ellie eagerly agreed, wheeling herself to the area Jean had indicated.

As she waited for Jean, she smiled at a couple of new mothers who were preparing to take their new babies home.

'Oh, she's beautiful!' exclaimed Ellie, peeking at a tiny bundle, warmly wrapped in a soft pink-and-white blanket in a carrycot.

The baby's mother sat with the cot on her lap, and gently stroked the little one's cheek with her forefinger.

Ellie was amazed as the tiny form glowed with a rose-pink light that lit up the cot.

'Ah, here's my husband, with the car.' The woman smiled at Ellie and waved to a man hurrying through the entrance door. 'Time to get this cherub home.'

Ellie watched them go, then turned her attention to the only other mother in the area. The smiling new mum was lifting her baby up to wrap more warm clothing around him in preparation for leaving.

Seeing this, Ellie stifled a gasp. The baby's aura was awful. Not bright and clear, and nothing like the other child. In horror, she saw the area around the baby's abdomen was a dark, turgid, muddy colour.

Ellie spun her chair around and headed for the reception desk, but before she got there, she saw Jean approaching her.

'What's wrong, Ellie? You look like you've seen a ghost!'

'Jean! There's a baby in the seating area, waiting to go home. You can't let him go! He's really ill! Don't let them discharge him, please!'

Jean's face creased into worry lines. 'Come with me,' she whispered urgently, and led the way into a side cubicle. 'Look, I know about the lights and colours that you see, but the doctors have given that child a clean bill of health. How can I go against them?'

'Believe me, Jean, that child has something terribly wrong in his tummy, and I mean *serious*.' Ellie wondered what she would need to do to make Jean act.

Luckily, she didn't have to, as Jean gritted her teeth and said, 'Okay, I'll find a reason to check him over again, even if my job is on the line. I'd never live with myself if I ignored a warning and a child suffered.'

'You won't lose your job, Jean, I know it. But that baby will die if you don't get help fast.'

Outside, Ellie watched as Jean pulled on a wide smile and said, 'Oh, Mrs Wilman! So glad you are still here. I'm so sorry. I'm just checking the discharge paperwork. We have new admin forms to fill in, and I need to do one final check on baby Harry. Just pop him back into the cubicle, and I can generate some aftercare information for you to take home.'

Ellie sat and watched, sick with anxiety. Minutes passed, then she saw a doctor hurry out of the main unit and dive into the cubicle. In under ten minutes, mother and child were being rushed out of the waiting area, and a white-faced Jean was left staring incredulously at Ellie. 'You were right,' she breathed, as she passed her. 'I'm afraid my coffee break is off for today. I'll try to see you later.' Then she was racing after baby Harry Wilman and his distraught mother, leaving Ellie wondering whether to laugh or cry.

* * *

At four that afternoon, Ellie had a second visit from Carl Thomas. He sat down heavily and stared at her. 'Nurse Jean Brady told me everything, and frankly, I'm at a loss as to what to say to you.'

'Harry? How is he?' It was all Ellie wanted to know.

'He's out of theatre, and he's doing fine, thanks to you,' replied Mr Thomas.

Ellie thought the surgeon looked positively haggard. 'Then that's all that matters, isn't it?'

'My dear young woman! You *diagnosed*, for want of a better word, you diagnosed a rare defect in that child's abdomen. It showed no symptoms, and there probably wouldn't have been any, until the anomaly increased in size, and either ruptured, or twisted and caused an obstruction. I dread to think of the consequences if that nurse had not listened to you.'

Ellie sighed with relief and smiled. 'But she did, so crisis averted.' She wanted to say more, but he looked so worried that she sat back and waited for him to speak.

After a moment, Mr Thomas said, 'I cannot begin to understand what has occurred since your accident, Ellie. We have no other cases to compare with, and that means we have no way of knowing if it's a permanent thing, or something that will pass in time. I just want you to promise me that you will be careful with your health. You have a whole lot of healing to do, and this new ability is very powerful, so make sure you are fully recovered before you commit too much time and energy to it.' He stopped and gave her a weak smile. 'If I were a different kind of man, I'd tell you to come and work here with me. If this skill is as amazing as it appears, we could ditch all the scanners and MRIs, and use you!' His smile faded. 'But I am not that kind of man, and I'm fearful for Ellie McEwan, and what this gift could do to her.'

Suddenly Ellie smelled lilacs. She reached out and gently touched the man's arm. 'Please don't worry about me, Mr Thomas. I know I have a long way to go, and a lot to learn. I also know that whatever path I'm meant to follow will be shown to me, but only when I'm ready. One thing I do know is that I won't be alone. I have the wonderful support of friends around me.'

'Thank heavens for people like Mrs Meyer.' He then added, 'One more thing. I suspect you will be hearing from Dr Alice Cross. She is beside herself with your case. She's told me that she believes you could be the missing link regarding the Azimah Syndrome — one of a kind.'

Ellie grinned. 'Nice to know I'm special . . . I think?'

The wan smile returned. 'Listen, Ellie. Remember what I told you about taking time to heal. Don't get caught up in the hype . . . don't get pressured into spending too much time and energy on someone else's dream. Don't get me wrong, Dr Cross's case studies into brain trauma and chemicals are very important, and by all means work with her, but not at the expense of yourself. You've been through so much, so take it easy for a while.'

Ellie felt a rush of affection for this man who had saved her life. He saw her as a human being, not as a patient with a number, or a specifically interesting illness or injury. 'Trust me, Mr Thomas, I'm not going to throw away everything you've done for me. Life really is too precious. Besides, I have Carole, and no way will she let me step out of line!'

Thomas laughed. 'Now, that is a very good point!' He stood up. 'And on that note, I must leave you. You have a lot of people to say goodbye to, and hopefully by tomorrow afternoon you will be safely ensconced in somewhere called Snug Cottage! I'll see you before you go.'

The rest of the morning flew by, and after lunch, Ellie began to pack her belongings into a canvas holdall. Now that she had got her head around it, although it was a little daunting, she was looking forward to this next big step towards getting her life back.

As she was folding the last nightie, she heard a soft voice behind her.

'Bet you can't wait for tomorrow.'

'Dr Cross!' Ellie was surprised to see her again so soon. 'Yes, it's great news, isn't it? Going home at last. Well, sort of home. I'll be staying with a dear friend until I'm properly mobile again.' She pointed to the plastered leg. 'All the ops are out of the way, and I'm learning to get about on crutches, but it would be a nightmare on my own.'

'Ah, yes. Mr Thomas told me about Mrs Meyer, and he's rather impressed by her, I have to say. Seems you will be in safe hands.' Alice Cross sat on the end of Ellie's bed. 'That's why I'm here now. I wanted to see you before you left the hospital.'

As she pushed the floppy curtain of blonde hair from her eyes, Ellie thought she might have been wrong when she told Carole that the doctor was not gorgeous. There was something very attractive indeed about the woman.

'So . . . you look great, but how are you feeling? How is the sight now?'

Ellie dragged her thoughts away from the fanciful. 'I've got a long way to go, I know that, but one thing I do know is that I won't need medication. I can do this myself, Dr Cross. I'm already improving with each passing day.'

'Hey, we agreed that you'd call me Alice, remember? And whereas I'm delighted to hear you are able to manage your visual disturbances, I'll always be around to help if things go pear-shaped. It might not be the kind of help you want, but it will be right here, if needed.'

Again, she pushed that swathe of hair to one side and, realising that it was a nervous gesture, Ellie wondered why she should feel that way. She didn't have long to wait to find out.

'Can I ask you something, Ellie?' Alice sounded both anxious and excited.

Ellie nodded. 'Of course.'

'Can I keep in contact with you? The thing is, I'd love to use you as a case study for my paper on Azimah . . . only with your permission, of course.'

'Does that mean you believe I have the syndrome?' Ellie asked.

Alice produced a great sheaf of printouts and graphs from a battered old leather briefcase. 'All my findings so far, from the brain frequency readings and electro-magnetic scans, show a distinct link to the trauma and the chemical, Azimah. You only show signs of the auric sight, Ellie, but they are classical! Thank God you don't seem to have the full syndrome, with all its other anomalies, but the mere fact that you're finding a way to deal with the lights makes your case unique! I would love to do a follow-up history.'

At that point, Ellie had to tone her down. The lights that radiated from the doctor were dazzling in their intensity. Carl Thomas's words flooded back to Ellie, and she said, 'Of course, I'll help if you think I can, Alice, but there is a "but", a big one.'

Alice exhaled and grinned at her. 'I know! You must have time to adjust to life outside the hospital, and to heal, but I can wait, honestly. I just need to know that I can continue to work with you.'

'That's it.' Ellie tentatively touched the scar on her forehead. 'In a nutshell, it's scary leaving all the protection and security of having professionals to call on. Mr Thomas called it being institutionalised, and he's right. This is a big step, and not one I'm going to hurry. However, I'll give you my contact details, and Carole's too. We'll keep in touch, and as soon as I feel strong enough, maybe Carole could drive me to London to see you?'

As she spoke those words, she lost focus. Lights bombarded her, and a flash of a vision hit her; then it was gone. She grabbed her glasses and pulled them on, trying to calm herself.

'Whatever's wrong? Are you all right?' Alice's voice seemed to come from miles away.

Ellie swallowed. 'The boy. I saw the accident again, when I mentioned driving to London.' Tears filled her eyes. Then, through the blurry mist she saw a bright shiny hand grasp her own. She was surprised at the warmth of the touch.

Alice's voice was as gentle as her touch. 'It's quite understandable, Ellie. But nothing that happened that night was your fault. You were a victim, as much as he was. Try to consider it this way. You have been given a very rare opportunity to help others. You have already saved a life. Mr Thomas told me about Harry, and he would have died without you. By the time his symptoms started to show, his mother would never have been able to get him back to the hospital in time to save him. Without your accident, a family would have lost their newborn son, and without your boy, you wouldn't possess this wonderful gift. That boy is instrumental in every good thing you choose to do with it, and that makes him very special indeed. Think of him with love, and respect the fact that by his death, you can help others.'

Ellie sobbed and held on to Alice's hand. What the doctor had said was one hell of a responsibility, but it could be the answer. Finally, she stopped crying and said, 'Yes, Alice, I think, given time, I might be able to embrace that.'

They talked for a little longer. After Alice had left, Ellie felt as if the final brick had been cemented into the wall. Her time at the hospital was over; they could do no more for her, mentally or physically, and it was time to go home.

Alice had totally refused to hear of her travelling up to London, and they had left it for Ellie to contact her when she felt strong enough, and Alice would visit her. As it happened, she had a sister living in Surrey, so she would be more than happy to combine a family reunion with a trip to see Ellie. She'd said that, from what she had heard about Snug Cottage, it would be a far better setting to discuss her paper than some clinical, pokey hospital office.

Ellie spent the rest of the day saying goodbye to the lovely people who had become her friends over the weeks and, that night, she felt a rush of both excitement and anxiety. The excitement felt a bit like being a kid on the night before Christmas, too hyped up to sleep, and the anxiety came from leaving her safety net behind.

In the end, she gave in to both, and closed her eyes. A new chapter was about to begin, and she prayed she would be ready for it.

CHAPTER NINE

Snug Cottage, for all that its name implied, was neither snug nor a cottage. It was a lovely old lodge house constructed of warm red brick with sand-coloured stone lintels and two wonderful 'barley sugar twist' chimney stacks. High up, almost under the eaves of the roof, was a weather-worn stone plaque bearing the nearly unreadable legend, *Sydenham Lodge, 1824*. Vera had thought this altogether too pretentious and was not overly impressed by the fact that the only famous Sydenham she could recall was the physician who first discovered measles.

Before moving to Compton, they had referred to their, at that point undiscovered, 'dream-home-in-the-country' as a snug little cottage. The name stuck, and now a carved wooden plaque hung over the porch, declaring that this rather large lodge house was indeed Snug Cottage.

Inside, the rooms were spacious and refreshingly free from modern home-improvements. The courtyard, lawned garden, herb and vegetable area, the front flower beds and the orchard used to be cared for entirely by the two women, but since Vera's passing, Carole had enlisted the help of a retired local man. Scrubbs — Carole didn't know if he had a Christian name — had fallen hopelessly in love with the grounds, and spent an inordinate amount of time there, for a ridiculously small wage. As he totally refused what Carole considered a fair going rate, it had become a sort of game for her to find other ways of recompensing him without his realising it. This often involved an unwitting Mrs Scrubbs, who was a simple soul, and no match for her husband's calculating employer. As a result, the Scrubbs were rarely without fresh garden produce . . . 'But Scrubbs, how can I possibly eat all these vegetables!'

A freezer full of meals . . . 'Well! There I go again! I seem to have cooked far too much for one. Be a dear, Mrs S, and use this up for me.' Bills were strangely settled . . . 'I think you must be mistaken, dear, look it clearly says PAID, you've probably forgotten.' And once, when Mrs Scrubbs was in need of a small operation, the two-year waiting list miraculously disappeared and everyone was told, 'Honestly, lovey, I was looked after so well, you'd a' thought I'd gone private!' And so on.

Hence on the day of Ellie McEwan's return, the gardens, despite the winter, were still gorgeous. Heathers, hebes and Christmas roses vied for space with winter flowering jasmines and perfumed pink daphne. Mrs Scrubbs, who did a spot of cleaning, 'Just to help out now'n'agin, you understand?' held the door open for them, and Ellie's fears about being away from the hospital began to disappear.

The extent of Carole's hospitality became immediately apparent.

An electric wheelchair stood in one corner of the hall, and a huge vase of flowers, courtesy of the staff of Fleurie, graced the half-moon table next to the coat rack. All the loose rugs had been removed and the parquet flooring lacked its usual highly polished lustre.

'Can't have you breaking the other leg,' said Carole dryly. She led, the by now exhausted, Ellie into the library. 'This is your room for as long as you would like it.'

Ellie gazed about in amazement. She'd been in it many times before, but now it had been changed beyond recognition, and it was absolutely beautiful.

A log fire burned and crackled in the inglenook fireplace. French windows opened out onto the back courtyard garden, and Ellie noticed that a sturdy wooden ramp had been constructed to allow easy access to outdoors. Along one wall, a bed had been made up, with piles of fluffy pillows and a wonderful quilted throwover in an ivy design worked in a multitude of different greens. There was an old oak writing desk, a tallboy with drawers and hanging space for her clothes, a comfy armchair with a tapestry footstool; and still the books remained, hundreds of books. Shelves filled every blank bit of wall space. The overall effect was so warm and welcoming that Ellie felt a lump in her throat.

'This is just wonderful! I can't believe all the trouble I must have put you to.'

'For heaven's sake! It's nothing! Now, get that leg elevated and rest while I go and organise some tea. Probably be the first decent cup that you've had since you were here last!'

She left in a flurry of lovat tweed, and Ellie lowered herself gently onto the bed. She surveyed the room, all deep reds and dark greens — bookbinding colours, she thought. A winter room. Heavy drapes kept the draughts out and the warmth from the fire in. There was no central light. The study was lit by lamps, mainly electric, but she noticed two exquisite old oil lamps that appeared, from the brown singed wicks, to be regularly used. A closer inspection showed a small television with an integral video and a portable radio/cassette/CD player.

Her friend returned with a tray of tea and bone china cups and saucers, plus a plate of warm cheese scones.

'Far cry from the hospital, and just when I was acquiring a taste for polystyrene!'

'Yes, well you'd better start acquiring the taste for some proper home cooking again. I've planned some very nourishing meals. Both our diets have suffered over the past few months, and I intend to build you up again, my lady!'

Wiping crumbs from her chin, Ellie decided that she could easily put up with being bullied, if the cheese scones were anything to go by. 'Where are the dogs?'

'Marie Littlewood and her son, Daniel, have taken them over the Downs to wear them out. I don't want them bothering you just yet. You look lethal enough on those crutches without five dogs dancing around you. They can stay in other parts of the house for a bit. This is your domain where you can feel safe, though you may welcome little Digger for a cuddle; he's gentle enough and he loves a real fire! Oh yes, you may have noticed the wheelchair in the hall. Mr Thomas didn't want you overdoing things, crutches can be exhausting, so rather than curb your mobility, it's there if you need it.' Carole relegated several hundreds of pounds worth of generosity with a dismissive wave of the hand and got on to what she considered the more important issues.

'Tonight, we are having trout and almonds with fresh asparagus, and a rather tasty potato dish that I found on my last trip to France. Now, is there anything you would especially fancy as a treat tomorrow? Fillet steak maybe? Or perhaps a special dessert?'

Ellie was overwhelmed, but before she could answer, she was interrupted by the sound of excited barking coming from the orchard.

'Right, now you rest. I need to go and sort out my pack. I'll be back before you know it!'

And in a flurry, Carole was gone, and Ellie lay back and thanked the powers that be for such a wonderful friend.

* * *

''Fraid they need a bit of a wash, but they've had a lovely run. We've walked for miles,' said Marie. 'Dan, how about hosing those dirty paws for Carole? There is a reel on the wall in the courtyard.'

Without a word, the man walked off with the muddy animals.

'How is he, Marie?' whispered Carole.

'It's slow going. Some days better than others. He's just so uncommunicative, I don't think he's spoken more than half a dozen words to his father in the whole two weeks he's been home.'

'He's taken it very badly, hasn't he?' murmured Carole.

They looked across at Dan who was surrounded by wet spaniels, washing mud-caked feet, and unsuccessfully endeavouring to keep his navy slacks dry.

'Will you be at church next Sunday?' asked Marie. 'I'd really value a chat. I can't talk to his father. He's so busy, what with Dr Williams being on holiday, and the new clinic opening.'

'Of course! Ellie's friend Gill and her husband are coming for tea on Sunday, and they will stay with her until I get back, so we'll talk after the service.'

Carole thanked her friend for helping so often with the dogs over the last few months, and she made her promise to allow her to repay her, in some way, in the future.

'Oh, I've loved taking them out, and I hope that I can continue to come on walks with you and the boys, even though things are getting back to normal. Do you know I've visited places that I haven't been to since the doctor and I were courting, and that was thirty years ago! Without a dog, you get out of the habit of walking, and I do love the fresh air.' She touched Carole lightly on the arm and nodded towards her son. 'He's coming back . . . we'll speak on Sunday.'

Carole watched them go, noticing Marie talking, making the occasional gesture, but receiving no perceptible reaction from Daniel. The Littlewoods were not exactly candidates for the Compton Happy Families Competition.

When Carole entered the library, Ellie was asleep, so without disturbing her, she put some more logs on the fire and left the girl in peace.

Back in the kitchen she gazed about the spacious room, wondering whether to do some more baking while Ellie slept. She had already prepared scones, butter biscuits, and a Victoria sponge, added to which there was the delicious aroma of fruit cake issuing from the Aga. That was probably enough for today. Making another pot of tea, she contemplated the hours she had spent with Vera in their country kitchen, cooking, preserving, freezing, plotting and planning. She still spent hours here with the dogs, but the life really had gone out of what she did. There was little enjoyment in cooking for one, and even less in eating alone. It would be good to have someone here for a while. She hoped that Ellie would stay until she was one hundred per cent ready to face going back to Sefton Place alone.

Her last conversation with Carl Thomas invaded her thoughts. As she was about to leave his office, he had admitted a vague and unsubstantiated apprehension regarding Ellie. Nothing concrete, nothing to hold her in hospital, but something was bothering him. He suggested that Carole should keep in touch, and he gave her a number where messages could be swiftly passed to him. She had the feeling that he didn't do this for all his patients and had thanked him for his support.

She recalled his parting words.

'Mrs Meyer, that incident with the baby made a deep impression on me. For Ellie, it is the first shoot from a newly sown seed. The plant will need care and nourishment, prayer and provender, to keep it healthy and alive. It will not be easy for either of you, but I sincerely wish you well, and pledge any assistance that is within my power.'

Stirring her tea, Carole silently logged that information into her memory-bank file named 'For Future Reference' and hoped she would not need it.

* * *

Ellie awoke to the sound of a telephone ringing somewhere in the house. For a moment she expected to see Pauline in the bed opposite her, and it took a few moments to assimilate her new surroundings. A second or two of panic was soon dissipated by the fragrance of potpourri, woodsmoke, and what seemed to be a smell from childhood. She saw a fleeting vision of her mother beating cake mixture in the huge old biscuit-coloured mixing bowl that had been her grandmother's.

'Please, Mummy, can I clean the bowl when you've finished?' She remembered running a finger around the smooth sides of the bowl and plunging the creamy buttery mixture into her mouth.

The opening of the door broke her reverie.

'Ah, you're awake. I've made more tea if you'd like some? That was Gill confirming that she has arranged a babysitter, and she and her husband will be able to stay for tea and the evening, if you're up to it.'

Ellie was delighted. It would be so good to talk to her friends without the depressing surroundings of the hospital with its constant calls for bedpans and painkillers.

Carole was placing a plate of golden-brown butter biscuits in front of her.

'Lord! My crutches will be bowing under the extra weight if I go on like this!' exclaimed Ellie, happily nibbling her third.

'Nonsense! You could eat until next Christmas and you'd still look like a beanpole!'

'I wish!' A big easy smile crossed her face; then she noticed Carole regarding her with what appeared to be wonder.

'When I sat with you in Intensive Care, I never dreamed that, in a few months, you would be like this.'

Ellie knew that the shorter hairstyle suited her. The light fringe obscured the already fading scar on her forehead. The hair around the wound from the operation was doing a grand job of camouflage, and apart from the plastered leg and her paleness, there was little to show of the awful trauma she had suffered.

'I've been incredibly lucky, I mean physically, that's apart from this auric sight. And that reminds me, I must tell you what Dr Alice Cross said before I left the hospital.'

She recounted both the doctor's thoughts on the cause of her visual ability, and her philosophy for dealing with Joseph Edward Saville.

Carole nodded and sipped her tea. 'A bright young woman by the sound of it, with a sensible head on her shoulders. A bit of a rarity, I should say.'

'You'll be able to meet her soon, if it's okay for her to visit. She wants to use me as a case study.'

Carole's cup clattered forcefully into the saucer. 'You can have whoever you want here — this is your home for as long as you want. But, I'd think twice about being a guinea pig for some ambitious young whipper-snapper!'

Carole's lips were so tight they had practically disappeared, and Ellie burst out laughing. 'I thought you just said she was a "bright young woman!"'

'Yes, well, that's before you told me that she wanted you as a research animal!'

'It's not like that.' Ellie grinned. 'Really, I'd be glad to help her.' She paused. 'She's nice.'

'Nice! I hate that word, what is "nice"?'

'She was gentle and understanding with me, and her work is very important to her. Besides, her nearest patient with Azimah's Syndrome lives in Inverness. If I could be of help, I would be happy to assist her.'

'Ellie McEwan! I do believe that you are soft on her!'

Ellie felt a slight flush on her pale cheeks. 'Ridiculous!' she rejoined, fooling no one. 'She's just nice.'

'So you said,' grunted Carole.

Ellie couldn't stop giggling, and she had the feeling Carole privately thought that as long as the young doctor wasn't using Ellie, or cashing in on her in any way, then she was a far better proposition than the late lamented Stephanie had ever been. And she had to agree!

A timer rang in the kitchen, and Carole left to minister unto her cake, leaving Ellie remembering the warmth of Alice's hand on hers.

* * *

Dinner that night was a positive delight. They ate in the kitchen, at the old pine table that had no doubt witnessed thousands of family meals throughout its long life. Its honey-coloured surface would have been the support of banquets when the money flowed, and meagre fare in poorer times. It would have seen venison and game, and bread and cheese. Tonight, there were candles and flowers in the centre, and Carole served directly from the Aga to the table. Hospital food suddenly became a dark memory, and to Ellie, every mouthful of the moist pink trout was ambrosia to her taste buds. There was champagne in tall, fluted glasses to toast the homecoming, and as Ellie sipped the cold, dry sparkly wine, she reflected that this was her first drink for months. Her first drink since the night before the accident.

'Penny for them?'

'I was thinking about the accident. What I remember . . . and what I don't.'

'Do you want to talk about it?'

'I was just trying to recall my last proper memory, other than the boy. I can remember being here with you, and then you and I went out with the dogs . . . and that's about it. The rest is what people have told me.'

'It's strange that you remember the boy, but not the drive, or being in the car. How do you equate that?'

'It's weird.' Ellie took another mouthful of champagne and felt a very pleasant tingling sensation course through her. 'Perhaps this will help me find the words for what I have not been able to explain. It's . . . it's like a firework. Yes, imagine a stygian black sky, then you hear a firework rocketing up into the night. You see a tiny silver light, like an arrow to the heavens, and then an amazing burst of thousands of white stars in a huge circular exploding nova. It fills the sky, and although it only lasts for seconds, it seems like forever, then it fades and drifts to earth. It was just like that. I have a memory of a moment. Nothing about the car or the road, just a rectangular field of vision, bit like wide-screen TV. There was a sound, a sort of high-pitched noise, then his face. It was sideways on, and it slowly turned the right way up. Carole, he was beautiful! There was no fear, he looked

. . .' She paused trying to choose the right words. 'Ecstatic, as if he had just achieved something wonderful. The winning goal, the lottery, I don't know. And there was this haunting undertone beneath the elation. Just a lovely peace, then he faded down to earth, just like the firework, and he was gone. I described him to Jean Brady, the staff nurse who looked after me on ITU. She was in A&E that night and saw him. There was no doubt about it. It was the same boy, not just my imagination, or some illusion.'

Staring at the glowing candle flame, Carole sighed. 'I think you were meant to see him, my dear, don't you?'

'It seems that way, but I'm not really sure why.'

'You will understand as time goes by. Forgive the cliche, but it is early days yet. Don't force things, there will be answers, I'm sure. A short while ago you'd never have dreamed that you'd be able to manage the coloured auras that you see. Now, well, they are becoming part of your life.'

There was a grunt and a groan as two sleeping spaniels vied for the comfiest spot in the doggy duvet that nearly filled the huge bed next to the big old cooker.

'There is something that I meant to ask you about my colour sight. I worked a lot, especially in the week before I left the hospital, on identifying what different colours mean to me when associated with illness or injury. I also notice that emotions, moods and temperaments give off colours. Plants and flowers give off their emanations, as do other life forms. Everything is intensified when it's sunny or very bright, and it's much easier to see subdued conditions, the evening for instance. In a limited way, all this I can understand, but very often I see something that I cannot tie in with a living form.'

Ellie stared at the woman sitting opposite her and continued.

'Right now, you are almost totally sky blue. Yes, there are other colours as well, but your natural healthy colour is Aegean blue. Michael's main colour is a wonderful leaf green. I'm learning what these really mean, but just now I'm telling you what I actually see. The dogs in the box over there are giving off a muted sort of rainbow hue; their auras are all joined together in one glorious bubble of colour. But there is also something else. Just in my periphery vision, there is a glow, a shimmering halo of purest violet. It comes and goes, but it's here now, over near the dogs, in the corner.'

Carole smiled over the top of her glass. 'I wondered how long it would be before you noticed her. I'm glad you see her as violet. It is such a spiritual colour, and it reflects intuition and psychic ability. It also means protection.'

'You mean I'm "seeing" Vera!'

'Absolutely. Can't you smell the lilacs?'

CHAPTER TEN

At the same time as Carole and Ellie were finishing their champagne, two other people sat across a table, deep in conversation.

No fine wine here, just two tepid mugs of muddy looking coffee.

'Right, Sergeant, nine a.m. tomorrow, I'm throwing this lot at the team, but tonight, I'm giving it to you. I want to know if I'm missing something, before this show goes on the road.'

Detective Chief Inspector Bob Foreman shifted on the uncomfortable plastic chair. He and DS Vic Barratt were huddled in a corner of the deserted staff canteen. The heating had failed in the offices that afternoon and, now at nine thirty in the evening, the engineers were still no further to sorting the situation. The fault had not affected the canteen or the cells and, not fancying the cells, it was here that Foreman decided to hold his council of war.

Prematurely grey, DCI Foreman was a tank of a man who would not have looked out of place at Cardiff Arms Park. Not just his hair but everything about him was grey. His suit, his socks, his shoes, even his shirt was a silvery colour. He looked eagle-eyed across the ketchup-stained shabby Formica-topped table at his colleague. 'Two murders. Both women. Both bear the same trademark of their killer. Neither sexually assaulted. So, what have we got to tie them together?' He threw a thin file on the table.

Vic Barratt produced his notebook and thumbed through pages of tiny, neat script. Unlike Foreman's gargantuan proportions, the sergeant, although tall, was slim and wiry. He had pale, icy-blue eyes, a fine, straight nose, and surprisingly, considering his eye colour, dark-brown wavy hair that he kept cut short. 'Well, sir, frankly, nothing as yet, that is, nothing apparent.'

'Okay, Vic, give me what you've got, and we'll compare it with this.' He indicated to the buff-coloured file.

'Victim one. Melissa Crabbe. Twenty-three years of age. White, single. Lived at home with her parents in Hersham. Only child. No regular boyfriend. Worked in Kingston as a secretary-cum-computer operator for a small finance company. Father is an accountant; mother an aromatherapist. Both appear genuinely distraught by this. Popular girl, lots of friends, close family. Hobbies were swimming and going to the gym. Played the violin in a local all-girl quartet, sort of pop-classical stuff, Vanessa-Mae kind of thing. Mother said that they were hoping to cut a record soon, some agent was interested in them, reckoned they were very talented. Description, five foot four, eight and a half stone, slim athletic build. Light brown hair, long and straight. No scars or unusual features.' Vic Barratt paused, took a sip of awful coffee, grimaced and continued. 'Victim two. Helen Carbery. Forty-five. Second marriage. First husband died, and then she married again seven years ago, to a David Carbery. Businessman, family money . . . pots of it. No children, their choice. She was a plastic surgeon, specialising in facio-maxillary facial reconstruction. Family home in Woodham, big old property, lots of grounds, her mother lives in an annexe there. Father dead. Friends are mainly business associates. Neighbours rarely see them. No specific hobbies that we know of. Owned a Labrador retriever that she was walking when she was attacked. She was five foot six, short dark hair, ten stone. Academic. Wore wire-rimmed glasses. Small operational scar on upper left abdomen and another on her right knee. No other distinguishing features or marks. The Carberrys have a cleaning lady who comes in twice a week, and she raised the alarm when she found the dog, shaking and cowering on the back doorstep, when she arrived. David Carberry was away on business in Germany, which we've checked. Helen apparently walked the dog at about seven every morning around the edge of the golf course where she was found.'

He sighed. 'Apart from being female and the fact that there were identical mutilations, they were two very different women.' He sighed again. 'I can see no connection at all.'

Bob Foreman scratched his neck and yawned. 'Oh, there is a connection, my friend, somewhere there has to be a connection.'

'Could be totally unrelated, sir, just in the wrong place at the wrong time. Maybe he's a nutter who just came upon them, and the bastard took advantage of the isolation at that moment. Helen Carberry was killed at about seven a.m. — it was hardly light and no one had seen her walking that morning — and Melissa Crabbe was taking a shortcut through an alleyway off Caulfield Avenue, at just after midnight. She was going to stay at a friend's house after she'd finished the gig she was playing at. Both places were dark and isolated, with no one around.'

'Someone was around all right. Sorry, Vic, I think you're wrong on this one. There was nothing at either scene of crime to help us. He was very careful not to leave anything that we could pick up for DNA testing, and then there's what our killer did to both women. This was planned, it wasn't random, I'd stake my pension on it.' He ran his thick fingers through even thicker wiry grey hair, and took a deep noisy breath. 'The method of killing was identical. The victim was hit from behind, causing her to fall to the ground. Then something heavy, a bar or a piece of pipe maybe, was held across her throat, until she stopped breathing. Then he proceeded to execute his endearing little personal trademark. This animal came out well prepared and took his tools and his precious talisman away with him.'

'Are we certain it is a "him", sir?'

'No actual evidence, Vic, but this isn't a woman's way of killing, and the post-mortems indicate that a great deal of strength was used. In the Carberry woman's case in particular, the windpipe was crushed, and I mean, crushed. No, detective, it's a "him" all right and I can't wait to meet the bastard!'

Vic Barratt got up and pushed his chair back noisily. 'Want some more coffee, guv?'

'I think you are being generous with your description of this stuff,' he said pushing his mug towards the DS. 'But, yes, I suppose so. We haven't finished here yet.'

'Mind if I just ring Barbara, sir? I was meant to help my son with a project tonight. If he's still awake, she can sweet-talk him into forgiving me before I get home!'

He returned a few minutes later and placed two more mugs of the suspect liquid on the table.

'Go ahead, Vic. Ring her now. How are the wife and the kids?'

'They are good, sir. Barbara's got a part-time job now Hannah's old enough to keep an eye on Matthew. Not that he needs it, he's ten now. I don't know where the years go.'

Bob Foreman remembered the trouble that Vic and Barbara had experienced when they first tried to adopt the brother and sister. The officer's wife had been close to a breakdown with all the red tape and the legal minefield they found themselves embroiled in. Bob was glad it had finally worked out for the family.

Vic Barratt pulled out his mobile and spent a few moments chatting with his wife, then returned to Bob. 'Told her not to wait up, sir.'

Foreman was studying photographs. 'Weird, really weird. Where do you start with a case like this?' Then he answered his own question. 'With good old-fashioned police work. Psycho or not, there's a common denominator here somewhere. Let's get looking. Vic, at the breakfast meeting tomorrow, we'll get the team on checking anything that might link the victims. I mean anything at all. Hairdressers, window cleaners, dentists, you know, the usual list. Then we want past history, origins, where they went on holiday, any family connection, albeit a third cousin twice removed on Granny's side!'

'There doesn't seem to be any sort of physical tie-in, does there, sir? I mean, they are different ages, hair colour, appearance, lifestyle, and certainly background.'

'I know. And why the gruesome tokens that he took with him? What's he planning on doing with those, I wonder? Just our luck for this monster to begin his rampage in Surrey. Why the hell couldn't he have started on the Met's patch!' He handed the pictures to his sergeant. 'All right, Vic. Deep breath, and let's start again.'

* * *

At six o'clock on Sunday morning, Ellie awoke with the sound of heavy rain hammering against the windowpanes. It was not yet light, and even though every muscle, tendon and joint in her body was screaming at her, she painfully dragged herself out of bed and pulled on her towelling dressing gown.

The central heating had only been on for a minute or two and, without the fire, the room had a decided chill about it. She reached for her elbow crutches and put a slipper on her 'good' foot. The toes on her 'bad' one felt frozen and had a purplish tinge in the light from her bedside lamp. She leaned forward and massaged them for a few moments, and the circulation started to improve.

She hobbled over to the French windows and held back the drape. Outside, the garden was a frenzy of motion. The wind was thrashing naked branches back and forth as if furious that they bore no tender leaves for it to tear away. Confounded by the trees, it then gathered up water from the courtyard fountain, and with invisible hands, dashed it to the stone floor, leaving a shiny, oily-looking puddle that was soon absorbed into the wet, dark surface of the York slabs. Somewhere in the orchard, wind chimes issued a continuous carillon, calling desperately to the gales to treat them more gently; they shouldn't be played that way.

A light was on in one of the upstairs rooms, throwing sketchy illumination across the garden, and reflecting on the beaded drops of rain running down the window. A movement in the darkness caught her eye. Through the wrought iron gate, something furtive passed across the lawn towards the summer house. Just a shadow, a darker stain in the black morning.

The sudden sound of a toilet flush told her it was not Carole. It seemed too big for a fox; perhaps it was just a trick of the light . . . or the dark.

The whole garden was still dancing to the tune of the storm. Surely no one would be outside in weather like this, and at this hour on a Sunday morning? She stared at the area of lawn visible through the gateway, but saw nothing else. It had to be her imagination.

Ellie wondered if she should, or indeed, could, make a cup of tea. It was after all, her panacea for all problems. She gave one last glance out and, seeing nothing, let the drape fall back in place and made her way slowly to the kitchen.

When she arrived, the kettle was already on, and her friend was giving a handful of little bone-shaped biscuits to a waiting line of drooling dogs.

'Sit yourself down, dear. Don't want the hounds to have you off your feet, do we?'

The kitchen was warm and cosy, but the apprehension that she had recently felt, left a chill around Ellie. 'I thought I saw someone, or something, in the garden, on the grass through the gate.' She shook her head. 'I'm probably seeing things.'

'When?' demanded Carole, immediately on her guard.

'Only a minute or two ago.'

'Right! Badger! Benji! Orlando!' With surprising agility, Carole was across the room, flinging the back door open, throwing the switch to the security lights, and removing the largest of the chef's knives from the block. In seconds the door had slammed behind her and Ellie was left with the two smaller dogs. She limped to the nearest window with a view of the courtyard, and saw the old iron gate, open and swinging in the wind. There was a short spell of high excited barking, and then silence.

Ellie's heart raced until, finally, the halogen security lights showed the woman and three Springers striding back through the archway, the high-powered beams glinting off the Sabatier blade in Carole's hand.

The door flew open and Carole shepherded her dogs into the kitchen. She made them sit on the puddling quarry tiles while she got a dry towel for them. Before drying herself, she picked up the receiver from the telephone on the wall and dialled 999. 'Yes, this is Mrs Cavendish-Meyer of Snug Cottage, Compton. I've had a prowler in my garden.' She paused, listening, then said, 'Five minutes ago, and yes, certainly, my number is 01 483 3356. Ah, right, Guildford, you say. Thank you very much.' She hung up the telephone and grunted. 'He'll be long gone by the time they get here. Someone had been trying to get into the sanctuary by the look of it. There are wet footprints on the veranda, and one of the pots of winter pansies has been knocked over. The dogs heard or saw something, but they didn't go mad. Funny that, as Badger normally howls like the Hound of the Baskervilles if there are strangers about. Well, I'm going to get dressed before the constabulary arrive, if they bother to turn out for a prowler, when they've got a double murderer on the loose!'

Ellie watched Carole's expression and knew that she bitterly regretted mentioning the local murders.

'Sorry, Ellie, but I suppose you did know about them?'

'Oh yes, one of my physios talked about nothing else. Her younger sister played the cello in the band the first girl was in. She said that the murdered girl, I think her name was Melissa, was a real virtuoso, only in her twenties, but very talented. The physio thought the group would split up without Melissa, she was the real star. It's so sad, poor kid.'

Carole clearly didn't want Ellie dwelling on dead youngsters and made a swift getaway to get some clothes on before the police arrived. 'I'll have a quick shower, dear, then I'll get breakfast . . . the smell of bacon should attract our stalwart local bobbies to our door!'

* * *

The black helmet, and the bowler with the chequered ribbon, looked incongruous next to the delicate bowl of flowers on the table.

Sitting in the warmth of the kitchen, WPC Paula English wrote methodically onto a pad on a clipboard. Her hapless partner, PC Derek Bowman had been relegated to floundering through sodden flower beds and checking the surrounding neighbours' gardens.

'So, what actually happened?' asked the WPC.

Ellie recounted what, when and how she had seen the prowler, and Carole stated what she and her dogs had found on their sortie into the garden.

'You say you put the security light on to go out, do you not leave them on at night?' asked the police constable.

'Not when it's windy. They are so sensitive they go on and off all night long. It can be disturbing, so I switched them off last night at about midnight.'

The officer directed her next question to Ellie. 'You still managed to see something, even without the sensor lights?'

'Yes, there was a light on upstairs,' replied Ellie. 'It shone through the gateway. It was quite feeble though, which is why I really wasn't sure what I saw.'

'Right, now let me read this back to you,' said Paula, 'and you tell me if I've got it all correctly. Then we'll see what my colleague comes back with.'

Carole got up and poured boiling water into the waiting pot. 'I expect a cup of tea will go down well, especially when your partner gets . . .'

Her sentence was cut short by the back door opening, and a dripping wet figure asking if he could come in. PC Bowman's black Gore-Tex jacket was running in rivulets of water, so Carole took it to the utility, shook it, hung it up on the end of a clothes dryer and went back to pour the tea.

The offer of a bacon sandwich was readily accepted by both police officers as they sat warming their hands around steaming mugs of tea.

'That's very kind of you, Mrs Meyer.' The young bobby sniffed the air as the wonderful aroma of the bacon pervaded the kitchen. 'There has definitely been someone out there, but I think you, or the dogs, scared him off. As you said, the plant pot had been disturbed and the footprints were still visible because of the mud on the boot soles. I found similar boot prints at the far end of the flower borders at the point where there is a gap in the fence leading out to the orchard. I've walked right round the grounds, and the lane, and checked with the neighbours either side, but there's nothing.' His radio crackled unintelligibly. Both officers listened for a moment, but decided the message was not for them, and PC Bowman continued speaking. 'I noticed the summer house is a bit up-market, you know, not the sort of place you just store your old plastic garden chairs and table for the winter?'

WPC English gave her young partner an exasperated stare. She had noticed the elegant wrought iron patio set and stone benches as she came through the courtyard, and realised from the rest of the house that Carole had probably never heard of the word 'plastic' in relation to furniture.

'I'm not sure what you mean by "up-market", young man, but it is a well-used garden room, yes.'

'I was just wondering if there was anything of value in it and someone knew it was worth breaking in to, or whether it was just a vagrant looking for a dry spot to shelter in.'

'Nothing of value at all, an old CD player and a lot of books really. I can't imagine anyone wanting to break in for those.'

'I guess it's just a tramp then,' mused the PC before biting into his sandwich. 'Oh! I say, this is excellent!'

Paula English agreed about the sandwich, but not about the vagrant. 'Now that it's light, we'll drive around the village and make some enquiries.' Privately she felt uneasy about the whole business. She would like to know what the toerag was up to. It was the wrong time of the morning to be looking for shelter. He would have done that last night and got his head down there for a kip. No, it didn't feel right at all.

'We'll give the place a thorough check, Mrs Meyer, and we'll have someone keep an eye on the place tonight, just to be on the safe side. It probably was just some tramp, as Derek here reckons.' She smiled and hoped she looked more confident than she felt. This time it was her radio that spluttered into life. WPC Paula English spoke swiftly into it, and said, 'Drink up, Derek. Mrs Meyer, Miss McEwan, we'll be in touch.' She stood up and handed Carole a card with her name and contact number.

'Don't hesitate to ring if anything bothers you, or if you think of anything else. And we'll get a car to drive around tonight.'

Derek Bowman collected his jacket, and they were gone.

* * *

'Well?' Carole looked quizzically at Ellie. 'What did you pick up from our boys and girls in blue?'

'Sorry?'

'Come on, I was watching your eyes. Shifting focus, altering your gaze. You were analysing their auras, weren't you?'

'Hmm, I seem to do it automatically when I see new faces,' admitted Ellie. 'Well, they seemed a very genuine pair; they had healthy lights around them. The young man has problems with his shoulder. He has a gap in the aura line with some rather sludgy discolouration around it. Very localised, probably a sports injury. Lots of enthusiastic spurts of colour when he speaks. The woman was different altogether, more controlled; her lights were less brilliant, although nice clear shades. She has arthritis or something similar in her toes and ankles of both feet.' Ellie paused. 'There was one interesting thing about her though. I've never really noticed until now how the aura reacts when a person says one thing but means another, and I saw it then. She told you that it was probably a vagrant, but as she said it, her lights went down. She didn't believe what she'd just said. She made a positive statement and showed negative colours. Interesting.'

'It seems you might have a built-in lie detector there!' laughed Carole. 'Useful!'

'That's a new one on me,' said Ellie. 'Although Michael said that I will see and understand more and more as time goes by.'

Carole decided that Ellie seemed quite delighted by the thought that her skills were progressing, and fortuitously seemed to have missed the point of what had worried the police officer. If it wasn't a tramp, then who was it, and what did they want in the summer house?

CHAPTER ELEVEN

Sunday turned out to be one of those strange days, so uncharacteristic of the season. A bright blue sky was strategically spotted with fluffy white clouds like the ones children drew. With a stretch of the imagination, it was possible to almost feel some heat on your skin. Even though she was indoors, the brilliance of the day forced Ellie to hide behind her sunglasses. Her pleasure, however, at the thought of having a sociable afternoon and evening with her friends, was not going to be dampened by problematical sight.

The day was made even more agreeable by a call on her mobile from Dr Alice Cross. She assured Ellie that she was putting her under no pressure to see her, but just wanted to make sure she was settling in, and that her health was still improving. They spoke for perhaps ten minutes and Ellie was surprised, as she put the mobile back in her bag, that the conversation had been easy and amusing — more like old friends than a new, quasi-professional relationship.

Sitting in the library, sipping freshly ground coffee and enjoying a slice of orgasmic chocolate fudge cake, she decided that things were indeed looking up.

Outside the French windows, the sun was glinting on the water in the fountain, and she decided it might be the day to venture out and get some fresh Surrey air into her lungs. The incline of the ramp was quite gentle and she thought that it would pose no problem if she were careful.

Finishing her elevenses, she reached for the crutches, and slowly made her way through the French windows and into the sunshine. For one awful moment, she nearly lost her balance, as the full glare assaulted her enhanced sight, forcing her to stand still and try to regain her equilibrium. A fuzzy medley of muted colours ambled into her field of vision.

'Hang on, Miss! I'll give you a hand. Don't move.' A strong arm went round her waist. 'This was really meant for that wheelchair the missus bought you, not for skidding around on these dangerous looking things!'

Scrubbs looked disapprovingly at her silver metal crutches.

'Thank you, Scrubbs. Maybe I should have waited for Mrs Meyer before I started exploring.'

'You're right there, Miss. Still, you're out here now, so come on, I'll walk you over to the seat by the fountain. Just be very careful that the rubber ferules don't slip if there is any dampness or moss on these stones. We don't want you having another accident.'

Ellie sat heavily on the bench and made a mental note to use the electric wheelchair next time she felt adventurous. 'I had no idea that walking on crutches could be so exhausting and so hazardous!' Ellie wiped a hand across her forehead, its pressure decreasing as she touched the scar. 'I'm worn out!'

'Oh yes, Miss, I was on 'em for a time a couple of years ago. Bloody dangerous, if you ask me! Beg pardon, Miss, but I nearly broke me neck on the damn things!'

Ellie smiled at the man's vehemence. He was probably well into his seventies and had that weather-beaten leathery look that comes with working outside for most of your life. Carole had told her that for many years he had been the head gardener on a big estate nearby, and before that had spent his younger working life tending to the grounds of a stately home in Kent. He was short and stocky, and smelled of fertiliser, tobacco, and Imperial Leather soap. He continued to berate walking aids of all descriptions, and then chortled heartily as he told her about his most dramatic fall on a wet kitchen floor when he finished up, head down, in a washing basket.

Ellie thought that his face reminded her of a wet, screwed-up chamois leather when he laughed, and giggled along with him.

'The grounds here are a credit to you. I can't imagine what state my little garden is in. The shop didn't leave me much time for gardening, and I was about to get round to organising someone to come in when I had the accident. I should think it's a jungle by now.'

'Oh no, miss, it's fine! I've power-hosed the patio, cut back the overgrown shrubbery. I know it's the wrong time of year, but they'll be fine by spring. I've cleaned out all your tubs and pots, and got shot of the rubbish. The borders are all forked over and edged up. No, Miss, it's all tidy and ready for a bit of spring colour . . . pansies maybe? Or some polyanthus?'

Ellie was amazed. It was obviously Carole's doing, but as she had never mentioned it, it came as a surprise. 'I don't know what to say, Scrubbs. That's wonderful. I must pay you. Just tell me what I owe and I'll write you a cheque.'

'It's all been settled, the missus sorted it. Anyway, it's no big deal, that little pocket handkerchief of a garden didn't take me long, and I'll pop back over when you're ready to go home and give it a once over for you. It'll be all well under control for you to get a gardener to come in once a week, and don't get one of those Italian blokes with the big lorries, they don't know their abutilons from their astilbes!'

Ellie made her second mental note of the day, to have strong words with Mrs Carole Cavendish-Meyer about allowing her to pay her way!

Going up the ramp was decidedly simpler than the downward journey and, safely back in the study, she thanked Scrubbs for his help and closed the doors.

She was glad to see the fire blazing in the hearth, and suddenly realised, that for all the bright sun, she was freezing. Ellie sat in the armchair by the fire and warmed her chilled hands. She could hear Carole busy in the kitchen. Metallic sounds of saucepans and lids, running water and the fast, rhythmic tapping of a knife on a chopping board. Sunday lunch was lovingly being prepared.

A soft scratching sound at the door made her look up, and a small brown nose peeped in. 'Come on, Digger, come and enjoy the fire with me.'

It was the little dog's first expedition into her inner sanctum, and he looked around suspiciously, expecting at any minute to be ordered out. After a few moments, however, his tail was wagging furiously, and he settled at her feet on the rug in front of the crackly, applewood-smelling log fire. He was comfortably asleep in seconds.

Ellie marvelled at his ability to just drop off when he wanted to, but admitted to herself that a certain lethargy was creeping over her own body. The cushions moulded themselves to her back, and the sounds from the kitchen faded into oblivion, as her eyes shut.

Vera sat on the edge of Ellie's bed, looking across at her. She was dressed in a deep purple jacket and skirt with a lavender high-necked blouse. On the lapel of the jacket was an extraordinary brooch. Celtic in design but worked in an intricate weave of silver and many colours of enamel. At her feet was the large spaniel, Monty.

Digger stirred in his sleep but did not wake.

Ellie wasn't at all surprised to see her there, and she smiled at her old friend. 'Is dinner ready?' she asked sleepily.

Vera smiled. 'No, not yet. How are you?'

'I'm fine. Carole's being so kind to me. I'll never be able to repay her, not in a million years.'

'She doesn't want repayment. You know that, but you have to help her. At some point, my dear, she will need you, as much as you need her now. Be there for her. Please, for me . . . will you?'

'Of course! But what's wrong, is she ill?'

'No, she's fine. But when the time comes . . . ?' Vera fingered the brooch absent-mindedly.

Ellie surveyed the older woman gravely. 'I promise. I will be there. Whatever she needs, I promise.'

Vera smiled and then sighed the deepest of sighs. 'It will soon be time for you to progress further with your enlightenment. The next stage has to be learned. You are doing well. Continue to work with Michael Seale — he has much to offer you, and join Carole in the sanctuary. It is a good place. You will find it easy to meditate there and answers will come to you more readily. Don't trust everyone, Ellie; sometimes you have to say no to people. You now know you have a way to help others, but there are some that would exploit that gift for their own ends. Be cautious who you cooperate with. Even though you have a way of seeing what others do not, remember, not everyone is quite what they appear to be.'

Vera smiled at Ellie. 'And don't ever forget that I am here for you.'

Carole pushed the door open and boomed, 'Ah-ha! I thought I'd find you here, you little monkey! Is Digger being a nuisance, Ellie?' She stopped abruptly. 'Oh, sorry, dear, were you sleeping? Lunch is ready, would you like it here or in the kitchen with me?'

'Goodness, yes, oh, in the kitchen would be lovely. I'm sorry I must have dropped off, and Digger's no problem at all.' She looked down at the little dog. 'I've been dreaming, I . . .' She allowed the words to ebb away. 'I'll go and wash my hands and join you straightaway.'

As the dream came back to her, she decided to keep it to herself. She left the room, her peripheral vision noticing a round indentation on the smooth flat surface of the embroidered counterpane. She supposed that Digger must have climbed onto the bed while she slept.

* * *

At four o'clock, the elderly silver Subaru estate car belonging to Clive and Gill Edwards bumped and groaned its way down the lane to Snug Cottage. Ellie stood at the open door to greet them.

Gill and Ellie hugged each other until neither of them could breathe.

'Come on in!' Ellie led the way to the lounge, where Carole was putting more logs into the already blazing inferno. The covers, a necessity when the dogs were allowed in the room, were all gone from the sofas and the chairs. All the woodwork shone with polish, and china and crystal gleamed.

Clive shook hands with Carole and expressed open admiration for her lovely home. As usual, the woman pooh-poohed the compliments, but nevertheless showered Ellie's friends with her own brand of mannerly hospitality. She then went off to check the dogs, who were imprisoned in the kitchen, and prepare tea.

At five, she laid out the sideboard, buffet-style, with a delicious array of homemade foods. She left a large tray with a cafetiere, a huge pot of tea and various milks, creams and sugars. 'You will forgive me if I leave you. I'm off to church this evening. The dogs are quite happy in the kitchen, but, Gill, I wonder if you would mind coming and meeting them, then they won't bark at you if you want to go and make more tea or coffee. I would suggest Ellie does not roam around too much without me here, just in case one of the boys gets excited and jumps up at her. By the way, there are drinks in the cupboard if you prefer, please help yourselves.'

Alone in the kitchen, Gill declared that she could not have expected to see such an improvement in her friend, and it was nothing short of a miracle. She assured Carole that they would wait until she returned before leaving, and at last Carole felt safe to leave her precious charge to go and change for church.

* * *

When she was not there by six forty, Carole started to get concerned about Marie. She was never late and had made a real point about meeting Carole for a talk about her son. Just as the small congregation was making a feeble attempt to find the right key for the second hymn, Carole heard the scuffle of chairs being moved, and a familiar and very welcome soprano voice of Marie gathered up the failing hymn and restored it to its intended glory.

It was a pleasant service, but Carole found concentrating difficult. It was her turn to help with the refreshments, so she slipped out just before the end to put the kettle on.

Against the pile of cups and saucers, she found a note with her name on it. She tore it open and found Marie's spidery script telling her that she couldn't stay for the promised chat, they'd had a bit of trouble at home, and Daniel needed the car straight after the service.

Puzzled, Carole laid up the two old wooden trays, and hearing the last prayer come to an end, slipped back out to try and get a quick word with her friend. But then she heard the hall door slam, and saw the tail lights of Marie's car as it left the car park with enough speed to throw gravel in the air.

* * *

Ellie and her friends were still deep in conversation when she got home, so Carole slipped upstairs to her bedroom and dialled Marie's telephone number. An official sounding BT message minder offered her emergency numbers for MediDoc, as Dr Littlewood was unavailable at present. She hung up before the message finished and sat on her bed wondering what she could do. She had a most disturbing feeling that all was not well. She suddenly wished for the days, not so long ago, when all she had to worry about were Vera's occasional illnesses, and whether to worm the dogs this week or next! At present she seemed to be bombarded from all angles with vague anxieties, apprehensions, and brooding feelings of impending danger. Tonight, there was little she could do, and it was frustrating. Marie obviously did not want to talk in front of her son, and if there was no answer on the telephone, then she was stymied. Tomorrow she would go over on some pretext or other and get the woman on her own.

It was nine o'clock when Clive and Gill left to get home and save their babysitter from the twins. Gill arranged to collect Ellie one day the following week to take her back with her for lunch and, if she was up to it, combine it with a trip to Fleurie.

Back in the lounge, Carole poured them both a generous drink and they sat quietly in front of the dying fire.

'Gill's arthritis is in remission, her lights were much brighter than on the last couple of times I've seen her, and she's moving easier, too.' Ellie paused. 'Clive has something bothering him. This is one area I'm not clear on yet but, he's really worried about something. When is Michael coming next? I think it's time I picked his brains again. I get very confused by emotional problems. Clive's whole aura seemed "depressed" for want of a better word, and it's not a physical thing. I wonder what's on his mind?'

'Gill, maybe? She does get very poorly with that condition of hers. You said that she only has good spells occasionally, and they can't really cure her. Or, of course, it could be money, they are not exactly the Gettys are they?'

'Could be anything, I guess. It's more worrying because Gill tells me everything, and she hasn't said a word.'

'Perhaps she doesn't know about it,' suggested Carole.

'Clive doesn't keep secrets from her, he loves her very much.'

'Everyone has secrets.'

Ellie thought about the odd dream about Vera, and how she decided not to share it with Carole.

'Hmm, I suppose so,' she whispered, and then changed the subject.

CHAPTER TWELVE

The major incident room was massed with policemen and women awaiting the Monday morning briefing. The comments and insults that were being hurled around abruptly stopped when a young PC, nearest the door, called out in a dramatic stage whisper that the guv'nor was on his way.

The Red Sea parted as Bob Foreman, with his sergeant in tow, made his way to the desk at the front of the room. He looked around at the photo-boards mounted on the walls and stared hard at his team. 'Now . . . you are not going to tell me you still have sweet Fanny Adams for me, are you?'

Detectives and uniform alike gazed at the ceiling, the floor, their shoes, their notebooks, anywhere rather than at their boss.

'Okay. No more than I expected. So, what do we have? Rawlings! Have you checked both victims for family ties?'

'Sir! No ties at all, that we can find.'

'Windsor? How about hobbies or interests in common?'

'None, sir. They were worlds apart.'

'Brown, what have you got?'

WDC Wendy Brown glanced at her pad and read, 'Different doctor, different dentist, no registration at the same hospitals. I've checked all the physiotherapy clinics, and alternative health practices, in a twenty-five-mile radius — nothing. They've had no similar past medical histories to compare; in fact, there is no medical connection that I can see, or not within this area, at any rate.'

Bob Foreman felt his spirit sinking as the meeting progressed. 'Churches? Were they religious?'

Windsor spoke up again. 'Victim one, sir. Never went to church. Victim two was a non-practising Roman Catholic. Hadn't set foot in a church, other than the usual weddings, funerals and so on, for years.'

'Hairdressers?'

This time it was Wendy Brown who spoke up. 'Melissa's mother used to trim her daughter's hair herself, and Mrs Carberry went to a very smart salon near her hospital in London.'

'Utilities? Tradespeople? Gardeners, window cleaners, painters and decorators?'

'Sorry, guv,' said another officer. 'I've checked back over the last two years, but nothing at all.'

'For God's sake!' Foreman threw the sheaf of papers onto the desk. 'Has anyone got anything? Anything at all to connect these two women?'

'Sir?' A softly spoken detective in jeans and a sweatshirt raised his hand.

'Hallelujah! And what little gem do you have for me, detective?'

'I think maybe the only connection is what the killer did to them, sir. I mean, I reckon that *is* the link. The mutilation, I mean.'

'Oh, great! We know that connects them *after* death, Hudson, you plonker, but that can't be all.'

'Sir, I think it is,' insisted Hudson. 'Maybe we should be asking, why this particular mutilation? Could we get an expert in on psychos? Find out what makes him tick, and why he does what he does?'

Bob sighed. 'As it happens, Hudson, I have a meeting with Dr Gerrard later today. I'll be putting the M.O. to her, and seeing that we are getting abso-bloody-lutely nowhere, let's hope she comes up with something. But, please understand the word "budget". Believe me, it does not extend to some fancy profiler, okay? Now, has anyone suspicious been seen at, or around, the crime scene?'

'Couple of "iffy" sightings on the Crabbe case, sir. A woman was woken up by a cat or something yelling in her front garden. When she looked out, she thought she saw a figure in the bushes near her neighbour's gate. It is about two hundred yards from where we found the body. Too dark for a description, but she swears it was a bloke in a long raincoat, or something similar. We checked, but there was no evidence to support anyone having been there. We also had a call from Weasel . . .'

A groan went up from the team.

'Yes, I know he calls in on every crime in the south of England, but funnily enough, he thought he saw a man — couldn't describe him 'cos he was too pissed as usual — fumbling around in a bag of some sort, and leaving the alleyway where the girl was found. The time was very close to our estimated time of death, and when we combed the alley, there was a stain on the concrete, where Weasel allegedly saw this bloke. It was a single drop of blood, and forensics have identified it as Melissa's. I know what Weasel's like, guv, but for once in his life he might just have seen the killer. Just our bloody luck, ain't it? Our only possible witness was rat-arsed!'

The briefing continued for about another thirty minutes before the chief sent his Indians away to continue tracking their unknown killer.

'Hudson, got a minute? You too, Sergeant. I want you to get hold of Weasel. He should be sober at this time of the morning. Take him back to the spot where the blood was found, and get him to go over his story, see if he can remember anything else. If that doesn't work, give him a few bevvies and let him talk. There might just be something useful in that heap of shit he has for brains, and don't look so bloody miserable, you two. I know his form, and I know it's likely he saw fuck-all, but he's all we've got, right?'

'And he smells, sir.'

'I know he smells, detective! Now bugger off!'

Foreman threw himself down in a chair and rifled through reams of negative reports. It seemed that Hudson might have a point. He'd give the whole thing to Dr Amanda Gerrard and see what she could offer him. Gerrard was the criminal psychologist for the area, with a history of working the Inner City for years. There were not many varieties of nuts that she hadn't sunk her teeth into at one time or another. As he packed all his documents into his battered briefcase, he wondered what she would make of this little curiosity.

* * *

Luckily for Carole, who had spent a restless night tossing theories and consternations around with the pillows and duvet, the problem of contacting Marie Littlewood was alleviated by the lady herself.

At seven thirty, as Carole was letting the dogs into the orchard, she saw the familiar figure, walking hurriedly over the meadow towards Snug Cottage. She was pleased to see that the woman was alone, but as she drew closer, her pleasure faded as she saw the state of her friend. Marie looked positively haggard. Her pretty brown-shot-with-silver hair was straggly and obviously hadn't seen a brush that morning.

The doctor's wife always wore subtle make-up, the sort that made her look healthy and fresh, without actually declaring its presence. Today her skin tones were sickly and her shoulders were hunched as she hurried towards Carole.

'I'm so sorry about last night.' The woman seemed on the verge of tears. 'I've had the most awful couple of days with Daniel. Can I cadge a cup of coffee and I'll tell you what's been going on?'

'Of course, come on in. I've been so worried about you.' Carole shepherded her friend into the kitchen. 'Here, sit yourself down and tell me everything. Ellie's still in the land of nod, she had a hectic day yesterday and was tired out. We've got the place to ourselves for a while.'

As the coffee was being made, Marie launched into her story. Her voice was agitated and her sentences were disjointed. 'I couldn't believe it! The police came, they were only asking if we had noticed anyone strange around, or heard anything unusual, and Dan went mad! Absolutely mad, screaming and shouting at them to go away. Carole, it was dreadful! I couldn't calm him, and I thought he was going to hit his father! Then he ran off for over an hour. I just don't know what to do with him.'

Carole handed the distraught woman her coffee and tried to remember exactly what Marie had told her about Daniel's troubles. As far as she could recall, Dan had worked for a massive superstore, one of those built on the outskirts of major towns with their own huge car parks and restaurants. He was a branch manager and a conscientious one. It had happened on a bank holiday. Something had gone wrong with a refrigeration unit and he had an emergency call from one of his junior produce managers, who was in total panic. Although officially on leave for a couple of days, he decided that it would be quicker to go in and sort things out. His wife, Della, or was it Delia? — Carole could not remember — had been furious. She was in the throes of a migraine, and begged him to stay and look after their two children so she could take some painkillers and shut herself in a dark room until it subsided. Daniel had sworn he would only be away for an hour at the most, and promised to take the kids to the park when he got back so she could have some peace. Although generally a happy couple, Daniel's work was one thing they had difficulty with. Apparently, a well-rehearsed row had followed. Della accusing him of putting work before the family, and Daniel retorting that, as he was the only one bringing home a wage, she should be grateful that he had such a good job, even if it did mean him having to go in at short notice sometimes. That, as usual, incensed Della, herself a highly skilled draughtswoman, who had embarked on her famous speech about how she had had to give up her career to have his children . . . and so it went on until Daniel drove away, and Della headed for the medicine cabinet. True to his word, Dan had only taken an hour to telephone the correct engineers, pacify his staff, and drive home again. But it had been enough time for Della's migraine pills to put her to sleep, and for their four-year-old daughter to drown in the children's paddling pool. Daniel arrived home to find his son happily playing with his Thunderbird toys in the sandpit, blissfully unaware that the bright pink beach towel floating in the pool concealed his dead sister. It had been an accident, a horrible accident, but Della never forgave her husband for going to work and leaving them. Perhaps guilt played a large part; she had, after all, taken the strongest tablets, and she knew that they could knock her out, but she chose to forget about that, and directed all her hurt and pain at Daniel. The child's room was left as it was. She would not sort out the little girl's clothes or toys. She would not clean it and she would not allow anyone else in. The bed bore the same ruffled linen that it had when her daughter had got up that morning, and the Minnie Mouse hairbrush, sitting on her dressing table, still held precious, long baby-blonde hairs. The dusty shrine, forbidden to Daniel, drew him like a magnet. One day he forced the lock, and was found hours later by his hysterical wife, curled up in a tight foetal ball on his dead daughter's bed.

Marie sipped her drink and gazed, without focus, over the rim of her mug. 'I thought that dear little Phillipa dying was the worst thing that could ever happen to Dan but, well, now, this last episode, I think he's right on the limits of what any man could be expected to take.'

'Sorry, Marie, you're losing me. I thought he'd come home because Della was looking after a sick father or something, and he lost his job after his child died, didn't he?'

Marie stared at the floor. When she spoke, her voice was flat and unemotional.

'He didn't want me to tell anyone the truth. A month ago, he came home from work, and Della had left.' Marie stifled a sob. 'Carole, she's taken his son, and he has no idea where they are. You know how he idolises young Christopher, and he's still grieving for Pippa. He is at the end of his tether, and I can't help him.'

'What about the police, the newspapers? There must be something he can do to find them.' Carole looked exasperated. She thought about the mountains she would move in order to protect those close to her.

'Dan's a sick young man. He's not fit to deal with anything. He's refused all medical and psychological help. He told the psychiatrist what she could do with her therapy suggestions, and he won't take any of the medication that has been offered him. He won't hear of counselling. He can't fight this alone, and yet he refuses help. He even resents his own father trying to stand by him, just because he's a doctor. I'm the only one he'll talk to, and that's not very often, now I don't even know where he is. He met me from church last night, and as soon as I got out of the car, he was gone . . . without a word.'

Carole watched her neighbour carefully, noted her body language and her speech patterns and decided that, no matter how close Daniel was to going over the edge, his mother was not far behind.

'I don't know what I can do to help. I'm just thinking that you've been taking the dogs out and coming over and feeding them for me, and all the time, you've had this awful thing going on. I'm so sorry, if only you'd said.'

'To be honest, I think the walks and the dogs have kept me sane. My husband has got his work to keep him occupied, but me, well . . . Believe me, I've been grateful to have had them to look after. The only time Daniel talked to me at any length was when we were up on the Downs, or in the woods with your boys. Oh God, I wish I knew where he was now. I'm worried sick! And fancy behaving like that with those two police officers, heaven knows what they thought of him! I told them he was under a lot of stress, but the woman police officer looked at me a bit old-fashioned, if you know what I mean. I keep wondering if I should report him missing, but he's gone off before. Not for long, but he'd be furious with me if I caused him any more hassle. I just don't know what to do!'

Carole was about to answer when she had a picture flash into her head. She saw a tall hedge and big conifers with an iron garden gate leading through them. The black and white gables of a slightly ill-kept detached house showed over the top of the firs. On a post, practically hidden by the thick hedging, was a well-known green-and-red *For Sale* sign. Staring up at it, his back to her, was a young man wearing navy slacks and a chunky dark red jumper. As quickly as it had arrived, the scene had gone, but it left Carole in no doubt of where Daniel Littlewood was.

'Marie, is Daniel's house up for sale with William Bouverie and Son?'

'Well, yes! How on earth did you know that? I don't think I've even mentioned that it's on the market.' Marie Littlewood looked nonplussed.

'That's where Daniel is now. He's just very sad. He'll be back soon. I know that much.'

Marie smiled with relief. 'You've seen him! You've had one of your . . . your clairvoyant messages!'

'Sort of, more like a picture postcard, but don't worry, he's coming home.'

The women were interrupted by the entrance of the dogs. Having had enough of games in the orchard, they thought it time for breakfast, and invaded the kitchen en masse. Carole dished out biscuits and Marie fondled silky ears. The invasion was a welcome one, a break from the intensity of the conversation.

Carole offered any help that she could, be it only a sympathetic ear, and Marie left, promising not to bear the brunt of her son's horrible situation alone.

Alone with her dogs, her proxy-children, Carole tried to imagine what it must be like to have one young child die, and the other taken away from you. She remembered taking one of her pups to the vet, only to be told that it had an incurable tumour and would have to be put to sleep. The loss of the twelve-month-old dog had been a physical pain in the chest that went on and on, and she never forgot the bright little fellow. What it would be like to lose one's own child, your flesh and blood. What Daniel must be going through, she could not even begin to imagine.

Pushing a hand slowly through her wiry thick hair, she also pushed the thoughts of death away, and turned her attention to getting Ellie some breakfast.

CHAPTER THIRTEEN

Professor Michael Seale was delighted to receive the invitation in the morning post. It was time for a break, and although it was something of a busman's holiday, he relished the thought of a week in the lovely Surrey village with its exquisite Norman church, fascinating gallery, and various antique shops. Then, of course, there was the attraction of the inimitable Mrs Cavendish-Meyer's culinary expertise, and some company. That was what Michael missed more than all the cordon bleu cooking. His wife had died less than a year ago, and it was as if she had taken part of him with her. He thought it may have been the best part, because he did not always like the person that was left.

He called Janet into his tiny consulting room and asked her to reschedule all his appointments for the following week. He knew that it was fairly quiet, and he had briefly skimmed through the list of patients. Nothing stood out as being a problem, and the only important thing on the horizon was a lecture in Paris next month. Plenty of time to plan that when he got back from Compton.

Carole's request had stated that, in return for spending some time with Ellie, she would feed and water him, offer some bracing fresh air, and before he left, treat him to a dinner at the Carnack Arms Hotel at Pyrbridge. 'Crafty mare!' He laughed out loud. 'If anything could get me to leave London, it would be the rare malt whisky from that particular hostelry.' It was a small price to pay to spend some time with the delightful Ellie McEwan. In fact, and he suspected Carole Meyer knew only too well, he would have made the trip to see Ellie without any bribes being offered at all!

* * *

It takes someone who has been ill, incarcerated, or incapacitated, for some length of time, to appreciate the delights of a trip to a supermarket. What to most harassed shoppers was a nightmare — a chore of necessity not enjoyment — was to Ellie a great adventure. After eons of being reliant on others to provide her daily food, she had, at last, convinced Carole that she was ready for a shopping expedition. Carole needed to stock up in readiness for Michael's impending visit, and she wanted to go to one of the bigger food stores, in order to get everything she wanted under one roof. They decided on the superstore at Brooklands.

Rather than have her walk too far, Carole dropped Ellie off at the entrance, and drove away to park. Ellie made her way inside, and had a rush of panic sweep over her. The store was huge, and it almost overpowered her. After a swift mental telling off, she made her way slowly along the aisles, looking at the brightly coloured corridors of breakfast cereals, pickles and washing products. How things could change so radically in a matter of months amazed her. There were products on the shelves that she had never heard of, and some old favourites in completely different packaging. Nothing looked the same.

Carole appeared, pushing a huge trolley that already held several items. 'I'll be as quick as I can,' she informed Ellie, 'and if you get tired, go and sit down over by the check-outs. I'll find you when I've finished. Then if there is anything you particularly want, I'll pick it up for you.'

Ellie was unable to use either basket or trolley while on crutches, and now all the operations were over, she was counting the days until the plaster would come off for good.

She made her way up and down the aisles, enjoying looking at the merchandise and making mental notes of some things she might like to purchase. A couple of times she saw Carole industriously loading up her trolley with a mountain of goodies, then hurrying off to the next section. Michael is going to be well fed, she thought with a smile, and headed off towards the wines and spirits department. She decided she would like to treat Carole to a bottle of something special, an Islay, or perhaps a Glenmorangie.

A few yards ahead of her there seemed to be a bit of a traffic jam. Wary of her injured leg, she was about to turn around and look for a different route to the whisky aisle, when she realised there was something of an incident occurring.

A tall, heavily built man was bending over a child of about four or five, who was sitting on the floor with his back against shelves full of tinned fruit. A small crowd was starting to collect, but Ellie's view of the boy was, at that moment, uninterrupted. She automatically brought the lad's aura into focus and immediately saw a problem.

An old lady with a high-pitched voice was excitedly telling the woman next to her that she had heard the little boy say he felt dizzy, and the next thing he was on the floor.

The child had broken out into a sweat and was now crying. The big man, who Ellie decided must be his father, had swept the child up in his arms and was pushing away from the crowd and moving towards her. His fear and concern made Ellie's eyes hurt; the intensity was impossible to shut out. He slowed as he approached her. Even in his flight to get his son to somewhere quieter, the man was aware of her broken leg.

As he passed, she called out to him and urged him to wait. She hobbled to catch him up.

'I'm sorry! He's not well. I've got to get him out of here!'

Ellie realised that this was no time to prevaricate, and shouted after the man, 'I know what's wrong with him!'

The man hesitated. 'Are you a nurse? Can you help him?'

Not wanting to go into detail, she carried on with as much authority as she could muster. 'Get him to hospital, he has a foreign body in his right ear, and it's badly infected. Looks like it's been there for days.'

'How can you know that just by looking at him?' The man's consternation was momentarily overpowered by suspicion.

Ellie offered up a quick prayer for forgiveness, and lied proficiently. 'Oh, I see kids like this all the time; it's typical. Just get him some medical help, don't go poking around yourself. He'll probably need some antibiotics, as well.'

The man stared hard at her, and she thought he was going to challenge her, but instead he shook his head, muttered something unintelligible, then took off with his crying son held tight in his arms.

She watched as he hurried through the main doors and across the car park. She sincerely hoped he was on his way to the hospital; the child had been in agony. The foreign body, it looked like a bead or a button, was a long way into the ear. The kid must have been too scared to say what he had done or, like some children, just forgotten about it until it started to hurt.

'What was that all about?' Carole was by her side, her trolley groaning under the weight of all her acquisitions.

Ellie said she would tell her all about it on the way home, and did she think there was room in the trolley for three more items, if she really squeezed them in.

Carole gave her a withering look and they proceeded on to Wines and Spirits.

* * *

DCI Bob Foreman swore softly under his breath.

This was all he needed. The digital message strip above the hospital reception check-in bore the legend:

WAITING TIME IS APPROXIMATELY 2 HOURS. WE WILL DO EVERYTHING TO

ENSURE THAT YOU ARE SEEN AS QUICKLY AS POSSIBLE. A NURSE WILL ASCERTAIN THE SEVERITY OF YOUR ILLNESS OR INJURY AND THEN YOU WILL BE SEEN BY A DOCTOR ACCORDINGLY.

The message flashed on about major injuries arriving by ambulance and helicopter and having patience with people whose problems were more serious, etc., etc., etc. By the time he had read it six or seven times, his head ached and his patience was frayed to breaking point. He knew it wasn't Rosie's fault that the babysitter had let her down on the day she was sitting her final exam. He knew he couldn't shout at little Liam for stuffing God knows what in his ear. He couldn't even be angry at the dog for knocking the milk carton over, the reason he had gone to the supermarket. He guessed he had the dog to thank for his being there, and meeting that strange woman who knew exactly what was wrong with Liam. She had been right, spot-on right. The triage nurse had taken one look in the tearful youngster's ear and pronounced the probable presence of a foreign body, but it was a very long way in and the canal was very swollen and infected. He would be seen by a doctor as soon as possible, but they were very busy.

That was nearly an hour ago.

Liam was asleep on his lap, and gently stroking his son's straight dark hair, he let his mind wander back to the murder inquiry. He had given all the information he had on the killer to Amanda, and she had promised to come back to him as soon as she could with her observations. He badly needed a break on these two cases. He wondered how Vic and Hudson had made out with Weasel. He certainly wasn't going to hang by his eyelashes on that one, but it would be ironic if, as one of his team had said, it turned out after dozens of times of crying wolf, Weasel really had witnessed the murderer leaving the scene of the crime.

He wanted to get back to the station, but knew he had no chance until Liam was sorted out. For the twentieth time since his son had collapsed, he wondered about the woman on the crutches. She had given the impression, by the way she spoke, that she worked with children, paediatrics maybe, or a child minder perhaps. It just didn't feel right to him. Call it policeman's nose, or just being plain suspicious of everyone, but he thought she couldn't possibly have been so dead sure, without even examining the boy. He heard her voice call after him, 'I know what is wrong with him!' The emphasis was on the 'know'. No doubts or unspecific offers of help, just 'I know!' It niggled at him as he sat and surveyed the waiting area with its tatty, well-thumbed magazines and empty coffee beakers. He decided to tell the doctor, if and when he ever saw one, about the woman and her prophetic diagnosis.

'Liam Foreman, please!'

Bob carried his son through to a cubicle with Jungle Book curtains around it, and sat with the boy still on his lap, until the doctor arrived.

The young doctor confirmed that there was something wedged deep in the child's ear, and due to the swelling and obvious pain it was causing him, he was loath to delve around and make it worse. He said that he would give Liam something to make him a bit more comfortable, and he would be happier if his superior examined him. If they could not reduce the inflammation somewhat, he may have to be seen by a specialist in the ENT clinic the next day. Foreman's heart sank. Mainly out of concern for his boy, but also because he needed to be elsewhere, tracking down a killer. He needed to be focused on murder, not worrying about ears, noses and throats.

After a few minutes, a scarecrow of a man appeared through the curtains and introduced himself as Jack Barker, Head of Department. He talked softly to Liam, who responded well to the dishevelled smiling consultant.

'I think I can sort this out for you,' he said to Bob. 'I will need to sedate him and get the offending article out as quickly as possible. He'll be sleepy for a while, so watch him carefully when he gets home and, if I am at all concerned when I get a proper look in there, we'll bring him back in the morning, all right?'

In twenty minutes, Bob and Jack were staring at a mucky pearl button sitting in the bottom of a kidney bowl.

'Well, there it is! It looks as though it's from a lady's blouse to me,' said Jack.

'Could be, my Rosie wears the kind of clothes that may have that sort of button on them.'

'Young Liam is going to have a very sore ear for a few days. I've given him an antibiotic shot, and you'll have to pick up a prescription from the pharmacy for him. Some gentle painkillers will help too. It was very observant of you to realise what the problem was. I assume Liam didn't give you any clues? Kids rarely do.'

'Not at all, and the thing is, I never realised anything. It was this woman in the supermarket!'

Bob Foreman told the story and Jack Barker listened quietly.

'I cannot help you on that one,' said the consultant. 'As far as I'm concerned, without an examination, or Liam actually saying something about his ear, there was no way she could have known what the problem was.'

'That's what I thought.' Bob looked perplexed, then offered his thanks to Jack. 'Thank you, Mr Barker, I appreciate what you've done. I don't think my lad will be doing that again in a hurry.'

'Don't you believe it! He's a boy, isn't he?'

* * *

Jack assured the police officer that his sleepy, whimpering son would be fine with them while he went to the pharmacy. He called a nurse to stay with the little lad and made his way back to his office. Called the Pig Pen by the staff, Jack Barker's den was inhabited by piles of notes, plastic bone formations, reference books, discarded clothes and half-dead plants. 'Office' was a slightly grand term to describe where

Jack sat, behind the ancient desk, with its top so exquisitely etched with coffee cup rings and ink stains.

He absent-mindedly screwed up some very out-of-date Post-it notes and threw them in the vague direction of the waste bin. Why did he think that the woman the detective chief inspector had met in the supermarket was Ellie McEwan? He remembered her clearly. Apart from being a bit of a miracle, she had been a resident of the hospital for so long that everyone knew and liked her. Then there was her strange ability, brought to their notice particularly by her run-in with that baby leaving Maternity. Ellie would still be on crutches, of that he was sure, but how many other women were also in the same predicament? People recovering from strains and breaks, others having had operations, why should it be her? Perhaps some canny mother had seen it all before and made a lucky guess? Well, it wasn't up to him to give the policeman the benefit of his uncertain suspicions. The main thing was that the child was going to be all right, so everyone was happy, were they not?

* * *

Bob Foreman was far from happy. He hated unanswered questions. In his line of business this was unacceptable, and his brain found it very hard to put the pause button down on an incomplete inquiry of any kind. Rosie was home when he arrived, and she rushed to the door to greet their pathetic, grizzling son. She had picked up the message that he'd left on the ansafone, and had put Liam's Scooby-Doo hot water bottle and his favourite teddy in his bed, ready to welcome and console the little boy.

A few minutes later, Bob and Rosie sat, one each side of their son, as he drifted off to sleep. He told his wife about the whole incident and was surprised when she practically dismissed his scepticism about the woman.

'Bob, some mothers have a real empathy with kiddies, can read their body language like a book. She probably noticed him touching his ear, or perhaps her own child had done exactly the same thing. Forget it, darling, Liam will be fine now, and that's all that matters.'

With that she hung the little boy's blue jeans and his bright red sweatshirt over the back of his chair, picked up a discarded Action Man, placed him on his designated shelf, and went downstairs to get dinner ready before the other two got home.

Bob remained vigilant beside Liam until he was sure the boy was fast asleep. Then he went to tell his wife that, as soon as they had eaten, sadly he would have to return to the station, for what could be a long night.

CHAPTER FOURTEEN

Michael arrived late afternoon, bearing two large flight bags, a plastic cover with some clothes hangers protruding from it, a small attaché case, and a shoulder bag. Scrubbs had collected him from the station in the Morris, as Carole was up to her armpits in pastry, but she wouldn't hear of him getting a taxi.

'I did say one week!' said Carole, hands on hips, and regarding all the luggage that was being removed from the back of the elderly car.

'Well, don't you find it difficult to gauge the weather these days? Anyway, I've brought a selection of clothes for all temperatures and occasions. I didn't quite know what we'd be doing, so . . . ?'

'Man, this is Surrey, not New York! There is little we can do here, other than walk, eat, visit the local, and laze around the house!'

'Oh bliss! Just what I hoped. How are you, old thing?'

Before she could remonstrate about the 'old', Michael had swept her into a bear hug, kissed her loudly on both cheeks, and was making a beeline for Ellie, arms outstretched.

'Ellie, you are looking wonderful, my dear! How's the leg?' Without waiting for an answer, he said, 'And how's the head? Oh yes, that's looking so much better, and how—'

'Michael! Give the poor girl a chance! Questions later, let's get you settled into your room. I've put you in the large bedroom at the front that looks out over the orchard. I think you'll be comfortable.'

Michael, who had stayed once before, remembered the room with its en-suite bathroom, and very agreeable bed. Certainly not an orthopaedic delight, it had been deep and soft and had enveloped him with feathery hospitality. He was delighted to think that Carole was not one of those who believed the main attribute of an expensive bed was that it should feel like a barn door underneath you. He had slept like the proverbial baby, and was sincerely hoping he would do the same again.

Occasionally, London, with its continual flow of the halt and the lame knocking on his door, got to him, and he wanted to savour this sojourn in the country.

Together, they carried his baggage up to the light, airy room, hung with watercolours, mainly of the Downs and the local countryside.

As Carole was leaving him to unpack, he asked gently, 'How are things, really?'

'I'm not sure, Michael. I'm not sure at all.'

Michael looked at her. Then he looked past the everyday expressions and general demeanour and saw that her natural halo of Cerulean blue was diminished and, for a moment, faltering in its strength. 'We'll talk later. Does Ellie turn in early?'

'She might stay up a little later tonight, as you are here, but she's never late, she still tires easily.'

'Then, I think you should ply me with some of your excellent Irish malt, and my ears will be all yours.'

She smiled appreciatively and left him to settle in.

As he watched her go, he felt his notion about an idyllic week of peace, perfect peace, slowly ebbing away.

* * *

Detective Sergeant Vic Barratt threw the empty Coke can into the bin and swore loudly. From the first-floor window he could see the distinctive dark red colour of the guvnor's car pulling into the staff car park. Another two minutes would have seen him on his way home — now God knows what time he'd see his wife and kids. The DCI would want a full account of everything that had happened that day, not that there had been any earth-shattering developments. He'd already put a typed report on his boss's desk, but he knew that would not be enough for Foreman. He'd want it all, word for word.

He thought about trying to slip out through the cafeteria, but he knew that Foreman had suffered a pretty awful day with his son at the hospital, and he felt a pang of pity for the man. So, instead of escaping, he made his way to his boss's office, and prepared to give the most concise precis of the day's events, in the quickest possible time.

'Ah, good, Vic, thought I'd miss you. I'm glad you're still here. How did you get on with Weasel today?'

Foreman had taken his jacket off, the heating system now fully operational, and was settling down behind his desk to peruse the pile of reports that had gathered there over the day.

'To be honest, sir, I got caught up with some calls from the first victim's family. I let Hudson take WDC Brown rather than hold things up. I spoke to him earlier and they'd got one extra bit of info. Weasel added a description of the bag. It was a sports bag, very little help as it's one of the most popular brands going. There are probably about seven kids with the same one in my son's class alone. Still, it's something, I suppose. I reckon he really did see our man, sir.'

'Anything else?'

'No, sir. We are rather hoping that Dr Amanda Gerrard will give us a new direction to try. Did you manage to get to see her?' He paused, then hurriedly added, 'Oh, sorry sir, how's your lad? I meant to ask when you came in.'

'Silly little bugger stuffed a button in his ear! Nasty infection, poor little devil must have been in agony, but he never said a word. I thought he was a bit fretful over breakfast but, you know what children are like. He seemed okay later, then he collapsed in the supermarket! Still, he's all right now, sleeping off the sedative, brilliant doctor . . . but I had to wait forever to see him.'

'Couldn't you have pulled rank, sir?' suggested Vic.

'Not my style, Vic, they know what they are doing, and I saw the right man in the end. And, yes, I did see Dr Gerrard. Hopefully, we should have something from her tomorrow. Right now, I expect you'll want to get off. I'll read the reports, and we'll talk in detail in the morning. Give my regards to Barbara.'

With that, the sergeant, happily and unexpectedly, found himself dismissed.

* * *

After their evening meal, Carole, Michael and Ellie sat around the fire, sipped coffee, and chatted amicably. The subject of Ellie's supermarket experience came up when Michael asked if she had used her gift in any specific way of late. He was fascinated by the story and kept asking her to go over bits for him.

'So, what exactly did you "see"? How were you able to be so sure what was wrong?'

'I was never in doubt, Michael,' replied Ellie. 'It was as visible as it would have been if I could have seen into his head. The aura around the right side of his head was almost missing, the ear itself was sending little spears of angry red light from it, like pictures of sunspots erupting, only in dark red. Then, in the centre of the field of pain, was this tiny jet-black area. It was obvious what was wrong.'

Michael regarded her for a moment. 'You didn't, at any point, consider an ear infection, plain old earache? Kids get ear problems: glue ear, otitis media, there are lots of other things apart from sticking toys and foreign bodies down the ear canal.'

For a while Ellie did not answer. Then, as if she had only just realised it, she felt really puzzled. 'No, not for one moment. I just knew. As soon as the aura told me where the trouble was, I looked intensely at that area, and I clearly saw the obstruction. Is that unusual, Michael?'

'Very. Even I cannot do that!' He paused. 'I admit I work very differently to you. As you know, I use the aura as a diagnostic tool initially, and then I use colour as a healer, putting it back when it is missing. In essence, I try to repair damaged auras. I admit that I can spot colours and changes in their patterns better than most in my profession, but I have to read and interpret their meaning. I don't actually "see" the anomaly.' He leaned back in his chair and regarded her thoughtfully. 'Powerful stuff, Ellie! I think we might have to find a suitable candidate, someone with a known health problem, not known to you, of course, and you tell me exactly what you see. This could be very interesting.'

Carole placed her cup and saucer on the table beside her and joined in the conversation. 'I think I can help there. I've a friend who has never met either of you, and he has a very specific medical condition. Not an obvious one, either. I'm sure he will allow you to practise on him, in exchange for morning coffee and a slice of chocolate cake. He's a neighbour of Scrubbs. I'll get him to drop a note through his door in the morning.'

'Excellent!' Michael grinned. 'Let's set that up for as soon as possible. I can't wait to see this lass in action.'

'Oh dear, I hope I don't disappoint you.' Ellie felt suddenly apprehensive. 'I don't know if I can do it to order, it just seems to happen.'

Michael assured her she'd be able to tune in and pick up accurate readings every time and, with help, would be able to decipher all sorts of subtle messages from the aura. 'Depressions, moods, anger, happiness, suspicion, love, all our emotions and feelings,' he explained, 'cause auras to fluctuate and transform in different ways. Sometimes these changes are very tenuous and hard to see, and sometimes they are dramatic and impossible to miss.'

Ellie accepted the balloon glass of brandy that Carole offered her and settled further back into the settee that she shared with two tired spaniels. She ruffled Digger's ears with one hand and held tightly on to the glass with the other, gently warming the amber spirit that swirled and sparkled in the firelight. She felt warm and safe here. She had good friends around her and it would seem from what Michael said that there was a very high probability she would be able to use her extraordinary gift in a positive way to help others. Her original career path, making her one of the country's top florists, seemed to be taking a major turn in a very different direction to what she had planned.

Sitting quietly with her friends, allowing the ambience of the room to penetrate her whole being, she felt content and glad to be alive.

A tear slowly made its way down Ellie's cheek, and although she hoped it would go unnoticed, she saw that Carole's observant gaze did not miss it. Her friend, however, chose not to mention it. She seemed to know that it was not a tear of sorrow, and was more likely an expression of some inner feeling. Carole was very aware that Ellie was still rather sensitive to things.

She managed to stay awake until nearly ten o'clock, then was forced to leave the most pleasant of evenings, as her eyes were shutting. Making her way to her room, she realised this was the first moment in a very long time that she had felt at peace.

* * *

Foreman carefully read all the reports, making notes where necessary, and listing particular areas he wished to clarify with the members of his team the next day. It was around ten o'clock when there was a soft tap on the door, and Hudson came in. His clothes stank of smoke and there was a distinctly beery smell about him.

'Thought I'd find you here, sir. Sorry, I'm not at my best. I've been hanging around Weasel's watering hole, like you said.'

'I didn't mean for you to stay this late, Officer, and I hope you didn't drive like that.' Foreman pulled a face at the state of his detective.

'I didn't drink, sir. Some scruffy scrote tipped his pint down my jacket, that's why I stink like this. Anyway, it might have been worth the trouble, sir. After about his sixth drink, he started getting really chopsy with his mates; he must have told the story a dozen times. Funnily enough, he didn't change it, you know, spice it up for his oppos. Then I heard him say one other thing, well, it wasn't exactly saying something different, just adding something. This bloke drinking with him asked him if he recognised the villain, and he said yes. He didn't know who he was, but he had seen him before somewhere.'

'Didn't we ask him that question, Hudson?'

'No, sir, I don't think we did.'

'Bring him in tomorrow, and we'll start again on him. Good work. Now go home and clean yourself up. You stink worse than Weasel!'

'Thanks very much. Do you think expenses would extend to getting my jacket cleaned?' He looked hopefully at his boss, then grimaced. 'Okay, sir, I know . . . "Bugger off, Hudson!"'

Foreman smiled as the detective left. He sat for a while longer before straightening his files and reaching for his coat. Was there a possible chance that their alcoholic witness could make an identification? There was no way of using his statement in a court of law, as he would fall to bits, but he just might lead them in the right direction. It was precious little to go on, but along with the bag, as Barratt had said, at least it was something.

* * *

Carole heaped coal and a large round splintery log onto the fire, and topped up Michael's glass. 'Now, my friend, where are those ears you promised me?'

* * *

After his encounter with Hudson that night, Bob Foreman couldn't face his ritual one beer when he got home. Instead, he sorted through the sideboard cupboard, moving bottles of dry sherry and Vermouth, until he found an unopened Jack Daniels. It was so easy to drink too much in his line of business, but he loved Rosie and the kids, and he loved his job. Years ago, high-ranking officers could flout the law with impunity. Now, coppers came down hard on coppers. He was just as likely to get pulled over as anyone else, and he never knew when the phone would ring and drag him from his bed. However, he thought he had earned a small snifter tonight — it had, after all, been a truly shitty day. He broke the seal and poured a small measure into a shot glass. He smiled as he always did when he read the motto on the side of the cheap, heavy glass. 'My Dad's a Big Shot!' His eldest, Frances, had brought it back from a day in Brighton with her mother and younger brothers. Since then, he'd had to forgo the crystal in favour of his daughter's gift.

He smiled again and put the lights out. He hoped Rosie would still be awake as he hadn't had time to discuss today's exam with her. He looked in on Liam, who was sleeping soundly with a nightlight burning in a lamp shaped like Shaun the Sheep. Leaving the boy's door wide open, he went across the hall to their bedroom.

His wife was sitting up reading *Harry Potter and the Goblet of Fire*. She said that it was purely to check it was suitable for eight-year-old Max to read, but from the avid way she read it, Bob knew better.

'A quick shower and I'll be with you, sweetheart. I see the boy is sleeping the sleep of the just. I hope you've locked up all clothing with buttons on?'

'Actually, I've cut them all off,' replied Rosie, with a grin. 'So watch your work shirt for the morning!'

He smiled at his wife. There was rarely a day went by that he didn't give quiet thanks for their being together, and for their lovely family, and to wonder what the devil a beautiful woman like her was doing with a great lummox of a police officer like him. As usual, he had no answers, but he gave thanks anyway.

* * *

It was nearly two in the morning when Michael Seale's tired body renewed its acquaintance with the marshmallow of a bed, and nearly three before his eyes closed.

Murders, prowlers, unstable young men, apparitions, coincidental dreams, premonitions, and warnings, all swirled around on the backdrop of the gentle rolling Surrey hills and frightened the life out of him! He thought of his flat in the metropolis, and suddenly, the homeless in the shop doorways, the prostitutes, the junkies, the graffiti, the rubbish, and the muggings of the city, seemed very tame indeed.

CHAPTER FIFTEEN

'Oh, bloody hell! What now?' Bob Foreman groaned and reached for the bedside telephone. He lifted the receiver, acknowledged his name, and heard something he really did not want to hear.

He grabbed a pen and scribbled down the address. 'I'll be there, and for God's sake, don't let anyone contaminate that scene!'

He hugged his wife and left her, as he had a thousand times before.

During the drive to Weybridge, he thought about what he would find at the murder scene. In films they always looked dramatic: powerful and sensational. In life, he found them filthy, degrading places. When he thought about them, he always saw them in black and white, like a lot of dirty pictures. Human life put out with the rubbish.

When he arrived at the hotel, uniformed officers were hastily erecting a tarpaulin cover over and around the scene of the crime. Blue-and-white ribbon secured the area from the public, although no public had deigned to join the merry throng at two thirty in the morning.

The woman lay, face up, in a shrubby area, only a few yards from the entrance gate to the outdoor tennis courts.

Foreman knew the hotel, having attended a few official functions there, and he recalled his niece's wedding had been held in the banqueting suite, two or three years ago. Nice meal, but grossly overpriced, according to his brother.

The hotel was well known and very expensive. It was set in several acres of parkland and boasted a small well-kept golf course among its amenities.

The first thing that amazed the detective was the closeness of the body to the main building. The killer had taken one hell of a risk if he had actually murdered the woman in situ, and not killed her somewhere else and dumped her here.

The pathologist, encased from top to toe in a white protective suit, was already with the dead woman. Foreman struggled into his own suit and approached his colleague with careful steps. In answer to his question, the forensic doctor assured Foreman that this was the site of the killing, and yes, it had all the hallmarks of the other two.

Bob stared at the victim. He wasn't good on ages, but he reckoned she was in her early thirties. Her clothes were undisturbed — none of the women had been sexually assaulted, and it puzzled him. She appeared to be wearing dungarees and a tie-dye T-shirt. The odd thing was not so much the clothes themselves, but the fact that they were splattered, not only with blood, but with paint. She wore heavy boots, the type that men wore on building sites, high legged, and made of waterproofed soft camel- coloured leather.

A denim jacket was lying in a puddle of mud a little way from her, and a shoulder bag, made of pieces of multicoloured leather sewn together with large herringbone stitches, had been abandoned in a flower bed beside the path to the tennis court.

The pathologist gave Bob his preliminary findings and promised to make a full report as soon as he could. 'Death occurred between ten o'clock and eleven, I'd say. Hit on the back of the head with a heavy object. Smooth, rounded surface as before, then asphyxiated using, I think, the same weapon that was used to stun her. The trachea and the oesophagus have been crushed with a great deal of force.' The pathologist sighed and continued, 'Then, of course, he added his own unique mark to his handiwork. Any ideas on that one, Chief Inspector?'

'Absolutely nothing, Doctor. How about you?'

'A hare-brained theory or two, nothing I'd like to share with you though.'

'That wacky, huh?'

'Probably less wacky than the truth, whatever that might be, Chief Inspector. If you get really stuck for ideas, pop down to the mortuary, and I'll give you the benefit of my fertile imagination!'

'Thanks, I'll bear that one in mind.'

Bob ducked under the cordon and called over the uniformed officer in charge. 'Who found her, Mac?'

Sergeant Ferguson pointed to a young man in a black leather jacket who was in earnest conversation with DS Barratt.

'He's a waiter, French, I think. It appears he was coming back from some illicit meeting with his girlfriend, the path round the tennis courts leads to a side gate out onto the main road. It's not lit at night, and he practically fell over her. He's well shook up, but these Continentals are a bit highly strung, aren't they, sir?'

'So would I be if I was his age and had just fallen over a dead body in the pitch black!'

'You're all heart, sir, but we don't know yet that he didn't kill her himself, do we?'

'Look at him, Mac! Clutching at straws a bit, aren't we? He looks about twelve and scared shitless!'

The two men looked at the hapless young man who was in the process of waving both hands in the air in a dramatic gesture that seemed completely lost on Vic Barratt. After a minute or two he was dismissed by the detective, and made his way, slouch shouldered, and shaking his head from side to side, into the hotel.

Vic Barratt closed his pocket book and walked over to them. 'He's too shaken up to take a statement tonight, guv.

I've got the details verbally and I'll see him in the morning. He's in staff quarters here.'

'Okay, so what have we got on the girl? Do we know who she is?' asked Bob.

'Yes, sir, the hotel manager has confirmed her to be a Miss Adele Turner. She was working on some decoration in the banqueting suite. The hotel owners had brought her in to revamp some big picture.'

Bob thought of his niece's matrimonial bash and recalled an enormous mural on the wall behind the wedding party. Some Bacchanalian scene full of debauchery and grapes and wine, cornucopias of fruit, and tables of food. 'I know the one you mean. It was a bit faded and dull two years ago, could have used some restoring even then. So, Turner was an artist?'

'Yes, mostly seascapes, sir!'

'Very funny, Sergeant, and at this time in the morning . . . unappreciated.'

'Sorry, sir. Yes, very talented girl. She comes from Cornwall, and was staying at the hotel, courtesy of the management, until the job was finished. She has been working all hours, very early mornings, and late into the night, so that they didn't have to close the room completely. She'd practically finished, another couple of days at the most, according to the hotel manager. He's a Mr Julian Featherstone, guv, and he's frantic to keep this low key.'

'Impossible. Serial killers attract attention. I'm afraid his hotel is going to be famous, or more like, infamous. Tell him not to worry, his bookings will probably double once the killer is apprehended. People revel in a good murder; a bit of notoriety could do wonders for his takings.'

'And what about until then? We still have a murderer running loose in the neighbourhood.'

'Don't remind me, Vic. I'm painfully aware of that fact.'

He rubbed the back of his neck and suddenly felt very tired. Top brass was going to be screaming for results and he had nothing to offer them. He had held off calling in someone to replace his DI, who was on sick leave, hoping she would be back this week, but the latest report said she would probably not be fully fit for duty for at least another fortnight. As soon as the world had woken up, he would have to draft in some help, and fast. 'Vic? Why was she out here?'

'Well, she mentioned to one of the waiters that she might join a group of hotel employees for a drink in the local, the Water Gate, if she could make it before closing time. Looks like she tried to take the short cut. That gate comes out on the road right opposite the pub.'

'Why go drinking in the local when you are staying in a licensed hotel?'

'Have you seen the prices here? And anyway, it was a leaving do for one of the chefs, and the staff are not allowed to drink in the hotel. Miss Turner had been working here for over a month and had got friendly with the staff, so it was understandable that she went for drinks with them from time to time. English and Brown are taking statements from everyone who was in the Water Gate last night, and anyone who was on duty before she left the building. We will put it all together at the morning briefing and see what we get.'

Bob Foreman leaned against an ivy-covered wall and crossed his arms in front of his chest. 'Three talented ladies. No sexual abuse. What is he killing them for, Vic?'

Sergeant Barratt looked across towards the shrouded body that was being carried to a waiting van. His eyes were unfocused. 'Dunno, sir, but it's a bloody wicked world when things like this have to happen.'

The DCI pulled his coat around him and straightened up. 'I'd better go and see Mr Featherstone and assure him that his worst fears are about to be realised. Finish up here, and go and get a few hours shut-eye, Sergeant. I'll see you at the station for the morning meeting.'

'Thanks, sir. I'll just grab an hour or two and tell Barbara that I don't know when I'll be seeing her again.'

'The joys of being a copper's wife, Vic. I'm about to ring Rosie with the same good tidings.'

Julian Featherstone was distraught. He paced up and down, and ran long, well-manicured fingers through his expertly coiffured locks. 'I can't believe it! Why here? We are going to be bankrupted! Head Office will go berserk! They'll blame me, I know it, I'll never be employed again! And that poor girl, bludgeoned to death, right here. Oh my God, it's just too awful!'

Bob Foreman noted that the death of this young artist had been placed last on Mr Featherstone's catalogue of disasters. *Right charmer, this one,* he thought. 'I expect my sergeant has asked you for information on all your members of staff, Mr Featherstone, but there are going to be a lot of other questions that I will be wanting you to supply answers to. I hope you will make yourself available for my officers? Plus, we will need a room here, downstairs, and as near to the front reception as possible.'

Featherstone's face was one of abject misery. As if a murder wasn't enough, now he would have swarms of policemen messing up his Axminster.

'We will be as discreet as we can, Mr Featherstone, and it will only be required until our interviews with your employees and guests are complete. We have a major incident room already set up at the station. So, the sooner we get our questions over, the sooner you can get back to normal.'

Discreet and policemen were obviously an anomaly in Julian's book, and he voiced the opinion that he was certain the hotel would never be 'normal' again. However, he seemed to see the folly of procrastination, and offered Bob a small reception room off the main foyer.

'As soon as we have interviewed the guests, they will be free to go, until then, I'm afraid . . .'

'Yes, I know, your sergeant gave me that piece of disastrous news. They'll never come back, you know! We will lose dozens of important clients. Oh, it's a—'

'Yes, Mr Featherstone, you mentioned before . . . it's a disaster. Give it a break will you! If anyone deserves to think it a disaster, it should be Adele's family, don't you think?'

Bob was a good detective, but he had serious problems with keeping his temper under control when people put money before human life. As he walked out to the foyer his hands were stuffed deep in his coat pockets and gripped tightly into fists. He really did not like Mr Featherstone and thought perhaps he would leave the formal interview with the objectionable manager to Vic Barratt.

Before he got to the ornate front doors, he heard his name being called out. WDC Brown was hurrying down a corridor that led to the staff quarters.

'Sir! We've got something! Have you got a minute?'

They sat on one of the huge leather sofas by the deserted reception area, and the young detective spoke quickly, unable to keep the excitement out of her voice.

'I've been speaking to one of the chambermaids, sir. Her name is Mary Probart. She took the short cut to the Water Gate pub last night. She doesn't like the path past the tennis courts, but she had been working late, and didn't want to miss out. She said it was ten o'clock exactly, sir, when she left her room. She had a torch with her and, as she was approaching the gate, she heard something and stopped. She shone her flashlight towards the bushes and saw a man and a woman in an embrace. The man had his back to her, but she said that he was wearing a long dark coat, sir.'

Bob inhaled, guessing where this was going.

Wendy Brown continued. 'She couldn't see who the woman was, as the man was shielding her. When she realised it was a courting couple, as she put it, she moved the beam away from them and called out *Sorry to interrupt!* She said she giggled a bit, and went on past them. She forgot all about them by the time she got to the party, and returned later, with the others, by the longer route. Apparently, they were trying to sober-up a couple of the lads before they got back. Mary reckons the management are strict, and they could easily have got the push for improper behaviour on hotel property.' Wendy took a breath. 'Anyway, we have just been over it all again, sir, and this is important. When she thought she was interrupting a snogging session and tilted the torchlight down, she noticed two bags at the couple's feet. One was leather, made up of bits and pieces of different coloured materials, and the other was a sports bag, sir. It was the same as the one Weasel told us about this morning: a black Nike holdall.'

Bob's mind was racing. He exclaimed, 'Excellent work, detective. Get your young lady down to the station immediately. She's seen our murderer with his latest victim. She might well remember something more, and depending on whether the killer saw her, she could be in danger. Off you go, Brown. I need a word with the SOCOs, and then I'll see you back at the station.'

Wendy Brown hurried back down the corridor, and Bob pushed open the large carved doors and walked briskly back to the now brilliantly lit murder scene.

Two white garbed scenes of crime officers were carefully sifting through soil, leaves and grass, evidence bags ready for any suspect material that could be of use to forensics.

Lenny Chambers had been attached to the Force for as long as Bob himself, and he was pleased to see him there. Lenny was thorough to the point of obsession; plus, he had been at the other two murder scenes.

When Bob approached him, he was, as always, bemoaning the fact that the whole scene had been contaminated by Surrey Police issue footwear, and were young rookies these days specifically taught to obliterate as much of the evidence as possible?

Bob let him finish his ritual diatribe and asked him if he had found anything yet.

'Daylight will help, Bob, but it's a different pattern this time. I suspect a struggle, nothing major, not a big fight. It's just that with the other two lasses, it was as if the murderer didn't exist. He left nothing. This time there are clear-cut signs of an incident. There's a lot more blood, and not only in the area where the body lay, as in the other two victims. No, I think he was disturbed, or maybe hurried his work because of the proximity of the building. This is—' Lenny halted and turned as his name was called out by the other SOCO.

'Found something, Len!'

Dangling from a pen, glinting in the glare of the halogen lamps, was a blood-soaked ring. On closer inspection, it was a gold eternity ring, and from its size, it probably belonged to a woman.

'Bag it, laddie, and note exactly where you found it.' The older man looked at the chief inspector and shook his head. 'Certainly not Mr Cool this time, was he? By the time we are through, you could well find we have something the lab can work on for you, old friend! He's been careless.'

* * *

The morning briefing was animated. There was nothing like a breakthrough to fire up the team's enthusiasm.

The walls of the room were covered with photographs. A large area map with coloured pins in it was central behind Bob Foreman, and white soft-card boards, covered with relevant written information about the individual murders, were hung at intervals with the photos.

Bob asked each member of his team for their input, then talked them through the case, until a picture started to emerge. He stood quietly in front of the map, stared at some point in the distance and spoke slowly.

'Three women. All skilled at their profession. One a musician, a brilliant young violinist to be exact. One a doctor, with a special talent for delicate specialised surgery. One an artist, whose talents extended from incredibly detailed miniatures, for which she made her name in the art world, to restoring wall murals. Each woman murdered in the same way. Hit from behind and stunned, except, we suspect, in the case of Adele Turner, who died instantly from the force of the blow to the lower part of the cranium. They were laid on their backs and asphyxiated, using the same instrument that was used to knock them out. The pressure used on their throats crushed both the windpipe and the food pipe, along with the larynx, the vocal cords, and the hyoid bone. Then they were mutilated in identical fashion.'

At this point Bob stopped, turned, and indicated to the post-mortem photos. 'The murderer severed the three middle fingers and the thumb of the right hand of the first two victims, and the same digits of the left hand of the last victim. Melissa and Helen were right-handed, and Adele was left-handed.' Bob paused. 'The killer knew his victims. He knew what they did, and he knew whether they were left- or right-handed. He took the fingers and thumbs with him, and no trace has been found of them.'

The room was now silent. For once there were no smart comments or black jokes. And everyone present was feeling the weight of responsibility to find this killer before he attacked again.

'Melissa was wearing a ring that it appears he also took,' continued Bob. 'Helen's rings were on her other hand and were untouched. Adele's ring was found, drenched with blood that we assume is hers, at the scene of the crime. The killer, should he have decided to let them live and settle for mutilation alone, would have rendered each of them unable to work. He took away their skills and their talents. We can only assume that he hates them for their abilities.'

There was a murmur of agreement from the gathered company.

'You will see from the photographs that, in each case, he has been careful to leave the little finger unscathed, even though he used a small cleaver, a chef's implement rather than a butcher's tool, to remove the other four digits. The once accomplished hands, in each case, slender and beautiful, have been turned into something freakish and hideous. In an hour or two, we should have the report from Dr Gerrard, the criminal psychologist. We will take her observations and add them to what we already know and see what we come up with. The pathologist has promised to hurry through the post-mortem report on Adele Turner, and that should be with me this afternoon. Anything that shows up that we do not know about, I will notify you straight away.'

Bob Foreman straightened his back against the wall, reached for a glass of water from the table in front of him, and drank deeply before continuing.

'We have a witness this time. We may have one for the first murder too, but as it's Weasel, we won't be able to use his evidence in court. This time, the killer was seen with a woman, most probably our third victim, at the murder site, at a few minutes after ten o'clock. At his feet were two bags, one positively identified as belonging to Adele Turner, and the other a black Nike sports bag with the white logo on the side. A bag of the same description was also seen being carried by a man leaving the scene of the murder of Melissa Crabbe. It was described as "a black one of them sporty jobs, you know, the label with the big white tick". Very common, I know, but most likely, the same bag. Now, our new witness is terrified he may have seen her, although she has been assured that it is very difficult to recognise anyone when they are behind the beam of a torch. He also had his back to her, so I doubt she is in any danger. Her name will, of course, be withheld. She is screaming for protection, but with our budget, she'd have to be Salman Rushdie to get any.'

Before he could continue, a civilian entered the room and handed him a memo. He read it, grunted, and nodded his thanks.

'There has been another possible sighting. It occurred a little later in the evening. We have had a call from a man who had been taking his dog for a late walk. He was rounding the corner of Nettle Close and Barham Avenue, when he was knocked to the ground by a man running at full pelt down the street. Sadly, it seems the witness has very poor sight, and in the badly lit avenue, he could only say that it was a male, and he was carrying something clutched to his chest as he ran. It appeared to be a bag of some kind. The witness is in his late seventies, and I suggest we speak to him as soon as possible, but I don't hold much hope that we'll get any more from him.'

Bob stretched. He hated these long catch-up sessions with a vengeance, but they were vital to amalgamate all the evidence, and get everyone on the same wavelength.

'Okay, I want names of everyone who has been in contact with Adele Turner in the time she has been working at the hotel. Boyfriends, girlfriends, paint suppliers, dry cleaners, possible dates, anyone who has so much as passed the time of day with her. Brown, spend as much time as you need with your witness, and bring me your report when it's ready. Someone check out whether the hotel itself may have been another connection with the three women. Did Melissa ever play there? People do hire groups for parties and functions. Did Helen Carberry attend some gathering during the time that our artist was at work there, or while Melissa was fiddling her way through a concerto? Check all angles regarding the hotel as a link. And Sergeant Barratt, I want you to wring every scrap of information about the hotel staff, past and present, from our friend, Mr Julian Featherstone.'

Vic Barratt looked grimly at his boss, but muttered his acquiescence.

'Lastly, Detective Inspector Gerry Reader will not be back for another couple of weeks, so we've got a couple of chaps from Redhill being seconded to us, DI Leatham and DS Corbett. They are good old boys, and I think some of you will have worked with them before.' There was a murmur of assent. He finished by saying that, due to the seriousness of the inquiry, other officers would be drafted in over the next few days, to ease the pressure on the overworked team.

Bob finally retired to his office, phoned his wife to check on Liam's progress, then glancing at his watch, scribbled on a Post-it note not to forget to go and meet Adele Turner's parents, who were travelling up from Cornwall to see their daughter's body. He sighed. That was yet another reason the policeman's lot was not a happy one.

CHAPTER SIXTEEN

So that both Carole and Mrs Scrubbs could get on with their daily chores, Michael and Ellie decided to go to the summer house each day after breakfast. It was peaceful, an ideal spot for Ellie to bombard Michael with questions, and for Michael to inundate Ellie with his first-hand knowledge of dealing with auras. He had brought books with him on a variety of affiliated subjects. He told her about Kirlian photography, coronal discharge photography, colour healing, energy and chakra work, and harmonic induction.

He was delighted when Ellie began to perceive the depths that this science, for want of a better term, could go. It was certainly not a matter of seeing pretty colours around people; the human energy field was a highly sophisticated structure. It was composed of seven levels. Carole had been amazed that Ellie could perceive three when she first started to control her gift, but now Michael knew she was seeing more every day.

Michael coaxed her into a near perfect description of what she saw when she stared at him. Fixing her gaze into his auric field, she defined many levels of colour and light. Some were clearly structured, and others diffuse. Some like the glow you saw around a candle flame, and others more fluid, like oil on water. Others were more like mist over a damp meadow, vaporous and hazy.

Michael explained that the closer the level to the body, the more physical it was — that area dealt with sensations, mainly pain. The next level was about how you perceived yourself, your personal emotions, and feelings about yourself. He went on covering mental states of mind, relationships, divine and spiritual feelings, and love. Each field had a base colour, often lighter in sensitive people and darker in strong ones, that was present when the field was healthy, but dull and broken in sickness or negativity. He had also brought colour charts, and they spent a great deal of time discussing their depths and properties.

Over the past few days, and without overtaxing Ellie's aching head, Michael tried to explain how he healed people through their auras. He reiterated that there was a school of thought which felt that the human energy field showed the illness before it became present in the physical body. Hence, if you could heal the damaged aura, you could prevent the disease occurring. The same applied when the disease was active; if you rebalanced, re-energised and recharged the aura, then the body would heal. And that was what he did. His gift was of healing, and he firmly believed that Ellie's was a talent for perception and diagnosis. He appreciated that she was a very teachable student, and privately thought that her gift, with the right guidance, could become quite awesome.

He only hoped that she was emotionally strong enough to cope with such a powerful legacy. Something as extraordinary as this could change a person. Sometimes for good, but not always. He shivered when he thought about the other Azimah Syndrome sufferers. It had destroyed them.

Michael looked across to where Ellie sat, deeply ensconced in a book on colour therapy, and smiled. No, Ellie would not succumb. She had him and Carole and Vera to keep her on the right road. Ellie was special, and she would use her gift wisely, of that, he was sure.

* * *

It was mid-morning when Gill arrived to take Ellie back to her home for lunch with her and the twins. Clive was working, and they decided, as Ellie was feeling stronger, they would drive back to Compton via Fleurie. It would be the first time that Ellie had visited the shop and her staff since the accident.

Michael and Carole had arrangements to visit an old friend in Farnham for lunch, so everything fell into place rather well. Marie's troubled son had come back home, as Carole had said he would, and the two were going to walk the legs off the dogs for the afternoon. Ellie had a key to Snug Cottage, should they get back early, and she and Gill set off, twins firmly strapped in the back of her car, for Walton-on-Thames.

Although they chattered incessantly, at no time did Gill mention Clive having a problem, or indeed any problems within the family. Ellie finally decided that her skills were not proficient enough yet, and she had probably misread the signs.

Lunch over, Gill popped the children next door to her neighbour, who had promised to babysit while they went to Ellie's shop.

Ellie was surprised to feel butterflies in the pit of her stomach as they drew up outside. Gill had forewarned the staff, and the shop looked resplendent as she swung through the doors on her crutches. Most of the staff were there to welcome her, and even some of the part-timers who were not actually working that day had come in to see her. Ellie was delighted they had kept the shop looking so good. The flower display looked fabulous, and the windows were dressed impeccably.

She sat with Gill and Peter at the desk where the customers sat to write their cards, and Peter told her how things had been in her absence. He did not pretend it had been easy. Certain customers had protested bitterly that Ellie was not there to do their orders, and one or two of their business accounts had taken a lot of cajoling to leave their contracts in place, even though the famous Ellie McEwan would not be personally attending to their arrangements. But, apart from a few odd hiccups, things were running well.

True to his word, Philip was supporting Peter with administration, and Peter expressed how good it was to know there was someone there for him, should things go inadvertently pear-shaped.

After a quiet chat with other members of staff, Ellie was relieved to see that her manager was really coping very well, and there were no behind-the-scenes agendas to deal with.

The two women spent an hour at Fleurie and, when they left, Peter gave her a huge bunch of French Mona Lisa anemones, as a gift from all the staff. They all hoped she would be back with them before too long, and she had smiled, but decided not to mention that she would probably be leaving her beloved family business for good. She was not sure what the future held for her, but she felt strongly that it was not floristry.

Thirty minutes later, Gill pulled the car into the lane to Snug Cottage, just as Marie and Dan were returning the dogs. Carole's car was already parked outside, although the lady herself was not in sight. Marie pushed the last spaniel through the gate into the courtyard, and turned and smiled at Ellie.

'I don't think you two have met. Ellie, this is my son, Daniel.'

The man silently held out his hand to her, and then looked across at Gill.

Ellie explained that Gill was her dearest friend, and introduced her to Marie and Dan, but once again he did not speak, just mutely shook hands and stepped back.

They made some small talk about the weather, and as the conversation was starting to run dry, they were thankfully joined by Carole, who immediately boomed out her gratitude for having her 'boys' so beautifully exercised.

Ellie covertly observed Daniel and was shocked at the poor state of his aura. There was practically no energy to be seen. She made a mental note to try and get Michael to meet this man before he left, and give her some idea of his problems.

The little crowd dispersed, Ellie giving Gill a big hug and thanking her profusely for her trip out. Carole then shepherded her inside to help Michael devour a huge plate of homemade cakes, and enjoy the ever-present pot of tea.

'I don't know where you find the time for all this cooking,' said Michael, carefully trying not to get cake crumbs in his beard.

'Time is not the problem; it's getting motivated that I find tricky. That's why I enjoy having house guests, I get on with it. If I were on my own, well, I'd find a hundred and one other things to do rather than bother.'

'Well, I'm delighted that you're bothering! May I?' Michael reached for another slice of lemon drizzle cake. 'Speaking of cake, when is that old boy that you mentioned coming in for his coffee, cake and a quick diagnosis?'

'Ah, yes, he'll be here at ten tomorrow morning. I forgot to mention, Scrubbs saw him, and he's happy to help with Ellie's edification. His name is Moses, by the way. Moses Hoskins.'

'Moses? That's not a very usual name, is it? I hope I don't laugh.' Michael looked amused.

'So do I,' Carole admonished. 'He was one of ten children, all with biblical names. At least he did better than one of his brothers who was called Hezekiah, after some Old Testament king of Judah. I think the girls came off best, they were Rachel, Mary, Esther and Ruth.'

'It was certainly a good bet to be female in his family. Mind you, Hezekiah Hoskins does have a certain ring to it, don't you think?'

Ellie laughed, then asked more seriously as to whether he would mind having his afflictions discussed with two strangers.

It was Carole's turn to laugh. 'You must be joking! He will be delighted to have some fresh ears to batter about his medical conditions. It's his favourite subject! I am rather looking forward to seeing how Ellie does with this old fellow.'

Ellie wondered what Moses suffered from and was almost nervous about testing her skills in front of Michael. She felt like she was a teenager again, sitting an examination. She just hoped she would pass!

* * *

Rosie Foreman often passed comment that her husband was too soft to be a detective chief inspector. She went so far as to say that he was too soft to be a copper at all.

As he left Adele Turner's grieving mother and father at their bed and breakfast accommodation, and climbed back into his car, he thought that she could be right.

A glance in his mirror showed the vacant-faced man with his arm tightly around the waist of his wife. He was holding her so close, it seemed that if he loosened his grip for one moment, he would lose the other most precious thing in his life.

The dead girl's mother had made a supreme effort to help with their inquiries, but slipped time and again into that strange limbo state that accompanies grief and shock. He saw her now as he drove away, staring after his car, stock still, arms at her sides, seemingly unaware of her husband's vice-like grip around her. She had pinned her hopes on him and him alone. He felt her eyes boring through the back window, willing him to catch her baby's killer. He felt the weight of that responsibility, like a sack of cement across his shoulders, and he sagged slightly at the wheel, as he accelerated away from the small hotel.

He hated dealing with relatives at the best of times, but telling parents that their kids, no matter what age they were, were dead, was the worst of all. Too close to home, he supposed. You don't have a wife like Rosie and three great children, and not be scared for their safety. You can't help but make comparisons. What if it were little Liam, or studious young Max, or Frances, his lovely tomboy of a daughter. What would he, and what would his darling Rosie do? How would they ever cope?

Recognising the signs, the DCI aggressively changed gear and jammed his foot down. He did the same with his thoughts, and threw his previous contemplations into the back seat, and turned his weakness into determination to get the bastard.

By the time he arrived at the station, he looked sufficiently pugnacious to warrant any nasty nickname that his team cared to label him with, and his mind was back, one hundred per cent, on the case.

Before he had even put his briefcase down, Vic Barratt and DI Leatham were knocking on his door.

'Dr Gerrard brought your report down in person, sir. She's in the canteen. Shall I go and tell her you are back?'

'Send someone else, Vic, I want you here.'

Vic Barratt put his head back round the door and yelled for a young PC to go and find the psychologist for him.

Detective Inspector Jonathan Leatham was sitting by the window trying to speed read a great sheaf of papers that Bob had handed him.

Bob nodded towards him. 'Jonathan is cramming all he can on background, Vic, before Amanda gets here. Now, I know she's scary, but I want you both to listen to her opinions carefully. She's not a profiler, but she was doing the self-same job for ten years before they invented that smart job title. She's bloody good. I just hope there will be something for us to go on.' He brought another chair up to the desk for his guest and sat heavily in his own. 'Anything new while I was out, Vic?'

'Brown is back with her witness, sir, and Hudson is out with Rawlings on a hopeful. Apparently, when that old bloke who was walking his dog got knocked flying, he yelled blue murder, and we had a call from a woman who saw the incident.'

'Good, did she see the assailant running away?'

'Seems like it, sir. Hudson is getting a statement now, been gone a while so he shouldn't be too—'

Vic Barratt was interrupted by the entrance of the imposing Dr Amanda Gerrard. She swept into the office in a blaze of scarlet, and threw herself into the waiting chair. 'God! What a bloody day! Traffic's appalling. I've a thundering headache, and your canteen doesn't have decaf!'

She cast her vivid red mackintosh irreverently to the floor and rooted around in her equally red attaché case for her report.

Bob Foreman tried to hide his amusement at the looks on the faces of his two officers, and hurriedly made introductions that he knew from past experience would be totally ignored. True to form, she continued to fuss around with notes and typed sheets, did not look up, but irritably said, 'Yes, yes, whatever. Ah, now, here we are!'

She produced a pair of dilapidated half glasses that were so covered in finger marks that Bob wondered if she could see anything through them. She proceeded with her lecture.

Two minutes into her introduction into criminal psychology, Vic's phone burst forth with a tinny rendition of Ravel's Bolero.

Amanda's frown condemned the offending mobile to the fieriest part of hell, and Bob thought that Vic suddenly resembled a small schoolboy in a grubby, ink-stained shirt, and short grey trousers, about to be caned by some formidable maths master.

Vic stammered out a swift apology and took the call. 'I have to go, sir, trouble with a snout of mine. He's down in reception raising Cain about something. He wants to talk to me, won't listen to the desk sergeant and he's getting a bit agitated by the sound of it. I'll be back as quick as I can. Sorry, sir. Sorry, Doctor.'

Bob had the distinct impression that a recalcitrant third former had just left the room before he could receive a whack across his open palm with a ruler!

Amanda Gerrard, however, was just as happy with her audience of two, and coughed theatrically to get their attention, before continuing. After a brief recap, she got to the bit Foreman was waiting for.

'Oh, it's a man, no doubt about that. I think you are looking for someone with high moral values, a gentleman, to all intents and purposes. I know it seems incongruous, but he works in an extremely well-organised manner. It was not a sexual thing. He is not very young, probably in his late thirties or early forties. I would be pretty sure that he is employed, and probably a professional of some sort. He will be difficult to track down because he is intelligent.' Gerrard scanned her notes. 'We all know about the cunning and craft of serial killers, but this man, I think, has led a fairly "normal" life up until now. Something has happened to trigger off an old and very painful memory, something that was so awful to him that he is taking retribution for a crime against himself, or possibly someone very close to him.' She fastened Bob with a steely gaze. 'My money is on it being personal. Something happened to him when he was a child, and from the type of victim he chooses, I think that it was a woman who injured him, and it could well have been his mother, stepmother, sister, or another close female relative. Maybe even a child minder or a babysitter. Whatever she did to him, she used her hands, in particular, her first finger and thumb.' The doctor made a gesture, bringing her own finger and thumb together in a pinching movement. 'We aren't talking childlike pranks; we are talking torture.'

Amanda Gerrard paused to allow her words to sink in. She stared from Jonathan to Bob, then said, 'I think this man may be unmarried. Although, he could have found a suitable partner, so unlike the woman who hurt him that he can separate them. I doubt you will find any history of previous serious mental illness, either. This man has only recently been pushed over the edge. He's carrying out his revenge on dexterous women, with a fanatical enthusiasm.'

Gerrard gathered up her papers and handed them over to Bob, then with her last throwaway line, picked her raincoat from the floor, and prepared to leave.

'Oh, and I'm ninety-nine per cent sure that he doesn't know he's doing it. Got to go, Chief Inspector. It's all there in detail. Ring me when you've caught him. I'd appreciate a look at him.'

Jonathan Leatham sat like a statue for a full minute after the office door had closed, and then, as if waking from a deep sleep, looked at his boss and mouthed, 'Good Lord, what a terrifying woman!'

'Frightening,' agreed Bob. 'Both the lady and her findings!'

* * *

Hudson accepted a second cup of tea and smiled benignly at the middle-aged woman who sat comfortably on the matching two-seater settee opposite him. 'So, you live alone here, Mrs Long?'

'Yes, have done for the past three years. My husband left me. He worked abroad a lot. One day I had a telephone call to say he wouldn't be home, that he'd met someone else, and that was that. At least he gave me the house, and I'd got a bit of money from my mum when she died. He was away so much, I hardly know he's gone.'

Hudson noted the look on her face and decided not to believe her last statement. She was a pleasant looking woman, about fifty or so, he thought. Her hair was expertly streaked to blend silver with several shades of blonde, giving it a natural sheen that could have belonged to someone much younger.

Rawlings came back into the room. He had been looking at the view of the road from Audrey Long's bedroom window, and with his knowledge of the area, trying to decide where the perp had been running to.

Mrs Long looked apologetic and said for the second time, 'It's a pity the streetlight at the end of the road wasn't working. I'm sure I would have seen which direction he took. As it was, he just disappeared into shadow. He could have gone down the alley to the recreation field, or either way at the junction at the bottom of Barham Avenue.'

Rawlings sat down next to Hudson and picked up the cup and saucer from the coaster on the coffee table in front of them. 'Sod's Law that, Mrs Long. Still, at least you got a pretty good view of him. Do you mind if we just go over this one more time and then we'll leave you in peace?'

The woman repeated her statement. She had been pulling her bedroom curtains when she heard shouting coming from the Nettle Close end of the avenue. It must have been a bit after ten thirty, because she had been watching the ten o'clock news and decided to turn in when it finished. Her next-door neighbour's garden was open plan, so she could easily see the old man on the ground, his dog jumping around him. Running away from him, crossing to the other side of the road as he went, was a man in a long dark coat or mackintosh, she wasn't certain which. He ran in an unusual manner, and she realised it was because he was hugging a bag tightly to his body as he went. 'He was tallish, but not overweight, he looked quite fit, he didn't seem out of breath, just running really hard. He was white, but I didn't see his features, he was gone too quickly. Oh, and he was wearing proper shoes, you could hear them as they hit the pavement, not like trainers or sports shoes. He ran off in the direction that I showed you, and that's all I can tell you.'

'You have been very helpful, Mrs Long. Perhaps you could give one of us a ring if you think of anything else?' Hudson passed her a card with the station number on it.

'Certainly.' She stood, then sat down abruptly. 'Maybe it's nothing but I just remembered . . .'

The two officers looked sharply at her.

'. . . as he ran, the coat flapped open, and he was wearing a very light-coloured outfit underneath. I'd say white, but you can't tell with street-lighting, can you? Both his trousers and his top were the same pale colour. He reminded me of a penguin, for a moment.'

Hudson added her recollection to his notebook. 'Thanks for that, Mrs Long. I'll prepare a statement and perhaps you'd come down to the station and we'll read through it again. Sometime tomorrow would be good, if that's convenient?'

Audrey Long nodded. 'I'll go after lunch.'

As she saw them out, Hudson saw a distant look on the woman's face, and he had the feeling that something else might be lurking somewhere in her brain, just out of reach. Whatever it was, he hoped it would surface before the next day.

* * *

WDC Wendy Brown had used every method she could think of to calm her witness's fears, all to no avail. The frightened girl was certain that she was going to be the next victim. She had convinced herself that the killer had seen her clearly and was, at this very moment, searching her out.

Wendy had even demonstrated, in a darkened room with a flashlight, that you could not identify a person if they were shining a light at you if they were behind the light source, as Mary had been.

There was no reason to keep Mary Probart at the station — her statement had been completed long since, but Wendy did not have the heart to take her back to the hotel in such an upset state. Although she knew she was putting off the inevitable, she decided on one more cup of tea with the girl, and then she would escort her back to her room.

Since Mary had come to believe that she was going to be the fourth victim, she had rambled, almost deliriously, about the murderer and what she had seen. Wendy, although apparently only keeping her company, listened with a trained ear, waiting to pick up any discrepancies or details that she had omitted earlier. As her story unfolded for the umpteenth time, Wendy thought that if the killer remembered anything about his observer, it would be her broad Geordie accent. She had, after all, apologised for interrupting them. As the north country lass rabbited on, warning bells rang for Wendy Brown.

'Hang on there, Mary, say that again.'

'What? Oh, well, I was saying about that coat. How many men these days do you see wearing full-length coats? They're not exactly fashionable, are they?'

'No, in fact, I don't know anyone, except my cousin and he's very flamboyant. Funny that. You can't give us a better description of the coat, can you, Mary?'

The girl looked despondent. 'Sorry, no. The whole thing happened in seconds. It was just long and dark, nearly came down to his shoes. Black shoes! He had black shoes, Wendy! I didn't remember before. The torchlight caught them as I shone it down. Then I saw those bags, and then I carried on up the path.' Mary shivered at the thought of having walked down that dark path, after speaking casually to a murderer.

'Oh, my! I can't go back there!' Fresh tears flowed down the colourless cheeks.

Wendy put an arm around the girl and looked at her compassionately. 'Come on, Mary, I know you're frightened. Is there anyone you could stay with for a while? Have you got any family here, or maybe a friend?'

Mary shook her head. 'All my family are still up north. I don't want to lose my job, but I can't face that room on my own.' She sat staring at her mug of tea, then looked at the police officer hopefully. 'There might be a chance of me staying with Francoise. She worked with me until a couple of months ago. She's got a better position now at that big new hotel at Shepperton, and she doesn't have to live-in anymore. She's got a little flat in Hersham. Perhaps I could stay with her until you catch him?'

'Worth a try, have you got her number? We'll give her a call and see if she will help.'

Francoise Lascelles was not at all delighted to be woken up by Surrey Police after she'd been covering a night shift for a friend, but soon rallied and, in broken English, said that 'Poor Mary' would be welcome, if she didn't mind sleeping on a futon in the lounge. Wendy took the girl's address and prepared to escort Mary back to the hotel to collect some things and square it with her manager for a few days leave.

At three o'clock, WDC Brown felt much happier about her witness. She had finally dropped her off at her friend's place, where Francoise had greeted her with a hug, and welcomed them both into the tiny flat. Wendy made sure that Mary was settled and had got various numbers to call if she was worried, or if anything else came to her that she thought the police should know about.

Driving back to the station, she thought about Mary's comment about the full-length coat and found herself searching bus queues, watching men milling around outside public houses and betting shops, staring generally at the male gender of the public at large. No long overcoats.

She would definitely mention that to her boss when she got back.

* * *

Alone in his office for the first time that day, Bob Foreman took a few minutes to read in detail, the psychologist's report. She had skimmed over the major points with them, but in-depth reading brought up an interesting picture. She was certain the murderer was a professional of some sort. She thought he may have a demanding job that he threw himself into body and soul. A workaholic. Her last paragraph suggested he had recently suffered a major mental trauma in his life and, when they apprehended a suspect, they should look carefully into happenings around any female members of his family. Something had opened a very nasty can of worms in his head. Something powerful enough to send him on a crusade of killing. As to her assumption of his being unaware of his actions, she explained thus:

> *'The killer in his "normal" guise, probably a gentle, hard-working man, would find the actions of his alter-ego quite abhorrent to him. He would look, as others do, in horror at the deaths of these women. Up until now he has been able to brush aside anything that has reminded him of his past and what "she" did to him. Now an incident has occurred that has brought it all back, and as he could not*

possibly do anything about it himself, he has unconsciously called on a dark side of his mind to sort it out. He has a split personality. He's like the paid killer, sent out to do a job, but the hirer does not want to know any of the details.'

The doctor had then scribbled in bold handwriting:

'Bob . . . The problem is this . . . alter-egos, when allowed out too often, have a horrible habit of wanting to stay out, and they have little regard for their good host and his Holy War. I respectfully suggest that you catch this man before the killings become enjoyable to him, because at that point he will forget his cause, and anyone who presents him with good sport will be fair game. Amanda.'

Thanks a bunch, Doc. He looked once more at the sheaf of papers, took an A4 pad and began to note relevant points to make to the team. His writing was interrupted by DS Barratt's knock on the door.

'Switchboard wants to know if your phone is off the hook, sir, the Super's trying to get hold of you. Sorry about earlier, sir, hope I didn't miss too much.'

DCI Foreman hunted beneath folders and piles of reports, only to find the handset of his telephone upside down next to the cradle. Absorbed as he had been in the doctor's report, he had vaguely wondered what the faint buzzing noise was.

'Thank you, Vic, I'll ring him straight back and, yes, you missed plenty. I'll give you a copy of her report when I've finished with it.' He stretched and sighed. The Super is going to want to know what I will be saying at the press conference tomorrow, and I wish I knew myself. Any updates?'

'Hudson and Rawlings would like a word, sir, and Brown, too.'

'Bring them all in when I've finished on the blower. We'll see what they've got for us.'

Before the meeting could commence, there was a major exodus from the office after a message left for DS Corbett about a tip-off that might have a connection with the second murder.

'What was that all about?' asked Bob, as his four officers trooped into his office.

'Couple of women popped into the Woodham Arms at lunchtime, sir, overheard some old lag mouthing off about his mate having seen the murderer of Helen Carberry. The landlord has seen this bloke around quite a bit recently, nasty looking piece of work apparently. DI Corbett has taken a couple of PCs to talk to the girls and the pub landlord and see if they can apprehend the scumbag.'

'Good, now what have you got for me?'

Rawlings gave an account of their meeting with Audrey Long, and WDC Brown added Mary Probart's observation regarding the killer's fashion wear. They both agreed about the shoes being 'proper' shiny black shoes.

'Sir?' Wendy Brown raised her hand. 'Audrey Long mentioned that he was wearing light or white clothes under the coat. He has worn the coat, as far as we know, at each killing, certainly at two of them. Do you think he is only wearing it to cover up what he has on underneath? As in a uniform of some kind? Something that would be easily recognisable?'

'You have a point there, Officer. White trousers and shirt, or jacket, are not your average winter wear, and why wear white when you could easily get covered in blood? Who normally wears white in their line of work?'

The others listed all they could think of. Food chain workers, bakers, butchers, lots of food preparers, abattoir workers, chemists, hospital workers . . . the list went on.

'Some stores have corporate uniforms, sir,' added Hudson. 'Then there's cricketers, bowls players, and tennis freaks.' Hudson ran his fingers through short and spiky baby-blonde hair. 'We are probably looking at a shift worker, or why would he be out in his work clothes in the dead of night?'

Brown let out a sigh. 'Perhaps we are barking up the wrong tree after all, sir. I mean, who would go out in their works uniform to commit a murder, it's too much of a giveaway. Such a shame that old guy who got knocked over had bad eyesight, we could have had a photo-fit in the papers by now.'

The meeting broke up at about five thirty, leaving the five police officers with little more to go on than before. As Hudson said, as they walked out into the incident room, 'All we need is the suspect, then a quick check on his employment record, and sporting interests, make sure he has a quirky family history, and we've got him.' He rolled his eyes. 'So, simple!'

Before anyone could answer, DS Corbett hurried in and was speaking so excitedly that Bob had to slow him down and make him start again.

'We've brought him in, sir! I don't think he's just a witness, I reckon he could be a suspect! He tried to do a runner but, bloody hell, sir, your PC Windsor ain't half got some legs on him! Went off like Seb Coe, he did, had the toerag in no time!'

'Okay, Corbett, excellent. Get him through custody, and as soon as he's fit to interview, we'll see what he has to say.'

For some reason Bob didn't feel Corbett's enthusiasm about the possible suspect — it all seemed a bit too easy. An overheard conversation in a pub, a loud-mouthed lag and a very conveniently apprehended suspect.

He decided he was getting old and sceptical, but at least it was something to give to the Super for his press conference.

CHAPTER SEVENTEEN

The following day, Ellie realised she should not have worried about her competence.

Moses Hoskins sat in an upright chair beside the big kitchen range and beamed with delight. Ellie watched him and noted the care that the old gentleman had taken with his appearance. He seemed in awe of being summoned to Mrs Meyer's court, and had dressed to give the best impression possible. He looked, to Ellie, like a photo she had been given of her maternal grandfather. He wore a dark suit with a waistcoat that sported a gold watch chain, and she knew without a doubt that there would be a fob watch concealed in the pocket. His shirt, although old, had been carefully pressed, and his tie was knotted with precision and perfectly centred between the points of his collar. His pride and joy was a 'handlebar' moustache, exactly like her grandfather. The Victorian picture was completed by the shiniest pair of boots Ellie had ever seen.

Carole introduced Michael and Ellie, and then let Michael explain what they were going to do. When he asked Moses whether he would mind confirming or denying Ellie's diagnoses of his conditions, and perhaps tell them a bit about his medical history, his eyes positively sparkled. At that point, Carole left the room, her eyebrows raised to her hairline.

Ellie took a seat facing Moses and drew several deep breaths. She calmed herself and tuned in on the old man's human energy field, then gasped as his aura burst into rainbow hues around his body. She had clearly been expecting that an elderly person in their eighties, suffering from some medical problems and general debility due to old age, would have depleted and dim lights. She could not have been more wrong. True, there were the dark lines of pain, hugging close to his physical frame, but as the layers worked outward, the colours were exquisite. The most astounding feature was the outer level. It was of purest gold and radiated out almost a metre from his body. Above all, Ellie was astounded at the clarity of the colours — they seemed to contain a spiritual element that had somehow cleansed all the impurities and left simply flawless colour.

It was very hard not to stay immersed in the quality of this energy. She had never seen anything like it before, not even in those early days when she had been blinded by glowing lights. Then they had been harsh and glaring — these were wholly beautiful.

Hardly aware of the passage of time, Ellie floated and bathed herself in the golden rays, then something inside her reminded her of what she was supposed to be doing. With difficulty, she pulled her sight away from the shining corona, and looked at the man and the closer levels around him.

She allowed her eyes to travel around the man, from the top of his head, down his neck, down the arm, round the hand and up to the armpit. She continued around the whole outline, finishing back at his crown. It took about three minutes to complete the trip, and at that point, she took several deeper breaths, closed her eyes, and allowed the lights to retreat.

Opening her eyes, she blew out her cheeks and expelled air with a loud 'Phew!'

The kitchen, with its occupants, including Carole who must have slipped back in while she was working, were all back to normal.

Michael's smile almost exceeded that of Moses, and Ellie realised that, with his natural gift, Michael would also have been party to that amazing light show.

'Brilliant! That alone was worth the trip to Surrey!' exclaimed Michael. 'Okay, Ellie, if you've had time to get over the shock, your analysis, please, of Mr Moses Hoskins.'

Ellie was silent for a second, then pitched headlong into her interpretation of what she had seen. 'Mr Hoskins is basically in wonderful condition. Mentally and spiritually, he is perfectly balanced. I assume, although I have no personal knowledge yet of the subject, that this is very rare. He is completely at ease with his self and his Maker. His outer level could only be described as Divine. I'm sure that I will be very lucky to perceive another aura with similar qualities. On the physical level, however, there are two replacement knees, the prostheses cause a gap in the continuum and their presence is clearly seen. Then there is an interesting phenomenon in the upper parts of both legs. Large quantities of shrapnel, I believe, they extend from just above the knees and up to the pelvic cavity. Other than rheumatism and arthritis, Moses is fighting fit, and the most remarkable man I have ever seen!'

Michael got up from his seat and clapped his hands loudly, in a standing ovation for one. 'Well done, our Ellie! Amazing! What do you reckon, Mr Hoskins, is she right?'

The old man nodded furiously.

'Oh yes, it was the War in the Desert, Miss, I was in the Tank Corps. I was doing some work, repairing the track of my old Matilda Mark II, when a Jerry shell made a direct hit on the tank next to me . . . next thing I knew was . . .'

Carole suddenly remembered an urgent telephone call she had to make, and smiling from ear to ear, left the room.

Twenty minutes later when she returned to make another pot of coffee, Moses was just completing the gory details of the surgeon's search for the shrapnel and the fight to save his legs.

'Of course, these are new-fangled, bionic knees, you know, but they didn't have things like this back then. They just patched you up as best they could. Still, they did a pretty good job under the circumstances and now modern science has let me walk, as long as I have my old stick, as well as most my age. I'm almost ninety, you know!'

As he politely sipped his coffee, Ellie steered him on to other topics, keen to know how he could have developed that golden aura. As the conversation went on, it became apparent that the old man, a gentle and kindly soul, was quite sincerely a good person. He was non-judgemental, and heaped praise and forgiveness where he felt it was due. Ellie had summed it up when she noted that he was at ease with himself. He had, in his late eighties, seen it all and come to terms with everything that needed addressing. He accepted himself, warts an' all, as he put it, and knew that his God would do the same, when his time came.

As he left, upright and smiling, Ellie thought that you'd have considered his stick more a fashion accessory than a walking aid for two artificial knees. She felt privileged to have met him, and she was made aware of the enormity of her gift, for without it, she would have hardly noticed Moses, perhaps just thought what a nice old man, but never had that glorious glimpse of an earthbound angel.

* * *

That evening Michael was in his room sorting through his wardrobe. This was the night for dinner at the Carnack Arms Hotel, the high spot of Michael's stay. Or it had been until he had seen Ellie at work with old Moses. There was no doubt she had been endowed with the most awe-inspiring ability, and that she was learning at a faster rate than he could teach.

He laid several shirts and ties on the bed, trying to decide which he would wear tonight. He chose a lavender hand-finished shirt and a silver-and-purple striped tie. He had brought a dark grey suit with him, and when he held the ensemble up in front of the long dressing mirror, he thought that his wife would have been proud.

His work over the last week had kept her from being uppermost in his thoughts. She was always there, but for the last seven days, her presence had not dominated his every waking moment. He sat on the bed and considered what had been achieved in that time. It was more than he would have dreamed possible. He had planned on limiting their sessions to a few hours each day, but Ellie had thrived on his schooling, begging him to tell her more and more. Now his stay was nearly at an end, he was planning on catching the midday train on Sunday, and he had done little other than coach his prodigy, and stuff himself on goodies from the Meyer kitchen. He smiled to himself and softly muttered, 'Can't be bad!' He had done a few token rambles over the Downs, and enjoyed a couple of trips out with Carole in her antediluvian motor vehicle. He had also taken pleasure in an afternoon pottering around Compton, and now there was tonight, and that single malt to relish.

While he searched for cufflinks, he offered a little prayer of thanks that, up to now at least, he had been spared the appearances of any of the dire happenings that seemed to be hanging around Carole, prior to his arrival. She seemed more relaxed than she had to begin with. Even the bulletins on the radio and television about the third murder had not phased her unduly. Surely the police would catch the monster soon? Michael felt sorry for them. They must be beside themselves over this case. He would hate to have to deal with something like that. In fact, he didn't know how they did it for a living. He silently added another prayer to his last, and wished the police force swift success. Here at Snug Cottage, he hoped things would remain as calm as they were at present, and stay that way, long after he had gone back to London.

Calm or not, he still felt an enormous amount of apprehension at the thought of leaving two women on their own in this big old house, with a killer on the loose.

He shivered and tied up his shoelaces. He only had a small flat, but he considered asking them to go back with him until it was all over. He was not sure how Carole would take that, but he decided to drop it into the conversation over dinner anyway.

The finished product that smiled jauntily back at him from the mirror looked pretty good to him. Smartly pressed clothes, clean shoes, although maybe not up to Moses' standards, he reflected. Well brushed hair and clean teeth. He completed his wife's mantra, grinned wolfishly at his reflection, and said out loud, 'Okay, ladies! Michael's all dressed up, now let's have a good evening!'

* * *

Downstairs, Michael's 'ladies' were also ready for a good evening. Although Carole was well-dressed in expensive clothes, and Ellie suspected the green check jacket to be Laurel, she still did not have the polish that Michael's immaculate, although inexpensive, suit offered. Carole always managed to look as if five spaniels had just climbed off her lap. Ellie noted the strands of dog hair and decided they probably had.

Ellie was not exactly overly impressed with her own, far from fashionable, but compulsory accessories. Silver elbow crutches and a bright blue leg cast was not really the statement she wanted to make. Luckily, she had managed to resurrect an old pair of wide-legged black evening trousers that, with difficulty, she stretched over the plaster and with the help of a multicoloured floral shirt and a black linen jacket, made an acceptable outfit.

Carole shut the dogs into the kitchen for the evening, and they set off.

The Carnack Arms was an old coaching inn, nestling firmly in the heart of the small town. There was still the archway through which the carriages had driven, and the restaurant was situated around three sides of the cobbled courtyard beyond the wooden arch. They had chosen to eat early, for Ellie's sake, and the dining area was quiet. They were shown to their table by a tall young waitress, who introduced herself as Jessica, and said that she would be looking after them.

Carole did not like the new trait of using first names and being over-familiar with staff, but she came from an era that used Sir and Madam to clients. However, she was forced to agree that the excellent food made up for having to memorise the name of your waiter.

Michael sat with Carole, facing Ellie, in order to give her as much leg room as possible. They sat back and took in the atmosphere. Soft music played, Strauss sashayed among silver spoons, and delicate flowers waltzed across the satiny fabric of the drapes and their tablecloth.

'Very nice. Very nice indeed,' sighed Michael, as he accepted the wine list from the willowy Jessica.

They ordered and were waiting for their meals to arrive when Ellie suddenly looked at Carole. 'You said that you had an ulcer! On the night of my accident, we were at the Poachers! You looked awful! Oh God! I remember!'

She tried to regulate her breathing but noticed that her hands were shaking. Suddenly another hand reached across and enveloped hers in a great, reassuring bear paw.

'Steady, Ellie. Things are going to come back to you. Something will just jog your memory, just like now, sitting in a restaurant with Carole. It's only another tiny fragment of the past floating back. It can't hurt you.'

'I think there are a lot of things I would prefer not to know about, Michael. I'm frightened of remembering too much.' She took one hand away and unwittingly touched the scar on her forehead.

'You could be recalling what I told you when you were unconscious, of course,' Carole added thoughtfully. 'I did tell you all about that evening at the restaurant. Mr Thomas told us to keep talking to you as you may be able to hear us. I think I probably rambled on for England.'

Ellie was not convinced about that, but was sure there were some occasions in the hospital when she knew there were people around her. She had definite memories of hearing music, especially Eric Clapton.

She sipped her wine and decided that Michael was right. It really could not hurt her to recollect things. That awful time was over, and once her leg had healed, she had a whole new life to look forward to. Even if it did come back to her, her past would not affect her future.

She smiled up at her friends. 'Sorry, folks! Forgive the shaky moment.' She gave a little laugh. 'It's all over now! Let's eat!'

* * *

As Ellie spoke, Carole felt a cold chill pass over her heart. *Oh no, please, not again, not now!* An iciness gripped her, making her catch her breath. She knew without a doubt that it was far from over for Ellie McEwan. Another misty, dark vision was slithering into her mind, but this time she pushed hard with all her mental energies and sent the blackness back to whence it came.

She hurriedly bent down on the pretext of picking up her handbag, and rifled through it, ostensibly hunting for a tissue. She fought to gain control, snorted loudly into the handkerchief, and waded back into the conversation. She'd be damned if she would frighten the girl again, and she silently sent a message to who or whatever was sending her these awful premonitions, that they could bloody well send them when she was alone, and not around her precious Ellie.

Although it was a struggle on Carole's part, the three friends enjoyed the rest of the evening, and it seemed that in no time at all, Michael was bewailing that it was the very last sip of malt whisky in his glass, and he wanted it to last forever. They thanked the willowy Jessica, Carole paid the bill, and they left the restaurant.

They were quiet in the car during the short drive, each in his or her own world for a while. Despite the good food, none of the worlds were very pleasant places to be.

Carole's world was probably the darkest. She drove carefully, and concentrated her mind on the road, but in the background was the niggling idea that she should not have been so quick to push the images away. What if it had been something clearly recognisable to her? What if it were something she could have dealt with? What if it had been a warning? At that point she stopped the rush of questions in her mind, and once again thought only of the road ahead.

She couldn't know it, but Ellie was looking out into the dark night and thinking of those three murdered women. All out on a night such as this, but they never reached home.

Carole noticed the girl draw her jacket tighter around herself.

And if she could have read Michael's mind, she would have known that he was suffering vague fears of an unknown origin. He had noticed a surge, of what looked like terror, emanate from Carole's aura during the evening. Invisible to everyone, except Ellie, and thankfully at that moment Ellie had been avidly staring at the menu. He had watched Carole fighting to keep her mental balance, and thankfully, winning. But what had happened? He had no idea and it was making him sick to know that, as soon as they got home, he was going to have to ask her.

Carole looked in the mirror and saw him looking at her thoughtfully. He knows, she thought, then stared hard at the winding black ribbon of a road in front of her, and bit her lip hard enough to make it bleed.

* * *

Ellie went straight to her room, pausing only to hug Carole and thank her for the wonderful meal. She apologised again for her outburst, and was assured that she must always say when she felt, as she had put it, shaky.

Her recovery was still in its infancy in so many ways, and Carole went to great pains to convince her she was not alone, and her friends wanted to be with her every step of the way, and that included the odd bit of stony ground she may stumble upon. Carole wished her sweet dreams and returned to Michael, who was fixing a nightcap in the lounge.

The fire was not alight, and the room seemed gloomy and cold without it, so they took their drinks back to the kitchen and pulled the farmhouse pine chairs closer to the Aga and the dogs.

As soon as she had taken her first sip of the fiery whisky, she saw Michael looking at her. 'All right, old girl, spill the beans! What happened in the restaurant?'

Now she knew for sure that her private battle had been observed, Carole decided there was little point denying it and told the truth, as far as she could understand it.

Staring into some place that existed within the realms of his whisky glass, Michael considered her words. 'I see your point. You think it would have been better to know if something awful is going to happen. Now you suspect something terrible will occur, but have no clue as to what it might be.'

'Exactly. The thing is, last time, if I'd comprehended what was being shown to me, a vision of the accident before it happened, I would have never let Ellie go that night.'

'Hmm, and she would not have been hurt. But, and it's a big but, she would not have been given this incredible gift, and that baby would be dead, and that young child in the supermarket would have gone through a lot more pain than need be, and that's just the beginning. You have to consider the big picture.'

'That Saville boy might not have died,' she added doggedly.

'From the sound of things, he would have been hit by someone else. You don't bound across six lanes of busy road and get away scot-free, Carole. Sorry, but I think this smacks of karma.'

'Then why was I shown the accident?' she asked. 'It does not make sense.'

Michael looked at her thoughtfully. 'Perhaps you weren't. Maybe you picked it up somehow, not as a warning, but as a sort of preview.'

Carole remembered her own thoughts concerning Ellie's pre-accident nightmare. She had said it was just a glimpse of something. 'Possibly, possibly. But it still means that there is another trauma, or some kind of happening, to come.'

'But it might not involve you or Ellie. It might have nothing to do with you. You know how sensitive you are, perhaps you are being used as some sort of receiver, a witness, maybe. It's like that weird occurrence up on St Martha's. I'm pretty sure that you were an unwilling witness to the Surrey murderer in action. He has nothing whatever to do with you or Ellie, but you saw it, didn't you?'

Carole nodded mutely. That strange apparition, and Ellie's coincidental dream, had bothered her ever since it happened. Her saving grace in all this was Vera. She had lifted the darkness that day and restored the sunlight to that grim woodland on the hill. All she could do was pray that, whatever was happening around them, Vera and their guardian angels would be there for them and see them through.

She was dragged from her contemplations by Michael.

'So, what do you think? It would only be until the police catch him, and I'm sure they've got leads by the score.'

'Sorry?'

'You and Ellie. Will you come back to London with me on Sunday?'

Yes, yes, yes, screamed her heart. *We'll pack now, we'll leave tonight, why wait till Sunday.* Her voice was calm as she said, 'Michael, that's very kind, but it's not really practical. You have a small flat and you have to work. Two women interfering in your daily routine would be far from satisfactory. Then there's the dogs, and Ellie herself. She has follow-up appointments coming up, her plaster to come off, and she still needs the wheelchair if she overtires herself. I really appreciate your offer, don't think for one minute that I don't.' She paused for a moment, and with uncharacteristic softness said, 'Michael, I truly wish I could say yes, but I think we are going to have to stick it out here until the storm passes.'

Michael watched as she straightened her back, shook her head slightly, and summoned back the old indomitable Carole. 'Yes. We'll weather this. Stiff upper lip, and all that. Don't worry yourself about us, Michael, we will keep in touch, let you know all that's going on, and we will come and visit. I'll have no choice in the matter. Ellie has made it clear that she wants to continue draining your brain!'

'I have no problem with that,' replied Michael. 'But I do have one with leaving you here with such a bad situation around you. I would willingly drive Ellie back for her appointments, and maybe Mrs Littlewood and Daniel could house and dog sit for you? I'm not worried about the size of the flat, I'm sure we could all bounce off each other nicely!'

'No, Michael. With all the good will in the world, we would be in your way. Just promise me that I can ring you when I need to, and if you have a spare weekend, you'll come back and give us some moral support. You have done wonders with Ellie, you know that, don't you?'

'I'm just glad I can be around to guide her on her path. It must be very daunting to have all this thrust upon her, but I think she is going to be a very sought-after lady, when she masters her art.'

Michael twisted her arm into a 'tiny top-up', and they talked on into the late evening. At around midnight, the conversation found its way back to the interrupted premonition in the restaurant. Carole was a little uncomfortable with the suggestion she was about to put to her friend, but she forged ahead anyway. One of the dogs climbed onto her lap and she stroked its silky coat as she cautiously said, 'Of course, there may be a way . . . a way to recapture whatever it was I was supposed to see.'

'*If* you were supposed to see anything, that is, and what exactly are you proposing, Carole Meyer?'

'I think I could summon it back.'

There was a deathly silence.

'You'll do no such thing!' Michael's voice rose several decibels. 'I have no doubt of your capabilities or your mediumship skills!' He remembered Ellie, sleeping a few rooms away, and lowered his tone. 'But I know what you're considering, and, no, no, it's far too dangerous. Perhaps if you were in a circle, or at least with others to help you, but alone? Definitely not! No way, absolute madness, Carole!'

'But I'm not alone, am I, Michael?'

'Oh no!'

'You believe what I believe, my friend, so why not? I would simply ask you to be with me, to pray with me. If I am well protected, and I know how to protect myself, I'm sure there would be no danger. I would simply . . .'

Michael raised his hands, palms out, as if he were a rotund and grim-looking traffic policeman, halting her progress on that particular road. 'There is nothing simple about what you are considering, woman, and well you know it!'

'Michael, I will only ask to be made aware of what I was going to see anyway.'

The professor's eyes narrowed as he stared at her. 'Don't try to make it sound so straightforward. You could be opening yourself up to Lord knows what. We have no idea where your "message" came from, and besides, if it was, well, only some psychic waveband that you accidentally tuned into, the chances of finding it again are negligible. It'll be floating around somewhere in the ether for a million years.'

'So, there's no harm in just asking, is there?' she persisted.

For a while he said nothing — then he seemed to change his tack. 'Look, old girl.' He paused, obviously waiting for the usual rebuke, and when nothing was forthcoming, he continued. 'Why not give it a while. It may come back anyway. If something wanted you to know something important, then it won't go off with its tail between its legs after only one little rebuff from you. It will try again, I'm sure.'

Carole gently lifted the dog from her aching legs and watched it fondly as it climbed into the enormous bed with its 'brothers'. 'I'm going to do this anyway, Michael. With or without you. But I'd prefer it was with you. Last time, if I'd had someone to talk it through with, I know that I would have realised what was going to happen. I appreciate everything that you've said to me but, if there is the slightest chance I can do something to help, then I want that chance.

As you said earlier, it might be something we have to let take its course. Well, so be it, but at least we can discuss it together and I would be prepared. I *need* to be prepared, for whatever it is. Can you understand that? Will you help me?'

Michael stared at the floor, his hands doing a silent imitation of Lady Macbeth. 'If, and I stipulate, if . . . what have you got in mind? How? When, where?'

'Now, tonight. And there's only one place I would ever consider for this, and that's the summer house. I have no special rites to use. I will ask for protection, ask for Vera to be with me, go into a deep meditative state . . . and open myself up. I will allow whatever is out there to come to me, and we will take it from there. All I ask of you is to be with me, pray, keep the protection up around the summer house, and listen. There may be something that comes to you and I miss it, or am not privy to. And that's all, my friend.'

'That's all, is it?' Michael looked torn. 'You are asking a lot, old girl, and I'm not happy about it, but I suppose it's better than letting you go it alone . . . and you will, won't you?'

'Oh, undoubtedly, but . . .'

Michael tilted is head enquiringly, a puzzled expression on his face. She decided that Michael had the feeling he was missing something. Something important. Something he should know, but was just beyond his grasp.

Carole hurriedly stood up, indicating to the back door. 'Shall we? There are jackets in the utility. I'll get them. The garden room will be warm, the heating stays on low all the time.' She turned to the sleepy heap of dogs and told them to be good, they wouldn't be gone long, and strode purposefully out into the night.

CHAPTER EIGHTEEN

Although wearing one of Carole's oversized gardening jackets, the iciness of the night tore into him like steel knives. Since they had arrived home, a diamond covering of frost had shrouded the grass. Silver-green blades crunched and broke under his step. The security lights had bathed the whole garden with their eerie incandescence and Michael voiced the concern that Ellie would be disturbed by them. He was certain the glare would penetrate even the library's thickly lined drapes.

Carole assured him that, after being advised by the police to keep them on, they had been going off and on at odd times every night. Digger often made nocturnal sorties through his cat flap, and the local vixen's food hunting route took her directly through the beam that activated the lights. Even if she should wake, and Carole thought that very unlikely, Ellie would not be bothered by them.

Carole unlocked the door and they were greeted by a welcome rush of warm air. They took off their jackets and Carole began to prepare the room. Michael selected himself the comfortable chair in which he had sat so recently, opposite Ellie, as her tutor. All the time he had spent in this peaceful garden room, he had felt happy and confident. Tonight, his body was wracked with shivers, and he had an unsettling feeling of wrongness about what they were about to do. Several times he was on the verge of leaving and going back to the cosy kitchen. He thought of the marshmallow bed, and wished desperately that he was being enveloped by its intimate, feathery embrace. Miserably, he accepted the fact that he could not leave his friend out here alone. He would see it through and, hopefully, there would be a satisfactory outcome to their evening's work.

Carole had lit candles and incense cones. Already a heady fragrance of sandalwood, lavender and frankincense perfumed the air. Michael noticed she was taking a considerable amount of time selecting a CD. After careful deliberation — all the impatience of earlier had dissipated — she chose one and put it in the player, starting it, and then putting the pause button down. 'Are we ready?' she asked gently.

Michael sighed and nodded.

Carole began with a prayer. She spoke out loud and Michael mouthed amen, as and when he saw fit. She asked that they both be kept safe. She asked for a ring of white light to be placed around them, around the summer house, and around their hearts. She asked that her spirit guides gather near to advise and protect. She prayed for understanding for all that may be shown to her that night. She then quietly started the music and took several very deep breaths.

'Push aside all unwanted thoughts, acknowledge them and deal with them later. Keep your feet firmly on the floor and relax, palms upwards, resting lightly in your lap. Concentrate now on your first chakra. Its colour is red, the deep blood-red of a rose. Open that chakra, dwell for a minute on the colour, immerse yourself in it. Move on to the second chakra. Its colour is orange . . .' She continued through the seven main energy centres, pausing at each one to allow for its opening and for the colours to gently wash through their bodies.

Michael, well-practised in meditation, dropped easily down into a deeply relaxed state.

'Allow the music to carry you to a place of tranquillity and safety . . .'

Michael's eyes were already closed, and he felt himself drifting away with the strange music. On some level he vaguely noticed the difference in the timbre of his friend's voice. He could have sworn that he was not listening to Carole at all, but to his other old friend. He wanted to look, but his eyelids were too heavy to open, and the voice was seductively hypnotic. It dropped to a soft litany, and Michael followed the words, a guided meditation taking him away from the summer house, and into another realm.

A small part of him that retained awareness was fascinated by the music. He used new-age CDs all the time with his healing work. It was calming, evocative, uplifting, tranquil, elevating, or sublime, and he chose what he felt best suited his patient. He owned an extensive range of this genre of music, but this... the sounds that softly invaded his senses were nothing that he could ever remember hearing before. It was music of the higher consciousness.

He not only heard, but felt, a wind blowing. A subtle noise that you heard as you snuggled down into bed on a winter's night. Muffled by the covers and the double glazing, you hear it distantly, but it is no worry to you, safe and warm in your cocoon. But tonight, he felt part of those woven strands of air, keening through branches, and tearing at wet slates on oily-looking roofs. He heard water, dripping in an underground cavern, falling soundlessly from rain-soaked leaves, driving against windowpanes, and he was that crystal-clear teardrop that fell from a mother's eye. Instruments, unknown to him, formed patterns and tunes that were unfamiliar and mystifying but, at the same time, nostalgic in their recognisable closeness.

Michael heard voices that sang without words, sounds of the spheres, of the depths of the oceans. Sounds of new growth in spring, and that of the slowing of a heartbeat as it gently slides into death. He slowly and silently, on the breath of a zephyr, slipped into the deepest meditative state of his fifty-eight years.

* * *

Carole was aware of Michael's descent, and knew from his inherent goodness that it would be a place of beauty that his soul was now exploring. She needed his essence of light here with her. The knowledge that she was sitting an arms-length away from a pure heart would strengthen her, and she sorely needed that strength.

She felt a good strong protective field around the summer house and knew from her usual communion with spirit, the situation was perfect. But tonight, it was different — if answers did not come from the sources that she hoped, maybe she would have to step a little beyond the light.

She would not endanger Michael; she would never break the protective shield that circled them. But she could, if need be, transport herself outside it. She gravely hoped it would not come to that last-ditch attempt to find the truth, but she was prepared to try, if there was no other way.

She let herself fall into, what an observer would have thought was, unconsciousness. Her blood pressure dropped, and her breathing slowed.

In a magical place, their special place, she sat with her friend and watched sunlight filter through the grey-green leaves of the eucalyptus trees. The deep evergreen shades of tall pines interspersed the delicate gum trees and scented the air with their aromatic aroma. Between the tree trunks, their bark a patchwork of creams, browns and greys, a glimpse of azure sea sparkled and glittered. High on the hillside, Carole felt a soft breeze caress her skin, making the tiny fair hairs on her arm tingle and rise.

Vera sat opposite her on a red check blanket that they used for picnics. Carefully selecting a sandwich, she looked first at the golden-baked bread, and then at her friend. 'I know what you are looking for, and I do not want you to continue with this search.'

'Can you help me?'

'Not with that which you choose to pursue.'

'I need to know what was being shown to me.'

'No, my dear. You don't. Leave it alone and look after the girl as you are doing. Do not delve too deeply.' Her voice was serious, and her brows were knit into untypical furrows. A smile slowly lifted the corners of the severe lips. 'You are a stubborn, old fool, Carole Meyer, but I love you, and although I can look after you a lot of the time, please understand that there are some regions not open to me. I do not want you straying into them!' She took a dainty bite at the sandwich and chewed slowly and appreciatively.

Carole gazed at the familiar features and noted the subtle changes that were etching themselves on the woman. Vera was more upright, her body moved with more fluidity, and her previously heavily lined skin was smoother, and possessed the old glowing quality that Carole remembered so well. She had watched it fade into a sallow pallor, its bloom stolen by illness and age.

Vera continued. 'You always were a tenacious old terrier, could never let something go once you'd got your teeth into it. You haven't changed, have you?'

Carole hung her head in mock shame, and then tilted it to one side and looked up with a sheepish grin. 'I have actually . . .' She paused, and her expression changed from childlike humour to intense sadness. 'It's not the same without you, there is no fun left in my life. Until Ellie came and asked for help, I felt as if I were just marking time, waiting until . . . well, you know . . .' Her voice trailed off leaving the obvious unspoken.

'That's wrong, and you know it! Your time on earth is precious beyond words. Don't waste it dreaming of the hereafter, that will come about in the blinking of an eye, so don't fritter away those priceless moments with morbid thoughts. You have plenty to do and plenty to learn.'

Carole accepted her admonishment with a sigh and fiddled aimlessly with the ruby ring on her wedding finger. 'Then help me as far as you can. I'll try not to overstep the mark. Just help me understand whether I am directly concerned in something, or observing some other person's troubles. Can't you even tell me that?'

Vera looked at her old friend with great compassion. 'It's just not in you to leave this alone, is it?' She sighed and put her sandwich down unfinished. 'I was not privy to what happened in the restaurant. There are forces at work, that do not want, or if their strength permits, will not allow me, to be witness to their activities. I would never meddle with them. They are very distasteful to me, but . . .' She paused. 'As my loved ones become involved' — she positively glowered at Carole — 'then I have already been forced to intervene.'

Carole knew she was referring to the apparition up on St Martha's. 'You must know, my dear, that such an altercation can deplete my energies or make me stronger, depending on their outcome. If I should find myself weakened, then apart from the danger to myself, I would put you and yours in the gravest jeopardy. Unprotected, and in peril of losing more than your lives. Last time it was easy, there was no battle, I simply stopped you seeing a . . . a sort of hologram that was being played in order to frighten you. These are often used to scare people off, and they generally work. Sensitive souls, enlightened or otherwise, pick up these fright shows and back off. Others get sent nightmares, dreams so bad that they never forget them. They are all deterrents, warnings to leave well alone, and if you don't, my dearest Carole, they find more permanent ways of halting you. Please do not let that happen. I could not bear to see you hurt, or worse.'

Carole was all too aware of the powers of good and evil. Light and dark. She was not so naive as to believe that good always triumphed, and she never underestimated the dark side, but there was a part of her that could not, would not, let her abandon her mission. She had no intention of taking on the powers of darkness, but a brief foray into a greyish area was not beyond her.

She smiled at Vera and held out her hands. 'I'm going to let you go with love, my friend, just for a little while. Don't be angry with me, and never put yourself at risk on my behalf. I know you would be there for me if you could. I cannot allow myself or Ellie, or any of those close to us to be threatened and frightened like this. It's not right.'

Carole's sense of justice and fairness gave her a strength that she knew Vera would understand, and not fight her over. Not at present, anyway.

Their fingers touched and, in a burst of light, Carole watched her angel, the sea, and the waving trees evaporate into wisps of amethyst, green and blue mist. It spiralled upwards, and in its place, a cold midnight sky descended upon her.

* * *

Michael and his wife were climbing, sure-footedly, up the cobbled steps and uneven paths that took them through the white-washed village, and up to the monastery that topped the hill. It was a daunting climb, darkness and the faint bobbing lights from their torches could have made it treacherous. Michael and Georgia had done it many times before, and in the depths of his meditation where all things were possible, their feet almost floated above the stone track of the Greek island. Soon the last dwelling was left behind, and in front of them they could just make out beyond the twisted silhouette of an ancient olive tree, the gate to the deserted monastery. As the beam from his flashlight sought out the latch, it illuminated ornate metal braids of wrought ironwork, its once carefully painted surface, blistered and flaked by the hot Sporadian sun. The gate swung open silently, they crossed a courtyard, ducked their heads under lintel topping a low aperture in a wall, and found themselves again out under the dark Grecian sky. A few hundred yards ahead was the outline of the chapel. Their pilgrimage was nearly at an end. The rounded cupola roof, crowned with a plain cross, still intact after hundreds of years exposed to the salty breezes, stood out in relief against the lightening sky. Daybreak, the reason for their journey, was about to dispel the darkness and paint the awaiting canvas of the sky.

They sat on a crumbly wall out on the cliff edge. Below and all round was the vista of the age-old town, built into the very hill itself, and the sea. The sea, scattered with its myriad of tiny shadowy islands.

They sat and held hands, as tightly as they had done on the day they met. Michael looked out to the line of the horizon, seconds away from the coming of dawn, waiting impatiently like a child, for the great burning globe of the sun to make its emergence from the depths of the sea.

Georgia gazed beyond the hills to the purple mountain ranges that rose and fell in the distance. They never spoke at times like this, but communicated with a little tightening of the fingers, a gesture, or a touch. They sat, totally at peace, and watched and listened to the sunrise. They learned a long while ago that the sun rose in your ears as much as in your eyes. From the occasional faint night sound, there issued the noise of the dawn.

It started with the chugging sounds of the fishing boat engines, as the three little boats made their way back to the harbour after a night in the silky black waters. A cock began to crow and a dog barked in answer. Other dogs joined in the chorus, their voices rising from different parts of the town that nestled below them. A metallic scraping noise took a little while to identify, but they had watched the peasant women, up with the lark, making traditional bread and baking it in strange outdoor stone ovens built into the walls of their backyards. They used long, flat metal spatulas to feed the loaves into the oven, and it was those, scraping against the stone oven floor, that they heard, way up on their cliff top.

In a while, along with birdsong, came the shouts and calls of fishermen and farmers, babies and grandmothers. It took a very short time to go from silent darkness to the brilliant cacophony of the awakening day.

Georgia squeezed his hand and smiled. The blood-red sun caught her flaming auburn hair and he was dazzled, as he always had been, by her beauty. She gazed at her husband,

and in a voice that was little more than a whisper said, 'She's going to die, Michael. You've made a mistake.'

* * *

Michael clawed his way back to the summer house, his heart racing and blood pumping dangerously through his veins. His temples thudded, and he sweated profusely. 'I knew! I knew! Why on earth didn't I . . .'

Gasping for breath, he begged his eyes to open and focus again as the realisation of their folly washed over him, and then he saw the lifeless figure slumped on the floor.

'Carole! Dear God!' He forced his leaden weight to rise from the chair and he fell beside her on the carpet. Praying to every deity he could think of, he checked her life signs and found a weak pulse. He pulled her unceremoniously into the recovery position and dragged a blanket that had been draped over a rattan chair down with him to cover her. Unsteadily pulling himself up, he found an unopened bottle of mineral water that Ellie had left behind. Shakily, he tore off the plastic seal and, bending down, he moistened the white lips. He was horrified to see flecks of white foam on her chin, his imagination perversely reminding him of cappuccino coffee. He rubbed her cold wrists and felt a shudder pass through her — then her limbs and her whole body shook in a kind of convulsion.

The shivering was fierce and frightening, but after what seemed an eternity, the spasm passed and her breathing began a ragged but encouraging rhythm.

He sat on the floor and hugged her to keep her warm. He talked continuously, and employed his own form of healing, showering her colourless body with every rainbow hue that his fatigued mind could muster. He wanted to call an ambulance, but he did not dare leave her. Her eyes opened, but to his great concern, they seemed empty and unseeing.

Michael began to pray. His voice gained strength, and in about five minutes, her eyes closed again and her breathing settled to a regular pattern. Her temperature rose, and when her eyelids fluttered for the second time, there was life in the eyes that looked back at Michael.

They remained, like a strange tableau, sitting on the summer house floor for nearly an hour. During that time, the heady perfume of lilacs washed over them and they both drifted in and out of a light sleep.

Carole muttered a little, mostly odd words and unintelligible phrases, but after a time she became coherent and expressed the wish for them to get back into the house.

With Michael's help they made the journey back, pausing to sit on the stone bench in the courtyard, and praying that Ellie would not wake and see them.

In the kitchen, Carole slumped in the chair closest to the heat and begged Michael to make her a strong cup of tea. Michael, amazed and delighted she was even alive, yet alone asking for a drink, did as he was bid, but demanded that she let him get her to hospital for a check-up. Her answer was an emphatic no. She insisted that she badly needed sleep, and they would talk in the morning, but no doctors and no hospital.

She sat, five mute dogs at her feet, and drank the hot tea in silence. She drained the last drop from the cup and surveyed the worried looking man seated by the table. 'I'm sorry, Michael, but could you help me up the stairs. I am better now, but my legs are still weak. I need to rest.'

He helped her up to her room and she fell, fully clothed, onto the bed. He removed her shoes and pulled the duvet over her. One of the bigger dogs had padded quietly up the stairs behind them and leaped up on the bed beside his mistress. He stared balefully at Michael as to make his position perfectly clear. He would guard her tonight.

As Michael left the room, he heard her whisper, 'It's okay, Michael. I'm safe now. Try to get some sleep, and thank you.'

* * *

In his own room, Michael undressed, pulled on his pyjamas, and reached for his mobile telephone that lay, unused until now, on the bedside table. He dialled his own office number and left a brief message for Janet. She would pick it up early tomorrow morning — she always popped into the office, even on Saturdays, to check for messages, and could deal with his requests appropriately. He said that there had been some health problem with his hostess and he would not be returning until the following week. He would notify her of the exact day when he knew himself. He asked her to telephone any appointments and to give his mobile number to any of his patients that may need to speak with him urgently. He would, if necessary, burn the midnight oil to prepare for the Paris lecture.

Even the glorious bed did not make him welcome that night, and at three thirty he was back in the kitchen making yet another hot drink. Returning to his room with the steaming mug of tea, he sat with the lights still on, duvet wrapped around him right up to his chin, and went over the horrors of the last few hours.

From the second that Carole had made her intentions plain, he had alarm bells ringing fit to wake the dead, and yet, somehow, *somehow* he had ignored the golden rule. He was a healer, for heaven's sake. Before any session, be it meditation, a creative visualisation, or a full healing therapy, he always followed his own ritual practice. He bathed, if he hadn't already; he had a very light meal or sometimes fasted, and he *never* drank alcohol. Tonight, after a huge dinner and copious quantities of wine and whisky, he had followed Carole, like one of her small dogs, to the summer house and gaily opened himself up to the unknown.

Carole had not drunk at the restaurant, but she had consumed two huge home-poured doubles later. You never messed with the occult, in any shape or form, when you had been drinking. He was at a loss to know where his brain had been. And Carole? Had she realised . . . something had crossed her mind before she hurried them to the summer house. Was it that? She knew the dangers, and had gone ahead anyway?

He pulled the duvet up even higher, and hoped the tea would help take away the chill that had settled into the very marrow of his bones.

He felt awful, but suspected that tomorrow, he would look a whole lot better than his hostess. What were they going to say to Ellie? One look at the two of them should provoke more than a raised eyebrow.

He reverted to worrying, once more, about Carole. She should have had some kind of medical attention, but he understood her reticence, and he was not even fully aware of what had happened. What on earth had she tried to do, and what had gone so terribly wrong?

With a heavy heart, he realised they had some serious talking to do in the morning.

CHAPTER NINETEEN

Although sleep had not been his ally during those last few hours before dawn, Michael rose early, pulled on his shoes and his dressing gown, and went out to the summer house. He doubted that, in their troubled state, he had remembered to lock the door, and if Ellie made her way out there before either of them, she may fear the intruder had returned.

There were still crisp white patches of frost on the grass and the air was fresh enough to make the little hairs in his nostrils tingle. The door, as he thought, was closed but not locked. He wearily made his way inside, fully expecting to have to tidy up after their nocturnal episode. He stood for a moment, rubbing gritty sleep from his eyes with a chubby fist, and tried to fathom what he was seeing.

The blanket he had used to cover Carole, which he'd left on the floor by the table, was neatly folded on the seat of the rattan chair. The chairs were carefully placed under the table. The cloth was straight and the cushions were all puffed up and tidy. The CD player was switched off at the mains, something he never did, not even at home, and the plastic water bottle was missing altogether.

Michael sat down heavily and ran his tired eyes once again around the orderly garden room. He was certain Carole could not have been fit enough to get back out here after he'd left her last night. She was exhausted and practically comatose by the time he had left her room. He had dozed only fitfully for the rest of the night and would have heard her if she had got up. She was not exactly light footed on the stairs.

He absent-mindedly picked up a piece of quartz crystal and turned it over and over, passing it from one hand to the other. Surely Ellie hadn't been out here already? It was not yet seven o'clock and Ellie, on her hostess's orders, rarely rose until breakfast time. He stared out across the lawn, feeling drained of all energy. He could hardly find the strength to ponder over the puzzle. Whatever, there was nothing he could do out here. No doubt, as they say, all would be revealed. He had better lock up and get indoors. He must discuss with Carole what she had in mind to tell Ellie. One thing was for sure, it would not be the truth.

Carole was washing a glass in the sink as he came in the back door. She looked up and gave him a listless smile. 'I saw you go out there, I realised what you were doing. Thank you, I expect we left it in quite a mess, didn't we?'

Michael was silent as he dropped into a chair. He looked at her steadily and said, 'Yes, we did, but somehow it had all been sorted out by the time I got out there.'

'That's impossible!' Carole's back snapped into ramrod position, and she rounded on her friend with almost aggression. 'Quite impossible!'

'I know that as well as you. Go and see for yourself if you don't believe me. I've done nothing out there, and it's all spick-and-span. Go on, go and check!'

Michael's uncharacteristically irritated voice calmed Carole almost immediately. 'Michael, I'm so sorry! Of course I believe you! It's just . . . who? I mean, no one . . . ' She made an exasperated noise through her teeth. 'I don't understand, that's all.'

'I know, old girl, nor do I. I was totally dumbstruck when I opened the door. But listen, you and I must not fall out over this, and you know that you've got a lot of explaining to do, so get your act together. The first thing we have to do is form a united front with regard to Ellie. What are you going to tell her happened last night? You must have looked in a mirror this morning, you look ghastly! Oh, and I haven't even asked you how you feel?'

'Ghastly will suffice, although it's an understatement. And you?'

'"Knackered" springs to mind.'

Carole smiled ruefully at him, and for the first time that morning, he noticed how ill she really looked. 'Lord, you make haggard look good.'

'Thank you, Professor, for your expert observation, but I am more than aware of my appearance! In fact, thinking about it, this particular image could be the aftermath of one monstrous hangover. Your own sallow, sickly complexion, hiding embarrassingly behind your beard, could also attest to a night of excess.'

'Hmm, probably our best bet.' Michael leaned over and took her hand. 'Listen, my friend, I can only guess what you were trying to do last night and I'm sure you would prefer not to talk about it, but Ellie will not be up for at least another hour and, first, I need to know if you need any form of medical attention.' He stopped her as she began to bluster his comment away. 'No! Hear me out. Apart from anything else, you had some kind of fit out there last night, it could have been some sort of mild stroke, you really should have a check-up, without delay. And second, I must know exactly what happened. You involved me, and you owe it to me to explain.' He spoke firmly, but his obvious care for his friend shone through his strong words.

All signs of fight drained from the weary woman. She got up slowly and took the boiling kettle from the hob. 'You are right, of course. I will tell you all that I can remember.'

The making of her cure-all was automatic. As she talked, without emotion, stiff fingers lifted the silver teaspoon and heaped dark pungent leaves into the pot. 'I was unbelievably foolish. My complete disregard for you, as well as myself, is unforgivable. I would only say, in my defence, that after I made the initial decision to pursue the knowledge I required, to whatever ends, well, another influence took me over, and my thoughts were not my own from that point on.'

She shivered and Michael realised the difficulty she was going to have in reliving the evening.

He gently took the two mugs from her shaking hands, placed them on the familiar warm pine tabletop and went to the refrigerator for milk. She sat silently, her eyes tracing patterns in the knitted tea cosy that Vera had made.

Michael poured the steaming hot tea and listened intently. In broken sentences and erratic speech, Carole pieced together the part of the night that Michael had not been a party to.

As he had suspected, she had been aware of their drinking, but chose to proceed anyway. Her idea was for Michael to simply be there for her, deep in a meditation, happily giving off good vibrations. She, on the other hand, had intentions of tracking down her lost vision, even if it meant leaving the protective circle of her 'sanctuary'. She sadly told him that she had even ignored the cautions of her dear Vera and ridden roughshod over the advice of those who knew much more than she. 'Vera said I was stubborn, but how could I have been so half-witted to think that I could challenge such power!'

Michael listened as she described how she had sent Vera away, and asked for direction to whoever or whatever had sent her the unfinished presentiment. She had felt herself sucked into a cold, dark place where a foul-smelling wind blew. She could hear cries and sobbing, and then silence. Complete silence. She seemed to be suspended in an icy black nothingness. She had called for Vera, and although she felt a slight warmth for a moment, and the merest hint of perfume, there was no break in the darkness. She then began to be truly afraid. She had prayed to the Great Spirit, her Heavenly Father, to help her and bring her from this void. She no longer wished to know anything. She shouted her stupidity to anyone who would listen, but the words had no form, and she shrieked soundlessly into emptiness.

After what seemed to be both an eternity and no time at all, the wind returned, howling louder and battering her this way and that. She was forced to breathe in its foulness, and the stench that invaded her lungs made her retch. As she had fought for breath, she became aware of a sound. A low chuckling sort of a laugh rippled through the wailing of the wind. She had thought that even the terrible silence was better than that diabolical mirth.

Then she had heard a voice.

At this point, in the warmth of Snug Cottage, Michael thought he may have to call this recollection to a close. It was his friend who said no, she was hoping it would be a catharsis. She had to rid herself of the memory and so continued.

The voice, discordant and ugly, had declared its willingness to endow the woman with the vision that she had been so stupid as to push away. In fact, as she had gone to such lengths, such pains, would she not prefer to see more than just that paltry helping of clairvoyance that had been tossed her way? Yes, she should see a little of what was really around the corner, waiting for her. Waiting for her, and for her dear friend.

It had giggled in a perverse parody of a child. Fear consumed her, and knowing herself to be hopelessly out of her depth, with an evil whose presence was draining the very life from her, she began, once again, to pray. Quietly and persistently. The voice sneered at her litany and assured her that as she had asked for the knowledge, she would get it. Although she persisted doggedly with her prayers, the awful vision was played out to her in its hateful entirety. When the darkness descended again, she found her voice carried some substance and she called to her God to take her home. Another wind had enveloped her, a gentle fragrant cloud, that cocooned her within itself, and brought her out from the darkness. She was held in feathery wings, bathed in cool water, and dried in the healing rays of the sun. She had been placed on a silver-sanded beach with the enormity of the ocean before her, and watched the sun rise in a blaze of red and gold. Finally, she was lifted by unseen hands and brought back home.

As she slowly descended through the starry night sky and drifted down to the summer house, she was snatched by bony, dead fingers, a skeletal hand holding tight over her mouth and nose, and flung, with air-starved lungs, to the ground.

The last thing she remembered before she blacked out was a satanic cry of victory; one that turned to a choked scream of terror, as she witnessed in the seconds before her eyes closed, an army of gold, led by a violet warrior, fall upon the darkness and throw it back into its abyss.

Tears ran unashamedly down Carole's cheeks and she slumped forward, head in hands, onto the tabletop.

Michael laid a reassuring arm over her heaving shoulders. 'Nearly there, old girl. Tell me, if you can, what you were shown.'

'I can't.' Her voice was almost inaudible.

'You have come this far, you are very brave, now finish it and you can let it go.' He was persuasive, but her answer was again in the negative.

'I mean, I can't, not won't. It's gone, and I hope forever. All I know, Michael, is that there is something terrible out there. Something is walking this world, and the powers of darkness are very pleased about it, and will give this thing every bit of help they can. The worst part is that it involves Ellie.'

As if perfectly on cue, the sound of the downstairs shower being turned on drifted into the quiet kitchen.

'We must get dressed, Michael. All I can say is that Vera and some others. Angels? Healers? Spirit guides of some kind were with us last night while you helped me. They spoke to me. I am only in danger if I interfere again, and I won't. This will take some getting over and, yes, I will get a check-up as soon as Dr Littlewood can fit me in, but please, please, keep all this from Ellie!'

'Carole, I do not understand this myself and it frightens me to death. I'm hardly likely to go sharing this with our young friend! Now go and shower. I'll confess to leading you astray with the "fire water" last night, and we'll take it from there.'

Carole mouthed her agreement and with a final, 'Thank you, my dear friend', disappeared upstairs, and soon Michael heard the second shower start to run.

His role as the 'rock' in this strange saga was starting to weigh heavy on his heart, and with a determined intake of breath, he prepared to take to the boards and act out his part as the apologetic, drunken guest.

* * *

Ellie was late for breakfast and hurried, as best she could on her crutches, into the kitchen, calling out cheerful 'good mornings' to humans and dogs alike. 'Good grief!' she exclaimed as her exuberant greetings were returned in hushed tones.

Michael's bleary eyes reminded her of a bulldog and, Carole, well, she had never seen her friend look so under the weather. 'How much did you two put away last night? she asked in amazement.

'Quietly, child!' said Michael with a pained expression. 'My head can't take anything above a whisper at present.'

Carole mumbled some sort of agreement and turned to slice bread for toast.

Ellie practically doubled over with laughter. 'By the look of the pair of you, it's a good thing I missed your party! You both look awful!' She narrowed her eyes and Michael saw that she was reading their energy fields. At a guess, he reckoned she was seeing a muddy blur where the healthy lights should be.

'I suggest you both get another few hours and try to sleep it off. I've never seen such dreadful hangovers! You should be ashamed of yourselves,' she giggled. 'When on earth did you get to bed? I never heard either of you go up. I slept like the dead last night.'

'How fortuitous, I'm glad we didn't disturb you, we, eh, were rather late . . .' Carole seemed to be slipping into a trance but then hastily pulled herself together. 'I can't imagine what made us go on drinking like that, talking over old times and reminiscing, I suppose. Well, we're paying for it today all right!'

'Poor dears!' laughed Ellie. 'Look, I had a call on my mobile this morning. Dr Alice Cross is driving down from London today to visit her sister in Gomshall for the weekend. She wondered if I would like to go out for a drive with her, and perhaps stop for lunch somewhere, before she goes on to her family. I said that I'd discuss it with you guys and ring her back, but by the look of you, some peace and quiet with me out of the way seems like a very good option, doesn't it?'

Michael and Carole both nodded like naughty children caught out in a lie.

'I'll be back just after lunch. It will be nice to see Alice again.'

'Ah, yes, Ms Nice, isn't it?'

'Sarcasm does not become you, Mrs Meyer!' said Ellie, with mock severity.

'I don't know, I think I've thrived on it for the last sixty or so years! You go and enjoy yourself. Michael and I will have a small restorative that I discovered in Bermuda. It is . . . let me recall, mostly angostura bitters, raw eggs and . . .'

'Oh, please!' exclaimed a pained Michael. 'You go ahead, but I'll give that a miss, thank you!'

Ellie rang back, and the doctor told her she was already on the road, and with luck, she would be in Compton in about an hour. She gave Alice some directions to find Snug Cottage, said that she was looking forward to their excursion, and hung up with a smile. She finished her breakfast and tried not to laugh at Michael, as he aimlessly pushed a slice of cold toast around his plate.

'Excuse me if I go and get ready. Alice should be here within the hour. I'll leave you two to recover.' Her next words were directed to Michael. 'Maybe, if you feel better, you would like to meet Dr Cross when she brings me back. I know she would be very interested to talk to you about the energy fields. Anyway, see how you feel later. I'm sure you would find her interesting.'

'And don't forget . . . nice,' simpered Carole, with an attempt at a grin.

'You're impossible,' laughed Ellie, throwing a tea towel at her friend, and hobbling off to find her handbag and jacket.

* * *

Michael and Carole sat hunched over the table. The professor's hands were clenched around his third mug of tea, and Carole sat staring at her dogs, trying to find the energy to take them out to the orchard for a game of ball.

Ellie had long gone, waving happily to her two hungover friends from the window of Alice's little Micra.

Carole's head ached badly. It felt as if a pressure were building up inside her temples, and pulsing pains ricocheted around her skull. She wanted nothing more than to go back to her room, draw the curtains and fall into bed, but that wasn't really an option. If she could just get herself outside with her boys, the fresh air would do her far more good. 'Come on, Michael. Get your coat and come with me to the orchard. Those lovely dogs need some exercise, and so do we.' She painfully stood up, using the table for support, and let a moment of dizziness pass.

'You look more in need of some sound sleep to me, old girl. I'll get the dogs out. You lie down for a bit.'

'It's not just fresh air, I need to get back into the summer house, to my sanctuary. I need to know it's . . . well, safe again, a good place to be.'

'The sanctuary was always safe, Carole. You left that safety and went outside it. You never broke the circle.'

'I still need to sit for a while and feel it for myself. I would never forgive myself if I ruined such a special, such a hallowed place.'

The portly professor was feeling much recovered. Apart from a weariness and heaviness in the lower limbs, he was nearly back to his old self. He fetched their coats, and together, they shepherded Carole's flock through the archway and into the orchard. The frost had lifted and a weak wintry sun shone on the glistening furry coats of her playing dogs.

'Not so rough, Orlando! He's not as big as you!'

The big Springer barked with delight as he bowled Tug, the little cocker spaniel, over and over in the grass. Undaunted, the small dog dashed back into the fray, barking at the top of his voice.

'Do they ever fight?' asked Michael, pushing his cold hands further into the deep pockets of his sheepskin-lined jacket.

'Good heavens, yes! They have to straighten out the pecking order occasionally. Nothing serious though, it's all noise and gnashing of teeth, no biting. They have never fallen out in earnest. They are my pack, and I am their leader. They all know their place, and we exist in harmony because of that.' She produced a couple of hard rubber balls from her old and shabby thorn-proof coat and threw them half-heartedly between the apple trees.

They stayed there for twenty minutes, and when the dogs had settled down to nose around quietly by themselves, the couple walked slowly towards the summer house.

As he unlocked the door, Michael felt tension emanate from his friend. She faltered on the step, and for one moment, Michael thought she would be unable to enter. She drew deep breaths and slowly stepped through the doorway. It looked to Michael as if she were expecting, at any moment, to be struck down. He supposed, on reflection, that she was. She walked around, picking up this, and moving that, until suddenly she collapsed into the rattan chair and sighed. 'Thank God. I really believed I might never be able to use this lovely room again. Well, not as a sanctuary, that is. I think, as you sat with me last night, the whole place was cleansed. The energies feel stronger than they did before.'

Strength was returning to her voice, and Michael felt a shiver of apprehension — an icy finger insidiously traced a path down his spine. 'I hope you are not considering any more madness! Don't ever forget that the last expedition nearly killed you. You will be a lot of help to Ellie, if you go on the way you are going!'

'Michael! Believe me, no more experiments! I'm just so relieved I haven't lost my precious refuge, that's all.'

His anger subsided and he looked around the room. 'Who do you think came in here after we left? Who tidied up, Carole?'

'I have no idea. It obviously wasn't Ellie. Scrubbs would never wander around in the garden after dark. It certainly wasn't you or I. I keep thinking it has something to do with that prowler we had here, just before you came. Maybe it is a vagrant . . .'

'Vagrants stink. The room smelled fresh and clean when I came in.'

The two friends slipped into their own thoughts, sitting peacefully in the quiet garden.

'I think Ellie is rather fond of that young doctor, don't you?' commented Carole.

Michael nodded assent. She certainly seemed pleased to hear from her and had been quick to agree to the outing. 'Good for her. I'll make a point of having a chat with Dr Cross when they come back and I'll tell you what I—'

His plans were interrupted by the sight of Marie Littlewood hurrying across the lawn to the garden room. Stumbling in the door, she stared at Carole, and then pent-up tears coursed down her face. 'They've taken him! The police, they've taken my Daniel away!'

It took them several minutes to calm the woman into coherence. When she was more composed, Carole gently questioned her. 'What's happened? What is he supposed to have done?'

'I don't know! They came to the house this morning and talked to him for ages and, oh, you know the state he's in, he started to lose his temper. And they took him away. A lady police officer said if he wouldn't cooperate with them at the house, then they would have to take him to Guildford police station. At that he got worse, so they took him. Carole, I don't know what is going on. I just know my son is sick, and he shouldn't be held in a police cell!'

'I'm sure he's not in a cell, if they only need to talk to him. Look, he'll calm down soon and realise that he is not helping himself by being so aggressive. He will see sense, answer their questions, and they will let him go. After all, he hasn't done anything, has he?'

'I don't know,' stammered Marie. 'He keeps going off, and I don't know if he has done something wrong or not.' The distraught woman put her head in her hands and sobbed.

Carole whispered to Michael, asking him if he would see the doctor's wife safely home. Seeing his fervent nod of the head, she spoke softly to her friend. 'I think you should be at home, dear. Daniel may try to ring you. You really should be there for him. Michael will look after you, and if you like, I will ring the police, and see if I can find out anything for you. Where is Dr Littlewood, by the way?'

'Thank God, he is on call with Medi-doc this weekend and they are flat out. I haven't told him yet. I'll wait till he gets home.'

Michael looked apprehensive and voiced his opinion that she really needed him with her at this time.

She vehemently shook her head. 'I'll be fine. But I'm afraid he's not coping with Daniel's problems very well.'

'Whatever you say, but let's get you back in case he calls.' Michael put a comforting arm around Marie and led her out onto the lawn.

Carole looked after them and thought how commendable it was that Michael was never afraid of giving a hug or touching your hand. So many people these days, herself included, were averse to physical contact. Would shun it even if they were crying out for it. Yes, she thought it an admirable trait, to be able to reach confidently beyond today's self-imposed restrictions.

Back indoors, she found the card WPC English had given her, rang the number and left a message asking her to return her call as soon as possible. She planned on using the return of the prowler as a red herring to find out about Daniel Littlewood. As it was, her plan failed miserably. Some fifteen minutes later the police station duly called back, but informed her that WPC English was working on an urgent case and perhaps they could help. She lamely explained about the summer house, and was told that in their experience, ne'er do wells rarely did a spot of cleaning and tidying. If nothing was stolen or damaged, then there was little they could do. The officer said he would make a note of it and Carole decided she would get nothing out of this young man about Daniel, so gave up and waited for Michael's return.

* * *

Michael was saddened at Marie Littlewood's reticence to involve her husband. He was a firm believer that partners should share everything, good, bad and indifferent, but as he sat and talked to her, he realised that their disturbed son was driving a wedge between the otherwise happily married couple. Dr Littlewood, Michael deduced, didn't have much time for those who would not make their own contribution to recovery. His son's refusal to accept his help, either as a doctor or a father, had made him angry. His wife's 'softly-softly, give the boy time' attitude made him even angrier.

As the fly on the wall, Michael realised that both husband and wife were battling each other out of their complete inability to help their only son.

Phillippa was not Lazarus. They could not bring her back from the dead. They could not make Della love Daniel again, and they could not make her give the sick man his son back. They were helpless. They could not get through to Daniel, so they fought each other.

The iron gate to the courtyard swung open silently as Michael made his way to the house. Such a sad situation. Two caring parents making their lives an unnecessary hell. If only they would support each other, things would become more manageable. He hoped that his beloved Georgia and he would have coped better if they'd had worries about their children. But, being childless, who was he to moralise.

Carole held the kitchen door open for him, and as he fought to get a stocky arm out of the jacket sleeve, he regarded her, thinking she now looked almost human. A singular improvement on earlier. He hoped her obvious progress would not deter her from getting a medical check-up. He shuddered when he thought that, only eleven hours ago, she had been lying, almost lifeless on the sanctuary floor. If Georgia had not warned him, deep in his meditation, Carole would be dead. When he contemplated that fact, his mouth went dry and he felt a sticky sweat form on the palms of his hands.

Michael heard a small bleeping noise and realised that his mobile phone's battery was low. He wandered up to his room to find the charger, and having plugged it in, kicked off his shoes and lay back on the bed. It felt softer than it had last night. He lay, hands behind his head, musing over the last twelve hours. He still had trouble accepting that Carole, normally so careful and respectful when dealing with the occult, had made such a dangerous and stupid move. He could only accept the fact that once she had committed herself to her enquiry, a force far greater than anything she had anticipated had pushed her forward. Things were out of her hands before she had a chance to change her mind.

And what of Ellie? Carole seemed to think that the greatest danger was to her, and here they were, back to square one. The woman's in jeopardy, and we don't know how or why or when. His friend nearly died, and for nothing at all. Whatever she had been shown was obviously so horrible in Carole's eyes that her subconscious had chosen to bury it. Possibly forever.

He considered the Catch-22 situation. If the knowledge stayed buried, then Carole was safe, but Ellie was in peril. If Carole remembered what she had been shown, then they may be able to help Ellie, but the horrors of recollection could put Carole in danger.

Michael prayed that it was just a diabolical joke, and that neither of his friends were really in trouble.

The urge to run back to London was strong, and suddenly his lonely flat took on a magnetic appeal.

Then he heard Carole calling him for lunch, and realising he was starving, he managed to quash the desire to run away. His play acting with the toast at breakfast had only been to strengthen the lie about the hangover — he was now ravenous. Pulling on his shoes and brushing his hair, he decided to go with the diabolical joke angle. It felt safer all round.

* * *

Ellie returned at two thirty with Dr Alice Cross in tow. Michael was sitting in the lounge, thumbing through the Review section of the *Telegraph*, when they came in.

'A real fire!' Alice practically ran across the room to stand in front of it and warm her hands.

Ellie made the introductions, and Michael and Alice fell into easy conversation, mainly about their work and the Azimah Syndrome.

Ellie and Carole went off to organise a drink for Alice before she continued the journey to her sister's home, and Ellie mentioned that she was delighted to see that Carole, like Michael, was looking considerably less fragile. Then she raved on about what a good time she had had. 'We had a lovely run, Carole. Spring is nearly here, the bulbs are coming up, and there are snowdrops everywhere. We stopped at a pub for lunch, right out in the middle of nowhere. I had a ploughman's and Alice . . .'

Ellie's enthusiasm was a delight to see. Even in her depleted state, Carole could feel nothing but goodwill for the girl. She hoped if there should be a romance, this one would be better than the last. Ellie deserved a happy partnership with someone who would cherish her, not be totally selfish, as the departed Stephanie had been.

'... and as she said, there is no point in having a big car in London, so she ...'

As Carole placed cups on a tray, she wondered when she had last heard her friend so animated. Never, seemed to be the answer to that question. As Michael said earlier, 'Good for her'. Her cynicism returned as she qualified that statement with the thought ... *as long as she is all she seems to be, and not out to use Ellie in some way.*

'... and the Siddiq family have been really helpful to Alice with her paper and she ... Oh, yes, before we go into the lounge, Carole, may I ask her here to dinner next week, would it be all right? I know it's a bit of an imposition, but I'd really like you to get to know her, and we, that is, she and I, could start working together on the case study.' Ellie looked hopefully at her friend.

'Of course!' said Carole. 'Thursday is the only day that won't work, as you are seeing the orthopaedic surgeon and having that plaster removed. Then we have an appointment with Carl Thomas for a follow-up review. We could be late back, and you will most likely be exhausted.'

In the lounge, the others were still deep in vigorous conversation, and if Ellie had not reminded her doctor friend that she had family to see, Carole thought that Alice would have talked until nightfall. She happily accepted Ellie's invitation to dinner, and they settled for Wednesday evening, as Alice had a lecture that afternoon that she hoped would finish early.

After she had left, Michael commented that he found her to be a personable woman, and passionate about her work. Then being sure that Ellie was out of earshot, he said, 'She does seem genuinely fond of Ellie, Carole, but that case study appears to be very important to her. Very important indeed.'

Carole pulled a face. 'Hmm, and that's my worry too. I think we need to keep a watchful eye on that one, don't you?'

Michael just nodded.

When Ellie was back, Carole left Michael explaining about Dan being taken for questioning, and took the dogs for a walk over to Marie's house, to see if she had heard anything from her son.

She returned not long after to say that the house was empty, so hopefully she had gone to collect him from the police station. They spent the rest of the afternoon reading, and later, Michael did the unheard of, and went out and brought back fish and chips to save Carole cooking. They all dozed in front of the television until the regional news came on, when Ellie called out for them to watch the item that was being shown.

An imposing grey giant of a police officer was making a statement about the murders. The police had two men helping them with their enquiries. It was too early to make any conclusions but they were confident that, along with other evidence in their possession, at least one of the two men could lead them to an arrest.

'That man!' exclaimed Ellie. 'That detective — he's the father of the little boy in the supermarket!'

For a while they discussed the coincidence, and then settled down to watch a film on Channel 5. Carole brought them big mugs of hot chocolate, because for some reason no one fancied whisky. The film was dreadful and by ten o'clock Snug Cottage said goodnight to its three weary inhabitants.

Carole slept with the light on.

CHAPTER TWENTY

The grey light of Sunday morning slowly brought the dark shapes of the furniture in Bob and Rosie's bedroom into relief. It had been past three o'clock when the policeman had gently edged in beside his wife. He had not wanted to disturb her slumbers, but he needed the warmth and security of her body next to his. He lay, now, in the same position, holding her back firmly to his stomach. Spooning, they called it. Well, if that were the case, she must be a teaspoon, and he a serving ladle! He loved to lie like this. He ran his hand over the cool, smooth skin of her shoulder and felt the rise and fall of her regular breathing. It was now, in the quiet before the children awoke, that he did his clearest thinking. Unhampered by distractions, other than that of the closeness of his wife's nakedness, he allowed his mind to drift into the convoluted issues of the murder case.

Things had suddenly started buzzing at the station. They had brought in one man for questioning — DS Corbett's chap that he apprehended in Woodham. And now, a young fellow the Guildford police had had problems with was also sitting in his interview room, after being transferred to him early that evening. Strange lad. He had spoken briefly with him before handing him over to DI Leatham and Vic Barratt.

A sullen, angry man, who seemed to pass from violent temper to almost catatonia, in the blink of an eye.

A memo had been sent out to all police stations in the area requesting immediate knowledge of any odd or unusual occurrences involving white males. A Guildford based WPC had been making some general enquiries about a prowler. Talking to the local doctor's son, they found him abusive and aggressive. He had, apparently, run off after speaking to them, and according to his mother, disappeared overnight. Getting a second call from a different source in the same area, the WPC had once again spoken to this chap, and this time found him so unhelpful that she took him back to the station to question. After a while it had become apparent there were things he was hiding. He refused to say where he was on the nights of any of the murders and the Guildford police were certain that, if nothing else, he was probably their prowler. In the light of the DCI's investigations, they thought the murder team might like a word with him.

Bob moved even closer to Rosie, breathing in and savouring her particular sleepy smell.

The other fellow was an obvious petty villain. Foul mouthed and dirty, he had been put in a cell to cool down until the morning. Corbett had been dying to get his teeth into him, but it was considered prudent, considering the stench of beer he gave off, to let him get some sleep and sober up.

He had known little more than that, but the Super had insisted he bring forward speaking to the press to that evening. He was emphatic that the public believe there was some progress being made by the police with the murders. The press needed no encouragement to gather in haste, and the superintendent had even managed to secure a slot on the regional news that night.

He hoped he had sounded more confident than he felt. Nothing seemed right about these cases, and although it was good for morale to have some action, his opinion was that it would all come to nothing. He was facing a confident psychopath, who, if Dr Gerrard was correct, was going to veer away from his cause, and take up murder for the pure love of it. The Villain and The Nutter just did not seem quite right to him, but still, he would wait and see what their interviews brought forth. He might be pleasantly surprised, or most likely, not.

Another ten minutes and he would have to get up. He kissed the back of his wife's neck and felt her stir in his arms. At times like these, he wished he was not a copper, and that they could share the sort of Sunday morning he thought she deserved. Breakfast in bed, with the Sunday papers, the kids and the dog.

He buried his face in her hair and tried to identify the hint of fragrance her shampoo had left. He thought it may be coconut. 'Sorry, baby, got to go . . . I'll ring you later.'

Half awake, she turned and held out her arms for a goodbye kiss. 'Love you,' she whispered to the granite-faced man, before falling back into sleep. 'Take care.'

* * *

Carole sat at the rosewood escritoire in the bay window of the lounge. She had felt so awful yesterday that she had not even opened her post. But she had been pleasantly surprised to have slept for eight hours without waking, and even though it was Sunday morning, she rose early and went down to the lounge. She gazed out of the window. It was barely light, but she thought that Ellie had been right when she said spring was nearly here. Buds were showing their tender green growth and the forsythia bush near the gate was a fountain of acid yellow flowers. She surveyed the ornately tooled leather inset on the top of her desk. She had neatly stacked her post for opening to one side of the leather-edged blotter. Her Mont Blanc pen sat ready for use on the soft cream blotting paper, with a silver letter opener shaped like a dagger next to it. For all the sleep she had enjoyed the night before, she still felt listless and there was a dull, rhythmic thud in her temples.

The opening of the post had become a major task, one that she hardly felt capable of.

She gazed at the heavy glass paperweight that sat towards the back of the desk. A magical swirl of kingfisher blue and dioptase green formed a whirlpool of colour in the clear quartz-like crystal. It was motion frozen in time. She tilted it, this way and that in her hands, feeling its smooth coldness permeate her own cold skin. It had been a rare gift from her brother. He had never been given to shows of affection that involved showering his loved ones with presents. It was more his way to offer time, support, or the benefit of his substantial knowledge. She had loved her older brother fiercely, and William, in his rather more dignified way, had felt the same about her. She had been a feisty child, quick to leap into battle and slow to hold her tongue. Will saved her from many a beating. Both verbal and physical, as she recalled. The one he defended her from most, of course, had been their mother. An involuntary shiver, like ice-cold water, rippled across her back and sent a glistening of frosty prickles down her arms and into her fingers. Now in her seventies, she would have thought the long dead woman would have held no power over her. But even now, the thought of the tight-lipped, steely-eyed matriarch, caused her chest to tighten and her heart to beat faster. To say that her mother had hated her was somewhat of an understatement. The adoring love of her spineless father was no anodyne to the daily quota of cruel insensitivity and sarcastic scorn that her mother had poured so abundantly on her. Will had once sagely observed that, with Carole's acid tongue and mulish reticence to give in, and their mother's glacial antipathy to her daughter, it was a wonder she survived childhood!

She smiled sadly as she remembered her handsome brother, blown away by some sniper's bullet, in a country she could barely pronounce the name of, yet alone care about.

She was the last of the Cavendish-Meyers: the last of the line. The family could be traced back practically to Adam, but it would march no further forward, and from its bloody history of feuds and madness, she decided, not before time either.

A blackbird burst into frantic song outside the window and brought Carole back from her daydreams and down to the job in hand.

She slid the fine blade into the first envelope and, in a strange continuance to her thoughts, found a letter from the family solicitor. Why she still kept him, his small office situated in the old market town of Boston, in the heart of the Lincolnshire Fens, she never knew. Tradition, she suspected, and the mere idea of trying to explain the complexities of the Meyer Estate to someone else was too daunting to contemplate. Messrs Brothertoft and Singleton — Singleton being long since departed but always mentioned in dispatches — were requesting the pleasure of her presence in those dingy little Fenland rooms, at her soonest convenience. Another year had gone by. It seemed only months ago that she had sat, in a most uncomfortable chair, and waded through heaps of boring legal documents, amending this and altering that. Mr Brothertoft, a cadaverous looking man, with thinning hair and very odd taste in ties, had drawn her attention to certain articles and advised her of the various wisdoms of selling, holding, or investing.

So, it was time once again to re-evaluate the state of the Meyer inheritance. Boring, but necessary, she supposed. In fact, the letter had arrived with perfect timing. She had planned only last night to ring the old codger and make a few radical changes to her will. Excellent, she could kill two birds with one stone.

An hour later, all her correspondence dealt with, she realised she could no longer put off taking some paracetamol. Damn it, but she may have to see Littlewood for that blasted check-up after all.

The thought of visiting the doctor brought back her concerns about Marie and Daniel. She had rung at intervals throughout the evening, but to no avail. As soon as it was decent, she would call round and check on her friend and her wayward son.

* * *

Outside the interview room, DI Jonathan Leatham leaned against the wall and plunged his hands into his pockets. 'I hear what you say, Vic, but I don't think he's on anything. I reckon he's sick. Anyway, the duty doctor should be here shortly, we'll leave it to him to see if he's up to questioning or not.'

Vic Barratt pulled a face. 'Yeah, and if he's not capable of being interviewed, we'll have to send him home until he is . . . and then he'll do another runner. Back to square one!'

'You know the rules, Vic. He's got to be fit enough to answer questions, and you've seen him in there . . .' His statement hung in the air, as they both recalled the difficulties of the last hour.

Daniel's silences were not the stuff of the belligerent thug clamming up about his misdeeds — they smacked more of a complete disassociation with everything. It was as if something else drew his attention out of the spartan interview room, and on to another place and time. He was not actually refusing to answer the policemen — he just kept slipping into the strange fugue state that had made Vic think he was on drugs.

Vic Barratt chewed his bottom lip and absent-mindedly kicked at a grey dried piece of chewing gum that was stuck to the corridor floor. 'I know you're right, sir, but doesn't it get to you? All the wasted time because of red tape. If we could just get a few straight answers from him, he'd probably be on his way home, anyway. He's a nutter, all right, but he doesn't particularly fit our killer's profile, does he?'

Jonathan yawned. 'He can't, or won't, remember where he was on any of the dates or times we've thrown at him, and by the state of him, I'm hardly surprised.' He glanced at his watch. 'The boss will be in soon, and depending on what the doc says, I'm going home for some shut-eye. How about you?'

'Yes, my wife, Barbara, has taken the kids down to her brother's place at Arundel for the weekend, so I'll be able to crash out in peace for a few hours, thank God!'

A door slammed at the end of the corridor and a harassed looking young man in a smart sports jacket was escorted towards them.

'Dr Watson,' said the constable with a smirk, 'to see Mr Littlewood, sir.'

'Don't!' growled the doctor, before either man could make a comment. 'I've heard it too many times for it to be amusing! My name is Trevor, so let's leave it at that, shall we?'

DI Leatham opened the door and held his hand out for the on-call doctor to enter.

Before he went in, Trevor Watson glanced at some hastily scribbled notes, and stepped away from the door, beckoning the detective to follow him.

'I have it here that the patient is Daniel Littlewood from Compton. Would you know if he happens to be Dr Morgan Littlewood's son?'

'That is correct.'

'Oh' — the doctor looked concerned — 'is he under arrest or helping you voluntarily?'

'He was arrested by Guildford police for a breach of the peace, but has since been further arrested on suspicion of murder. Do you know him, Doctor?'

'His father and mine play golf together. I've met him once or twice, but that was ages ago. I can't believe he would be involved in murder though. Still, better take a look at him, Inspector.'

'Would you like an officer with you? He is not exactly rational, although his aggression seems to have evaporated since he got here.'

'No, I'm fine, thank you.'

The door shut behind the young police doctor, and DI Leatham went back to the incident room to grab a coffee and see if the DCI was in.

Bob was in but missing from his office when Jonathan got there. The familiar grey jacket was carefully hung over the back of his chair, and the man's desk looked like a war zone. Leatham smiled to himself and, not for the first time, wondered how such an impeccably dressed man could work in such chaotic conditions.

He ambled to his own desk and collapsed into his chair, wearily debating whether to start on some paperwork, or go back and wait for the doctor's verdict. The decision was made for him by a bright-eyed constable, fresh on duty and whistling chirpily. 'Doc's ready for you, sir.'

'Thanks, Constable, I'll be down, and do me a favour and belt up will you? Not all of us have had a night's sleep!'

'Sorry, sir.' The constable left the room, and seconds after the door closed, Jonathan could hear the resumed warbling making its way back down the stairwell.

'Sorry, Inspector, but I have to declare him unfit to question or detain.' The doctor closed his bag and looked up from the form that he was filling in.

'I thought as much,' said Jonathan. 'It's not drugs, is it?'

'No, far from it. Drugs are what he needs in his condition. He is a very sick man, Inspector. I cannot discuss his problems with you, patient confidentiality and all that, but I have given him some diazepam and would request that you have him taken back to his parents' home, as soon as possible. He seems to think his mother may be here. Is that right?'

'Not to my knowledge.' Leatham frowned, then called a uniformed officer over to him. 'Check as to whether we have a Mrs Littlewood anywhere here. She would be waiting for news of her son. And get back here pronto with the answer.'

The officer nodded and hurried away.

'When can we talk to him, Doctor?'

The doctor chewed on the end of his pen and gave Jonathan a thoughtful stare. 'It's difficult to say. Normally

I'd ring his own GP and get him to see him straight away. He really does need serious medication, but apart from a couple of Valium, there is not much I can do. He isn't registered with a local doctor and has refused to let his father or his father's partner help him. I gather that he has domestic problems, but he is not able to give me any details. I'm hoping his mother may shed a little light on what is wrong.'

Before Dr Watson could continue, there was a tap on the door and a sheepish looking constable asked to speak to the DI alone.

Outside, the officer explained that they did indeed have Mrs Littlewood with them and she was less than a happy bunny. Apparently, there had been a mix-up at Guildford, and the poor woman had been left waiting there long after her son had been transferred. She had only just arrived and was upset and angry.

'Bring her down immediately. I'll speak to her myself, and organise the lady some refreshments, on the double!'

Jonathan Leatham was a compassionate man who had been brought up properly. He hated this sort of cock-up that gave a less than rosy view of the Constabulary and the job he loved. He looked at his watch and decided that the poor soul must have been stuck in some waiting area for most of the night. The least he could do was give her his undivided attention, let her speak with Trevor Watson, unite her with her son, and then get them both safely home.

Marie's anger quickly abated under the genuine concern voiced by the detective inspector. A hot drink and a dubious sandwich helped to assuage her physical discomfort, and gentle words from both policeman and doctor calmed her fears for her son.

It took her some fifteen minutes to explain how his family and his world had fallen apart with the death of his daughter. Sadly, she could not provide an explanation of his whereabouts on certain dates and times, as he had been so mercurial in his habits since arriving at his parents' home. She skimmed briefly over the absence of his father through all their son's traumas, looking desperately at the young doctor for help and corroboration when she declared that he would surely understand the pressures on a GP these days.

Watson nodded but said nothing.

Jonathan watched and realised that this poor woman was having to shoulder everything alone. It was rejection and loneliness the woman was feeling, and he silently hoped that if he ever had a child, he wouldn't give up on it so easily.

When she had told them all she could, Jonathan gently explained that the custody sergeant would set bail for Daniel, who would then be allowed to go home with her. It was imperative that the police speak with him as soon as he was fit enough. He was careful to make her understand that he was referring to hours, or possibly a day or two, no longer. They wanted to eliminate him from their inquiries, and the sooner the better for all of them. He promised that as far as possible he would deal with Daniel personally, but there must be no more running off or unacceptable behaviour. He was firm but kind and Marie promised to do all she could to get her son to take Dr Watson's medication regularly, and to keep him calm enough to be interviewed.

The doctor accompanied her to her son and noted that there was no impassioned greeting. He simply allowed himself to be hugged and uttered a quiet, 'Can we go now?' as he pushed away from her.

Marie Littlewood, happier now at having her son back, refused his offer of being driven home and her own car delivered to her later. She certainly looked stronger, and Jonathan hoped that her strength would hold up through what was clearly going to be a rough time. As they left the room, he silently prayed that the disturbed young man would not do another disappearing trick on them.

* * *

DS Corbett was having a very different time with his detainee.

Stuart Fletcher was as foul-mouthed sober as he was when inebriated. Although hungover, he still managed to find a plethora of profanities to shower upon the unimpressed sergeant. Barry Corbett was delighted to realise that Fletcher's garrulous mate was getting as much verbal flack as he was, for 'opening his fucking great trap in a bleedin' pub in the first place!'

Stuart Fletcher sat, legs akimbo, with his elbows resting on his knees and his chin on his entwined knuckles. He smelled of stale beer and something like vomit. His filthy stained vest top gave credibility to the puke theory, and Corbett thought that not all the dull patches on his combat trousers were authentic camouflage design. His calloused and nicotine-stained fingers clenched and unclenched against his chin, making his bony face nod in a jerky and rhythmical fashion.

The sergeant and the police constable were not enjoying this singularly unpleasant man's company, but took the interview slowly, and gave the impression that they were happy to be there with him if it took all day for him to answer their questions.

So far, they had ascertained that he was unemployed, was dossing with the mate with the big fucking gob, and held a deep and well-advertised loathing for the 'filth'.

The sergeant stoically pressed on, monotonously bombarding the odious fellow with the same enquiries and queries repeatedly.

Fletcher had not wanted a solicitor, and for the first half hour insisted that his mate had just been trying to be 'Jack the Lad' in front of some piece of skirt. He denied having seen anything at all, and claimed the story was a load of bollocks, made up by his wanker of a friend.

His story changed somewhat when DS Corbett cleverly put it to him that his reticence in simply telling them where he had been and what he had witnessed on the night of the murder was indicative to very suspicious behaviour — perhaps he was more involved than just being a voyeur? Perhaps he knew the victim? Was he near the golf course to meet her for some reason? Did they argue?

'Fucking hell! You ain't gettin' me fer that one! Pigs! Yer all the same. Yer don't 'ave a clue, do yer? Just pick up any bastard off the street 'n' fritten 'im wiv bloody murder! An' why? . . . cos you ain't got no bloody suspect, 'ave yer?'

'On the contrary,' said Corbett softly, 'if you think about it, you tell your friend you saw a murderer, now you tell us you didn't, sounds suspicious to me. Can't blame me for thinking the worst, can you?'

'Look! A'right so I saw this geezer, right? An 'e frightened the shit out a me. Looked like soddin' Dracula.'

'Dracula?'

'Yeah, dead creepy.'

'Where were you?'

Fletcher sighed. 'Can I 'ave a fag?'

'Just give me a few answers and I'll get you a packet. Where were you?'

'On the path that runs by the copse next to the golf course. The one that goes along the backs of all them big 'ouses.'

'And what were you doing there?' As if I didn't know, thought Corbett.

'Nuffin', just walkin'.'

'Casing some nice big drum, were we?'

'No, I wasn't!' Fletcher looked indignant. 'Bust up wi' me bird, if yer must know! I was just walkin' okay?'

'Sorry, Stuart,' said Corbett mildly. 'I didn't take you for the kind of chap to commune with nature, swallowing up the winter's morn, heart breaking with unrequited love . . .'

'Don't take the fucking piss! I was smarting, that's all, so save yer fancy trap fer those that'd twig wot the hell yer talkin' about!'

'What time was it?'

Fletcher blew his cheeks out and thought for a moment or two.

'S'pose it must've been about sevenish. I was 'ome at 'alf seven, and it's only a twenty-minute walk from there.'

'So, what did you see?'

'I reached the end of the path and, well, I didn't know wevver t' go 'ome or wander over to the fairways. Sometimes I picks up some lost balls that the rich toffs can't be bovvered to look for. But it was still too dark for that, so I turned round and there he was . . . Fuckin' Dracula!'

'Describe him . . . what was he doing?'

'Can I have that fag?'

The sergeant made a sign to his constable and spoke towards the tape recorder. 'The time is now nine forty-five a.m. PC Windsor is leaving the interview room. DS Corbett and Stuart Fletcher remain. Go on, Stuart.'

''E weren't doin' nuffin'! 'E was just there! That was bad enuff, standin' under a tree in the bleedin' dark, talkin' to 'imself and 'uggin' a bag or somefin'. Fucking weird!'

'So why did you decide you'd seen a murderer, Stuart? The world is full of weirdos, but they are not all murderers.'

The door opened and PC Windsor approached the table, throwing a packet of Benson and Hedges ahead of him. 'PC Windsor has entered the room, the time is nine fifty-seven a.m.'

Fletcher fumbled hungrily at the pack and looked hopefully at the two policemen for a light.

Windsor produced a disposable lighter, flicked the catch, and held the flame towards him.

Drawing deeply on the smoke, he continued. 'Cos I saw her, didn't I! The poor cow!'

'You saw the murdered woman and didn't report it!'

'It weren't as simple as that,' grunted Fletcher. 'Listen, first I sees Dracula, then by the time I've caught me breath and looked again, 'e's bleedin' gone. Then this bloody dog nearly has me off me feet, runnin' like 'e'd got the 'ounds of 'ell behind him! By now I'm finkin' I'm out of 'ere, and I started to run back towards the main road. Before I got there, I saw that dog again, he was whinin' and yelpin', an' sorta pawin' at something layin' on the ground under the trees. I didn't go and look, but after, well, I kinda put two an' two togevver, didn't I? Musta been 'er, the poor cow who got done!'

DS Corbett shifted in his chair and tugged at his shirt collar to loosen it a bit. 'Why didn't you come forward with any of this?'

'Ain't none of my business and I don't 'ave no dealings wiv you pigs if I can 'elp it.'

'What makes you call him Dracula?'

''E was 'alf turned away from me when I saw 'im . . . I thought for a minute 'e was wearin' a cape, a long dark cape . . . finkin' about it now though, I guess it was just some long overcoat or mac, creepy bastard!'

Barry Corbett continued to question Fletcher for another hour, but came up with little more than he had already managed to extract from his unforthcoming witness. He terminated the interview and sent in coffee and a sandwich for the man. It was time to give the guv'nor an update on his findings.

* * *

'Badger baiting, guv. He'd been out in the copse the previous night and dropped his torch. He went back just before first light to try and find it, when unluckily for him, he practically fell over our killer and his victim. He gave me some garbage about being out for a walk after an argument with his girlfriend, didn't want us to know about his nasty little nocturnal occupation, but he coughed to it in the end.' Corbett screwed his face into a perplexed frown. 'There is one other thing, sir. He does a bit of jobbing for a bloke he knows. Painting, decorating — he's a plasterer by trade, and sometimes stoops to a bit of honest graft, cash in hand. I asked him for a list of the last six jobs he'd done and guess who the last two were for? Dear Mr Featherstone at the Waters Meet Hotel in Weybridge!'

'Well now, what an interesting coincidence! And we don't believe in those do we, Barry?'

'I've sent Windsor down to the hotel to get a list of the jobs and the dates when he was there. Fletcher does not remember the dates, but that Featherstone chap should have records of work done.'

Bob Foreman bit a thumbnail anxiously. 'Having a connection with two of the murders, no matter how tenuous, is fluky to say the least, but I don't know, something isn't right, is it?'

DS Corbett nodded furiously. 'I totally agree, sir. He's a right cop-hating little shit, but to be honest, I don't think he's bright enough to have concocted a double-bluff.' He frowned and continued. 'It doesn't make any sense, and not only that, he is about as far from the profile as you could get.'

'Exactly, but I still don't like the involvement in two out of three deaths. Get back to him, Barry, and make quite sure there is no connection, no matter how sketchy, with Melissa Crabbe.'

'Right, sir.' Corbett got up, then paused as he turned to leave. 'Any luck with the Guildford bloke, Daniel Littlewood, sir?'

'Not fit to question. Doc sent him home. Strange fellow, and he does have domestic problems. We are not ruling him out yet. DI Leatham will speak to him as soon as possible.'

Foreman leaned back in his chair, making Corbett concerned for his safety, given the delicate woodwork and the size of his chief.

'Sergeant, it's the same as your chap. No evidence to say otherwise, but I'm damn sure he's not our man. We need some help on this one, and we need it fast. The Super is snapping at my heels almost hourly for a result, and as far as my hunches go, we have sweet sod all! No more than when we bloody started.'

He lurched forward, his chair legs crashing to the floor and making the detective sergeant jump back with surprise.

'Do you know what really gets me! The bastard's been seen! On each occasion, he's been eyeballed! With Crabbe, by a woman looking out of her bedroom window and by Weasel. With Carberry, by your low-life, Fletcher. And with Turner, by the chambermaid, Mary Probart, then another woman, Audrey Long, also from her window, and some old guy walking his dog! He's been seen! He wears weird clothes, and still we've got nothing! Bloody nothing! It's inconceivable!' Foreman was about to go on, but his phone rang. 'Okay. No, no, I'll go myself. Royal Surrey County Hospital, did you say? Yes, on my way!'

Crashing the receiver down into its cradle, Bob Foreman swore briefly and wrenched his jacket from the back of his chair, 'DC Rawlings has been injured on his way to work. Don't know the details yet, but it could be bad, they think it's a hit and run. Inform DI Leatham and Vic Barratt for me, will you? Then keep on at Fletcher, Sergeant. I'll be back as soon as possible.'

CHAPTER TWENTY-ONE

Being early, A&E was less crowded than the day he had brought Liam in, and this time he was on official business. The burly officer was taken straight to Jack Barker's office, where he was greeted like an old friend by the casualty consultant.

As scruffy as ever, Bob wondered if the man slept here, or if he even had a home of his own. They shook hands and Jack proffered a chair to the policeman, then sat himself and began to explain what he knew.

'Your young detective has sustained mainly internal injuries; he is on his way to theatre now. He was in a collision with a motor vehicle and apparently the driver did not stop. When it's man versus machine, man's delicate tissues rarely come off best. He had a pneumothorax on the right side and his lung collapsed. Not actually as terrible as it sounds, Chief Inspector, we've sorted that, but there was a nasty blow to his abdomen and a scan showed some bleeding into the peritoneal cavity. There may be other damage in that region, too. The surgeons will find out soon enough. Luckily, apart from the rib that penetrated the pleura, there are no fractures, just very nasty bruising. Depending on the extent of injury to his stomach, he should be fine. He won't be back on duty for a good long while, I'm afraid, which isn't the best news for you, with all the work the force has on at the moment!'

Bob pulled a face. 'You're right, but at least Rawlings sounds as if he's going to pull through okay, and that was my first concern.'

'Not having much luck, are you, Chief Inspector? First your son. How is he, by the way? Fighting fit by now, I expect?'

'Oh, yes, he's just as you said. Up to all sorts again, hospital forgotten.'

'Good.' Jack Barker paused, then added, 'You never saw your woman in the supermarket again, I suppose?'

Bob shook his head slowly. 'Still bothers me. Apart from not understanding how on earth she knew what was wrong with him, I really want to thank her. She was so positive that I acted on her advice immediately, and with your help and expertise, she saved my son a lot more unnecessary suffering. I really would like to meet her. I expect if I were not so busy with my work, I would have tried to track her. I hate unsolved mysteries.'

Bob watched as Barker stared at him intently. He seemed to be weighing something up.

'Look, detective, I'm a pretty good judge of character, and I can see how much you care about both your family and your fellow officers. I get the feeling that this unexplained mystery will nag at you constantly until you've finally met that woman again.' He drew in a deep breath. 'This is entirely off the record, so to speak, so please be discreet with the information that I'm giving you.'

Bob Foreman stiffened as he noted the serious intonation of the doctor's voice.

'We had a woman in here some time ago, she'd been involved in a bad RTA. I suspect it's the same woman.'

Bob's eyes widened. 'Why would you think that?'

'To cut explanations to a minimum, she had a head injury that left her with, well, an anomaly. She developed the ability to "see" energy forces around living things. Don't laugh, I know what you pragmatic coppers are like, but it is an accepted phenomenon, I promise you. Rare, but it does exist.'

Bob knew he was looking totally perplexed.

Barker laughed. 'Don't worry, I'm not going to lecture you on brain chemistry, but just know that we are not talking weirdos or freaks. I have the greatest respect for this lady, and so do my colleagues. There was an incident here before she left that defied explanation. She made a diagnosis on an infant, and suffice it to say, the child would have died without her intervention.'

'Like Liam! I know he wouldn't have died, but the scenario is the same!'

'Exactly. That's why I'm telling you this. I don't think it would be right, ethically, if I handed over her name and address to you, so, if you would be happy with this, I will contact her and explain that you would like to meet her. If I'm right, she will be wondering how your son is, and I will let her make the decision whether or not to contact you, okay?'

'Perfectly. That's wonderful news!' Bob rose and offered his hand to Jack. 'Thanks, and once again, I owe you one! Now, I'd better get some wheels in motion for DC Rawlings. I hope his operation goes well and things are as good as they can be for the poor devil; your help and care with him is much appreciated. He is a good officer.'

* * *

Alone in his Pig Pen, Jack Barker smiled to himself. He was pleased he had told the policeman about Ellie McEwan. After all, it couldn't hurt, could it?

* * *

Ellie had heard noises, both canine and human, coming from the kitchen. It was Sunday and her bed was comfortable with downy warmth. She moved slightly to try and make out the shadowy hands on the face of the clock. It was almost nine! Still, Carole had forbidden her to rise early during her convalescent stay at Snug Cottage, and this morning she was more than happy to comply with her reversed curfew. The plastered leg was for once in a position that it was happy with, moderately pain free and relaxed. Her head had stopped aching, and apart from the occasional unpleasant itch from the scar, Ellie McEwan was feeling good.

She allowed her sleepy mind to wander back to her trip out with Alice. It had been such a pleasant morning — a rare treat to spend time in an easy-going and stress-free manner. She recalled the regular hiatus caused by trying to run the business and juggle Steph and her unpredictable moods. Invariably, whatever they planned would be put off, altered, or cut short. It was usually her fault, she conceded, but Steph had known the score when they first met. She had been a dedicated career woman running a thriving business. There were no set hours in floristry. If the work was there, you did it, even if it was a huge funeral, ordered three minutes before closing time, and to be delivered by ten the next morning. Many times she had closed the shop and worked on, arranging flowers until one in the morning, then driven straight to Covent Garden market to do the buying. She would grab a bacon sandwich in the cafe and drive hurriedly back to Weybridge to try and see Steph before she left for work. It hadn't all been bad, of course. Steph had benefited from her labours in a variety of ways, mainly financially. Fleurie had some very influential customers, some from the world of commerce, others in show business, and those who were just plain, stinking rich. They all showed their appreciation in different ways — a bottle of champagne here, a healthy tip there, dinner at an exclusive restaurant one week, theatre tickets another. One client, a travel agent extraordinaire, Ellie still recalled with amazement, had sent her an all-expenses paid weekend for two in New York. Okay, so that was an exception, but Steph had been by her side as they did up their safety belts and prepared for take-off. At first, Steph had seemed quite content with their erratic existence, although words like peace, or calm, were never part of her vocabulary.

Wriggling further under her duvet, Ellie considered words that really summed up her time with Steph. Hectic, emotional, sexy, guilt-ridden and moody came to mind. Even given the fluctuating state of their relationship, she had been shocked and hurt when Steph left, with her weak excuse of searching for the real Steph, and her convenient omission of the fact that she was not going alone.

Ellie now considered adjectives to describe time spent in Alice's company.

With delight, she softly counted, comfortable, amusing, amicable, untroubled and sensual. No mention of romance or relationship had been broached by either side, but there was an unmistakable chemistry that begged for attention. It was almost an irrelevance as to whether anything ever came of it. The almost tangible, but unspoken, attraction was enjoyable enough in its own right.

Ellie experienced a pleasant quivering in the pit of her stomach when she relived the merest touch of her hand, or the affable closeness of Alice as she helped her into the car. It was satisfying just to feel attractive again — both physically and mentally.

Her rejection by Steph and the disfiguring accident had done little for her self-esteem. A huge helping of Dr Alice Cross was exactly what her ego required right now, whether a transient encounter or something more, she did not care. She would just sit back and bask in the attention for a while. One thing was for sure, if she found another woman, one who she really loved, then there would be no three-way split — her partner, herself and the business. It was time to let go.

Pulling her pillows up behind her and dragging her heavy plastered leg into a sitting position, she made the decision to ring her brother today and discuss the disposal of her beloved florist shop.

She must have drifted from thoughts to sleep, for when she next looked at the clock it was 9.45 a.m. and there were distinctive sounds and smells of Sunday breakfast permeating the air. Ellie got up.

Opening the door, she found Carole and Michael deep in a conversation that stopped abruptly as she entered the room.

Michael grinned and welcomed her with the news that they were just talking about her, and how pleased she must be to be getting rid of the leg plaster the following week.

Ellie, noticing some odd colours around Michael, decided that for some unapparent reason, he was lying, and her broken leg had not been the object of discussion at all. Suspecting it may have something to do with her liaison with Dr Cross, she decided to keep her own counsel, and ignore Michael's poor attempt at deception.

As she accepted her plate of eggs, bacon, fried bread and tomatoes from Carole, she privately marvelled at the natural way she was coming to terms and using her gift of auric sight. There had been no hesitation or dithering as she looked at Michael and his unnatural aura — she simply knew he was not telling the truth.

'Michael is staying on for a few more days. He wants to spend a bit more time with your tutelage.' Carole's voice lacked its usual robust timbre, and as Ellie smiled up at her, she saw the same odd lights around her friend. *That's not true, either!* Her thoughts spun. Michael might be staying on, but it had nothing to do with her instruction. What was going on? Carole's life lights were awful. A second glance showed her to be suffering head pains, and a general lethargy that reduced her aura by half. Surely Friday night's binge was not still to blame, unless it had set off some kind of migraine attack.

Ellie's bright start to the day was fading, her cheerfulness being darkened like a storm cloud drifting across the radiant smile of the sun. She felt, rather than saw, a despondency about Carole, and when she regarded Michael, there was a shadow of burden, a cloak of concern, draped about his shoulders. She was gripped by unease, and Michael's forced banter did nothing to alleviate her apprehension.

Carole ate little and spoke even less. At the end of the meal, she told them she would be walking over to Marie's, as she had been unable to contact her and was worried about her and her son. She would go the long route around the lane and via the post box. She indicated towards a pile of stamped envelopes lying on the dresser. 'I'll take the dogs and come back through the orchard. Why don't you two go out to the summer house for a while, it's a lovely morning and it would be peaceful out there.'

'Fine by me, but would you like a hand with the dogs first?' Michael looked at her enquiringly.

'No, we'll be fine. I won't be long, unless Marie needs anything. It must be a terrible time for the poor woman, and for Daniel, of course.'

Ellie and Michael nodded their agreement, but Carole's lacklustre intonation mystified Ellie, and she determined to buttonhole Michael as soon as they were alone together.

Ellie decided to telephone Phil before going out to the summer house. She had made a final decision about the shop, and promised herself to act immediately. It would be easy to procrastinate and let what could be a quick and reasonably painless exercise become a long and drawn-out soap opera. She knew that her brother would not try to change her mind. He knew her better than that, and would fully appreciate that she would not be letting their family business, the one she had sweated blood and tears over, go without very careful consideration.

He answered on the second ring, and after a few pleasantries, Ellie outlined her plans to sell Fleurie. Phil listened with interest, and afterwards admitted that he had been half expecting it. He immediately put on his professional hat, and verbalised his opinions on the business.

'Well, it's in fairly good shape, considering all the knocks small independent traders are taking with the multinationals and superstores these days. Gross profit margin has dropped a bit since you're not there in person, but that's to be expected. I'm not too sure of the best way to market it. You'll have to give me a bit of time on that one, Ellie, and you know you won't make a fortune out of this, don't you? A flower shop, even one as innovative as Fleurie won't fetch much, and the building itself is leasehold, so not the most lucrative situation. You know I will do my best but . . .'

Ellie stopped him. She was more than aware that she would not become Ivana Trump overnight, and with small businesses going to the wall daily, she'd be glad for whatever Phil could arrange. 'The house is paid for. I have that small legacy from Dad and Mum, same as you, Phil, and it's well invested. Once I've fully recovered, I'm sure my vocation will lie in a completely different direction. I won't starve, and if things get really tough, I will throw myself on the mercy of my darling brother!'

Phil laughed. 'I wouldn't wish that on my worst enemy! Right, I'll make some calls and see what I can do. I'd say come over, but I guess the leg is not good enough yet for my flight of stairs?'

'It won't be long. I'm seeing the surgeon this week, the plaster's coming off, and I can start working on getting mobile again. I promise to visit as soon as I'm fit.' Ellie's voice softened. 'How are you coping, Phil?'

There was a short silence, into which Ellie read, 'Not very well.'

'I'm fine, although Andrew's been acting a bit odd. Can't exactly explain what I mean, but he seems a bit distant, a bit subdued, it's probably nothing. Other than that, everything is hunky-dory. Your Peter is going great guns at the shop, he's taken to the buying like a duck to water. The staff will be gutted, you know that, don't you?'

'That is the downside of this transaction. I hate to do it to them, but hopefully the new buyers will recognise a good team when they see one and hang on to them. Whatever, when Fleurie finally closes, I will make a payment to each of them, by way of a thank you.'

'I would have expected nothing less of you, Sis! And by the way, well done, your decision could not have been an easy one.'

Ellie had a sudden flash of the little boy crying in the supermarket. 'Easier than you may think, Phil. I definitely have other things to do with my life now.'

She put down the phone with a feeling of lightness. A major change in her life had been confronted and was now underway. She thought about that boy and his policeman father, remembered the baby in Maternity, and realised that the signposts were pointing in a very new direction.

Her exhilaration from earlier was returning and she set off with renewed enthusiasm to pin Michael down and thoroughly grill him!

* * *

The sun shone brightly into the garden room and cast deep shadows across the corpulent professor's face. He looked sheepishly at Ellie and admitted that he had forgotten, or maybe underestimated, her gift. 'It's almost impossible to tell porkies to someone who can see auras, but I do wonder at the speed you're catching on to all of this. It's quite astounding.' He folded his arms over his bulbous belly and sat back in the rattan chair. 'You're perfectly correct that Carole is unwell. Migraine, of some sort, I would think, and her immune system is deficient too.'

'I can't help thinking there is more to it than that, Michael.'

'Maybe, but I'm sure she will say, if she wants us to know. She is a very private person when it comes to herself. How much do you really know about her history? Very little, I would guess?'

Nicely side-stepped, Michael, she thought. Then she listened to what he was saying.

'I've known Carole Cavendish-Meyer for many, many years and apart from her time with Vera, and the fact her only brother was killed in Africa, I know nothing about her, other than inconsequential chit-chat, stories of her world travels, and so on.'

Ellie picked on a frayed edge at the top of her plaster bandage. 'I've never thought about it before. Now you mention it, I don't know where she comes from, her actual age, or anything at all about her family, other than the fact that Granny was a witch and mother was a bitch! You're right, all I really know are gossipy things like . . . well, yes, travel stories, very good ones at that, and tales about other people, never herself.' She looked directly at Michael. 'How very odd. She has been the best friend anyone could have, and I didn't even realise that I don't know her at all. I certainly never knew about her brother. I didn't even know she had one!'

'A very private lady . . . a wonderful one, but very private.'

'I could not fault her as a friend, and I hate to see her looking so ill.'

'Hmm, me too,' agreed Michael. 'So, how did you meet her?'

Ellie told him about the delivery of flowers, then about her florist shop, which led into her very recent decision to sell the business.

Michael tilted his head and smiled thoughtfully. 'I thought maybe you would come to this sort of conclusion, sooner or later. So, would you please give this some thought . . . my clinic is humble, I have a small clientele of loyal patients, but that's because I have chosen to run it that way. Every day I turn people away. I never advertise, and the work still pours in. If, and only if, you ever wanted to, I would be proud to extend my clinic to include your particular field of diagnostic aura reading.' He spoke slowly, obviously trying to find the right words. 'There is no pressure, absolutely none. It's just a thought. You have such a talent, and I'm sure we would get on well enough to work together. Do think about it, Ellie.'

Ellie felt a rush of warmth for her friend, leaned forward, and clasped his hand in hers. 'I will certainly consider it, Michael, and thank you, I'm very honoured by your offer. I just need a little more time to get my head around all of this.' She beamed at him. 'And in the meantime, how about some schooling, there are some things I need to ask you . . .'

* * *

As Carole approached the neatly manicured garden to the Littlewood's house, her headache intensified to the point where she feared she may collapse with the pain. Tomorrow she would take an emergency appointment at the surgery. They always kept a few slots for urgent cases, and although it went very much against the grain, she was forced to capitulate to Michael's theory that there may be something wrong.

She leaned on the gate, her dogs gathered close at her feet and unnaturally quiet. The house was quite obviously empty and she was unsure whether she was relieved or disappointed by that fact. Her worry remained as to Daniel's fate, but at the same time she felt too sick to talk coherently. She advanced through the gate and sat heavily on a stone bench beneath Marie's lounge window. The walk home normally took her only six or seven minutes, but now the trip was taking on the proportions of a coast-to-coast marathon. A gentle paw laid itself on her knee and she looked down into the soulful eyes of Orlando, and on to the other dogs. Their intuition regarding their mistress's well-being bordered on supernatural. Carole never ceased to wonder at animals' intelligence and courage. She loathed it when humans who did inhuman things were referred to as animals. Animals would never behave in such an appalling manner.

She regarded her pack now, each one had deep concern flowing from limpid eyes. Their combined strength would get her home. She stood and took a shaky step forward, each pace accompanied by a deep painful breath. She closed the gate behind her and began her long journey to the orchard next door.

Halfway across the field that adjourned her property, she caught the sound of a car braking on gravel. Leaning heavily on the gnarled bark of an ancient apple tree, she could just make out the figure of Marie getting out of her Fiesta, closely followed by her son. She sighed. There was no way she could make it back until this pain lifted, but at least Daniel was safe home. Now it was up to her to do the same, but although the gables of her Snug Cottage were beckoning to her on the other side of the red brick wall, she seriously doubted her ability to reach them.

* * *

Michael, who was returning to the house for a textbook on colour resonance, glanced up when he heard a sharp yelp from one of Carole's dogs. The little spaniel came racing around the arch to the orchard, barking urgently. Michael then heard the other dogs take up the call, and as he peered through the aperture to see what was happening, he saw the slumped figure of his friend. She looked like a ragged heap of wool and tweed, discarded in the long grass among the fruit trees, with a protective cluster of dogs surrounding her.

Her furry guard broke ranks as he raced to the stricken woman and fell on his knees beside her. She was not unconscious — the pains in her head had simply been too much to bear. Michael gently helped her up, and, draping her arm over his shoulder, half carried, half dragged her back to the house.

He took her straight to her room, helped her off with her outdoor clothing and carefully laid her on the bed. Wrapping the duvet around her, for the second time in three days, he was swamped by the feeling of déjà vu.

He pulled the curtains and left the room. In the hall, he called the emergency MediDoc number that he found on the flyleaf of Carole's address book. He knew she would be furious with him, but he felt it totally preferable to face a healthy Meyer wrath, rather than risk her life by procrastinating.

After a few moments the doctor himself rang back, and when Michael described the severity of the pain, he promised to make Snug Cottage his next port of call. After swiftly checking on Carole, Michael puffed his way out to the summer house where Ellie, her nose buried in one of his books, was blissfully ignorant of the drama in the orchard.

They sat with Carole until the locum arrived, when they slipped out to allow the doctor to examine his patient.

Michael considered his options and decided to face a double dose of Carole's anger, and tell Ellie the truth. He then reconsidered, opting for a diluted and slightly amended version of the facts.

With a suitably shamefaced expression, he confronted his younger friend with his watered-down account of Friday night. He was careful to avoid lies as he now realised that fooling Ellie was not a possibility.

He told her that, although they had been drinking, they had decided to contact Vera, that he had fallen into a very deep meditation and was unaware that Carole was in trouble until it was nearly too late. He believed her violent headaches were an aftermath of taking a wrong path while under the influence of alcohol and falling into some sort of stupor.

He sighed and admitted they had been unbelievably stupid, but people did the most foolhardy things when they drank too much. He shook his head despondently and thought to himself that he'd told no proper lies. He had simply omitted to tell the reason for Carole's walk on the dark side.

Ellie made no comment but sat staring distantly out of the casement window. After some time, she looked intently at Michael and asked, 'What do you mean by the wrong path?'

'I think an entity, something bad, was waiting for her. She strayed from the light, the protection of her sanctuary and, who is to say what was out there.'

Ellie's jaw jutted forward in a disbelieving manner. 'Carole is a stickler for precision. That would not be her way. She is too respectful of all things esoteric. And you, Michael . . .' her voice was not accusatory, she was just repudiating a situation that she found totally out of character '. . . I have been working with you for a week now, and I have nothing but admiration for you, for your morals and your ethics. You honestly expect me to believe that the two of you behaved like a couple of inebriated college kids, climbing the bell tower to hang a pair of Matron's knickers on the flagpole!'

'You saw the state of us the next day. I am ashamed to say that your analogy is actually quite good.'

'I cannot believe that Carole would undertake anything without being completely protected . . . it would have to be a life-or-death situation to tempt her beyond the light.'

Michael desperately hoped that Ellie had not noticed the flashes of alarm that must have leaped from his body at that innocently profound statement. Looking in her direction, he breathed a small sigh of relief as he saw her, once again, staring through the window and into either the garden, or empty space.

The sound of a door opening brought them both back to the present. The doctor was an elderly man, probably close to retirement. He had weather-ravaged, leathery skin that spoke of years in the tropics. His permanent tan seemed out of place with the heavy flannel trousers and thermal fleece. 'Can I have a word? Are you relatives of Mrs Meyer?'

Michael indicated towards the kitchen and offered the doctor a chair.

'I can't stay long, but I will sit for a minute, we are so busy this weekend, I'm exhausted!' He lowered himself gratefully onto the pine seat and completed a half-written note on a MediDoc pad.

'So . . . relatives?'

'We are close friends, doctor. Mrs Meyer has no relatives that we are aware of. Whatever she needs, we are happy to help.' Michael regarded the doctor with an anxious expression. 'How is she?'

'I am writing her up for some much stronger painkillers, if you could collect them for her tomorrow. I have given her enough for today and to get her through the night. She says she had bad migraines as a teenager, but I do not feel quite comfortable attributing such intense head pains to a reoccurrence of a historical event.'

Michael tried unsuccessfully to imagine Carole as a teenager. Try as he might, Carole was Carole, frozen in time. Surely, she had always been on the far side of middle-age, grizzly grey, imposing, intimidating, possessing of that sardonic wit and a brain, both enquiring and academic enough to encompass countless subjects, scholarly and mystical.

The doctor was rubbing his chin with one hand and still scribbling, in a spider-like and unidentifiable scrawl, with the other. 'The problem is, her insistence on not going to hospital. I would like to call an ambulance and get her in for tests, an EEG, in particular. I have to say, I have rarely met a woman who is in such obvious agony be quite so emphatic in refusing treatment. I cannot make her go, but I strongly advise that you keep a very close eye on her, and if you notice any change for the worse in her condition, that you dial 999 immediately and get her to hospital. I will leave a message for her own GP, Dr Littlewood, to call on her in the morning. Pity, he is on call with me this weekend, but he was already out on another visit. Perhaps, as her next-door neighbour, he can talk some sense into her, whereas I as a doctor, cannot! I will leave you a covering note. Should an emergency arise, give it to the ambulance crew. It should speed up her admission through casualty. Keep her quiet, although I doubt she will have the energy to do anything else other than sleep and, as I said, be vigilant. Although she seems free of most of the symptoms — her speech is fine, if somewhat caustic, no weakness or paralysis of either side of her body — but even so, I'm not ruling out a cerebral haemorrhage. An EEG is imperative for a correct diagnosis, and I urge you to exercise any influence you might have over your friend to encourage her to go to hospital without delay!'

He placed the promised letter, sealed in a manilla envelope, on the table, touched an imaginary cap to Ellie, and left.

A silence fell over the couple as they allowed the doctor's words to sink in.

'We'd better go and see her.' Ellie limped slowly to the door. 'This seems to extend beyond her usual bloody-mindedness, don't you think, Michael?'

Michael left the question floating. He did not answer but walked slowly behind her up the stairs to the bedroom.

Carole, a shadowy mound in the depths of her duvet, slept silently. They sat for a while, like watchers of the dead. Later, when they felt satisfied that her breathing was regular, and her drug-induced slumber had enveloped her sufficiently, they rose as one and left their dormant companion in the arms of Morpheus.

* * *

In the same room, but in a different realm, Carole drifted, searching and calling for her friend. A familiar fragrance spiralled fleetingly through her senses. She was tantalisingly close, but as yet, unseen. She whispered her name, and over and over, voiced her anguish, 'I'm sorry, so sorry. I didn't listen. Vera? Can you hear me? So very sorry.'

In the perfumed air, she caught the faintest of murmurs. The sigh of silk on silk. 'Oh, my love. What has he done to you?'

And as the fragrance faded, the gentlest lament. '. . . too strong . . . I was too late.'

* * *

It was two o'clock, neither Ellie nor Michael had eaten, but they were not hungry. They needed to be away from the oppressive atmosphere of the warm house, so they stood out in the courtyard and breathed in the cold, fresh air. The sun still shone and some brave blooms were unfolding their glorious colours in celebration of the impending spring.

Michael, hands thrust deeply into his trouser pockets, expressed his belief that they should take turns to watch her throughout the night. Ellie agreed and slipped her own hand through Michael's arm, linking them in their concern. Looking gravely into his anxious face, Ellie smiled wanly.

'Time to tell me what's going on, my friend . . . all of it this time.'

CHAPTER TWENTY-TWO

As Vic Barratt eased his navy Mondeo into the space between the conifer hedge and the Winnebago, tiredness caught up with him. A wave of total exhaustion washed over him in a sick tide. *Sleep, all I want. Sleep.*

The case was getting to him. His mind stayed with it, on and off duty. He should, after all his years in the service, be able to put it on the back burner when he got home. He should be able to play football with his son without visions of dead women lying between the goal posts. He should be totally engrossed in his daughter, as she excitedly described her last pony ride. He should not allow her happy piping to be drowned out by forensic reports.

But he could not. It lurked in part of his mind, every minute of every hour of every day, waiting to jump up and take precedence over all else.

As he turned the key in the lock and pushed the front door open, he felt a pang of guilt at his relief in his wife and children's absence. He loved them fiercely. He had fought for his kids. Literally. Everyone had said it would be a doddle. The fact that they desperately wanted mixed-race children should make adopting straightforward, but it had been far from easy. If Barbara could have had kids with him, then they would certainly have been mixed race, so that is what they set their hearts on. Two children that could have been naturally theirs. Then the nightmare began.

As he wearily hung up his jacket, his eyes fell upon the artist's copy of a photograph he had taken last year of Hannah and Matthew. The beauty they portrayed had nothing to do with fancy lenses or clever brushstrokes; it was that natural loveliness that belongs specifically to the child.

He smiled at his two angels and muttered an apology for his delight that they were elsewhere today.

Below the picture on the hall table was a letter. Barbara had left it for him to open. She had most likely recognised the copperplate script of his father. He groaned and left the envelope untouched. He knew what it would contain and was far too tired to contemplate wading through one of his parent's epistles.

The house was unnaturally silent, and although desperately tired, he was forced to put a radio on low, to combat the disturbing, childless stillness that had settled on his family home. He pulled the curtains against the daylight and stripped to his underpants. He wanted a shower. No, in truth, he needed a shower, but his eyelids were made of lead, and deep, dreamless sleep was all he craved.

He let himself drop onto the bed, and as his head nestled into the clean, fresh smelling pillowcase, he heard himself promise the world that they would get him. They would nail the bastard.

* * *

Jonathan Leatham was staying with a barrister friend in Hook Heath for the duration of the murder case. It made sense to be nearer while on secondment to DCI Foreman. He could have stayed, temporarily, in the section house of course, but his days of mucking in with twenty other sweaty-footed bobbies were well past. His sensibilities preferred the landscaped garden and the self-contained annexe provided by his old university mate.

He was in a pensive mood now, as his eyes took in the stately cedar of Lebanon that ruled majestically over the rest of the estate. He sat on deep, plush cushions on the four-seater sofa, strategically placed in the bay window to give the best view of the lawns and beds, the gazebo, and the folly. Gregson had done well for himself, a bit of family money, a good job, and a rich wife. What's not to like? He glanced briefly at the paintings, hung carefully to make the most of the natural light. All originals, not masterpieces, but still expensive. *And this is the annexe*, he thought with amusement. His own bachelor studio flat was by no means a garret, but Gregson Halliday's residence made it suddenly seem that way.

He rose and strode purposefully into the kitchen. He had earned himself a beer. Pulling the ring, he carefully angled the red-and-yellow can away from him and took delight in the hiss of gas that burst from the container. He returned to his carefully tailored botanical panorama, sipped the cold beer, and considered the murders.

In his mind, he reconstructed the white storyboards on the incident room walls. There were three of them. One for each victim. Each board held the history of a woman's life, and the manner of her untimely death, in an area six feet by four feet. Not exactly an auspicious biography for three such talented ladies.

He sighed at the pitiful waste. Sipping more beer, he felt a sleepiness creep through his veins. Jonathan was lucky; he knew a couple of hours solid sleep would rejuvenate him for another sixteen-hour stint. He carried his beer through to the en-suite bedroom, kicked off his shoes and pulled the counterpane down to reveal deep-purple silk bedding. He carefully folded his clothes and selected clean underwear from his neatly packed case. He showered slowly, luxuriating in the hot water running over his aching body, and after towelling his hair practically dry, slipped into the silken bedding. Taking deep relaxing breaths, he wondered what the connection was. The killer had to have known or met all three women. He knew their particular talents. But how?

As he drifted off to sleep, he decided he would get the team to double check all possibilities of a connection with the three victims. It was there somewhere, and damn it, he would find it.

* * *

DCI Foreman groaned as he saw the stack of folders, files, reports, memos, and nasty scrappy bits of paper on his desk. He vaguely wondered how anyone had found space for them — it had been loaded with paperwork even before he left for the hospital. He had waited until Rawlings was out of theatre and settled in the high dependency unit. Bob had spoken with his surgeon and spent time with his officer's distraught wife before he felt able to get back to the station. It did not appear that the young policeman had been targeted for any reason. There were witnesses who described an elderly person in a big old silver Ford, whose driving was less than exemplary. One witness thought that they might not have even realised it was a person they hit, and had driven off myopically, to avoid taking the blame for some damaged property.

It would be easy to trace, but that would not help Rawlings or the murder inquiry.

Bob tried to create some form of order to his shambolic desk. Everything he touched seemed to cry out to be dealt with first. Everything was important and it all needed his undivided attention. He admired those organised souls who could categorise their work, and steadfastly plough through until all tasks were complete. His own pathetic attempts at organisation left him in a worse state than before.

Finally, he piled everything onto the floor next to his chair, and proudly examined the scratched and stained empty surface in front of him.

He then sat back and reached down, taking one article at a time, reading it carefully, marking it for filing or for action, and moving on to the next. He wanted a coffee but knew it would just be delaying tactics if he got up and left the office.

He sat, working uninterrupted for an hour and a half, when his hand fell upon a yellow folder marked with his name and a large red URGENT sticker.

At his request, forensics had run some further tests to try and narrow down what had been used to bludgeon the victims. The report stated that, without doubt, the women had been hit ferociously with a piece of scaffolding pole. The same implement was then held, with great pressure, across their windpipes until they died. Tiny traces of the base metal used in the construction of scaffolding, along with sand and cement, and small deposits of blood other than the victim's, had been embedded into the damaged tissues of each woman's neck, with the exception of Melissa Crabbe, the first to die. No blood other than her own was found with the metal traces and the cement. Magnifications of the injury sites all matched, indicating that the same piece of metal was used in all three cases. For all the killer's care in keeping the scene of crime clear of evidence, he did not even bother to wipe the murder weapon before using it on his next victim. Perhaps the mingling of the blood was significant.

Bob made a note to contact Amanda on that score plus she would need to take a look at their suspects, if either of them proved able to be questioned.

'Can I get you a coffee, sir?' Corbett hung round the door and raised his eyebrows at the accumulation of paperwork that surrounded his chief. 'Blimey! Rather you than me, sir! I take it it's a "yes" to the coffee, then!' He ducked out of view and returned a few minutes later with a tray carrying two large mugs, two sugary doughnuts, and several bars of chocolate.

'Sustenance, sir. Looks like you could do with it, tackling that lot.' He pointed to the heap of reports that did not seem to decrease, no matter how hard Foreman worked on them.

'You're a diamond, Corbett.' He brushed sugar from a typed record referring to Melissa Crabbe's musical career. 'Any more from Fletcher?'

'Not from him. Windsor has just brought in the list of jobs that Fletcher may have been involved with. The company they use, called 'Konstrukt', uses a pretty dodgy database of self-employed and moonlighting sub-contractors. Even their office is not too sure who does what; their books are dubious, to say the least. It is highly likely he was at the hotel at the same time as Adele Turner. A couple of employees recall Fletcher, those tattoos are a bit of a giveaway, but no one seems to remember him having anything to do with Turner. He swears he never saw or heard about her. Said he did his job and buggered off — he didn't hang around the hotel at all.'

'Probably true. I wouldn't want a specimen like that gracing my upper-class establishment any more than he had to!'

'I'll push him a bit further about the hotel but I don't think I'll get much more from him. By the way, sir, any more news on Rawlings? We got your message about getting through the op all right. Sounded nasty.'

'Poor devil was in the wrong place at the wrong time, it seems. He won't be back for quite a while. I've asked Welfare to speak to his wife, see if she needs any help and we'll send a "get-well" something to the hospital when he's feeling a little better. Is DI Leatham around, Barry?'

'No, sir, both he and Vic Barratt have gone home for a break. They were here all night.'

'How about you, have you managed to get a rest?'

'I'm fine. I caught up last night, while I was waiting for Fletcher to sober up. Speaking of smelly Fletcher, I better get back to him, sir. Best of luck!' Corbett left with a last glance at Foreman's never-ending paperwork.

Before toiling on, Bob allowed himself a moment or two to reflect on his conversation with Jack Barker at the hospital . . . at least he might hear from the woman with the broken leg in the next day or so. The consultant's story had sounded a bit wacky to him but, as he had not come up with a better explanation himself, he decided to keep an open mind until he met her.

Draining the mug to the bitter dregs, and finding no more chocolate on the tray to distract him further, Bob Foreman leaned down, and with a despondent exhalation, lifted the next document from the pile.

* * *

Carole drifted from deep and peaceful sleep to restless and disturbed half-slumbers. Her friends had heard some whispered words and a few mumbled but unintelligible sentences. Other than that, she had not woken fully enough to talk to them.

Ellie sat, her injured leg resting on a pile of pillows balanced on a foot- stool, and watched the darkened outline of her friend, huddled in sleep. She was not proud of the way she had extracted the strange and thought-provoking story from Michael. She realised he was only trying to protect her. Endeavouring not to frighten her and trying to avoid breaking the promise he had made to Carole, which was to keep Ellie unaware of the possible dangers that surrounded her. She had made him break that oath and tell her everything. She had stated that Carole's serious health problem negated the need for concealment. They, Michael and herself, would have to work hard together to help Carole, and they could not do that if Ellie was only in possession of part of the plot. She had dug and delved, poked and prodded, used guile and craftiness, had pleaded and cajoled.

Now she sat in a dim room, with all the information she had demanded, broiling around in her head.

She shifted, trying to make as little noise as possible, and sank back against the hard wooden slats of her chair. There was no doubt in her mind that ignorance was bliss, but it was too late for that now. She would need time to assimilate the strange and unbelievable happenings that Michael had haltingly revealed. She just hoped she would be allowed that valuable commodity, and staring at the fallen Colossus in the bed beside her, she was not at all sure about anything.

Behind her, the door opened a crack and Michael whispered her name. As quietly as she could manage with the crutches, she inched her way out of the room.

Michael asked how the patient was, and on hearing that she still slept, asked Ellie to come to the kitchen for a while. He had taken the dogs out for a walk and had returned with a hollow, rumbling stomach, reminding him that they had not eaten since breakfast. On the table was a small cold collation that he had prepared. He urged her to eat and she soon found herself enthusiastically tucking into the ham and cheese as if she were starved. He had made huge mugs of tea, and after passing her one, he fished in his trouser pocket and produced a small scrap of white paper on which was written a name and number.

'There was a message on the ansaphone when I got back with the animals. A call for you from the Royal Surrey Hospital.'

Ellie noted Jack Barker's name and looked questioningly at Michael. 'On a Sunday? That's a bit odd. I wonder what he wants.'

'The message just said to give him a ring in A&E, when you have time. He is there all day today.'

Michael seemed subdued, and Ellie wanted to hug him and tell him that he must not feel bad about speaking out, but looking at him she realised he needed to make that conclusion on his own.

She finished her food and put the plate in the dishwasher. 'If you'd sit with Carole for a while, I'll ring the hospital and see what Jack wants, then perhaps I'll light the fire in the lounge. It's getting chilly.'

'Give me a call when you're off the phone, and if Carole is still sleeping, I'll give you a hand. I know it's not easy doing anything practical on those crutches.'

'Not for much longer, only four more days and let's hope it's healed as well as the surgeon thinks it will.'

Michael gave her a small smile and trudged back upstairs to continue his vigil.

Jack Barker expressed his pleasure that she had returned his call and launched into the tale of his meeting with the detective chief inspector.

Ellie confirmed that she was his 'mystery woman'. She was relieved he had gone to the hospital with the boy, and even more delighted that it was Jack who attended to the little lad. She had no problem with speaking to the policeman, although she privately wondered what such a down-to-earth man would make of her unusual ability. Jack passed on the man's mobile number and Ellie promised to visit the department after her appointment on Thursday. Wishing him well, she ended the call, and sat for a moment, tentatively considering whether she was up to this next call. Her head was still spinning from the earlier revelations.

Plucking the receiver from its rest, she decided to get it over with; after all, a few minutes polite chat, and it would be dealt with.

She recognised the deep tone of his voice from the television report on the murders. He declared his surprise at her ringing him so promptly and immediately suggested they meet. Ellie had not been expecting that and was completely caught off guard. Before she knew how it had happened, they had arranged for him to send a car for her at three o'clock the next day, to take her to his police station for coffee and a chat. The DCI was so effusive about seeing her that he would not take no for an answer, and when she hung up the telephone, her mind was in turmoil. Her brain felt addled, and when she told Michael how she had agreed without even giving Carole, or him, a single thought, he laughed out loud.

'Now you know how I felt after your interrogation!'

They grinned at each other sheepishly and Michael assured her, that so long as Carole had not taken a turn for the worst, he would be fine while Ellie made her trip to the nick!

He returned to check on their friend, and Ellie sat in the lounge, twisting newspaper into knots to make a base for the fire. She managed, with great difficulty, to finish placing the kindling and coal in the grate, but before she could light it, she heard Michael call. She got up the stairs as quickly as her leg would allow, pulling herself up by the sturdy old banister.

She hobbled into the bedroom and, to her astonishment, found Carole sitting up and demanding food. Michael sat on the edge of the bed and gripped her hands tightly in his.

'How's the pain, old girl? My God, but you gave us a nasty shock there!'

'The pain is awful,' she croaked, 'but those bloody tablets are a damned sight worse, for heaven's sake. Michael, stop hanging on to my hand like a love-struck sissy, and get me some toast!'

Ellie was a mass of mixed emotions — she did not know whether to laugh or cry. So she opted for both.

'Good Lord, whatever is the matter with the pair of you? Haven't you ever seen a migraine before?' Assuring the girl that she would be right as rain in the morning and did not know what all the fuss was about, Carole sank back into her pillows and wanted to know why on earth Michael was taking so long with her food.

Shaking her head in amazement, Ellie almost believed the bit about the migraine.

CHAPTER TWENTY-THREE

She knew that she should always work on fact. WDC Wendy Brown had no room for the fanciful and there was no earthly reason why she should feel such unsubstantiated concern for her witness.

She rubbed absent-mindedly at a tiny ink stain on the cuff of her white shirt, and pondered over Mary Probart. The girl had been terrified, with good reason. She had stumbled across a murderer with his victim. She had spoken to him, for God's sake.

For all her demonstrations with the torch in the dark room, Wendy was not at all convinced in her heart that the murderer would not go after Mary. She was as safe as she could be, without proper protection. Wendy had made it more than clear to both Mary and Francoise that her presence in Hersham should remain a closely guarded secret. They must tell no one. The local beat bobbies were keeping a low-key watch on the house, as and when their duties allowed, and Wendy herself had paid one visit, in order to ease her mind on Mary's safety. But was it enough?

She picked up the post-mortem report on Adele Turner and read it for the third time. She was struck by the closeness of the estimated time of death, and Mary's nocturnal stroll past the tennis courts. The report stated that Adele Turner had been killed not later than ten o'clock.

She flicked through her notebook and stabbed her finger on the notes she had made on the night of the murder. Mary Probart left her room on the stroke of ten, hoping to get a drink before closing time.

An unpleasant scenario played itself out in her head.

The killer attacks Turner. His location, so close to the hotel entrance, and only feet away from an occasionally used pathway, are far from ideal. He hurries his work. Then he hears the main door close. Wendy recalled a grating noise and a heavy thumping sound as it shut behind her. His victim, by now dead or dying, is lying in the shrubbery at his feet. He peers through the bushes and sees Mary Probart approaching the path to the tennis courts. He has not got the time to conceal the body so . . . Oh God, he picks her up and drapes her around him in the semblance of an embrace! The bags and Adele's jacket are where he left them, no time to hide them and if they had really been kissing then they would put their bags down anyway.

Wendy felt a slight nausea rise in her throat.

She looked across to Hudson, a few desks away and typing furiously with two fingers, and called for him to give an opinion on her theory.

'I think you've got something there, Wen!' The young DC puffed out his cheeks in amazement. 'Cool as a fucking cucumber! She was already dead when Probart thought she caught them snogging! Bloody hell!'

'Something else is bothering me, Hud. Will you come with me to the hotel? There is a little experiment I need to try out.'

Ten minutes later the squad car drew up in the hotel car park. The two officers could see the tarpaulin and the blue-and-white tape still in position. They showed their ID to the PC on duty and Hudson took his place just behind the bushes that flanked the path.

Wendy walked over to the main reception door and went inside. A few moments later she reappeared, stood for a second on the top of the steps, looked around her and then made her way towards Hudson. She walked briskly, but did not run. She met her colleague at the scene of the crime and studied him expectantly.

'Yep! I think you have it right. I realise it is daylight now, but the whole entrance is floodlit until midnight. From here in the shrubs I could clearly identify you, and just have time, if I kept a cool head, to lift the woman's body and hold it there until Mary had crossed the main gravel driveway, walked along beside the wall and the grass, to this point here.'

'You realise that means our killer, not only heard Mary's very distinctive Geordie accent, but had a bloody good look at her as she left the hotel!'

'Shit! Let's pick her up!'

The journey to Hersham took six minutes and the door was answered immediately by a smiling Francoise. Her smile faded when she noticed the concern on the two officers' faces.

'But she phoned me at work, this morning, just a short call, the company does not like personal calls. She said she'd had a visitor and was popping out for an hour. I wasn't to worry about her, she was quite safe, she knew him. I have only now come home from my shift, and when I see she is not back, I think maybe she feels safer with this person than alone here. I think she will return when she knows I am home.'

'Are you sure she did not say anything about the man she went off with?'

'Absolutement!' Francoise reverted to her native tongue in her distress. 'She sounded perfectly normal. I had no reason to feel the concerns about Mary!'

'You've got our numbers. If Mary returns, ring us immediately. And let no one in. No one at all. If Mary comes back, keep her here, and we'll pick her up. I'll arrange for an officer to keep an eye on the house tonight as well. Just ring us, okay?'

Francoise nodded. 'Poor Mary, poor, poor Mary!'

Hudson radioed in as Brown drove back to the station. A description of Mary Probart was issued and a full-scale hunt for the girl was organised.

DCI Foreman seemed bigger and greyer than ever.

He praised Brown for her work, but sat smashing one meaty fist into the other cupped hand, swearing repeatedly. 'If it's him, and not Mary being stupid and running off with a boyfriend without telling us, the bastard either knows her very well, and the addresses of her close friends, or he's been following us. You, in particular, Brown. He may have watched you when you went to get her things from the hotel and organise her some temporary leave. She was in the car with you, wasn't she? On the day after the murder, when you took her to Hersham?'

'Yes, sir. She went up to her room with me and we collected some clothes and toiletries. I left her locked in the car when I spoke to that Featherstone chap, as she said she couldn't face him herself. Then we drove straight to Francoise Lascelles's flat in Hersham.'

'Which makes the Waters Meet Hotel the place we should be concentrating on. Take that place apart! Hudson, I want the staff records double and triple checked. Someone was watching Brown, with Probart in the car, so the hotel is the obvious place to start. Brown, have a word with Mac and get some uniform to help you. I want a door to door in the Lascelles woman's road and the surrounding area. He has put himself out in the open this time, someone must have seen them together. Get to it!'

Vic Barratt and Jonathan Leatham arrived at the same time, both having received emergency calls to ruin their slumber. Leatham got straight on to the Littlewoods to make sure that Daniel was where he should be. To his chagrin, he was told by a tearful Marie, that although he was there now, he had wandered off for a couple of hours earlier and she had no idea where he had been. Jonathan grabbed Vic and they tore off at breakneck speed to Compton. It would have been difficult to get to Hersham and back in two hours, but not impossible. He timed their trip from the station, just to be sure. Doctor or no doctor, he would interview the man this time, whether he liked it or not.

* * *

As the shadows deepened, and evening closed curtains and blinds across Surrey, DCI Foreman's mood adopted a dismal greyness that was a match for the night sky.

The murder room buzzed with life. Computer printers chattered and spat paper into plastic trays. Telephones rang, buzzed, and played ridiculous tunes. Voices from all over the huge office joined in a cacophony of meaningless babble.

Bob regarded the room silently and realised that every single person and piece of machinery was doing the same job. Looking for one girl and one man. A victim and a murderer.

The computers were running constant checks, sifting through thousands of pieces of information that had been fed into them. Searching constantly for links, for connections, not only data specifically pertaining to the three murders here, but to other crimes and other deaths.

Bob considered Mary Probart. Who had she naively opened the door to? Whoever he was, he certainly had not been wearing a long dark coat this time, or she would have run a mile! She had said, quite confidently, that she knew him. Francoise had picked up no fear in her voice. The French girl was positive that she was not being forced to say something under threat. A friend? A deadly friend?

The big man, his square shoulders slightly hunched, returned to his office and put through a call to Rosie. It would be . . . Kiss the kids for me, big hug, see you when I can, love you, babe. How many times had they repeated that mantra? He smiled sadly. The answer was simple, as many times as there were murderers on the streets, rapists stalking innocents, terrorists planning their own brand of insidious horror, arsonists with matches burning holes in their pockets and thugs mauling ninety-year-olds for their pension book. As many times as he had taken up the sword against the evil that threatened property and life, and therefore threatened Rosie and the children, and every other honest person's family and loved ones. All the while there was a Mary Probart, a Melissa Crabbe, a Helen Carberry, or an Adele Turner, he would gladly repeat the mantra.

His resolution fortified and his shoulders once again squared against the world, he strode back outside and demanded updates.

* * *

In the warm confines of her bedroom in Snug Cottage, Carole sipped cold water and swallowed the two blue-and-white capsules the doctor had left for her. The pains were easier but she wanted to get through the night without waking in agony. She knew that she had been the virago from hell to that poor man. He had a very valid point in saying that she needed hospital care. No one knew that better than she, but she also knew that she could not, would not, leave Ellie. So, she had played the dragon and bought a little more time. She would have to leave her soon, albeit only for a day, but as soon as the headaches were under control, she must get to Lincolnshire, and Messrs Brothertoft and Singleton (dec'd).

She was sensible enough to realise that driving the three-hundred-mile round trip in her present state was not a possibility, but help had come from an unusual source.

She had told Michael and Ellie of her being summoned to Boston as soon as possible, and her dilemma apropos getting there. Ellie had disappeared into her room and returned wearing a Cheshire cat grin. Carole recalled their conversation.

'Sorted! I've just spoken to Phil and he has offered you his Saab, complete with Andrew as chauffeur. Any day next week to suit you.'

'Your brother does have a habit of saving the day, doesn't he? I will gladly accept his kind offer. We will go directly this migraine has subsided enough to travel without too much discomfort. Maybe Tuesday?'

'Phil has asked for a small favour in return. He feels that Andrew is not very happy just now, nothing specific, but he seems rather preoccupied. Phil wondered if you could draw him out a bit on the journey. He might just say something in a casual conversation, out of his boss's earshot? You know how valuable Andrew is to Phil, with his myriad problems. He would hate to lose him if it could be avoided.'

'I'll do my best, although chit-chat is not exactly my forte.'

As she lay in the quiet room with the ghost of a pain swirling around her head, she remembered Pauline's tasty geezer with the sharp suit, and placed a wager with herself that it would be woman troubles of one kind or another.

* * *

Downstairs, the professor and his student discussed Carole Cavendish-Meyer's 'migraine'. The fire crackled loudly, and a glowing spark spat viciously from the grate and onto the fireside rug. Michael grabbed at it swiftly and threw it back into the flames, licking his scorched fingers.

'I suggest that tomorrow, in the cold light of day, Ellie, you look at our friend in a diagnostic manner. The doctor said an EEG is the only test to see what is wrong. I think you can do as well, or maybe better, if you try.'

'I did find myself trying to analyse her earlier, but everything was in such a fever, I couldn't concentrate properly. I only saw her pain.'

'That's understandable. Things should be calmer tomorrow. Try again and tell me what you see.' Michael got up and went to the writing desk in the bay, where he picked up a heavy looking bag. 'This is for you. It is probably not the kind of bedtime reading that a flower lady would have, so I bought you a copy for your new work.'

He handed the shiny carrier bag to Ellie and she gently pulled out a shrink-wrapped volume of *Tortora's Atlas of the*

Muscular and Skeletal System. 'There will be times when you will see particular areas of pain or injury that you are unsure about, it will be essential you learn the design of the human body. This will help.'

Ellie felt a tug somewhere in the region of her heart. She was truly on her new path now, and certain there would be help for her every step of the way. Pulling herself unsteadily to her feet, she gave Michael an unreserved hug of thanks, kissed his beard lightly, and returned to enthusiastically remove the book from its protective cover.

Somewhere out in the dark evening, she heard a siren wail and tried to determine whether it was the police, fire or ambulance. Coming to no conclusion, she returned wholeheartedly to her textbook.

* * *

Hastily pulling the curtains could not keep them out, and pretending she had not heard the doorbell didn't seem like a very good idea. With a heavy heart, Marie Littlewood opened the old oak door to DI Leatham and Sergeant Barratt.

Jonathan Leatham seemed sincerely sorry when he insisted that they speak with Daniel. Marie led the two officers down a wood-panelled corridor and into what Vic Barratt would have described as a den. It was a fairly small, almost claustrophobic room, overstuffed with heavy old furniture, gilt-framed pictures, bookshelves and house plants.

In an elderly winged armchair, facing the window and staring, with eyes fixed on infinity, sat Daniel Littlewood.

'Sir, we are sorry to bother you again. You will probably remember that I am Detective Inspector Leatham and this is Detective Sergeant Barratt?' Jonathan waited for a reply but Daniel was unforthcoming, and remained, still as a statue, before the window.

'We are making enquiries about the disappearance of a young woman. Mary Probart?' He paused again. 'Do you know Mary Probart, Daniel? Can you tell me where you were today between the hours of twelve o'clock and three?'

Slowly Daniel turned, and transferred his unfocused stare to Vic. His face was gaunt and Jonathan thought he had the saddest eyes he had ever seen.

'Where were you, Mr Littlewood?'

'Nowhere.'

His voice was without emotion. Jonathan could not believe that a couple of Valium were responsible for this, but they needed answers. 'Daniel, we know you were not here, so where were you?'

'I don't know.'

'Why don't you know?'

Silence.

'I am now going to ask you where you were on the nights of . . .' Sergeant Vic Barratt listed the dates and times of the deaths of the three murder victims.

The man shook his head forlornly, and lifted his shoulders in a painfully slow shrug. He still said nothing.

Vic looked across at Jonathan, his enquiring expression requiring no articulation. Jonathan nodded imperceptibly.

'Daniel Littlewood. As you are unable to furnish us with satisfactory information regarding your whereabouts on the nights in question, I am arresting you on suspicion of murder, and in connection with the disappearance of Mary Probart. I must caution you that you do not have to say anything. But it may harm your defence if you do not mention when questioned . . .'

Jonathan recorded the time and date of the caution in his pocketbook and held out his hand towards Daniel. For one moment, no one moved. The detective inspector saw his own hand frozen in front of him. Saw Vic's head tilted to one side, his lips slightly apart, waiting. In his peripheral vision he saw Marie, fixed in the doorway, both hands over her open mouth in a silent scream.

And Daniel . . . Daniel looked like he belonged in the Great Hall of Madame Tussauds. Jonathan was reminded of a glass case that had stood in the biology lab at school. He could remember standing in front of it, trying to make the long dead ferret move. Just the twitch of an eyelid, the ripple of a muscle, the tiniest hint of a heartbeat . . . but it had never come. The needle-sharp teeth had remained ready to tear and shred whatever the glassy, beady eyes held in their hypnotic stare. As far as he knew, although now probably motheaten and worn, the ferret still sat in its glass case and mesmerised small boys.

Marie's stifled gasp broke the tableau. Jonathan moved closer to Daniel and gently escorted him from the room. He thought it would serve no purpose, other than to cause the mother further distress, to use restraint. The fight had gone out of the man and he put up no resistance to his arrest.

Before driving away, the sergeant told Marie that they were taking him back to the station and suggested, considering her son's silence, she should contact the family solicitor, if they had one. He assured her that Daniel would otherwise be entitled to use the duty lawyer.

The shock of her son's arrest abating somewhat, she confirmed she would make a phone call immediately and have their own law firm represent Daniel.

Vic then contacted the DCI, informed him of the arrest and asked if his boss would arrange for a search to be made of the house and outbuilding by the local officers.

As they pulled out of the Littlewoods's drive, the troubled young man sat bolt upright in the back of the car, his eyes once again taking on the glazed expression of the dead ferret.

* * *

The search for Mary Probart continued, but as the clock ticked forward into dawn, Bob Foreman knew that hopes of finding her alive were disappearing, like the frost under the rising sun. At three in the morning, a computer had matched a man to two of the murders. Again, the hotel was the link. Gary Patterson had been a porter there for six months, until about three weeks ago. He would have known both Mary Probart and Adele Turner.

The main connection, however, was the fact that he had been part of a small team of helpers, employed to fetch, carry, and set up equipment for a group called Vivaldi. The group in which Melissa Crabbe had played violin. The connection had not been straightforward, as Vivaldi was originally a trio of three girls, Vivienne, Valerie and Diana, and the group name constructed out of the first letters of their names. Melissa had been headhunted into joining them, and for a time, they kept the title of Vivaldi. Later they thought they would update it to something a bit trendier, something that would not omit Melissa, as the original had. They became 'Viola d'amour', the group with whom Melissa had always been associated.

A couple of officers had been dispatched to the man's address to talk with him. After a lengthy informal discussion, in which Patterson was more than helpful, considering he had been roused from his bed, the policemen were satisfied that he had verifiable alibis for all the murders. Yet another blank had been drawn.

The house to house would be resumed as early as possible but had, up until late in the evening, provided no useful leads. Mary had walked out of her friend's safe house, unseen and unnoticed by anyone. If a strange car had been parked outside, then no one noticed. Because of the nature of her stay there, the neighbours were unaware even of her existence. No one recognised her photograph, except a woman who lived opposite. She had seen Mary with Francoise a few times, especially when the French girl first moved to Hersham. She certainly had not been seen recently. Hudson had come up with nothing new from the hotel, and a group of policemen and women were still wading through employment histories of the Waters Meet's staff, both past and present.

At seven in the morning, Bob, who lived only ten minutes from the station, capitulated to tiredness, and leaving strict instructions to be called should there be any developments, took himself home for a few hours rest. He knew he would suffer physically for the duration of this inquiry.

Unlike Jonathan Leatham, he required at least six hours solid sleep a night to retain the appearance of a human being! The hastily grabbed hour, here and there, did nothing for his looks or his composure. By the time his felon was behind bars, Bob would be wrecked, and probably sleep the clock round for at least two days before he emerged from his pit to start again.

CHAPTER TWENTY-FOUR

Monday brought a depressing anti-climax to the investigation. Leads led nowhere and new information dried up. Bob returned to the office at eleven o'clock and considered telephoning the McEwan woman to cancel their meeting.

After thumbing through a heap of negative reports and deliberating over the lack of movement, he let things stand as they were and found himself relishing the idea of talking to someone other than a police officer, about something other than murder!

Ellie arrived a few minutes after three, and made her way, wide-eyed, through the incident room to the DCI's office.

Bob Foreman greeted her warmly, made her comfortable on a rather plush chair he had discovered in the rest room, and ordered some refreshments for them both. After talking briefly about Liam, Foreman pressed her about her strange, new ability and the form it took.

Ellie explained in simplistic terms and confessed that, although she was working with a friend, a professor with a similar aptitude, she was very much a novice and was still somewhat in awe of her gift. Seeing his scepticism, and feeling the need to justify herself in some way, she sipped her coffee and, lowering her voice so she would not be heard from outside the office, said, 'How long have you had that elbow injury? It is an injury, isn't it, not just a recent knock?'

Bob spat coffee noisily back into his tilted mug.

He sat, without moving, then with unconcealed admiration replied. 'It was broken years ago. A drug addict in custody thought he would give me something to remember him by. It still hurts in the cold weather.' Then he threw up his hands and laughed. 'You have one heck of a talent there, Miss McEwan! I suspect you are going to be one busy lady when you get to grips with employing this . . . er, gift!'

They talked a little longer about energy fields, and Bob was intrigued by the way they indicated areas of sickness or injury. 'Tell me something. If, as you say, your sight picks up emotions, would it recognise mental illness? Or perhaps the evil in a person?'

Ellie considered his question carefully before replying. 'I have never witnessed extreme wickedness in a person, but I am sure that evil would be almost instantly apparent. Mental illness would manifest almost like any other physical problem — depleted auras and diminished colours.'

A prickle of excitement ran the length of the policeman's spine.

'Miss McEwan, I can't ask you to do this if you do not want to . . .' He paused, unsure of how to continue. 'If I showed you a seriously bad man, a man who is both self-confessed, and proven to be, a black-hearted criminal, would you look at him and tell me what you see? You would be perfectly safe. If you agreed, I would escort you myself to the establishment I have in mind, and introduce you to a very unpleasant character indeed.'

Ellie was obviously puzzled. 'To what purpose?'

'I'm not sure yet, but I think you might be able to help me with this investigation.'

'Can I think about it, Chief Inspector? I'm not sure I'm experienced enough for such an undertaking, and I would want to talk to Michael first.'

'Please do, but say as little as necessary to as few as possible. I would like to keep this between us to begin with.' He looked apologetically at her. 'For one thing, coppers are notoriously dismissive of anything that smacks of the supernatural, and whereas I realise this is very different, some could struggle to get their heads around it, and they can be bloody rude! I'd hate you to be embarrassed, and frankly I have no wish to have some of their mess-room humour directed at me either! So, talk to your professor, if you think he would be discreet about it, but no one else.'

'I have no doubts about Michael's integrity,' replied Ellie immediately. 'I would trust him with my life. Forgive me, but I thought we'd just be chatting about your son and foreign bodies in ears. I'm afraid the subject of interviewing murderers never crossed my mind. It's all a bit of a shock, actually.'

'I'm so sorry,' exclaimed Bob, realising his enthusiasm regarding his sudden brainwave had carried him along too fast for his new associate. 'I am used to issuing orders and being brutally blunt about things. Of course you must consider this, and naturally, discuss it with your friend. I only urge you not to delay for too long, because lives are at stake, and a young woman is missing. I am prepared to accept help from any, and every quarter. If there were any way you can assist me, then I would be more than grateful.'

* * *

The fact that the man was sincere was beyond doubt, and from the intense lights that surrounded him, Ellie knew whose side he was on. She had the almost uncontrollable urge to throw in her lot with the Surrey police force and take up Bob's crusade immediately. Only sensibility held her back, but she promised to ring him by the next morning with her answer.

As the driver dropped her safely back in Compton, she knew without a doubt that she would be seeing Detective Chief Inspector Robert Foreman in the very near future.

* * *

The Saab purred northwards up the A1 towards the Hatfield Tunnel. Andrew was proving to be the exception to the rule, as far as Carole's concept of young men driving fast cars went. He was confident but not cocksure, and seemed comfortable and in control of the speeding machine. To Carole, after years of driving a Morris Minor, the dashboard of Phil McEwan's car seemed more suited to one of the Tornado fighters that so frequently tore through the Lincolnshire skies.

The boy had been polite but uncommunicative for the first part of the journey. The older woman did nothing to stimulate the conversation, believing that everyone needed his or her wits about them when engaging passage around the M25. They had left at nine thirty, allowing the worst of the early morning traffic to disperse. Carole knew by experience that the Surrey end of the trip was purgatory, but by the time you reached the dual carriageway that circumnavigated Peterborough, you would be hard put to spot more than four cars together on a three-hundred-yard stretch. From then on, the only traffic you saw, as you headed across the flat, agricultural ground of the Fens, were lorries. Great colourful refrigerated wagons, carrying all manner of fresh produce to every corner of the country. Hold ups, if any, were caused by tractors and farm machinery, making their way from one vast field to the next. In her experience, these drivers were constantly aware of any small build-up behind them, and courteously pulled in to allow traffic to pass.

Her headache, although still suppressed by analgesics, had reduced itself to a low-grade nagging — annoying, but not as disabling as before.

She was amazed at the progress they were making. As her only comparison was her faithful but elderly station wagon, she had allowed far too much time to get there. Ah, well, she would buy the young man lunch in the market town of Boston, before leaving him to his own devices while she surveyed the scattered remains of the Cavendish-Meyer empire.

Andrew had asked her if she minded if he played a tape. It helped him to concentrate. She had acquiesced, he was the driver after all, but added the proviso that it should not be of the head-banging variety. He laughed softly and pressed a button. To her surprise, a most agreeable version of Pachelbel's Canon in D Major gently wafted through expensive speakers and filled the car with the evocative melody. For a moment, her breath had caught in her throat, and something closely resembling a tear was threading its way from her tired eyes. She had chosen this simple and beautiful piece of music for the beginning of Vera's funeral service. The peace and warm ambience it conjured seemed the epitome and essence of everything that had been her very dearest friend. Prior to her passing, it had been her favourite CD to provide a relaxing mood for meditation.

Carole observed the young man next to her — his eyes alert to his surroundings, his hands and feet responding efficiently to what he saw — with different eyes. When he made comment about the splendid medieval cathedral that was clearly visible from the sweeping, and nearly empty, carriageway at Peterborough, she once more reviewed her earlier observations about him. First impressions, it would appear, could be hopelessly wrong.

'It's got that fairy-tale quality of Notre Dame, don't you think?'

Carole agreed and asked him if he liked Paris.

Andrew's eyes lit up with the firework of memory, and he spoke enthusiastically throughout the next few miles, pausing only briefly to check directions with his passenger, and to take care negotiating some hairpin bends on the winding roads towards Spalding.

Listening carefully, she enquired when his last trip to that romantic city had been.

'Only a couple of weeks ago; the weather was wonderful, considering the time of year. We took a Bateau Mouche up the Seine. That was what made me think of Notre Dame. It was only a three-day break but it seemed like so much longer.'

Andrew seemed to slip away into private thoughts.

'You said we . . . Would I be rude to ask who you went with?'

'Sorry? Oh no, of course not. My girlfriend, Rachel. We went once before, on Valentine's Day. Do you know, one of the bridges was completely covered with red and pink balloons? The French really know how to express themselves, don't they?'

'You sound like a bit of a romantic yourself, young man!' The picture painted by Pauline, of the sharp and tasty geezer, was fading by the minute. The boy now looked to be a sensitive and thoughtful lad, and Carole was growing to like him more and more as the trip continued.

'I suppose so. I just wish I didn't work such demanding hours. I would like to get engaged.' He drew in his breath, as if making a confession about an unspeakable sin. 'But it wouldn't be fair on Rachel. I am at Mr McEwan's beck and call.' He hesitated again. 'He has a lot of problems, and sometimes he needs me at really odd times, in the night or early mornings. Don't get me wrong, he pays me well, very well, in fact. And that's the problem. My salary is what would enable me to ask Rachel to marry me. If I left Mr McEwan, I would never find work to pay me what I'm earning now, and I want things to be just right for her, she is a very special girl. Her parents are not well off, and I want to give her a proper wedding and a good life.' He sighed. 'So I need money. The trouble is, every time we plan something, Paris excluded, I have to cancel or cut it short. It's difficult. We just want to be together and it keeps going wrong.'

Carole heard Ellie bemoaning the fact that her business had been the downfall of her own relationship with Stephanie, and although Steph's departure had pleased Carole no end, she did appreciate the dangers to even a good relationship. 'Do you love her?' asked Carole bluntly.

'Yes,' replied Andrew, without hesitation.

'Then remember, employees can be replaced. Especially if the wages are good, but a true love, well, you might only ever find that once in a lifetime. Talk to Phil, I'm sure he would be able to do something to help.'

'I don't know how,' replied Andrew miserably. 'He's my boss, and he's sick. I can't.'

'Would you like me to speak to him, informally. Not drop you in it, just say it's an impression I am getting?'

Andrew's expression lightened. 'Would you?'

'Leave it with me. Now, last exit at the next roundabout, and we are only about fifteen minutes from our destination.'

The huge skyscape of the county of her birth was getting to her. She began talking, partly to Andrew and partly to herself. She rarely, if ever, spoke of her unhappy and lonely childhood. The desolate time spent in the company of a mother who hated her had never inspired her to reminisce about family life. She did, however, tell her chauffeur about growing up in the Fens. He could see a little of what she was describing by the uninterrupted vista across flat lands, ribboned across with water. Water in the form of rivers, streams, dykes, ditches and drains. And above it all, the sky, 360 degrees of visible sky.

Carole's home, or maybe it had been a prison, was a manor house. Imposing and grand, it had stood, a fortress alone on the bleak landscape, fighting off the winds and the mists that blew and swirled around its weathered grey stones. There was no other county, and in her lifetime, she had traversed quite a few, that she could both love and hate with such intensity.

It was a place where the memory of a sunset could stay with you from childhood until your dotage, such was its immeasurable beauty. And on another day, the melancholy mists could creep into your soul, bringing a depression that lay as heavy upon the heart as cold, hard winter ground.

She told him of Bomber County, and of the evenings when, as little ones, she and her brother had tried to count the dark silhouettes in a sky filled with heavy bomb-laden Lancasters, making their way towards Germany. She recalled the fighters, the Spitfires, and the Hurricanes, and the American C-47 troop-carrying Dakotas, all engaged in the defence of the realm. Then there had been that faltering, stuttering sound she could still hear today, of a broken plane, coughing and choking its way home to Lincolnshire, to safety, or sometimes to death. But it would be death in your home country, not in some foreign field, but in that rich soil of England, where you belonged.

As they drove across the River Witham and into the market square of Boston, Andrew sighed. It seemed to her that something she had said had appealed to the poet in him, and for a moment he was envying her living in such terrible times, under that big sky.

* * *

The journey home was a quieter affair. They spoke only occasionally, but the silences were contented. The powerful car ate up the miles, and Carole gratefully accepted the fact that the unwanted voyage had been almost a pleasant affair. She smiled inwardly, as she considered the time spent with the skeletal Mr Brothertoft. She recalled his placid agreement of her instructions, punctuated only with the sporadic raising of an eyebrow.

As she settled further back onto the sumptuous leather seat and looked out over the shiny bonnet, Carole felt a great deal of satisfaction about the day's work. In fact, if she had been free of the bludgeoning thump of the returning headache, and the constant concern about Ellie, Carole would have felt very good indeed.

* * *

While Carole and her young chauffeur were passing through Hinxworth, her two house guests and five dogs were playing a somewhat unorthodox game of Frisbee on the lawn at Snug Cottage. Concluding that it was not practical to tackle such an energetic pastime while on crutches, Ellie sank gratefully onto a wooden bench that Scrubbs had carefully constructed from two tree stumps and a fine old piece of oak.

Leaving the dogs to play among themselves, Michael joined her, and they sat in friendly silence, admiring the spring morning.

'Do you really want to visit a convicted murderer?'

'I have to admit to a certain fascination. You see enough violent criminals on the TV, but in real life it's hard to believe people like that really exist. I am tempted.'

Michael screwed his face into a grimace, and asked how such a delicate flower girl could harbour a notion as barbaric as going to visit an authentic Hannibal Lecter.

Ellie laughed and declared there was a little of the ghoul in everyone, that we all concealed secret desires or naughty fantasies at some level of our existence. 'And no questions about my fantasies, Michael Seale!'

Head hung in mock shame, Michael smiled, but continued in a more thoughtful vein. 'Carole is so worried about something happening to you, she seems to think, as we said earlier, that there is a connection with these murders and the danger she thinks is hanging over you like the sword of Damocles. I have to admit that odd vision she had up on St Martha's did seem a bit like a view of a murder, and the nightmare you had before the accident. I know you can't remember it now, but Carole described it clearly. Ellie, do you really want to get involved with this policeman and his killings?'

'I saw the murder room, Michael. Photos of those poor women. Women like me. Ghastly pictures stuck on the wall; they were horrible. If I can help, and I don't even know if I can, I honestly think that I should try, don't you?'

'I really don't know. My first concern is always you. I know these murders are terrible, but neither Carole nor I would want you to be at risk in any way.' He grimaced. 'And what on earth would you tell Carole? She is obsessed with keeping you safe.'

'That's what bothers me, Michael. But I'm convinced that going with the chief inspector and seeing what evil looks like in the aura, might help me in the future. Maybe not with this case, but if I am going to use this ability properly, I am going to have to study all sorts of conditions, aren't I?' She paused, tracing her finger around the rings of a knothole in the wooden seat. 'Michael, come with me. DCI Foreman knows about you, why don't we analyse this man together?'

'I really don't like it, Ellie. Did you look at Carole's aura this morning before she left? It's better than it was, but it's still awful. This will only make her worse.'

'Then I won't tell her. I don't want to hurt her, that's the last thing I want to do. She has been a rock, all through my accident, and then looking after me like this. I could never repay her. But, and you have to admit it, she is the first to say "use your talent" and I must not back away just because something is unpleasant or frightening to me. Do you understand, Michael?'

'As I see it, it's a bit of a no-win situation.' Michael stroked his beard and looked glum.

'I agree about her aura.' Ellie stared at her feet. 'She used to have the most amazing blue hue surrounding her, it made me think of Greek summers. Now it's hardly visible at all, and there is the strangest discolouration at the site of her headaches. I don't know what it means. I have nothing to compare it with. It's not like a tumour, I saw several of those at the hospital, and I saw a man who had a cerebral bleed, that was different, too. Carole's is weird, it's like a cloud swimming around in her head. Do you see it, Michael?'

'No, but my sight is not as refined as yours. I've only noticed the depletion of her aura and the awful pain she suffers.'

Standing up and stretching, Michael seemed to come to a decision.

'Okay, you tell your policeman you will go with him, but no promises to help. I'll stay with Carole, and you will just have to tell me what you think when you get back. If the old girl is strong enough, we will tell her, and if she's not . . .' There was a long pause. 'Well, I don't want her hurt, so let's just wait and see, shall we?'

'I'll ring him now and he can make his arrangements, and I agree, no promises.'

CHAPTER TWENTY-FIVE

Bob Foreman put the telephone down with a sigh of relief. Maybe something would go right today. At least McEwan had agreed to his plan. He scratched his head, heavy fingers raking through thick grey waves. Whatever was he doing? Clutching at straws came to mind, and if the mess room found out the lengths he was going to, he'd never live it down. He could hear the comments now. 'Oooh, where's Mystic Meg today, Bob?' 'Is that a Ouija board I see in your briefcase, Bob?'

He groaned and pushed the thoughts aside. At least he had correctly assumed from her general attitude that she would help him, so he had gone ahead and organised a visit to a top security prison, not far away, where Albert Courtney Brazil was residing permanently.

He had also been correct to believe that Brazil would grant them an audience.

He loved to talk. He loved to talk about murder. His murders.

Bob shuddered when he thought of the tall, slender, slightly balding man with the faintest hint of a speech impediment. He resembled a Victorian parson, and indeed, his strange sanctimonious manner had earned him the name of

'Father' Brazil. He had committed some ten murders that the police knew of, and although he was horribly proud of those, he only ever hinted at others. A lot of others.

The visit was set for the next day and he decided to collect Ellie himself, let her see the monster and get her home again. Despite his fears of ridicule, he did not feel guilty about taking the time to follow his strange hunch. His inquiry was going nowhere, and Mary Probart, who occupied his every thought, was still missing. The search of the area around Daniel Littlewood's home had brought nothing to light. The house to house had done the same. Even the computers were quiet, and Hudson's extensive enquiries at the hotel had revealed no more than they knew already. Her friend, Francoise, had made an impassioned speech on the TV news for any information, and there was a recorded message, a plea for her safe return, from her bedridden father in County Durham.

A dreadful waiting had begun. Waiting for Mary to return. In one form or another.

* * *

'Don't worry, young man, I shall do as I promised.'

Andrew's wave was energetic, and his face shone with appreciation as he pressed the button for the electric windows and drove carefully out onto the lane.

She walked up the path to the front door, fumbling in her pocket for her key. The door opened before she had time to find it, and Michael greeted her with open arms. He made her a drink. Between them, he and Ellie had prepared her a light supper.

The food, delicious as it no doubt was, made her feel nauseous, and she only managed to force down a few mouthfuls before excusing herself to go to her room. The headache was returning with a vengeance, and she had no option but to take two of those damned pills and lie on the bed.

At least she had accomplished everything, and more, than she needed to.

One last phone call, and she could succumb to the little men with the pneumatic drills inside her head.

The telephone being picked up immediately, she thanked Phil profusely for his kindness, then proceeded to explain what she considered to be the matter with his employee. She was diplomatic and, considering the agony she was in, made the whole account seem as if it were her deduction, and that his young man had been the soul of discretion and loyalty.

At the end of her diatribe, she made a few sage suggestions that she hoped Phil McEwan was wise enough to accept, and with repeated thanks for the loan of his chauffeur, Carole hung up.

She closed her eyes and finally acknowledged the pounding pains in her head. 'All right, you bastard, do your best. I'm ready.'

* * *

Before she left Michael and prepared for bed, Ellie decided she should contact Alice. The woman had been expecting to arrive for a delicious home-cooked meal, and all that would be on offer was a take-away. Carole was in no fit state for anything, let alone cooking. Ellie herself found standing for any length of time excruciatingly painful, and there was no way she was going to impose upon Michael any more than she was already.

Alice's ansafone was switched on, so she left a short message, briefly explaining that Carole was unwell, and although she was still very welcome, the food would be of the fast variety, and her own ability to concentrate on the case study might be impaired.

Five minutes later Alice returned her call, saying she was happy to risk the food, and perhaps they could just make a start on it — if it proved too much for her then, no problem. It would simply be nice to see Ellie again.

Happy with that reaction, she told Alice she'd be really pleased to see her again too, and that there was lots of news.

Alice promised to arrive as near to five as she could, allowing for the traffic.

It was one of those peculiar calls where neither party wanted to be the one to hang up, so although she decided not to mention her proposed trip to the prison in the afternoon before seeing Alice, they chatted on for another ten minutes about nothing much at all. In the end, it was Alice's bleep going off that decided who should be the first to say goodbye and the amicable conversation came to an abrupt halt.

Later, as she pulled the duvet around her and turned out the light, she wondered why she had been so hesitant in mentioning her intended outing to one of Her Majesty's prisons. It was after all, apart from Alice's visit, going to be the high spot of her day.

* * *

As Bob Foreman retrieved various items of paperwork and a briefcase from the boot of his Sierra, Ellie gazed in apprehension at the monstrous building in front of her.

The facade was about as inhospitable and austere as was possible in an architectural design. They had already driven through a gated archway in a wall topped with razor wire, and that was only the car park.

Bob had warned her of the security checks that they would have to go through, but still she was staggered at the lengths security went to, to ensure she was not in possession of anything she should not be. She was searched to the extent of a woman peering in her ears, had metal-detecting wands passed around her body, was asked to remove her shoes to have the heels tapped, and to her total wonderment, was made to give up her crutches, in order for them to be X-rayed.

They then proceeded from waiting area to waiting area, each time being called by name and official documents being produced and checked. A phone call would be made, and a metal door would slide open, leaving them together in a small, sealed space until the facing set of doors were activated, and they could move on.

On the drive down, Bob had given her a skimpy history of the man they were going to meet. He had insisted that she did not speak to Brazil, no matter how much he tried to goad her into conversation. He had a silver tongue, said the policeman. He was eloquent and well educated, but he was also a brutal and emotionless killer. She must not lose sight of that fact, and remain only an observer. Bob would ask questions that he felt would stimulate reactions from the man, and Ellie should monitor his aura. If at any time she wanted to leave, she must touch Foreman's arm, and he would terminate the interview.

He ran through a little of what he had prepared, and she had complied with the suitability of the material.

The last great door hissed shut behind them and they stood in a large room with a few high windows situated some ten feet above her. The only furniture was a table with a single chair in front of it. Both were bolted securely to the concrete floor.

Bob ushered her to a spot on the far side of a white painted line on the floor, and motioned for her to stay there.

The room was circumnavigated by a thick rubber strip that housed an emergency warning bell. Hit it sharply at any point, and a well-practised crisis procedure would ensue.

Ellie wondered if anyone could hear her heart thundering in her ribcage. She hoped she was giving off an air of quiet composure, but she doubted it.

Foreman pushed a buzzer and spoke into a small grill set in the wall. He then retreated to stand on the line, just in front of her.

The door opened again and four officers brought in Father Brazil. He was manacled at the feet and handcuffed to two of the prison guards. They escorted him to the table, where he sat, but not before a courteous bow towards Ellie. The two other men proceeded to attach the foot chains to two iron loops embedded in the floor. They released the cuffs from their colleagues and they all stepped away.

Foreman greeted the man formally and introduced Ellie as a consultant working with a special criminal investigation unit. He confirmed that Ellie would not be speaking to Brazil, simply observing, and that he should address all his conversation to Foreman.

'Such a pity.'

Brazil's slight lisp and innocent remark made Ellie's skin crawl. He smiled at her, and her stomach turned over. She swallowed hard and tried to get on with the job she was here to do, but she was totally unprepared for what she saw.

There was not one single healthy light around the whole of his body. Instead of flaring rainbows of colour, sick, filthy scum oozed its way around the man.

Perceiving the detritus that writhed and squirmed from him was bad enough, but listening to his sibilant speech as well was making her feel physically sick.

The DCI asked if he would be prepared to explain how he felt when he had taken the life of another human being.

The man looked perplexed and with his head on one side said, 'If I had done the job well, then I suppose I would feel satisfied, as one would when achieving excellence in anything.' He shrugged slightly. 'If the job had been poor, badly handled, then I would be very disappointed, and make it my business to do better, in future.'

Ellie noticed no change in his energy field.

'Please, would you recall in your mind, the job, as you referred to it, that you feel was your masterpiece.'

For a second nothing happened. He seemed to be selecting the victim of his choice, the most pleasurable of his grisly undertakings. Then his eyes lit up with recognition, and Ellie was practically knocked from her feet by flashes of dark, blood-red light. They emanated from the man's hands, chest area, and his lower abdomen. These were followed by streaks of a metallic dirty silver colour and then a barrage of jet-black lightning bolts that erupted all around him.

Ellie grabbed for Bob Foreman's arm and spun away from the wicked light show she was watching.

Bob immediately had the man removed, and put a bear-like arm protectively around her.

Their passage out of the prison was a blur, and sitting in the car, still shaking, Ellie was left with no doubt whatsoever that she would recognise evil, if she was ever unlucky enough to see it again.

With faltering words, she told Bob as much as she could, but did not mention one thing. The worst thing, the really bad thing to come out of the meeting, was that as those shards of horrible light had sprung from the monster, she realised she had seen all this before, but she did not know where or when.

* * *

Bob was tactful and left her at Snug Cottage without any further delving or questioning. He was fully aware that whatever Brazil had given off had shaken Ellie badly. He had felt a pang of self-reproach when she haltingly tried to tell him what she had seen. He made no mention of her coming back to the police station, or of helping him at a later stage. He thought it best to leave her for a while. He thanked her for going with him and apologised that it had been such a harrowing experience. He secretly hoped that after talking it through with her professor friend, she would be able to look at the incident in a more detached manner, and might possibly give him a ring.

Driving back down the A3, he considered the three victims and the missing girl, and although he still felt bad about Ellie's traumatic visit, he admitted to himself that he would do it all again if it would help him to catch the killer.

It had taken him nearly a year to catch Brazil.

Gripping the wheel until his knuckles turned white, he swore to God that it would not take him that long again.

* * *

Michael had fretted unnecessarily over Carole's reaction to Ellie's trip out that afternoon. Before Bob had come to collect her, Carole had taken two more painkillers and gone to her room to sleep. Ellie was home before she awoke. There was even time for an unhurried discussion about the prison visit.

Ellie had calmed down considerably and they took two mugs of tea and went to the sanctuary to talk. She explained in detail what she had seen, and also the terrible feeling of déjà vu. Michael confirmed her suspicion that it may have something to do with the nightmare she had experienced a few days before her accident. As she had absolutely no memory of the awful dream, it was difficult to compare the two incidents. She certainly was not going to bring the subject up with Carole again, and seeing her poor friend's present condition, she decided to shield her from as much worry as she could. She fervently wished she'd put Alice off for the evening, but she had harboured the hope that Carole would be much improved, and deep down, she did want to see Alice.

Before they left the sanctuary, Michael asked if she were planning on seeing the DCI again. Ellie did not answer immediately. Several issues were swimming around in her head and she needed to think carefully before she made any decisions.

Initially she had been so disturbed by Brazil that she wanted to be as far away from him as possible. Now her thoughts kept returning to those unfortunate women who had not had the opportunity to run away from evil. She felt a duty to them. But there was also a duty to her friends. If she were to put herself on the front line, then she would be taking them with her. It was not fair on Carole or Michael.

She thought of those pictures on the murder room wall. The youngest one, so beautiful in life, smiling and holding her violin. The second woman, so serious with her handsome, bespectacled, intelligent face. The third, the artist posing in front of one of her pictures, had a cheeky, boyish grin.

Below each of these were the last pictures to be taken of the women. Murdered and mutilated.

She suddenly realised that Michael was waiting patiently for her reply.

'It rather looks as though I will, Michael. I don't think I have a choice.'

He lightly touched her arm. 'I thought that's what you would say. Well. I'll help you all I can, but we have to consider Carole too. Now I know you have the hospital tomorrow, and Carole still wants to go with you, if she's well enough, but I must go back to London for the day. I have to see my assistant and make some arrangements to take some more time off. I might have to go back for one day a week to see any patients that have emergencies, but we'll see. Janet is a real angel when it comes to handling the clients for me. She'll do her best to hold them off until I get back. By the way, Scrubbs has volunteered to be your driver if Carole's not up to it.'

She smiled at her friend and mentor. 'Michael, what are the chances of getting Carole to see a doctor about those headaches. I really do not like what I see.'

'Remote, I should think. Hey! What about your Alice Cross? She specialises in neurological problems!'

'Of course! Why didn't I think of her. She'll be here within the hour, let's ask Carole to speak to her. Well done! Let's just hope she will talk to her; you know what Carole's like.' Her enthusiasm suddenly faded. 'But what can we say happened? We can't tell her the truth.'

Tugging his beard, Michael thought hard. 'It's more a case of what Carole will tell her. I think I should go and have a word with her now. Tell her how worried we are and ask her to speak to Alice for our sakes. It might work.'

He did not sound too hopeful, and although it was a great idea, Ellie realised that if Carole dug her heels in, it would be yet another non-starter. Oh well, she could but hope.

* * *

Michael left Ellie at the sanctuary door and strode purposefully across the lawn and through the courtyard.

He found Carole, sitting in the kitchen, feeding charcoal biscuits to her dogs. She said the sleep and the pills had done wonders and she felt so much better. In fact, she was well enough to cook for their guest.

Michael cast his trained eye over her and had to admit that she certainly had more colour around her. Nowhere near what it had been, but nevertheless, considerably improved. He expressed delight at the news, but went ahead with his appeal that she speak to a doctor. Dr Alice Cross, to be more precise.

Her answer was an emphatic no. She utterly forbade either him, or Ellie, to mention a thing to their visitor. She insisted that it was totally unnecessary. Migraines could be hell; it was lifting already. End of story.

'We both know that it's not a migraine, Carole,' said Michael softly. 'I was there, remember?'

She dropped her gaze to the floor, then slowly looked up at her friend. 'I'm sorry. I shouldn't try to bully you, should I? I know, for your sakes, I should see a doctor. I know I should have a scan, but I cannot speak to Ellie's young friend. To begin with, I couldn't tell her what happened, she would never understand, and . . .' She sighed. 'I'm afraid that whatever happened to me . . . is not going to get better, and I don't want to be told that. I was an irresponsible fool, and I am paying for it. If I'm meant to recover, Michael, then I will, with no help from doctors or hospitals. So, bear with me, will you?'

'Do I have any choice, old girl?'

'Not really.'

He moved towards the door. 'Then I'll tell Ellie not to mention anything to her doctor friend tonight.'

'Michael . . .'

He turned back to her.

'Thank you.'

'Stubborn old fool!'
'I know.'

* * *

When Alice Cross left Snug Cottage at ten that evening, Ellie was uncertain as to whether she felt elated, or disappointed. Carole had concocted a wonderful, if simple, evening meal and saved them all from a Chinese take-away. She said that she was feeling much better, but Ellie had watched her dicing vegetables and preparing pasta and decided that Carole was flying on automatic pilot.

They all ate together, and then Michael and Carole had retired to the lounge, leaving the doctor and her guinea pig to begin work.

Alice had seemed in high spirits, making Ellie wonder if it were her company, or the fact that the thesis was getting underway at last. Ellie's mind had been awash with subjects other than Azimah's Syndrome and she had found it very hard to concentrate. She realised just how important it was to Alice and had made a gallant effort to work with her.

Alice had finally put down her pen and asked Ellie what the preoccupation was. Without thinking she had blurted out about being asked to assist the police and having visited a murderer that very afternoon.

At that, Alice's whole manner towards her had changed. The doctor urged her to seriously rethink involvement with the inquiry, and had asked, somewhat brusquely, what on earth Michael and Carole thought about her reckless decision.

She immediately told Alice, that because of her not being well, she had not told Carole about the visit, and she'd be grateful if Alice would keep it to herself. She then remembered feeling slightly hurt by Alice's tone, and not a little irritated, but she hoped that the sharp words were spoken out of concern for her safety.

They had worked on for another hour, but a shadow hung over them. Alice told her she was going to stay overnight with her sister, and return to London early the next day. Ellie had expressed interest in her family, and she had softened considerably as she told her about her adored younger sibling and their family. When she had mentioned her parents, however, the shadow returned, and Alice simply said that they, her sister and herself, never spoke of them. They were dead and that was all there was to it.

She had then steered the conversation adroitly back to the case study. Her passion for her work was genuine, and Ellie had seen so much of the old Ellie McEwan in the doctor that she was forced to accept, if ever there was to be a relationship, it would come second to the love affair Dr Cross had with her work. Alice had kissed Ellie lightly on the cheek as she left, the anger had abated and she did not mention the subject of the police again. The chemistry had still been there and when she promised to ring the next day, Ellie found herself sincerely hoping she would.

Now, sitting alone in the kitchen, she was a tangle of mixed emotions. She liked the woman's company and the thrill of being near her, but to her surprise and sadness, she had not enjoyed working with her as much as she thought she would. She had originally been so kind and understanding but now it seemed the dissertation and her impassioned thirst for knowledge about Ellie's trauma and the Azimah link were overpowering their obvious attraction to each other.

She made herself a mug of chocolate and sat a bit longer in the warm room. She was not at all sure how she felt about her doctor, and she had to admit to being shocked by the outburst. The harsh words and the anger had hurt her, but then she recalled Alice's lips brush her cheek, and the confusion returned. The thrill of electricity that had coursed through her had been undeniable.

She sipped the hot drink and thought that she should really get some sleep. Tomorrow was her hospital appointment and she could say 'au revoir' to the plaster.

Encouraged by that positive notion, she washed her mug and limped slowly to the library. There were two positive thoughts on her mind as she slipped into bed. Getting rid of the plaster and shortly after, the crutches, and telephoning DCI Bob Foreman to offer him the services of her rather unusual gift.

CHAPTER TWENTY-SIX

The murder room had lost the buzz of earlier.

Mary had been missing for five days, and it was generally agreed among the team that she would not be found alive. It appeared that Wendy Brown had been right about the murderer seeing her, and he was taking no chances.

Fletcher had been allowed to leave. It seemed that his connections with the hotel and his witnessing of 'Dracula' by the golf course had been coincidental after all.

Daniel Littlewood had been no help to anyone. He had fluctuated between long periods of silence, depression, and angry ramblings.

On Thursday morning, Bob Foreman asked Vic and Jonathan to try again with the neurotic young man, and although Vic thought it was going to be a total waste of time, to their surprise, they found him calmer and more lucid than on previous occasions.

Jonathan switched on the tape, gave the date and time, and introduced those present. Daniel's solicitor, Graham Smart, sat next to his client, with the two police officers opposite them.

Jonathan recapped on the questions they had put to Daniel before. Mainly his whereabouts at the times of the murders and the disappearance of Mary Probart.

'I can tell you where I was on several occasions.' The voice was slow and deliberate. Daniel looked enquiringly at his brief. Smart nodded and he continued. 'I couldn't say before, well, I didn't want to. I, er, I've had a lot of problems, my child. My wife . . .'

Jonathan spoke gently. 'We know about your little girl, Daniel, and about your wife and son. So go on, where were you?'

'This friend of my mother . . . she has this garden.' He paused. He was plainly having trouble imparting this secret of his. 'There is this summer house, that's where I go. It's quiet. I can think there. If I've been upset, or done something silly like getting angry or running away, I go there. Late at night, sometimes all night. It's special. She leaves the heating on, and some nights I've slept there.'

'Surely she locks it, this friend of your mother?' asked Vic.

Daniel hung his head and looked thoroughly miserable. 'I've got a key. My mother looks after Mrs Meyer's dogs sometimes. She spent a long time with a friend who was in a bad accident. Mother got me to help her with the animals. I took the summer house key and had a copy made.'

It seemed to Vic that the occasional nocturnal use of this summer house was weighing heavier on Daniel's heart than the fact that he was being held on suspicion of murder.

'I'm sorry. I did not want to tell anyone in case I couldn't go back; it's been like a sanctuary to me during these awful dark days and nights. I never did any harm or damage.' He looked appealingly at Graham Smart, who assured him that was not an issue.

'Did anyone ever see you there, Daniel?'

He thought for a moment. 'Sort of. Early one morning, I hadn't been able to sleep so I thought I'd go to the summer house for an hour before the household woke up. When I got there, I couldn't find the key. Then I saw a light on in the house. Next thing, all her dogs were racing across the lawn. I wasn't frightened of them, they knew me, they're nice friendly fellows, but I didn't want to be seen there, so

I ran away. Mother told me that Mrs Meyer thought she'd had a prowler. But it was me.' He paused, as if trying to get his mind in order. 'Then, one night I got there and the place was a mess: chairs turned over, a blanket on the floor . . . and the door was unlocked. I was very upset that night. I was considering doing something . . . well, something drastic to get my son back . . . but I couldn't think of anything that wouldn't hurt him in some way. I don't know why I did it, probably too wrapped up thinking about Christopher, but I tidied up before I left. Stupid, really, I didn't want to draw attention to myself, and I went and cleaned up!'

'We can check that easily enough, but did anyone actually see you there?'

'No one I knew. One night, I think it was when Mrs Meyer was visiting her friend in hospital, I fell asleep in the rattan chair. When I woke up there was this thin woman sitting at the table and looking at these big cards, tarot cards, I think. Anyway, she just sat there with this big old dog at her feet and smiled at me. She said she wouldn't tell on me, and I could go there whenever I wanted. She said I should speak to Mrs Meyer, and she was sure she would let me use the summer house, I only had to ask. But I couldn't. I never did. Well, I must have gone to sleep again, because when I woke up, she and her dog had gone. I don't know who she was, but I'd recognise her if I saw her again. She seemed to know all about Snug Cottage and Mrs Meyer. She was a very kind old lady. I liked her. She had a mauve-coloured suit on with this extraordinary brooch on the lapel. She smelled of flowers.'

Daniel drifted away from them. His eyes lost their focus and Jonathan called the interview to a close. There was no more to be obtained from Daniel Littlewood.

* * *

Back in the murder room, Jonathan Leatham was about to dispatch his sergeant to check out the summer house story, when DCI Foreman called him into his office.

Leatham told him of Daniel Littlewood's story of spending nights in his mother's friend's garden room, and he showed his boss the address of Snug Cottage. To his surprise, Bob Foreman snatched the piece of paper away from him and stared in amazement at the name Cavendish-Meyer, the telephone number, and the address in Compton. 'Good Lord! I was only there yesterday!'

'I was just going to get Vic to go over and get Littlewood's story verified, sir. Is it someone you know? Did you want to handle it yourself?'

'Yes, maybe I will. But I'll ring first. If Mrs Meyer is well enough, I believe she will have taken a young friend of hers to the hospital today. We could have a wasted journey. Yes, leave this with me, Inspector. I'll keep you posted on it.'

Jonathan left, and Bob rang the number Ellie had given him. Her mobile was switched off, so he dialled Snug Cottage. This time he was greeted by an ansafone. He left a brief message asking Ellie or Mrs Meyer to ring him when they returned from the hospital. Rather than worry them, he said it was in connection to their prowler.

He wondered how Ellie was faring. She had been truly shaken up by her meeting with Brazil. He hoped that she would have good news at least from the surgeons and, feeling happier, perhaps consider talking to him again.

His gaze wandered out into the big incident room, and he noticed WDC Brown striding across the floor with a couple of carrier bags under her arm. She marched straight to his door and, knocking quickly, pushed her way in.

'Bad news, sir. Look.'

She emptied the two bags onto his desk. 'I've been over at Francoise's flat in Hersham. These are Mary's.'

It took a moment for the items on the desk to relate to Wendy's sombre tone and worried face.

He breathed out ferociously. 'Damn! Damn! Then it's definitely him! He has got her, hasn't he?'

'Looks that way, sir. She fits his criteria, even if she hadn't been a witness to one of his bloody murders.'

Together, they stared at the dozens of pieces of delicate and intricate embroidery. Not just a casual hobby to fill in a quiet evening in front of the telly, these were professionally tailored pieces, obviously ordered by someone. Mary was a skilled and talented needlewoman. Or had been. Maybe she was now just skilled and talented victim number four.

Bob's mind raced. So where was she? This was the first one he had abducted. He had spirited her away, in broad daylight . . . to where?

'Sir!'

Vic's cry rang out across the room. 'Guildford have found a woman's body. She's been mutilated, sir. From their brief description, it sounds like Mary Probart.'

'Where did they find the body, Sergeant?'

'St Martha's, sir. In the woods on the hill, by the church.'

* * *

The detective chief inspector gathered his team and sent Leatham, Barratt and Brown directly to the scene of the latest murder. Bob was certain it would be Mary Probart they'd found in the woody piece of countryside. Brown would be able to make a positive identification of the girl. He felt sorry for Wendy Brown — she had done the best she could for Mary, and the system had failed. They had all failed frightened Mary Probart from County Durham. Poor kid had been certain the killer was out there looking for her, and she had been right. Even so, she had happily let him in when he came knocking on her door. Sad that she had not chosen her friends more carefully.

He grabbed the phone and put a call through to Dr Amanda Gerrard.

She picked up the telephone immediately and agreed to come down the following day to be updated on the case and have a quick look at Daniel Littlewood. His stories of sleeping alone in someone's summer house were still unsubstantiated, and although he could not see the lad as a killer, he certainly was an oddball. Bob wanted her opinion of him, even if just to enable him to be released. He hoped there would also be more information by that time from the body at St Martha's that could assist Dr Gerrard in her profile of the murderer.

He needed help badly on this one. He could not afford a rerun of the Brazil case. That bastard had run rings around him, leaving death and destruction in his wake, for a whole year. The worst year of Foreman's life. He had nailed him . . . finally. But not before he had butchered ten living souls. Today, they were at number four and he had no leads, no clues and no hope of a swift arrest.

He silently prayed that Ellie McEwan would help him. If the mutilating murderer gave off the same dreadful lights that had burst from Brazil, then McEwan would spot them a mile away. He would have her look at every member of staff that had ever worked at that hotel, every guest, every manager . . . he'd have her walking the streets on her broken leg, if necessary, until she saw those awful lights around someone and then . . . then he would have the sodding butcher . . . and put him away for life.

* * *

The old Morris bounced up the lane and Ellie did her best to protect her tender and unprotected leg from the reverberations. Although Carole was doing her best, the elderly suspension was coming to the end of its long and stalwart service, and she saw Ellie wince more than once before they drew into Snug Cottage.

Scrubbs was there to help Ellie inside, and the two women made straight for the kettle. It had been a long but very successful day. Ellie and Carole had been treated like long lost friends at the hospital, and all the news regarding Ellie was good. The orthopaedic surgeon was delighted with her leg and the way it had healed. Another forty-eight hours on the crutches and he wanted her to start weight bearing.

The bones had knitted perfectly with a great deal of help from Mr Royston's Meccano set! The stitches and the wound were looking good. There would be scars but nothing too hideous. Ellie said that she was just delighted to have something that resembled a human leg after Carole had told her of the initial X-ray she'd been shown. She had declined to look herself.

Carl Thomas had been delighted to see them both. The head injury was giving her no problems at all, the scar was fading fast and he was very pleased with his favourite patient.

When the appointment was over and Ellie was making her way towards A&E to see Jack Barker, Thomas had called Carole back to his office. The two women had agreed to meet in Casualty, and Carole went back into the consultant's room, sank back into one of his comfy chairs, and accepted another cup of tea.

Carl looked at Carole with suspicion. 'So, what's wrong? Has it been too much for you, looking after my patient?'

'Your patient has been a dream, Mr Thomas. I'm afraid it's me that is the problem. The return of migraines, after a short break of some forty years!'

'Are you taking anything for it? You appear to be in considerable discomfort.'

'Oh yes,' she said, trying to dismiss his concerns. 'But you know what migraines are like, nothing works for long, does it? It will pass.'

Carl Thomas looked unconvinced, but noting her reticence to talk about herself any further, allowed the inquisition to drop.

'And Ellie's new gift. I heard from Jack Barker that she helped a lad with an ear problem?'

'Ellie will make very clever use of her talent of that I am certain. Her mentor, Professor Michael Seale, is more than impressed with her progress. She has an amazing ability and she is handling it well.'

'I am glad to hear it.'

'That young doctor, Alice Cross, who did the scans on her brain frequencies, has visited her. She wants to use her as a case study for her paper on Azimah's Syndrome.' She pulled a slight face, and Carl observing it, immediately interrupted her.

'And you do not approve?'

'Not exactly, she seems very pleasant, but I'm just not sure Ellie is ready for it yet, although I have to say that she does seem rather taken with the young woman. I know she told you she . . . ah, prefers women.'

'Ah yes, and Dr Cross is a very good doctor, kind and full of compassion. She is also rather attractive, but as far as I can tell, she is completely tunnel-visioned where work is concerned. If you will forgive me for saying this, and it's not being uncomplimentary to Ellie, but I am surprised that other than being a very interesting specimen, Alice has even noticed her!'

'Well, she has most certainly noticed Ellie, in a big way. I think. But it is this passion for work, almost obsessive, that bothers me. I'd hate her deep involvement with Ellie-the-Azimah-link, to get Ellie-the-person, hurt!'

'I have to say I agree, and I did warn Ellie to put herself first until she was stronger, but one cannot really get in the way of these things, can one? And they do have a habit of sorting themselves out. Now . . .' He sighed. 'Sadly I have a round to do, but ring me if you need any help, what I said before still stands. Ease up a bit, especially if those headaches continue. I know a good man, if they don't get any better. I will gladly refer you.'

Carole had thanked him and made her way to A&E to retrieve Ellie and get her home.

* * *

The two women were drinking tea and watching Scrubbs sweep the courtyard down, when Carole noticed the green light flashing on the ansafone. She pressed the button and a deep voice introduced himself as a Detective Chief Inspector Foreman. He needed either Ellie or herself to ring him as soon as possible after they got back from hospital. He had left a mobile and a direct line number. Before Carole could question how he knew where they had been that day, Ellie interrupted and explained that it was the boy in the supermarket's father, the man on the TV news programme. As Ellie had met him, she volunteered to ring him back and Carole, who was in dire need of more painkillers, cheerfully acquiesced.

Foreman answered gruffly, but softened immediately he heard Ellie's voice. He explained that there had been some recent developments that needed his immediate attention, but he wanted to speak to Mrs Meyer about a neighbour's son. Ellie asked if he meant Daniel Littlewood, and the policeman said that was correct.

As Carole was in her room, Ellie asked Bob if he would mind not speaking of their visit to see Brazil. She told him her friend had not been well and she did not want to worry her by telling her she had been hobnobbing with murderers. Bob agreed and arranged to call at about six o'clock that evening for a quick word with Mrs Meyer.

Ellie then hurriedly divulged that she was prepared to assist him, if he thought she could be of any help. The silence down the phone made Ellie wonder if he had heard her, or maybe was regretting his request after her distraught display in the prison. He dispelled her concerns as soon as he spoke.

'Thank God for that! I assume you do not want me to mention this tonight?'

'For the time being. I don't want to be devious, but I cannot hurt someone who has been so good to me, all right?'

'Fine by me, I'm just glad to have you on board. We'll talk as soon as is convenient . . . and thank you. See you later.'

* * *

The policeman's visit was a short one. Carole confirmed Daniel's story about tidying up, and both Ellie and Carole filled him in on the date and times of the prowler story. Carole was relieved to have an answer to the Summer House

Cleaner Mystery, and thought Michael would be even more thrilled to have the puzzle explained at last. She had noticed on several occasions that things were not exactly where she thought she had left them, but she'd put it down to the advancing of the years! The last thing the DCI asked was about the elderly woman and the dog that Daniel said he had spoken to.

Carole was silent, and Ellie completely dumbfounded. After a pause, Carole got up, went out of the room for a moment, and returned with a photograph. 'Show him this, and if he says this is the woman he talked to, then believe him, Officer, and I advise that you let him go. Daniel Littlewood is no murderer.'

Bob Foreman studied the older woman with deep interest, tucked the photo in his wallet, and thanked them for their help. He stared directly at Ellie and said he would phone again soon. She nodded, and an understanding passed between them.

As he left, Ellie looked knowingly at Carole. 'I suppose the photo was of Vera?'

'Of course. Now if you will forgive me, I think I'll lie down until Michael gets back. Then we'll eat.'

Ellie nodded. 'And considering the day we've had, I think I'll do the same.'

* * *

The team were back from Guildford. Mary Probart had been identified by WDC Brown and they had left Vic Barratt with the scenes of crime officers, until their job was finished.

Lenny Chambers, the SOCO friend of Foreman, had sent a message via Leatham saying that he was almost certain Mary had been killed elsewhere and dumped on the hill. Until the forensic reports were complete, he couldn't say much, but the pathologist estimated that Mary Probart had died sometime on Sunday afternoon. The mutilations and method of killing was the same as before.

'He took her and killed her, he didn't hold her anywhere, well, not alive anyway. How long has she been out there in the woods, any ideas?' asked Bob.

Leatham looked at his notebook. 'Lenny reckons about ten to twelve hours at the most, but don't quote him on that.'

'So, he stored her dead body for, what, about three days, then dumped her up there. How did he get her there? You can't drive right up to the top, can you?'

Leatham said that there was a car park a few hundred yards down from the church. No chance of getting tyre prints, St Martha's had lots of visitors and it was a dog-walker's paradise up there. With a few heavy showers recently, the muddy surface of the car park was a quagmire. Mary had only weighed about eight stone, so a fit bloke, and from all the descriptions of the Running Man, he could have carried her without too much difficulty to the spot where he left her. Little effort had been made to hide the body. Some leaf mould had been scooped away and the girl laid, face up, in the shallow grave, with sticky brown leaves clinging to her bloody clothes. Again, forensics noted the lack of evidence.

The team were despondent, and after Bob had issued them with their various tasks, they went back to their desks with a singular lack of enthusiasm. As Leatham had noted, they would have to release Littlewood. According to the timing, he was in custody when the body had been taken to St Martha's, so unless he was working with an accomplice, he had the very best of alibis. He had also instantly recognised the photograph that Carole Meyer had given Bob, and the woman was wearing the brooch that Littlewood had previously described, so that was that. Bob was back on the merry-go-round again. Dealing with the relatives. Waiting for Pathology. Speaking to the press and, God forbid, talking to the superintendent. Oh, what a joy that would be. Their second suspect released, and another death. He could hardly wait.

* * *

Vic Barratt's wife, Barbara, looked out of the upstairs window. She had heard her husband's car pull into the drive and she waved as she saw him walk around the back of his old Winnebago. Unroadworthy, but still parked in the front garden, it waited for overworked Vic to get the time to start doing the repairs it needed to make it legal again.

She smiled; they had had some wonderful holidays in the old camper. In its heyday, and before they adopted the children, they had toured France, Holland and Germany. Good times, she thought. Good memories.

She ran down the stairs and hugged her husband. She had kept a late supper ready, just in case he made it home that night.

He was in low spirits and although she usually tried not to ask him too much about his work, she knew from his face and his general demeanour that they must have found that poor missing girl. The papers were full of the disappearance, and the police were getting a lot of flak from the press about the murders and their lack of progress.

He picked at his supper and flicked idly through his mail. When he came to yet another letter in his father's instantly recognisable writing, she saw him sigh and put it on one side to read later. She thought about telling him to read it now and get it over with but changed her mind.

They sat for a while on the sofa, wrapped in a close embrace. A late-night film was showing but it did not hold their attention, and at one thirty in the morning they wearily went up the stairs to bed. He briefly looked in on his slumbering kids, staring down at their sleeping forms with undisguised love.

He kissed his wife good night and lay beside her, holding her hand tightly.

As she drifted off to sleep, she heard him say over and over again, 'We have to catch him. We have to stop him.'

* * *

In a police house in Addlestone, Wendy Brown tossed uncomfortably in her bed, Mary Probart's dead face swimming under her closed eyelids. In the gloom of the bedroom, she muttered an apology and a promise to her unwelcome guest. 'I'm so sorry, Mary, but we'll get the bastard, I promise, we'll get him for you.'

* * *

Hudson lay next to his new girlfriend. After half an hour of attempted love making, they had given up for the night. The murders kept marching through his mind and he couldn't let go of the case.

'Where are you, you murdering madman? I want to see you banged up for good. You're ruining my sex life!'

* * *

As the clock on the murder room wall flashed two o'clock, Jonathan Leatham wearily closed the file on the Waters Meet Hotel. His eyes were closing and he needed to be awake enough to drive back to Woking. As he pulled on his jacket, he looked once more at the whiteboards. There was now a fourth. A picture of Mary was centre top, the estimated day and time of her death, and little else, until the lab coughed up a report.

'Come on, girls, give me a break! You tell me the connection, and I'll nail the bastard for you. Deal?'

* * *

Windsor slept, but in his sleep he was running. Running fast, but the man in the long black coat was closing on him. He glanced behind, trying not to slacken his pace, and he saw a dull glint, as some unseen light fell on the piece of scaffolding that the man held tightly in his hand. Windsor woke up, coated in beads of sweat and shivering.

* * *

Barry Corbett sat behind the wheel of the unmarked car and watched a few late-night guests and staff pass in and out of the hotel doors. He had been there for an hour. He did not know what he was there for but still he sat, and watched . . .

CHAPTER TWENTY-SEVEN

At nine o'clock the team assembled for the DCI's morning briefing. It was Friday and the group were in unusually sombre frame of mind. There were no catcalls, no jokes, no laughter, and when the chief strode up to the front. All eyes were on him.

'You can imagine what the Super is saying about us, can't you? This investigation has gone to rat shit! We have four dead women and no suspects. This morning we will be releasing Daniel Littlewood. Dr Gerrard is looking at him now, and as soon as she has finished, he will be allowed home. His claims of hiding in a summer house have been validated by the owner and, as you know, he was here in custody when Mary Probart's body was taken from the place of the murder and deposited up on St Martha's Hill. We have cordoned off a three-mile area there, and Guildford are manning the search for us. You all have your allocated jobs to do, but before you get on' — Bob paused, uncertain of the reception his next words were going to get — 'I have to ask for your cooperation with a consultant that I am bringing in to assist us . . .'

A few eyes narrowed and a moan came from one corner of the room. 'Oh hell, it hasn't got bad enough to call in Mystic Meg has it?'

A ripple of laughter ran through the ranks.

'Not exactly, but . . .'

'Oh, sir, you haven't, have you? Not a bloody clairvoyant? Did someone pop down to Brighton and grab her out of her tent on the pier?'

'Shut up!' Bob's voice held an edge that stifled the sniggers. 'Our record on this case is crap! And I'm not turning down help, no matter where it comes from, and, no, Detective Smart-arse Hudson, she's not a clairvoyant. This is a lady with a very unusual gift. I have seen it in action, and she has some admirers in very high places, so do yourselves a favour and hold your judgement. If she needs to prove herself to you, I'm sure she will, but I for one am convinced she could help our investigation. So, as we have little else to go on, give her all the help she needs. And for fuck's sake, you lot, be polite! Okay?'

There was a bewildered murmur of assent and a scraping of chairs as they left the gathering.

'DI Leatham, a word in your shell-like, if you please!'

Jonathan followed the big man to his office, closed the door and sat down as directed.

'Jon. I am out on a limb here and I know it, but let me tell you a bit about Ellie McEwan . . .'

* * *

The doorbell rang and Ellie, unplastered leg encased in a thin tubigrip stocking, hurried as best she could to let Michael in.

'Oh I say! I bet that feels easier!' he exclaimed.

'I can't tell you how much!' laughed Ellie. 'Although it still feels weird, and really vulnerable. But how was the trip?'

'Successful. I don't know what I did to deserve Janet, but she is a life- saver.' Michael struggled out of his coat and hung it on the hall rack. He fought for a while with several carrier bags and yet another holdall. 'These are a few more clothes and things, just in case . . .' He looked guilty, but his love for his wardrobe had overcome Carole's inference that he had far too many clothes for a travelling man. He grinned at Ellie. 'She'll never notice.'

'I wouldn't be so sure, my friend!' A voice boomed out from the kitchen.

'Oops! Hello, old thing. How's the head?'

'Better. Ellie got on very well today. A bit of physio, and she'll be ready for the London Marathon!'

'Hardly! But it's doing fine, good news, huh?'

'The best! What's for supper, I'm starving?'

As they ate, Carole told Michael about Daniel's use of the sanctuary and his admission of tidying it up. As she thought, Michael was relieved to finally have an answer to his conundrum, but even more pleased for Marie that her son would most probably be off the hook. The conversation turned to the murders, and contrary to everything she had planned, Ellie suddenly decided to tell Carole that she was thinking about helping DCI Foreman with his investigation.

She put it tactfully and played her role down to a minimum. She simply said that if the police were questioning someone, she might join them as an observer, to see if she could pick anything up from the suspect's auras.

Both Carole and Michael were quiet, and Ellie felt bad that she had not discussed this with her professor friend first.

Finally, after a long silence, Carole said that she had been expecting it. 'In my mind, things are following the awful pattern I'd been hoping to avoid. I'm sure, Ellie, that you're being drawn into a dangerous situation, but if I try to dissuade you, I'm guessing that it will make you all the more determined.' She gave Ellie an anxious look. 'I sincerely hoped that you would not do this, but all I can say is to keep your involvement as limited as you can, and always have someone with you when you are around these unsavoury people.'

Ellie thought of Brazil's lustful smile, and decided to go along with Carole on that one. She promised to be careful, and swiftly changed the subject.

* * *

At ten they drifted off to bed.

Ellie, for the first night of comparative comfort without the plaster.

Michael, to fall heavily into his fluffy bed and a deep exhausted sleep.

Carole, to lie wide awake until the early hours, her headache thundering, praying fervently for protection for her friend.

* * *

It had been music to Bob's ears when Ellie had phoned that morning, asking if she could come down to the station. She had wondered if she could meet some of his team and get to know them a bit. She had promised not to get in the way but she felt she needed her presence there to be accepted. She was more than aware that her appearance among his tough, probably cynical, workforce, would not necessarily be appreciated. She was not far enough into her new enterprise to be able to deal with the ridicule that was sure to come her way, and she was not too sure how she would handle it. She felt that the friendly approach would be her easiest way in.

Bob Foreman had wholeheartedly agreed, and told her that he was assigning her to DI Jonathan Leatham, a thoroughly likeable and well-educated man who she would liaise with while she was at the station.

He had sent a car to collect her and she arrived at eleven o'clock. He introduced her to Jonathan and left her to the inspector's gentlemanly care, while he steeled himself to plough through Amanda Gerrard's latest report.

* * *

Jonathan Leatham's aura had a good deal of red in it, a healthy colour intermingled with predominantly greens and yellows. Ellie felt that he was suited to his job, with well-directed energies and a good sense of reality. From talking to him she gathered that he was analytical without losing his enquiring mind. In Jonathan's company, she enjoyed his polite but not condescending manner and felt safe in his openness.

He took her to each of the team in turn, introduced her, and in most cases left her for a short while. She was not too sure what they had been expecting when they were told they would have a consultant working with them, but she was fairly certain it was not a very ordinary looking young woman, with a friendly smile, and a pair of crutches.

There was no open antagonism, although she met with an underlying scepticism and slight suspicion from one or two of the officers, but mainly she found simple curiosity.

Ellie had told herself before she began that she would not show off. It was not ethical, and she hoped it would not be necessary. After a while she sensed that there was only one officer who needed a little bit of convincing. She felt that if she could bring him around, there would be no need to prove herself to any of the others.

PC Windsor was not actively taunting her, but she picked up a bit of the heckler in him. After his third 'amusing jibe', she politely suggested that before he exerted any more energy on baiting her, he took himself off to the dentist and sorted out that bothersome filling that was giving him such discomfort.

His face went scarlet. He had purposely not mentioned the toothache, and had been careful not to be seen rubbing his aching jaw. He had a reputation to uphold, after all, and if the team discovered he was terrified of the dentist, it would not do much for his street cred.

He started to babble, uncharacteristically, about not having had time to make an appointment, what with the murders . . .

His peers were astounded, and as Windsor had been too taken back to deny anything, Ellie McEwan made her quiet mark on the team and quelled her heckler in one unremarkable move. The rest of her trip around the department was easier.

WDC Wendy Brown gave off a considerable amount of emotional disturbance, nothing unpleasant, but Ellie suspected a kind of guilt had a great deal to do with it. Sergeant Vic Barratt was completely dedicated to his work — it showed clearly in his aura — and Ellie watched in awe as his energy fields glowed with a shower of pink and green lights when he talked to her of his two children. Hudson displayed lots of orange combined with other bright colours. She was very much aware of the young policeman's sexuality. Nothing threatening, he was just a healthy, red-blooded male. Corbett was a deep thinker. His aura was not so bright and it was apparent to Ellie's eyes that he was suffering. There was no specific site of concentrated pain but she felt an all over fatigue. After chatting for a while, she was interested to see him reach in his pocket for some extra strong paracetamol, mentioning that he thought he was coming down with something.

She had a brief sighting of one of the SOCO team. Leatham told her he was called Lenny, and both his aura, and his whole manner, exuded dedication and complete involvement in the job in hand. He had come and gone in a flash, but left quite an eruption of colours on Ellie's retinas.

It took her an hour to get around to meeting everyone, and then she flopped into a chair in Bob's office with a feeling of enormous tiredness. She was beginning to get an idea of what her new exercises would take out of her. Michael had warned her not to over-tax herself to start with, and here she was, positively knackered, and she had only accomplished her introductions!

WDC Brown brought them coffee and biscuits, and smiled warmly at Ellie. After a momentary pause before leaving, she said that she was pleased Ellie was there and, although she hadn't a clue how she worked, she sincerely hoped she could help them track the killer.

Ellie was overwhelmed by a feeling that the woman officer was taking this case very personally, and she could not help but think that it was not a good thing.

'Need to run a few things by you, Ellie,' said Bob, helping himself to a biscuit. 'As you know, police officers and those working closely here are subject to the Official Secrets Act. I have to make sure you understand, that although you haven't signed the Act, while you are here on an informal basis, you are still bound by it. The penalties for breaches are severe, so what goes on here, stays here, okay?'

Ellie said she understood, then Bob added that there was a need for discretion in what she chose to share with Michael. It had been agreed that, as her tutor, he should be privy to some information, but there would be certain aspects of the case that she would have to be silent about.

She stayed for a further hour discussing a variety of elements of the murders with the chief inspector, then said that she must get back to Compton.

As her driver pulled out of the station and through the building site that was to become the new Surrey Area Forensic Laboratory, Ellie was too wrapped up in the severity of the operation to even hear the wolf whistles and shouted comments from the hard-hatted workmen.

She sank back into the fabric seating of the police car, and felt the burden of finding the man responsible for the deaths of four talented women, slowly descend onto her slight shoulders.

CHAPTER TWENTY-EIGHT

As she walked across the lawn, Ellie realised how much better her leg was feeling. Her limp was far less pronounced, and she could hardly believe that it was six weeks since she had first walked into DCI Foreman's murder room.

Today's breakfast with Michael and Carole was a little different to usual. They all sat in the summer house with the doors and windows wide open, and the warm rays of the spring sun pouring in all around them.

Scrubbs's efforts in the garden were paying off. As they walked out, they were greeted with banks of gold and white daffodils, and an early showing of deep purple tulips.

Carole's headaches had receded over the weeks and she was almost back to her old irascible self. She spent more and more time alone in the summer house, and it seemed, much to Michael and Ellie's relief, that she was becoming more at ease and comfortable with her young friend's police involvement.

Michael had settled into an acceptable routine of two days up in his London clinic, and the rest of the time at Snug Cottage, in his role of tutor and mentor to Surrey Police's newest, and only, aura consultant.

The investigation was going badly. Other suspects had been questioned and released. A hoax caller had them following a red herring for days, until Ellie had sensed a destructive mischievousness around the bogus witness. The unpleasant scrote, as Vic termed him, was arrested for attempting to pervert the course of justice by the making of false statements, and Barry Corbett took a grim delight in reading the time-waster his rights.

The case was turning depressingly cold on them, and the only thing that was keeping Bob Foreman sane at present was the fact that the killer had not resumed his grisly vendetta against dexterous women.

During the last month, Ellie had prowled the cells and the custody suite, talking to every form of low life that she could find. She had met some obnoxious and frighteningly disagreeable characters, but never once witnessed the revolting display of energy she had seen emanating from the murderer, Albert Courtney Brazil. Last week, a celebrity crime presenter had dedicated half of his prime-time show to asking the public for their help. The switchboards had been flooded with calls and a ton of new information had been fed onto their computer. The description of the Running Man, Dracula, was circulated nationwide. To no avail.

Bob Foreman had been careful, through all the press and TV coverage, to keep Ellie McEwan's association with them concealed. She was his only secret weapon and he could not afford her alliance with them to be discovered.

This situation had suited Carole to the hilt. The less her Ellie was in the public eye and, therefore, the murderer's eye, the better.

They sat in the summer house, sharing toast and marmalade, tea and gossip. They had all taken the morning off from their various duties, and Carole wanted to discuss plans for building a rather adventurous water feature close to the garden room. She loved natural sounds for meditation, and felt that water splashing and falling close by would make a significant difference in her ability to relax. The others were simply delighted that she had her old drive and enthusiasm back. Michael thought he would have agreed to her building a scale-model of the Taj Mahal in the courtyard, if it made her happy.

After a while, Carole wandered off to discuss their initial ideas with Scrubbs. He was the logical one, who would either make her innovative plans concrete, or send her back to the drawing board.

On their own, Michael once again brought up the subject of Ellie joining him in his clinic. He realised that it would be well into the future. She would need to study, and pass examinations. He explained that it was actually a criminal offence to diagnose and treat without a certified licence, or unless you were a doctor. He thought she would probably enjoy the studying, even though it would be hard work. He would continue to coach her and he still felt she had a marvellous future if she combined her gift with a solid medical background.

She was about to answer him, when the pager that the chief inspector had given her started to vibrate. She pressed the receive button, and a text she had been dreading unfurled across the screen. 'Required at station immediately. Car on way. Possible number five. Foreman.'

Later that day, Ellie and her friend Gill had planned to try to get her behind the wheel again, for the first time since her accident. She quickly rang Gill and cancelled their date. Time enough for that she thought, when all this is over. She swiftly filled Michael in on the news and asked him to relay it to Carole, who was missing along with her five boys. As he wished her luck, a police car sped down the lane, oblivious to the damage on the suspension, and screeched to a halt at the front gate.

* * *

At the bottom of the orchard, gently retying Vera's favourite wind chime that had come loose from the apple tree branch, Carole looked up into the sunny blue sky and saw dark clouds approaching.

'It's starting, isn't it?'

A slight gust of wind, heavily perfumed with the scent of flowers, blew gently through her hair and she heard the single whispered word.

'Yes.'

* * *

'So, are you prepared for this? You do not have to. In fact, I'm not sure why you want to anyway.' Bob Foreman was none too happy about Ellie's request to attend the scene of the crime. 'Photos are bad enough, but actually seeing a young woman's body, Ellie, I'm really not sure you should.'

Fifteen minutes later the three cars made their way up the tree-lined drive to the main doors of the school. Ellie got out, and stood beside Jonathan, looking up at the ornate portico with the school crest centralised in the rounded arch. The private school on the edges of Chartsford had a fine reputation, not only for academic excellence, but for the arts and practical hands-on subjects.

Inside the reception hall, with its magnificent high ceiling and curving staircase, stood a collection of worried and nervous teachers and older pupils. For a second, it reminded Ellie of a Victorian scene with the staff lining up to welcome back the master and mistress of the manor. Their agitation and fear soon dispelled her fanciful notions and she was brought sharply back to earth by the chief inspector's booming voice, asking who had found the body.

Two girls stepped forward, clasping tightly on to each other. Ellie thought they were probably sixth formers. The one with more braid sewn on to her blazer, apparently a prefect, stammered that she and Annette, the shaking girl next to her, had found it.

WDC Brown and another woman police constable stationed themselves each side of the frightened teenagers and spoke gently to them. In broken and sob strewn sentences, the girls told how, before morning assembly started, they had gone to the Art and Craft block to look for a pencil case that Annette thought she may have left there the afternoon before. The classrooms and studios were empty, and not finding the missing article anywhere obvious, they widened their search to the cupboards and store rooms, thinking that the cleaners may have put it away with other art equipment. In a large storage space, used for both equipment and unfinished ceramic works, they discovered, not the pencil case, but the mutilated body of Miss Jenny Davis, the craft mistress.

Too distressed to continue, the women police officers escorted them to a side room, where they waited with the terrified girls until their parents arrived.

Ellie went with the rest of the team to the art block.

She felt a peculiar throbbing, high in her chest, and realised that her pulse was racing. She had insisted that she be here, and now as she donned her protective suit, along with the others, she was not so sure she had made the right decision.

A uniformed officer held the blue-and-white tape up for them to pass underneath. Time stood still, and Ellie found herself watching what felt like an old, silent black-and-white film.

She saw images of the scenes of crime officers stepping away to allow the DCI to approach the woman's body, camera flashes exploding, and the strange, almost pagan way they circled around the fifth victim.

There was an instant when their combined energies met and swirled together, filling the room with a confusion of colour.

Ellie blinked, and as she reopened her eyes, she was hit by a blast of bone-jarring force. The same evil discharge that had sprung from Brazil, as he recalled his dearest killing, had leaped from someone in the horror-charged room.

The shock had been so great that she could only utter the tiniest of gasps . . . something perhaps to be expected from a woman seeing her first corpse, and something that in an instant, she knew she must conceal.

She bowed her hooded head and tried to bring her reeling and terrified thoughts under control. She found herself staring at a young and distinctly dead young woman, lying on an uncomfortable bed of smashed pottery. There was blood that had seeped from a hidden head wound, and her throat was livid, bruised and damaged.

Ellie dragged her unwilling eyes to the right hand that lay in disfigured supplication. She swallowed bile and thought that she would throw up if she did not get away.

But she couldn't. She had to look, from the partial shadow of her hood, at every single person in this claustrophobic and stinking room. She gulped, knowing that one of those gathered there in attendance to the Late Miss Jenny Davis was also her killer.

Ellie shifted on her feet and looked away from the body, endeavouring to act naturally, if one could ever do such a thing in such circumstances. She quickly counted fifteen of them in the storeroom. But the awful lights had gone.

She looked from face to face, some she recognised, some she did not, but what they all had in common were the normal energies you would expect from shocked and excited human beings. The school caretaker stood by the door — had he let someone out? She thought not. He had stood, in shock, his huge bundle of keys in his hand, when she had entered, and he had not moved. There was no other way out.

Slowly, and in the fashion of a mantra, she began to recite in her head, the names or identities of all present, knowing that one was the murderer. When she got to the end of the list she started again. She could not allow herself to forget anyone there, and she must find out who the strangers were.

She left the building, tore off her suit, and walked back to the main block alone.

With every step she took she was made more aware of that terrible responsibility that hung around her like a shroud, and now she had another problem. With everyone she trusted, apart from Michael, in that room with her, who could she tell of what she had seen?

She found a notepad and a pen in her bag, and wrote name after name. She felt awfully alone, as she realised that the answer to her question was no one.

Hopefully the team would put her subdued mood down to her reaction to the sight of the murder victim in situ. That had been awful enough, but the dreadful realisation that she was sharing the room with a serial killer had somewhat relegated poor Jenny Davis's death to second place.

She systematically scrutinised her colleagues and the school staff who had been present, searching for the merest hint of malevolence or sickness. There was nothing.

Sitting in the front hall, she checked her list and made a simple diagram of their positions in the room, circling the people she did not know.

By the door was the caretaker. The prefect had met him on her way back to get help, and he had rushed to the Art and Craft block to make sure it was not a prank. To his left had been the headmistress and, next to her, the deputy head. Close to the body were two scenes of crime officers, one was Lenny Chambers, plus the pathologist. Bob Foreman had stood beside the forensic doctor, and the circle had consisted of herself, Jonathan Leatham, Vic Barratt, DC Hudson, PC Windsor and Barry Corbett. The last two occupants of the room had been uniformed officers; one had been on duty just inside the door, and the other on the far side of the circle.

She took a deep breath and crossed through the two school mistresses, as women were not suspects. She crossed herself off the list, and that left twelve suspects.

The caretaker, the pathologist, the uniformed officers, and one of the SOCOs, she knew nothing about, but everyone else she knew, or had spoken to.

As her mind slowed down, she tried to focus on the actual incident. Was there any way she could pinpoint from which part of the room the flash had come. She closed her eyes and reluctantly relived that horrible moment. She shuddered with the memory but was certain that it had just invaded the whole room space. There was no way of telling its origin.

Staring at the names, Ellie found herself looking suspiciously at the people who had been her working colleagues for the past six weeks. People with good auras — they were nearly friends, for God's sake! She had talked with them, swapping stories, and laughing about their families, and their escapades in the Force. Never once had there been a hint of a bad aura. This was ridiculous! It had to be the caretaker or even one of the SOCOs, surely not her colleagues?

She went over the list again. To suspect Bob Foreman was like indicting your favourite uncle. It could not be polite Gentleman Jonathan; it was unthinkable. With Vic Barratt's formidable love for his wife and children, you could not even consider him. Hudson's young Jack the Lad exterior hid a very likeable and dedicated hard worker. No, not him. Barry Corbett, she did not know so well, but he was as obsessed with catching the killer as they all were, and he was too, well, just too honest and straight. Sporty and enthusiastic Windsor? A great young guy, but without being disparaging, he did not seem clever or devious enough to plan a murder. Lenny Chambers, the team had told her that he had been with the Force since horse-drawn carriages, and he was as committed to providing the evidence to solving crime as it was possible to be.

She shook her head and tried to plan her next move. She had to find out about the other SOCO and the two uniforms. The routine investigation would cover the caretaker, and surely the forensic pathologist could not be a suspect, could he? She remembered looking at him as he stood over the dead girl. He was elderly, a mass of fluffy grey hair, and he was nearly as rotund as Michael. He could not be the Running Man by any stretch of the imagination. She crossed him off the list.

'The first one is always the worst, bit like post-mortems.' Ellie jumped; she had not seen Jonathan approach her. 'Sorry, I didn't mean to startle you, are you all right?'

'Yes, of course. As you say, not the kind of thing I'm used to.'

'You never get used to them,' said a deeper voice from behind the DI.

'You should get back to the station, Ellie. You have seen enough here, I think.'

More than enough thank you, thought Ellie, and as Foreman's tone left no room for argument, she collected her pad and her bag and stood up.

'PC Rushmore must go back with some information that I want put straight onto the computer. He will take you.'

Ellie was secretly pleased to see one of the two men that she needed to identify, waiting by the door.

'Thank you,' she replied. 'I'll see you back at the incident room later.'

Bob and Jonathan watched her go, and she knew they were both thinking that her attendance at the scene of crime had not been a good idea.

In the car, she was disappointed to find out that it was Rushmore's first week in Surrey. He had recently transferred from Cumbria when his father died. He had moved back into the family home in Esher to look after his mother and disabled brother. So, PC Rushmore was in the clear, and due to his short time with Surrey, would not know the other officer well enough to tell her anything useful. All she discovered was his name, PC Kevin Bell. Well, at least it was a start, and she could cross off Rushmore.

The murder room was practically empty, and she used Vic's desk to ring Snug Cottage. She wanted to be sure that Michael would be there when she got back. She did not dare speak to him over the phone, but was desperate to talk to him as soon as possible.

Michael, clearly sensing a problem, urged her to make her excuses and get home right away. The thought was tempting, but Ellie wanted to be there when the team returned. If it was one of them, discussion about the death could possibly induce another burst of energy from the killer. She told her friend to expect her early evening as there were things to do first. She assured him that she was in no danger, but she was glad he could not read her life lights, as they would have certainly told another story.

In the comparative quiet of the murder room, she explored her own position in this scenario. It was possible that she was as safe as she ever was. The murderer may not know about, or have even considered, her powers. If he had, the outburst was so brief, he might have assumed she had not seen it. It was also possible that she was under serious threat. He might have been very aware of her, and what she may have seen. In which case, what would he do?

She shivered uncontrollably, as she formulated the worst possibility. The one that left Ellie McEwan as victim number six.

The debriefing on the team's return offered no insights for the aura consultant. Her heart sank as she watched the fifth whiteboard being hung next to that of Mary Probart. It glared at her, devoid of pictures and empty of information.

This could be you, it screamed . . . next time.

She professed to be too tired and wrung out to be of any help at that time, and to Bob Foreman's concern, insisted on calling a taxi to get her home. She explained that she needed to run a couple of errands on the way, and could not justify using a police driver when they were so stretched as it was.

She had not wanted to behave in any way other than normal, but she needed to be completely away from uniforms and police-speak for a while. A cab driver with his trivial and inconsequential chat was exactly what she needed to restore the status quo in her mind. Then, in the tranquillity of Snug Cottage, she would brainstorm Michael with her discomforting news.

* * *

They had talked long into the night. Michael had listened intently as Ellie narrated the story of her day. He had stopped her only once to clarify a point, and afterwards sat in silence, digesting the information. He had said there were other things he needed to know about the investigation, and seeing that the goalposts had dramatically moved in the last twelve hours, Ellie felt no pangs of guilt about enlightening Michael with any and every aspect of the enquiry.

At the end of his deliberations, he had looked her full in the face and told her that they must take the very worst-case scenario, and work on that. It was the only way.

As she lay in bed, watching the last embers of the fire that she had lit for comfort, not for warmth, she recalled his serious speech.

'We have to assume that he is fully informed of your talent. If he has even the remotest suspicion you are on to him, he must remove you from the equation. Not putting too fine a point on it, but knowing his particular predilection for murdering women, we know what will be going through his mind. But, because of your close involvement with the police, it won't be easy. He may rethink, but I doubt it. What we must do, and do fast, is find out who you can trust within your group. So far there is only one thing you have told me that I think you're wrong about — that you can tell no one. There are two people who you can approach. One is your woman detective, Wendy Brown, isn't it? And the other is the profiler you mentioned. The criminal psychologist. You must use your regular detective to check everyone's whereabouts at the times of all the deaths. It will have to be a copper to get access to the right information, and if you start nosing around in staff records, it could alert him or draw too much attention to yourself. Now, I take it that the profiler is not based at your station, which is good news, because she can use her own staff to try and find some history that has to be attached to the killer. She will have to take each officer in turn, and make some very discreet enquiries about their background. Ellie, get to see her tomorrow. Go to wherever she is based and talk to her. Convince her. She could be your greatest ally. I have no doubt that Brown will do all she can, but make sure she is totally aware that she must not, I repeat, must not tell anyone else what she's doing. It could cost a life, yours or hers, or even both, make her understand that!'

He had paused and bit his lip. 'If anything starts to go bottoms-up, you get out, and get out fast. Keep your mobile charged at all times, and I think we should have some sort of emergency code. You know, something innocuous that you could say down the phone so I would know to get you help. How about . . . could I pick up your dry cleaning as you're too busy! Yes, dry cleaning, Okay? All I can do is to promise to be right here beside the telephone every minute you are away from the cottage, and using my mobile, I can do any sleuthing or checking you want.'

He had gone on to say that what he really wanted to do was bundle her off to London and anonymity, but he knew she would not leave five dead women to find their own killer, not when she had narrowed the search down to one of ten men.

She lay, her body still but her mind racing.

One in ten. She had to find him, before he decided how to deal with her.

She thought of Wendy Brown and Amanda Gerrard. From tomorrow onwards she may not be alone, and if between them they could find positive proof that other officers were to be trusted, then the odds did not seem quite so bad.

She shut her eyes and tried to sleep.

Damn it, she wasn't going to be number six.

* * *

The car was to be with her at eight o'clock, as Ellie had said she would like to be present at the morning briefing. As she dressed, she wondered if there was any chance she'd been mistaken about what she had witnessed. She had asked Michael if he thought she may have had some kind of flashback to Brazil, but from her clear description, he considered that unlikely. He reminded her to listen carefully to any information at the briefing about the school caretaker. He was the odd one out, after all, and if there was any chance he was the murderer, then she must tell the DCI what she had witnessed.

Michael waited with her in the hall of Snug Cottage, his smart check dressing gown stretching slightly over his corpulent tummy. 'Keep me posted. I want lots of reassuring calls, okay? And anything you want checked out from here, just ask. I won't worry unless I have cause to, right?'

Ellie was touched by his attempt to cover his obvious concern for her. Suddenly, as the sound of an approaching engine joined the morning birdsong, she frowned and asked, 'Michael, if it is one of the police officers, why do I only see good auras coming from him?'

The professor rubbed his eyes tiredly. 'I've been awake most of the night trying to work that one out, and the answer is, I don't know.'

CHAPTER TWENTY-NINE

The whiteboard now held a photograph of the young craft teacher smiling as she accepted some sort of award. She died, perhaps only two hours before her two students had found her, at around seven a.m. No strangers had been seen in the school or the grounds. Jennifer Sandra Davis had let herself into the craft block at approximately six thirty a.m. to put a tray of ceramic work into the kiln for firing. The injuries were as before, and even without the full forensic report, the pathologist had unofficially stated that he was almost certain the same sawn-off piece of scaffolding had been used. He had identified tiny flecks of old dried blood imbedded into the wounds, the same as the previous victims.

The DCI led them through the usual procedure, giving them facts, times, approximations and conjectures, and asking them for feedback, information and hard facts.

'Right, we have checked out the caretaker . . .'

Ellie stiffened.

'. . . no previous form, been with the school for fifteen years. The head has given him a glowing report as a conscientious and loyal member of the staff, and he was seeing in a delivery of oil for the heating system at the time the teacher was killed. He's clean as a whistle.'

An ice-cold ripple of fear trickled down Ellie's spine. She had not realised how much hope she had pinned on the caretaker, and just how much she had wanted it to be him. Now she mentally crossed his name off her list.

The meeting continued, and when they finally disbanded, Bob called her over to his office. As she entered, she had the overwhelming urge to tell him everything and be damned. It could not be Bob Foreman.

But it *was* one of nine men in the room, yet she had never felt so unsure of anything in her life.

This morning Bob was clearly exhausted, and wound-up like a spring. He was not his usual friendly self, but she had not expected otherwise. He wanted to know if there was anything she needed as he was going to be very busy later. He had yet another statement to make to the Press, and had been summoned to the Super's office.

Taking the opportunity, she asked him if she could have Dr Gerrard's number — there were a few things in the report he had given her to read that did not make sense. She hoped he would not mind if she had a quick word with the psychologist to clarify them.

Bob absent-mindedly handed her a card, and gave her a warning about the scarlet doctor's lack of social graces.

Taking the card, she thanked him and went in search of WDC Wendy Brown.

Brown was hammering away on her computer keyboard and glaring at the screen when Ellie sat down beside her.

'Bloody thing! Why does it have to give me all this garbage, when all I want is a blood group!' She cancelled the screen, and threw herself back in her chair. 'Ellie! Please tell me whatever you need has nothing to do with computers?'

'Sorry, Wendy, that might not be the case. Can I have a word, somewhere private?'

The policewoman picked up immediately on Ellie's grave intonation. 'I was just going to the ladies' room, will that do?'

Sitting on a hard bench in the ladies' locker room, Ellie abandoned all her carefully prepared speeches, and told the detective exactly what she had witnessed at the scene of Jenny Davis's murder. She did not have to spell out the implications.

Brown put her hands to her mouth and whistled softly through her teeth. 'Shit! Are you absolutely sure?'

'Without doubt. Will you help me?'

'These are my friends, Ellie! Surely it has to be someone else? Oh shit!'

'Listen, the caretaker is out, so is the pathologist. One of the uniformed men has only just arrived here in Surrey. All the women are excluded. That leaves two SOCOs, one beat bobby, the DCI, the DI, Sergeants Corbett and Barratt, and Windsor and Hudson. It came from one of them.' She gave her an intense stare. 'Wendy, I *have* to know who I can trust! Until we can place each person conclusively in the clear, I am an utterly unprotected sitting duck, with a killer spending his every moment trying to decide how best to get rid of me!'

'Jesus! You think he knows what you saw! Oh, Ellie, yes, I'll help. Of course I'll help you. Let me think. I can get a lot of this from the duty rosters, and my diary will help, too, and my pocketbook, yes, leave it with me. I'll tell you as soon as I've managed to put someone else unmistakably on our side. With luck, if I can exonerate the officers one at a time, we can build up a safe unit, until we are left with one. Oh God, and he'll be the killer.'

Ellie put her arm around the woman. 'Thank you, let's pray we get that far before he discovers what we are doing.'

Wendy left, and Ellie punched Dr Amanda Gerrard's number into her mobile and held her breath.

Ten minutes later, as Ellie made her way through the front door to the waiting taxi, she concluded that Dr Gerrard was the rudest and most arrogant woman she had ever had the misfortune to speak to. The psychologist made Carole Meyer seem like a lovable pussy cat.

As they drove towards Kingston, she was still smarting at being told that wasting an influential psychologist's time was tantamount to treason. She did afford herself a smile, however, when she remembered that the disparaging remarks had been tinged with curiosity. Ellie had asked to see her urgently on the pretext of having some vital information about the murderer that she could not possibly put before the detectives until she had the opinion of a highly qualified psychologist.

Well, she had managed to talk her way into a meeting — now she needed to capture this singularly blunt and discourteous woman's attention and solicit her help. She was forced to admit that she'd certainly make a strong ally. She was sure this woman got exactly what she wanted, when she demanded it.

As the cab pulled up in front of the enormous glass-fronted office block, Ellie felt her stomach turn over with apprehension. She took a deep breath and announced her name to the receptionist. The painfully thin and immaculately dressed girl checked Ellie's details against Dr Gerrard's instructions and pointed towards the lifts. 'Seventh floor, room 706, Dr Gerrard is expecting you.'

Room 706 was more a suite than a room, and Ellie realised that it was a consultant's clinic as well as an office.

She had met the doctor once before at the police station, although she doubted the woman would recognise her again. To her surprise she not only remembered her, but knew a remarkable amount about her work. Against her better judgement, Ellie simply told her the truth, right up to the point of enrolling the assistance of WDC Wendy Brown, and imploring her to help them.

The imposing and brilliantly garbed woman sat with her arms folded and considered Ellie's account. 'You obviously believe what you have just told me. You are giving me no reason to think that this is some strange fabrication you are feeding me.'

She paused and peered at Ellie, making the younger woman feel a bit like a bug under a microscope lens.

'This is a truly unusual request you bring me, and I cannot deny that I am intrigued, not only with your peculiar aptitude, but with the fact that you think I can delve surreptitiously into the private lives of my close colleagues and high-ranking officers.'

Ellie took another breath and fired back at the psychologist with uncontrolled emotion. 'Doctor. I need an ally. I need someone outside the murder team to make some very delicate enquiries for me. I *know* you could do it. You'll have friends in high places, senior police officials who would, I'm sure, assist you if they felt you were on the track of a killer. A killer, maybe within the Force. I'm sorry, Dr Gerrard, but I don't have the privilege of time to spare at present. I'm afraid it's too late for my good intentions of being polite and trying to cajole you into helping me save my skin, and possibly that of Wendy Brown. Can I count on you to help me, or not?'

Amanda Gerrard smiled. 'Now you are talking my language, Miss McEwan! I have much more respect for the plain spoken among us! I do, as it happens, have a few favours I could call in. I should think some locked doors could be opened for me, if I so desire. Give me the list of officers, I shall check for skeletons in their cupboards and bogeymen under their beds.' She skimmed the names, raising an eyebrow here and there, then smiled at Ellie shrewdly. 'If it turns out to be DCI Bob Foreman, I shall hand in my notice and check myself into one of my own facilities immediately!'

'I am making no accusations, Doctor. I am fully aware that eight of these men are "good men and true". But one is not, and that's the one we have to find, before I run out of time.'

'I will do what I can, Miss McEwan. Let me have your mobile number. I cannot call you directly until we clear a few names, and let me know what your WDC comes up with.'

Ellie added Michael's number to her own, and passed them over to the doctor. It would not hurt to have a go-between.

She left the suite feeling both exhausted and exhilarated. The confrontation had been a success, but a draining one. Her taxi arrived, and on her way back to the station, she was horribly conscious of a clock ticking in her head.

* * *

Audrey Long had been dozing on the sofa when she was woken by a shout and the sound of running footsteps. Lifting the curtain, she saw a teenager racing down the road endeavouring to catch another boy on a bike.

For one moment she had been thrown back to that evening when she had seen the Running Man, and the old chap and his dog.

'So that was what it was!'

Memory flooded back, and the tiny piece of the jigsaw that had evaded her was there, as clear as the night that it happened. It was a very small thing and she wondered if the police would consider it a waste of time. The two officers had been very nice, she reasoned. She went to her desk and sorted through some cards and memos. There was the white card with the Surrey Police insignia on it. DC Hudson and DC Rawlings, that was it. She picked up the receiver and dialled the murder room number.

* * *

'Hello. Surrey Police. Can I help you? No, I'm sorry, he's off duty at present, Mrs Long. Can I be of assistance? Ahh, no, DC Rawlings is off on sick leave — what is the problem? Right, okay, let me get that down. Really! Well, thank you for that. I will be sure to pass it on to Detective Constable Hudson as soon as he is back in tomorrow, and thanks again, you have been most helpful.'

He sat, the piece of paper screwed up in a ball in his clenched fist. His face was expressionless and his eyes unfocused. A thought, other than his own, passed across his mind. So, there was less time than he had hoped for. He would have to act quickly, and she would be his swansong.

CHAPTER THIRTY

Wendy was about to pull her hair out. Two hours work, and all she had managed to do was eliminate the SOCO, and that was by chance. If she had not heard Lenny Chambers referring to some aspect of the young man's honeymoon, she would not have had a hope in hell of tracking down the Scene of Crime personnel's rosters. They were, after all, civilians attached to the Force. The young forensic officer had been in Bermuda getting spliced at the time of Helen Carberry's murder.

Eight to account for. She had a feeling PC Kevin Bell had only recently returned after an injury on duty. A quick run through her diary told her what she wanted to know. Bell had badly torn the ligaments in his ankle in a chase through a shopping centre. No way could he have been the Running Man.

Seven to go. Wendy knew she should have started at the top and worked down, but somehow, she just could not face checking up on the boss. She had the greatest respect for Bob, and hoped against hope that she would come up with a suspect before being forced to do a check on him.

She sighed and got back to the point where she had given up last time. Hudson's hours had been a nightmare to track. He was always changing his shifts, covering other people, and getting mates to cover him. It took another hour to be reasonably certain that he had been on duty during two of the murders, but she could not be absolutely sure. She felt the pressure of time slipping away. This was by no means as easy as she had thought. She wished Ellie would get back. She was not happy when the woman was out of her sight, and she had been gone for hours. She prayed Dr Gerrard would help them, anything that woman did not know about psychos was not worth knowing.

She sincerely hoped that Ellie could be persuasive enough to recruit her.

Pulling out a new set of roster sheets, she started on Windsor.

* * *

In the summer house, Carole sat deep in meditation. When Michael saw her he was reminded of the awful night that he nearly lost her. Looking through the window, not wishing to disturb her, he saw a very different woman. She was composed, relaxed and serene. Her back was ramrod straight and the hint of a smile played around her lips. He turned to leave her in peace when he heard his name called.

Eyes still closed, her head was turned in his direction and a hand slowly beckoned him inside.

'Sit and relax, my friend. It is perfectly safe.'

'Ellie. I have to be near the phone, in case she needs me.'

'She is in no danger, at present. Please sit for a moment.'

He recognised the strange music that had almost hypnotised him before.

'That sound?'

'It is a synthesis of all things natural and beautiful. It is used to enable you to meditate on a different plane.'

'I've never heard anything like it.'

'You won't have. There are very few copies of it that I know of. Now listen, Michael, we know we cannot stop

Ellie's hunt for the murderer, but we will help her, if we can. Tell her that she must not forget we are here for her. She must ask for help, or we cannot intervene, do you understand?'

He nodded and whispered 'yes'. He was confused. One minute he was talking to Carole, then he had the distinct feeling that it was Vera speaking to him.

'Tell her this. "Forget your new vocation, remember the old one! Remember the skill and the artistic design, the fine wiring of delicate head-dresses, the intricate bouquets, and the gentle way you touched the flowers." Tell her.'

Carole drifted into silence, and Michael walked swiftly back to the house. He must get hold of Ellie. The message had been unmistakable. Why had he not realised it himself?

The line was bad, but he understood that she was on her way back to the station. He spoke succinctly, needing her to comprehend what he said, without frightening her more than necessary.

'It does not matter anymore, what happened in the storeroom, it's irrelevant. He wants you anyway. All your talents and artistic ability. You are perfect for him even without your new gift. You must be very, very careful. Keep people around you at all times, and you have to find someone to trust, to help you!'

Ellie said she was no longer alone. The doctor was in her corner and so was Wendy Brown. She would be watchful, but they had to catch him.

He gave her the message from Carole about asking for help. She accepted that she understood, and the line broke up, ending their conversation.

* * *

DI Leatham sat at his desk massaging his temples with his thumbs. There was something, something just out of his grasp. Something tantalisingly close. It was like a finger beckoning from around a corner, but when you got there, it had disappeared, only to be seen enticing you to the next corner, before you lost sight of it again. He bit his thumb hard and stared down at the pile of folders in front of him.

All these checks, all these enquiries, and still he knew, without a doubt, that he'd not asked the right question. The connection was there — the number of dead women had grown, but he knew if he could find that one question to ask, then he would have his answer, and his man.

His head started to ache. He could not afford to lose his concentration now . . . he was so close.

* * *

Bob Foreman was lucky to escape from his meeting with the superintendent with his murder team still intact. The senior officer had wiped the floor with him, and his lack of progress. Threats had been made to turn the cases over to another serious crime squad from outside Surrey. Bob had managed to buy them three more days grace. Only three days to nail him. He felt sick to his stomach as he returned to his office and his failing enquiry.

* * *

Amanda Gerrard cancelled all her engagements for the rest of the afternoon and immersed herself in the dissemination of the names on the McEwan woman's list. She had already brought up some interesting and gritty reading, but nothing that smelled of the psychopath. Her influential friends had provided her with a wealth of private and personal history of the officers in question, and her computer monitor flashed with yet another site to access. She glanced at the clock. Nearly six o'clock. To hell with it, she'd work all night if need be.

She adjusted her glasses and read the screen. Now this was some thought-provoking material, indeed. Warning bells rang in some deep, dark spot in her gut.

She picked up the phone with the secure line and dialled.

Ten minutes later, anxiously chewing the end of her pen, she stared at the faxed printout she had just received.

It did not make sense. She threw down the pen and returned to the keyboard.

Something was not right. Not right at all.

She grabbed a piece of blu tack from her desk drawer and stuck her original profile of the killer to the side of the monitor screen, where she could refer and cross-check from the screen itself.

She tapped the last button and waited for the file to download. 'Oh my!' she murmured. 'What have we here?'

* * *

As soon as she entered the office, Wendy Brown dragged Ellie, almost physically, into the locker room.

After checking all the cubicles to ensure they would not be overheard, Wendy listed everything she had discovered so far.

'Right . . . the SOCO is all clear. PC Bell, I've eliminated him. I'm ninety-nine per cent sure of Hudson, but he's off duty at the minute, anyway. Lenny Chambers, the other SOCO is difficult to trace, he's an associated civilian, we do not have their workload schedules at this station. He has been called out to all the murders, and in honesty, I do not believe he could kill someone, go home, then get a phone call, and dash back to work on the crime scene, do you?'

'Hmm, but the trouble is, we are not working with a normal person, are we? Anyone else?'

'That's all I've managed to do.' Wendy looked worried. 'Ellie, look, I reckon you should get out of here. We are down to the DCI, Jonathan, Vic, Lenny, Barry Corbett, and Hudson and Windsor. The last two are not proving easy to follow, they both change shifts and swap days as often as their underpants. If I'm having problems with tracing the two constables, what the hell is it going to be like tracking the higher-ranking officers? It could take days, and we don't have days. I need some help and until I can clear someone completely, I'm not going to get it. You really would be safer away from the murder room. I will ring you as soon as I can prove another person free of suspicion.'

Ellie knew the WDC was right, but did not want to be too far from the heart of the operation. At least here she had friendly colleagues around her. It was just sad that she did not know who they were. She wondered how Dr Gerrard was getting on. It was tempting to ring her, but Ellie knew the sort of reception she might get and decided against that idea. Wendy could hardly believe Ellie had managed to talk the doctor round. WDC Brown had been in her company on several occasions and had always come away feeling as if she had been through the office shredder. But . . . she admitted, the woman was one hell of a psychologist to have batting for you.

Brown returned to her desk, her diary, and her pocketbook, and Ellie pulled out the last report from the profiler, determined to try to understand the man better. There had to be something in his aura that would give him away. Perhaps if she provoked him, pushed a few buttons, she might get a reaction?

* * *

'Jim? Amanda. Yes, fine, fine. Listen, do you recall the Fyson case? Well, it's payback time! Yes, I would not ask, but I think we may have a lead on the Running Man killings, and I need two of the most reliable men you have, and I want them now. With a fast car. Here, as soon as you can. And, Jim . . . one more thing, keep this one to yourself, it may be someone involved in the Surrey murder team. Exactly, and thanks, all debts are now honoured!'

Amanda hung up and immediately dialled another number. 'This is Dr Amanda Gerrard. Criminal Psychologist for the Surrey Police. My apologies for contacting you at home. I need some information about a case that you dealt with back in 1994. I know it was a long time ago, but there are aspects of this particular file that I am sure you will recall . . .'

Amanda supplied all the relevant data she had, listened carefully to the replies, and then posed the question: 'You were bitterly against this, were you not? Could you tell me why?'

The voice on the other end of the telephone was emphatic — the old case was still a cause for some resentment, seven years later. 'It was my opinion that he was most unsuitable to accept such an undertaking. Quite the wrong sort of person. I fought it to the end, but the powers that be saw fit to remove me from the case. Oh no, nothing like that, Amanda, quite the reverse in fact, but it would still put them in jeopardy. Of course, I can only guess, money talks, or perhaps someone was in a position to pull a few strings, but it all went ahead and my professional judgement was disregarded. No. Oh, yes, obsessive to the point of paranoia. I suspected some sort of childhood trauma, although there was nothing to substantiate that in his history. That's all I can tell you, Doctor. No problem, goodbye.'

Dr Amanda Gerrard felt as if someone had slipped an ice cube down her back. Still, she needed more evidence before she could bring in the big guns.

There was a sharp knock on her door and two plain clothes officers introduced themselves. 'Okay, Andy and George. This has to be dealt with in the most diplomatic manner that you can muster. Whichever one is the driver out of you two, look this address up. I've got one more call to make, and then I want to get there, in a hurry.'

Tossing a piece of paper and a road atlas to one of the men, she made a short call, then reached for her bag and coat and strode to the door. 'I'll fill you in on the way. Now, drive!'

* * *

Ellie discovered that she really was not too good at disparaging remarks, and did not manage to ruffle a single feather in her attempts to evoke some sort of response from a damaged aura.

Wendy Brown had been given a task by the chief, and was back on her computer, hammering away indelicately, requesting files for him.

The incident room was very busy, and Ellie felt uncomfortable and impatient. The fact that she could not warn her friends that they were probably sharing their investigation with the murderer was eating away at her, and for the second time that day, she nearly went into the DCI's office to tell him everything.

Instead, she rang Michael. He suggested she get home, darkness was falling and he was not happy about her being in such close proximity to a killer, even if she were surrounded by policemen. She finally agreed, but being unsure who would drive her if she asked for a lift, ordered a taxi to Compton. While she waited for the car, she made sure Wendy had both her numbers, and she added Amanda Gerrard's mobile. The WDC promised to ring her as soon as she had found enough proof to trust another of their number.

She thought about slipping away without saying good night, but that would be most out of character, so stuck her head around the DCI's office door and mouthed that she would see him tomorrow.

Bob was talking on the telephone and raised his hand in acknowledgement. She called out a general goodbye, and went outside to see where her cab had got to. She was about to ring the mini-cab company again to confirm they would be with her, when she noticed that her battery was showing low. She cursed softly and opted not to use it again in case she needed it for an emergency.

Another five minutes went by and a familiar silver Peugeot estate car drove into the station car park. Her driver, the same one as the day before, apologised for keeping her waiting and blamed heavy traffic on the Seven Hills Road.

Sitting in the back, and half listening to her chauffeur's commentary on the quality of driving today, Ellie felt aggrieved that she had left without achieving more.

Gerrard had not contacted her, and poor Wendy seemed to be fighting a losing battle with the ever-changing shift rosters.

She stared out of the window. The night looked ominous, and as the darkness had stolen the friendly sunshine of the day, her mood had lost its determination, and fear gnawed away inside her. She thought of Michael and Carole, and the joyous greeting she would get from the dogs. She wished she could wave a magic wand and be sitting in front of the Aga with her friends, instead of being stuck in a traffic jam. Then she thought of Alice, and a terrible feeling of loneliness washed over her as she started to count the miles to Compton.

* * *

Wendy Brown was ready to climb the walls! She had thought it would be a doddle; after all, she was a bloody detective! But no! Everything she touched became a problem, and now the whole of the duty rosters for the previous month had gone missing. Frankly her urgent internal investigation had gone tits-up!

It crossed her mind to ring Ellie and tell her to go straight to Scotland Yard and dump the whole bloody mess on their doorstep. Let someone else do the flaming detecting. Nice thought, but they were this close to getting him. One of eight suspects, that was all. She leaned deeper into the big filing cabinet to look for the missing files and did not even bother to turn to see who had just come into the small office.

She straightened up, ready to try the next drawer, when a fierce blow to the back of her head turned her world into a fiery volcano of pain, followed by a fall into oblivion.

She never felt strong arms reach around her and drag her into the stationery cupboard. She did not feel the snap of steel around her wrists or the parcel tape wrapped swiftly over her mouth. And she never heard the door slam behind her, the sharp click of the key turn in the lock, or the slight metallic grating noise as the key was removed and slipped into a pocket.

CHAPTER THIRTY-ONE

The car sped through village after village. It was further than Amanda had thought, but there was no other way. She had to find them. If she had made all the right deductions, and her intuition meter was reading ninety-nine per cent, they would hold the key.

They would be quite old now, and she was loath to be the one to bring back the distant past, crashing around their elderly ears, but . . . damn that! If they had handled it differently, all those years ago, five women, five beautiful and talented women, would still be alive today. And maybe their son would not be hammering and chopping his way around Surrey, trying to avenge one woman's sadistic obsession of thirty-five years ago.

They were not far now, a mile or two at the most.

After years and years of keeping his torment under control, securely held deep down within him, something or someone had dragged it kicking and screaming to the surface. Something had to be very, very bad in his eyes to warrant such an awful revenge. It had to have come from the parents, she would put money on it. What in hell's name had they done to let this demon out?

It was a very expensive house. Gravel crunched under the police car's tyres as George slowed down and pulled up the handbrake, outside the impressive front porch. Security lights came on, and a tall, athletic looking man of about seventy, looked through wire-framed glasses at their identification. He reluctantly escorted them to their lounge, where his wife and he had been watching television.

They listened to what the doctor had to say, and although the husband remained aloof, his wife leaned forward, her head in her hands, and began to cry.

At first it was a stifled sob, and then as the reality of the situation, and the awful realisation of the outcome of their actions all those years ago, dawned upon her, her cries increased to almost animal intensity.

The man went to her side and put a firm hand on her shoulder, as if he thought that physical pressure could staunch the misery. 'We thought we had done the right thing by everyone. You are correct, he did have a sister. She was a little older than him. A very bright, very clever child. We didn't know about her, her cruel streak, shall we say? The boy was weak, if he had only come to us earlier, but he didn't. He could have saved himself a lot of, of . . .'

'Torture?'

'No! It was never that bad! Stupid boy, why didn't he tell us?'

'Probably because of what she threatened to do to him, poor little sod!'

'How dare you!'

'What exactly did you do then, that was "the right thing for everyone"?' demanded Amanda.

'We sent her to school in Canada. It was a tough place, no room for her little weakness there. She went on to university. She has done extremely well for herself. She is a surgeon now.'

Amanda felt sick. She could only imagine the delight this perverted woman got every time she drew her knife across soft living tissue.

The wife's sobs were now a soft background noise to the deep resonant tone of the tall and aristocratic looking man next to her.

'She is an accomplished pianist and water-colourist, very good with her hands, and as I said, she has done very well for herself. She married last December. A little late in life maybe, but her career had to come first, and now she is adopting a little boy.'

The words hung in the room like a spoken death sentence.

'And did your son know this?' Amanda tried to keep the tremor out of her voice. For once in her life she was shaken.

'I thought it was time he grew up and put that silliness of childhood behind him. Yes, I told him. I am proud of my daughter and what she has achieved! That fool of a boy and his pathetic whimpering lost me my daughter!'

Dr Gerrard examined the man before her, and deliberated that the real culprits, the instigators behind such heinous crimes, were not always the ones to be punished. She sincerely hoped that her look said it all. The contempt she felt for this pompous and despicable man left her speechless. Not a condition she enjoyed.

Her voice was harsh and her face like marble as she finally addressed them. 'You will be brought in to make a full statement. A car will collect you.'

She gathered her entourage and swept out of the house.

In the car, she swore constantly until the number she had dialled answered.

'Jim? Yes, it is one of the team! Use a secure line, please, and get hold of DCI Bob Foreman immediately! I want him to get to the officer's home address, pronto. I think he may uncover some very unpleasant evidence. I don't care how he handles the killer, it's over to you guys now, but for God's sake get to him, before he gets to Ellie McEwan! And, organise for these two people to be picked up and brought to Surrey. The address is Langton Manor House. Shipbourne, it's near Sevenoaks in Kent. The names are Major Lawrence and Mrs Edith Barratt. DS Vic Barratt's parents.'

* * *

Michael was literally pacing the floor. The dogs watched him with uneasy eyes. His nervousness had spread to them and they did not sprawl in their usual contented fashion, but sat alert, or trod the boards with Michael.

The phone rang and he jumped, nearly dropping the receiver in his hurry to speak.

'Michael? It's Alice. Sorry to bother you. Is Ellie there?'

The professor's disappointment and irritation at finding the caller to be someone other than Ellie was unconcealed. He rushed through an explanation regarding his concerns and, to his surprise, the young doctor said she would be straight over. She was at her sister's house some fifteen miles away, and the least she could do was put a car and a confidante at Michael's disposal.

He hung up. That news may have been good, but the fact that Ellie's mobile was constantly engaged, and she was now very late home, was not good news at all.

An hour ago, Carole had taken herself off to her sanctuary and told him not to worry about her. She was safe and well protected. She had work to do that evening and she needed time in prayer and quiet meditation before beginning. He had regarded her, initially with doubts, but on a careful examination of his dear friend, he found a strong and determined woman, ready for battle. He had wished her well, hugged her and settled down to wait for Ellie.

Now, as time ticked by, he sighed, pulled nervously at his beard, and continued his pacing.

* * *

The traffic was now at a standstill. Ellie opened her handbag and poked around, trying to find the half of a chocolate bar she had seen earlier. She had finally located it when her mobile rang. Thank goodness, it would be Michael, she hadn't wanted to use the last of her battery making a call, but she knew he would be worrying. She looked at the green glowing number that had come up but she did not recognise it. Static crackled in her ear. It was another mobile and the line was awful. She strained to make out the voice. It was a woman and she suspected it was Amanda Gerrard, but she could only understand the odd word. Before it cut out completely she thought she made out . . . 'Killer . . . trust Foreman . . .'

She sat, her brain in turmoil. What had she really said about the killer? Had she said, 'Trust Foreman' or 'Don't trust Foreman'?

She stared at the telephone in her hand, then jerked back with fright as it rang again.

'Ellie? Thank God! Are you all right? Has Wendy managed to get hold of you yet?'

Had that been Wendy and not the doctor?

'Vic? No, my battery is low, the signal keeps cutting out, but I'm fine.'

'Then I'll speak quickly. Wendy has cleared me from your list! She was trying to get hold of you to tell you, but the chief keeps interrupting her. Look, I can see your reasons for needing to be absolutely certain, but surely we can trust the guv'nor?'

'No! Vic, we can trust no one yet! Oh, I'm so glad she's exonerated you! This is awful having to suspect your friends.'

'It must have been terrible for you, Ellie. Now listen, I have come out to ring you, we obviously can't talk from the station. Wendy wants to see you. Where can we all meet? We have to talk. I think I might have a vague idea who it is, and as soon as Wendy has managed to check a couple more dates I've given her, we could have an answer. What about the pub round the corner? No, too many coppers go in there. Think, Ellie!'

Her mind swam with unsuitable places.

'Got it!' Vic's voice was starting to fragment.

'I'm losing you!' She started to panic. The increasing gaps and garbled unfinished words made it almost impossible to understand. Suddenly she filled in the missing syllables. Of course! It was close to the station. Wendy and Vic would be able to slip out easily and get there in a few minutes. She tapped her chauffeur on the shoulder and asked him if he could take some back doubles and get her back to Addlestone.

She breathed easier. She had never believed it was Vic. The sergeant loved his family far too much.

Seven more to go, and Vic had a possible suspect. She really looked forward to talking to another ally. She would borrow his mobile, and put Michael's mind at ease. It wouldn't be long now. The traffic was far less congested in this direction, and the old sports pavilion in the police recreational ground at the back of the station had been an inspired choice for a rendezvous.

* * *

Jonathan Leatham stood in the gents' loo, his back to the disinfectant-smelling tiles and tried to get his head in order. He had splashed cold water on his face, and still his mind felt like a tornado was ripping through it. A few simple calls — that's all he had to make. A few simple calls.

He slammed the door and almost ran back to his desk. Five minutes later, he stared with disbelieving eyes at the list in front of him. He always said he would find the connection.

Pushing his chair back, he walked like a man in a trance into the chief's office and placed the list in front of the big grey man.

DCI Foreman read the five sentences and grasped instantly why his inspector was standing in front of his desk, white-faced and silent.

He read it aloud, as if to convince himself of its veracity.

Melissa Crabbe. Spoke to police sergeant re. attempted theft of valuable violin.

Helen Carberry. Police called re. vandals causing criminal damage to her Mercedes.

Adele Turner. Police called to Waters Meet Hotel to calm a disturbance in the banqueting suite.

Mary Probart. Witness in the Turner case.

Jenny Davis. Sgt Barratt gave crime prevention talk to senior pupils and teachers last month.

They were the connection. The police were the question that nobody asked.

'And I found this in Vic's bin, sir.'

'Mrs Audrey Long?'

'I've rung her number, sir. She was the witness to the Running Man in Barham Avenue. She rang earlier with a piece of information. She gave it to Sergeant Barratt.' The detective swallowed and continued. 'Something bothered her about the appearance of the man in the long coat. She had seen it flap back as he ran. She stated that he was wearing a white top, and white trousers.'

'Yes, yes . . .'

'It wasn't quite like that. She has remembered it was an all-in-one suit, sir. Scene of crime overalls, I believe. That's why he left no traces.'

Before he could reply, a red light glowed on one of the chief's telephones and his own face turned ashen when he heard what Superintendent Jim Fisher had to tell him. 'Jon. Where is Barratt?'

'I don't know, sir. He was here about an hour ago but I haven't seen him since.'

'Right. We have to find him, Jon, and we have to go to his home. I'll take Brown with me, and I'll get Mac and some uniforms and get round to his house. You call in every man available and find him.' He stopped abruptly. 'God, Jon! Ellie!'

He dialled her number and got the no service message. He dialled Snug Cottage and a distraught Michael told him she hadn't arrived home.

'Which cab company did she use?' The DCI fairly spat the words at his inspector.

'I don't know but someone will. I'll get it checked.'

'Where the hell is Brown? God Damn it! Get yourself into the ladies' loos and see if she's there! I want her now!'

A brief search for the missing WDC showed nothing. 'Sir, do you think he's got her?'

'God knows! What else is going to go wrong with this sodding case? Jon, I have to get to his house, I'll take Corbett and Mac's unit, okay? I'll phone you if we find anything. You do the same, and those two women are your priority, got that?'

Jonathan turned on his heel — he needed no reminder of his priorities right now.

* * *

On the drive across country to Compton, Alice's concentration was mainly on sharp corners and narrow dark lanes with overhanging trees. Only when she reached the short bit of well-lit carriageway at Newlands, did she afford herself the luxury of thinking about Ellie.

She decided that she had been a prime arsehole. Her whole life for the past three years had been Azimah Siddiq's work, the syndrome, her death, and the bloody paper. All Azimah. Then she had met Ellie, and she was the Azimah link. She saw the woman as this amazing specimen, her prodigy almost, and she refused to accept her attraction to Ellie McEwan the person. Until she had mentioned working with the police that was, and she had flipped. She had been so rude to Ellie. She wasn't proud of it — she was just terrified Ellie would get into some kind of danger, and Alice had no idea how to handle her feelings. She had not even called her when she said she would. She had taken the time to decide whether she had room enough in her life for her work and a serious relationship.

Tonight, she had admitted to herself that she wanted to find that balance, and she had rung her. Only to be told that she was long overdue getting home.

She negotiated a nasty bend, accelerated and threw the little car into top gear as she approached the road into Compton.

She had prayed she would find Ellie safe at home when she arrived at Snug Cottage, but all she found was a distressed and fearful professor, waiting in the open doorway, his mind still full of the alarming news from the police station.

* * *

The cars squealed to a halt outside Sergeant Vic Barratt's house. They blocked the drive and men tumbled out and quickly surrounded the neat, and nicely painted semi-detached.

Bob Foreman had stipulated that they were not to frighten Barbara or the children if they could help it. He went to the front door with Corbett, keeping the uniformed officers out of sight.

Hannah opened the door and smiled broadly. 'Uncle Bob! Do you want Mummy? Come in and I'll get her for you.'

'Hannah, sweetheart. Is Daddy home?'

'Oh no, he's been very busy on your Big Case, hasn't he? Mummy says we're lucky to see him at all, until it's over.'

Bob looked at the beautiful child and a wave of nausea swept over him. This was not real. Not Vic.

Barbara appeared behind her adopted daughter, with Matthew following a few steps after her. She took in the cars, and the two serious-faced officers, without betraying her concern to the children.

'Okay, you two, go and watch TV while I talk to Uncle Bob.' She pushed the kids gently into the lounge and shut the door.

Bob, and Barry Corbett, followed her into the dining room.

'What is wrong?'

'Barbara, we have to search the house, and I have to ask you if you know where Vic is?'

The sergeant's wife slowly shook her head in disbelief. Corbett went out and brought in some of the other officers to begin the search. The children in the lounge were to be undisturbed until Bob gave the word.

He sat his friend's wife down, and as gently as he could, explained that they needed to find Vic to help them — he may have some information about the murders he had not shared with them. He asked her if her husband had been acting in a strange manner of late, or had he said anything to her about his father and mother.

She got up and opened a drawer in the sideboard. She handed him a small bundle of letters, all addressed to Vic in elegant copperplate writing. 'He hates receiving letters from his father. He never talks to me about them. He had a bad childhood, Bob. It left scars. We don't talk about it. He has Matthew and Hannah and me now. We are his family. Whatever happened before is in the past, we choose to leave it there.'

'I'm sorry, Barbara, but something still lives in the here and now for Vic. May I look at these?'

He thumbed through the letters and gritted his teeth at the contents. He stared out of the window, still disbelieving the facts that were becoming more and more damning with every moment.

He froze as his eyes lit on the old Winnebago camper in the front drive.

'Barbara! Do you have the key to the camper?'

She went to the kitchen and returned immediately, her hands empty. 'They've gone.'

'Corbett! Force the door, and no copper's feet inside. Just look and tell me what you see!'

'Go to the children, Barbara. You are going to have to be very brave and think of something to tell them . . . we will be moving you out for a while, until we find Vic. Can you do that?'

Corbett stood in the doorway, his face ashen. 'Sir. Can you come, please?'

The smell was bad, but not enough to be noticed through the closed door.

A black Nike sports holdall sat blatantly on the floor, and if you leaned in, dark stains could be made out under the long bench seat that ran down one side of the van. Next to the bag was a cooler box. Most of the equipment in the big camper was dusty. It had been some time since this vehicle had travelled the open road, but the box was clean and looked fairly new.

Bob did not need the forensic team, who stood by the front door donning their suits, to prove to him that this had been the last resting place of Mary Probart. Of course, she had felt no concern at leaving her safe house with a policeman. He could have easily spun her a story that she would have believed. She had no reason to doubt him.

Photos were being taken and, before the lid was opened, the saddened DCI knew exactly what the cool box would contain.

His mobile chirped into life and he spoke rapidly. 'But she's conscious? Right, get an ambulance for her but find out anything she can tell you before she goes. Thank God he didn't kill her too. What? Oh, well, think about it Jon! She did not fit his criteria at all. Wendy Brown is about as ham-fisted as a woman gets! She will tell you, she has no artistic flair at all, and that probably saved her life. He is not killing for the sake of it, Jon. His victims must have the benchmark. Dexterous, arty, and good with their hands, like Ellie McEwan.'

Jonathan had no news on either Barratt or Ellie, so Foreman swiftly brought his inspector up to date on what was happening there, and promised to return to the station as soon as he had spoken again to Barbara.

His heart went out to the Barratt family, and he silently agreed with his wife, Rosie's opinion, that he should not be a copper.

* * *

They drove in silence, each consumed by their own agony regarding Ellie. Michael had phoned Scrubbs, and the old gentleman and his wife had made their way over to dog sit, and take telephone messages. He had stood for a while in the summer house, prayed for Ellie's safety, then whispered that he was going, with Alice Cross, to Addlestone to help search for Ellie.

Unsure as to whether Carole had heard him, he had paused before leaving and looked fondly at his old friend. There had been an incredibly long intake of breath before she opened her eyes. She had spoken slowly and clearly, and seemed to be staring straight through him.

As the car accelerated out of a bend, Michael hung on tightly, hearing her words once more.

'She has gone back to where it all started. She has returned to her nightmare. That is where you will find her.' Her eyelids had slowly shut and Michael had seen that she held two tarot cards in her hands. Strength and the High Priestess.

Staring blankly out through the windscreen, he forced himself to remember everything Carole had told him about Ellie's nightmare. If the police did not know where she was, then it may be down to him.

CHAPTER THIRTY-TWO

Her leg was aching badly, but she had thought it sensible to walk the last few hundred yards to the recreation ground. She did not want to draw attention to herself or the meeting place. She shivered as she limped towards the darkened building and reproached herself for leaving her jacket in the back of the taxi. It had been stifling hot in the Peugeot; something wrong with the heater according to her driver, and she had slipped it off, as they sat marooned in the traffic jam.

The ground was soft underfoot and she wished she had a torch. She could not see or hear either of her friends yet, but she doubted that she would be first to their tryst. The two police officers had only to leave the back of the station and walk around the perimeter path to the old disused sports pavilion. She tried the first door, but saw the padlock glint dully with the reflection from a distant streetlamp. Further along from the main entrance was another smaller door, which gave to her touch. Glancing behind her and seeing and hearing no one, she pushed the door further open and stepped inside.

The first thing she noticed about the dark room was the smell. It was unpleasant and brought with it the shadow of a memory. She was trying to find her bearings in the darkness when she noticed subdued and flickering lights coming from the concealed end of the L-shaped room.

As the lights registered in her eyes and her brain, she was thrown forcibly back into her forgotten dream. Falling against the wall, she felt the expected, cold dampness of the tiles, even before her body touched them.

Every detail of her surroundings, from her heavy, unco-operative legs to her laboured breathing, was familiar.

The filthy colours were swimming towards her, the bloody brackish brown shot with the tarnished silver.

How could she have fallen for this simple deception?

She remembered that scream, that awful sound of shock, rising to a crescendo of terror, but as it tore from her throat, a distant part of her marvelled at the sound. In the dream, she had no idea the scream was hers.

He stood before her. The embodiment of everything that was abhorrent and unwholesome. She had never seen auras in the dark before, but the sickening shades oozed and festered from him in a repulsive, refulgent wave around his body. In her loathing of what she beheld, she realised that these horrible colours could not exist in daylight — they belonged in the realms of darkness.

It was Barratt, but no longer the friendly sergeant, devoted husband, and father of two exquisite children. The face in front of hers was twisted and ugly, like a melting wax effigy of the Vic she knew. It shifted and changed, as if each horrid thought that went through its warped mind were imprinted on the face for the duration of its stay, only to be replaced with something equally as revolting.

Ellie was frozen with fear. Some primeval urge to save herself was fighting to be recognised, but the sheer horror of the man, occupied the whole of her senses.

At some point he had reached out and gripped her right arm with a ferocity that practically cut off her circulation. She suddenly noticed the knife in his other hand. A knife?

Her brain had received the kickstart it needed and straightforward bewilderment forced her to speak. 'Where is the metal pipe? You always use the piece of scaffolding!'

Her voice was croaky, like she had aged fifty years in the blink of an eye, and her tone was petulant, as if he were not playing the game according to the rules.

His laugh made her feel bilious and she fought the tide of vomit that was forming in her throat.

'You . . . you are special, Ellie. You are the culmination of my work.'

'But Vic . . .'

She had been going to beg or say something inane, when she saw the faintest difference in his energy lights. In that millisecond that she had spoken his name, addressed him almost in the tone she always had, as a friend, his foul lights had diminished and a faintest hint of true colour showed itself.

My God, she thought. He is in there. Sergeant Vic Barratt is still in there.

The tiny rays disappeared and with a roar he pushed her further down the room to the concealed part where the old showers had been. He threw her to the floor and held her there with his foot. He had propped a flashlight in the corner of the cubicle, and in its feeble beam, Ellie noticed Mary Probart's nice, shiny black shoes. Proper shoes.

She lay, gasping for breath and desperately trying to find a way to get the other Vic, the real Vic, back. Her mind felt as sharp as a rain-soaked blanket — she had to be able to do something. If she didn't, she would die, there was no question about that.

She gasped again and caught the faintest whisper of a smell. No, a perfume, and one that did not belong in this filthy, ruined wreck of a building.

It was lilacs. She had smelled lilacs, and a memory came back to her, an insistent voice saying, 'Tell her to ask for help.'

The foot was pressing harder on her chest. Her newly healed rib was threatening to crack under the pressure, and her captor was raving about her being the vehicle of his retribution and revenge.

In a burst of pure agony, she pushed up against the foot, and called for help. She called to God, to her guardian angel, to Vera, and she called to Vic Barratt.

Caught off balance, the man staggered back. In the shadowy torchlight, he seemed disorientated. His lights rose and faded and his strange appearance fluctuated and altered, like special effects in a film.

Ellie saw this battle going on inside him and took the only advantage she could. She recounted all the things he had told her about his children. She shouted the names Hannah and Matthew over and over like a litany.

Then a familiar voice from inside the monster, which begged her to help him. 'Please Ellie, don't let him . . .'

The scent of lilacs was stronger. There was a glow of light in the room that did not come from the torch. Something was helping the policeman, the good man, to fight his way back.

The room went silent. The man stood over her, his head bowed. The lights that surrounded him were faint but clear. He spoke softly, like a child. 'She hurt me, Ellie, she did terrible things to me. She has to pay, doesn't she? She can't be allowed to adopt that little boy!' Tears were spilling down his cheeks. 'She will hurt him, like she hurt me, and I can't let that happen, can I?'

The knife lay on the floor where he had dropped it in his anguished battle with himself. Ellie slowly edged towards it, talking softly. She would help him. She would tell the authorities the truth about her. Oh God, she didn't even know who he was talking about. She would get him help. She would . . .

'Bitch!' His lights had died. A stench filled the room. 'Bitch!' The distorted face, a parody of the real man, leered at her and she saw the lascivious smile that Brazil had used on her. 'I think we will stick to my original plan.' The laugh was malevolent as he snatched up the knife and held it close to himself.

Suddenly Ellie was aware of something else in the room. She felt rather than saw, a surge of energy around her. Colours were swirling high in the beam of the flash lamp, strengthening, and brightening. A little way away from the rainbow of fast-moving ribbons of light was a single oval cluster of purest violet radiance. Ellie watched as it moved slowly towards the hideous creature that was jealously holding the knife. Suddenly there was another light, this time a brilliant sky-blue haze that moved swiftly to join and mingle with the amethyst.

Another battle ensued, and Ellie crawled into a corner of the shower room to be away from the strange maelstrom of opposing energies. It was like being tossed in a stormy sea — she felt battered and sick. The energies and lights had been joined by a weird cacophony of sounds and she thought she would drown in the uproar. The conflict seemed to last for eternity and then, to her dismay, she felt herself being dragged back towards the centre of this dreadful chaos.

The noises abated and she heard an iniquitous voice state, 'I will have her!'

She was dragged by unseen hands to within two feet of him and his silver blade.

There was nothing of Vic left, but Ellie screamed at him anyway. 'Yes! Go on! And prove to your children that their father is a monster!'

He stood stock still, and slowly his ebony darkness was enveloped by strands and wisps of amethyst and blue mist. The evil face gave way to that of the loving father.

'Oh no! No!'

He turned the knife from Ellie to himself and with a cry plunged forward.

She thought she had momentarily blacked out. She was dizzy, and couldn't open her eyes properly. It was cold on the damp tiled floor, and she started to shiver.

Something warm touched her hand. She moved fractionally and thought she felt soft silky fur brush across her face. Through a blur of fading colour, she thought she saw a woman. No, it was two women and a dog. Then nothing.

She fell back into unconsciousness, only vaguely aware of more lights and shouts, this time accompanied, not by wraiths and phantasms, but by black-and-white uniforms and policemen's boots.

She was helped to her feet by Bob Foreman, Michael, and to her surprise, Alice.

A blanket was wrapped around her and she was led out, shaking and chilled, into the clean night air. A young bobby she did not recognise ran after them. He held out her handbag and added, 'I took the liberty of putting your brooch in it, miss. It was on the floor where we found you, must have come off in the struggle.'

Not understanding, she fumbled in the bag and brought out the brooch. The enamel shone in the moonlight. A strange design like a Celtic cross in such wonderful colours. Where had she seen it before? She dropped it back in the bag and allowed herself to be led to the waiting car.

* * *

As Ellie and Alice sat in Bob's office, clasping big mugs of steaming hot tea and waiting for Amanda Gerrard to arrive, Michael was arriving back at Snug Cottage. He had been given a police driver to get him home to tell Carole of Ellie's rescue, and the death of the murderer.

Scrubbs answered the door and let the professor and his driver in. The elderly gardener told Michael that he had been out to the summer house about an hour before, but he didn't like to disturb the missus when she was in one of her trances.

Michael asked the police constable who had driven him if he would wait until he had spoken to his friend and made some arrangements with Scrubbs for the rest of the night, as he wanted to go back to the station to make his statement and to be with Ellie.

He put the security lights on and walked through the courtyard. He felt exhausted but could not wait to tell Carole the news.

The professor stood in the doorway. She had probably been dead for about two hours. Scrubbs' 'trance' had been of the permanent variety.

Michael walked quietly in, closed the door, and sat with his friend at the table. She was just as he had left her — serene, composed and peaceful.

This time she had not crossed any barriers that she should not. She had joined a fight for goodness, integrity and righteousness. She had been surrounded by light, and when she finally crossed that great divide, she did it like a hero.

He held the cold hands in his and wept.

CHAPTER THIRTY-THREE

Two days after Carole had died and Ellie had been saved, Bob Foreman called a meeting of his team, together with Dr Amanda Gerrard, Ellie and Michael.

The DCI stood before them, more haggard and greyer than ever.

The team was quiet. They had lost a valued colleague, and did not know how to come to terms with the circumstances of his death, or the terrible things he had done.

Along with the criminal psychologist and all the background history she had dug up over the last three days, Bob had pieced together as much as he could by way of an explanation for his unit.

He leaned against a table and looked sadly around the room, with its pictorial display of death and destruction.

'I know you are going to hear these words one thousand times or more. *"Sergeant Victor James Barratt was a bent copper."* Well, I do *not* agree, and I never will. Vic was a damaged child, who kept his demons in check for thirty-five years, until the same bastard who helped to make him the way he was, decided in his wisdom, to entice the devil out into the world.' He swallowed hard. 'Vic had an older sister: a delightful child, clever and artistic, who tortured him on a regular basis for some three years. We can only imagine some of the things she did, but the post-mortem on our colleague shows some unusual damage to internal tissue that seems to date back to what are termed as, childhood accidents. We do, however, know the incident that brought his suffering to light. His charming and nimble-fingered sibling inserted a large woodscrew into the little boy's penis, and left it there, refusing to allow him to pee until his retention was so great, that it nearly ruptured his bladder.'

Bob tried to ignore the groans of disbelief, and the mass crossing of legs from most of the male officers present.

'On this occasion, however, the little angel had gone a bit too far. The boy was hospitalised. Daddy and Mummy were well off, and deviously managed to squash a scandal. They sent their little charmer to Canada to be educated. The fact was, Vic's father hated him. He considered him weak, and the cause of his losing his precious daughter to the other side of the Atlantic. As soon as he was old enough, Vic left home, and lived alone.'

'Good for him,' muttered someone. 'Shame he didn't top his bastard father before he went.'

Bob coughed and ignored the comment. 'He joined the Force and committed himself completely. One day he was called to a rape case. The victim, a twenty-year-old Black woman, had been brutally raped by her father. His dealings with her were compassionate and caring. To her, Vic Barratt was a knight in shining armour. To him, she was the furthest thing he could imagine from his sister, and someone else who had been betrayed by family. She was as dark as his sister was fair. She was safe to love. Her name was Barbara. He married her, and they lived a life that suited both. Full of love and companionship, and without the one thing they both were terrified of, the sex act.'

Once again, Bob paused. This was not easy for him, but Vic's friends and teammates deserved to know the truth. He continued, 'Even so, they both loved children, and wanted to protect and nurture some kids who had suffered — kids who needed a family. They went the adoption route, but someone in the department had bad vibes about Vic. He failed some of the tests because he was obsessive about their safety. Somehow, he pulled a few strings with a friend on the board and after a long battle was awarded Hannah and Matthew. Last year the letters from his father started. At first, they were almost pleasant, commending him on his promotion, admiring him for taking on the children, and so on. Then he started to mention the sister, and how well she had done, how successful she was. All her attributes, her talents and her genius. Vic's wife has confirmed that the letters began to eat away at Vic. I suspect they tore at his insides.' He looked around the room, at the shocked expressions. 'This beast of a woman was a surgeon. Dr Amanda Gerrard believes he began to think about her more and more, hating the fact that she was prospering, when she should have been locked away. He knew she would never stop. She was a sadist, through and through. Then he received the letter that tipped the balance. It told him she was adopting a little boy. At this point Dr Gerrard is certain his mind could take no more. The horror of it brought out another Vic Barratt, an alter-ego, who decided that if he could not get at his sister, he would get at other talented and gifted artistic women in her place. The sadness is that he wanted to be caught, so she would read his name in the papers, and know that all those lovely women had died because of her. He would ruin the whole family, and drag their name into the mire with him.'

'Sir?'

'Yes, Hudson.'

'If he was this barking mad murderer, how did he fool Ellie? She saw nothing weird about him, except at the Davis scene of crime?'

'We think he fooled her by honesty, Hudson. Vic the copper believed he was a good man and a loyal officer. He knew nothing of what his alter-ego was up to. It seems that sometimes the murderer inside realised when things were not going to be easy, and he helped him along a bit. For instance, the killer could not allow Vic to hear Dr Gerrard's profile. He thought it might be too close to home for his host, so he arranged a bogus call to get him out of my office.'

'You've lost me, sir,' said Windsor.

'I wondered why the duty officer had called him on his mobile instead of an internal line to ask him to sort out some drunken snout in the front office. There was no fracas or snout. He had rigged his mobile to call his own number. He just could not listen to Gerrard and her psychologist's report describing him. Afterwards he believed his own story. He was completely unaware that he was the killer. He was trying his best to catch the murderer along with you guys. He changed when Ellie came on the scene. His other self hated her artistic abilities, and her odd gift of seeing auras was making it very difficult for him. When she saw his evil energy at the school, he realised she would have to die. He watched WDC Brown and saw her checking the staff rosters. It did not take him long to realise what they were up to.'

He turned his attention to Ellie. 'You were very lucky. Lucky to have a clever woman like Dr Gerrard working with you, lucky that Michael described the shower room in your nightmare so clearly, and lucky that the cab driver brought your jacket back to the station and told us where he dropped you off.'

He sighed and shook his head. 'And even more lucky that Vic turned the knife on himself. That surprises me more than anything. I would have thought that nothing would have stopped him with his grand finale.'

Ellie, still shocked by her ordeal, and grieving over the loss of her friend, knew she could never explain what had happened in that deserted pavilion. She was not sure herself, so preferred to let them believe that Vic Barratt had simply been unable to live with knowing the terrible things he had done, and had killed himself. Which, in essence, was the truth.

Bob Foreman closed the meeting by confirming that Vic had been responsible for all the deaths. The big Winnebago had been the place where Mary died. It had been parked at the back of the drive for months, waiting for Vic to do some work on it. No one took any notice of it. It was curtained all round and very spacious inside. He left her body there for a short time; when his wife was at work and the kids at school, he transferred it to his car and dumped it up on St Martha's. The bag had contained several disposable SOCO suits, a long black coat, a piece of blood-stained cut-off scaffolding pole, probably from the building site for the new forensic lab, and a small chef's meat cleaver. The cool box had contained the missing digits and Melissa's ring, packed in ice. He must have changed the ice blocks regularly, because when forensics opened it, the fingers and thumbs were perfectly preserved.

The DCI thanked everyone for their hard work and offered them all his condolences. He thought it may be the hardest case that his team would ever encounter. But then, you never could tell.

Right now, Bob was tired.

So very tired.

EPILOGUE

Michael and Ellie sat together in the cramped and stuffy office of Messrs Brothertoft and Singleton.

Through her grief, Ellie lethargically wondered how someone so painfully thin could ever find suitable clothes to fit him. She harboured the thought that Michael was probably wondering where the man could possibly have bought the bizarre tie he was wearing. Its colours and design were unusual to say the least, and she had the feeling that the solicitor was probably in possession of a drawer full of others, all equally outlandish.

Mr Brothertoft took an inordinately long time to organise and re-organise his papers. Finally, satisfied that everything was how he wanted it, he sat back in the elderly button-back chair, and surveyed his guests with the stare of a bird of prey.

'How well did you know the late Mrs Cavendish-Meyer?'

Ellie nodded to Michael to speak for them both. The passing of their friend was still raw, and she was content to sit and listen, rather than speak of her dead companion.

'She was our greatest friend, we spent a lot of time together. We both loved her, but of her history, we knew very little.'

'Then you would know she was of an unusual disposition, somewhat outspoken, and a little unorthodox?'

Michael nodded vehemently. 'Rather well put, that description. She was plain spoken all right, and sometimes unbelievably rude, but a wonderful, generous and brave lady to boot!'

'Indeed, and now I have to put a question to you both before we proceed. Mrs Meyer requested that I ask you, that if an amount of money was extended to you, would you be prepared to take and look after Mrs Meyer's dogs for the rest of their natural lives? The finances will be arranged to cover every eventuality, if you agree.'

This time Ellie answered. Her words held no hesitation. 'We had proposed to do this, even without financial aid. Those dogs were her life. We think too much of Carole to abandon them, or split them up. We're not too sure how, or where, but we'll manage somehow.'

Mr Brothertoft smiled benignly. 'Your answer has enabled me to proceed. This' — he indicated to an enormous pile of very legal looking documents — 'is the Last Will and Testament of Mrs Caroline Elizabeth Cavendish-Meyer. By the correct answering of one simple question, you, Miss Elena McEwan, and you, Professor Michael James Seale, are the main beneficiaries to her extensive estate. With the exception of three bestowals, the whole of her estates, properties, investments and monies are to be shared equally by you.'

He waited for the news to penetrate. After a short time had passed and no response other than a stunned silence was forthcoming, he rose, put his skull-like head around the office door and asked his elderly secretary to bring them some strong tea.

'I will mention the bequests first. Mr Andrew Fullerton, at the time of the signing of the will, in the employ of Mr Philip McEwan of Weybridge will receive the sum of twenty-five thousand pounds, and the freehold ownership of the property at 43 Rue St Antoine, in the Bastille area of Paris, France. Mrs Meyer has left a letter for the gentleman and it will be forwarded to him with the notification of his inheritance. The sum of twenty-five thousand has also been left to the Royal Surrey County Hospital. The figure to be disposed of, as he sees fit, by Mr Carl Thomas. Lastly, her car and the sum of twenty-five thousand pounds to Mr and Mrs Scrubbs of Compton, at present in her employ.'

He closed one folder and opened another, taking a deep breath before continuing. 'Which brings us to the remainder of the estate. It will take some time to inform you of her, now your, extensive assets. They are listed here, and Mrs Meyer gave me leave to answer any questions you may have about her family and her life. She was more than aware that she did not share much with you in her living years and has allowed me to furnish you with her history at a later date, if you should so wish.'

Neither Michael or Ellie trusted their shaking fingers with the bone china cups and saucers that were being proffered to them by Brothertoft's ageing assistant. She placed the tray on the desk in front of them and quietly left.

Brothertoft himself had begun to list properties in Lincolnshire, Rutland, Cornwall and Surrey. There was another apartment in France, and a small villa, at present let out as a holiday cottage, on the Greek island of Paxos. And there was money. Money invested in stocks, shares, businesses and bank accounts.

The solicitor droned on, leaving his two dumbfounded clients desperately trying to absorb even just a little of what they were being told. Some of the properties had belonged to Vera. They were bequeathed to Carole, who had now passed them to Ellie and Michael.

When they arrived, Ellie and Michael had been concerned as to how they would house five dogs in a small townhouse or an even smaller London flat. Then they had given the right answer to a single question, and . . . all this!

All Ellie could see was the Morris Minor, the old cord trousers with a patina of fine dog hair, and a thorn-proof jacket with a torn cuff.

Through a veil of tears, Ellie mutely held out her hand for the cream manilla envelope she was being offered. Michael did likewise.

From a great distance it seemed, the solicitor's monotonous voice was telling them that it had been Carole's request that they take the envelopes home to Snug Cottage, and open a large bottle of champagne; they would find a very special vintage, bottom row, second from the left, in the rack in the larder. They should then sit, with her beloved dogs around them, read the letters, and toast her reunion with the dearest friend in all her life, Vera.

* * *

That night Ellie brought in flowers for the table, and Michael lit candles. He had found the bottle of Bollinger when they arrived home, and put it in the fridge to chill.

According to Carole's wish, they sat at the familiar old table with her melee of spaniels at their feet, filled their glasses, and with tremulous hands, carefully opened the letters.

They didn't say much — they were brief and to the point, so typical of Carole . . .

Dearest Ellie,
   To ask you to use the money wisely would be an insult. All I ask is that you enjoy it. My boys are lucky to have you.
   Take your God-given gift to the heights.
   Be happy, and remember, we are always with you.
   Always.
   Carole

To dear Michael,
   Do you sometimes wonder what would have happened if you had said, 'No'?
   Have fun, my old friend, and watch that girl for me.
   Carole

THE END

THE JOFFE BOOKS STORY

We began in 2014 when Jasper agreed to publish his mum's much-rejected romance novel and it became a bestseller.

Since then we've grown into the largest independent publisher in the UK. We're extremely proud to publish some of the very best writers in the world, including Joy Ellis, Faith Martin, Caro Ramsay, Helen Forrester, Simon Brett and Robert Goddard. Everyone at Joffe Books loves reading and we never forget that it all begins with the magic of an author telling a story.

We are proud to publish talented first-time authors, as well as established writers whose books we love introducing to a new generation of readers.

We won Trade Publisher of the Year at the Independent Publishing Awards in 2023. We have been shortlisted for Independent Publisher of the Year at the British Book Awards for the last four years, and were shortlisted for the Diversity and Inclusivity Award at the 2022 Independent Publishing Awards. In 2023 we were shortlisted for Publisher of the Year at the RNA Industry Awards.

We built this company with your help, and we love to hear from you, so please email us about absolutely anything bookish at feedback@joffebooks.com

If you want to receive free books every Friday and hear about all our new releases, join our mailing list: www.joffebooks.com/contact

And when you tell your friends about us, just remember: it's pronounced Joffe as in coffee or toffee!

ALSO BY JOY ELLIS

ELLIE MCEWAN SERIES
Book 1: AN AURA OF MYSTERY

JACKMAN & EVANS SERIES
Book 1: THE MURDERER'S SON
Book 2: THEIR LOST DAUGHTER
Book 3: THE FOURTH FRIEND
Book 4: THE GUILTY ONES
Book 5: THE STOLEN BOYS
Book 6: THE PATIENT MAN
Book 7: THEY DISAPPEARED
Book 8: THE NIGHT THIEF
Book 9: SOLACE HOUSE
Book 10: THE RIVER'S EDGE

THE NIKKI GALENA SERIES
Book 1: CRIME ON THE FENS
Book 2: SHADOW OVER THE FENS
Book 3: HUNTED ON THE FENS
Book 4: KILLER ON THE FENS
Book 5: STALKER ON THE FENS
Book 6: CAPTIVE ON THE FENS
Book 7: BURIED ON THE FENS
Book 8: THIEVES ON THE FENS
Book 9: FIRE ON THE FENS
Book 10: DARKNESS ON THE FENS
Book 11: HIDDEN ON THE FENS
Book 12: SECRETS ON THE FENS
Book 13: FEAR ON THE FENS
Book 14: GRAVES ON THE FENS

DETECTIVE MATT BALLARD
Book 1: BEWARE THE PAST
Book 2: FIVE BLOODY HEARTS
Book 3: THE DYING LIGHT
Book 4: MARSHLIGHT
Book 5: TRICK OF THE NIGHT
Book 6: THE BAG OF SECRETS

Milton Keynes UK
Ingram Content Group UK Ltd.
UKHW021345310324
440331UK00004B/333

9 781835 263631